HELLO, DOVE

GILLIAN DOWELL

GILLIAN DOWELL

ISBN: 979-8-5231-1748-0

Dedicated to the souls that wander and the minds that wonder.

1982

A smile was plastered on my face as I walked behind my mother, shaking the hands of nearly everyone in the congregation. Weaving in and out of the church pews in orderly fashion with the ever-adored 'pastor's wife' is a tedious dance that I've performed hundreds—if not thousands—of times. The light touch from the women, the firm grips of the men determined to show their strength as the powerful providers that they felt they were—it was just as uncomfortable and exhausting as it had always been. Humid traces of peoples' nerves that built up upon the wait to touch the very God-given family that led their religious lives were now left upon my hand, and as I sat down in the pew beside my mother, I could feel the guilt seeping into my skin as I looked at my heavy palm.

They say that sin weighs upon the soul, but what was it that I carried that was crushing me beneath itself if I was without sin?

And I, in fact, was.

My thoughts alone were what smothered me.

"Be attentive, darling," my mother whispered from the corner of her mouth, so as not to let anyone know that she dared speak as my father began his sermon. "Your brothers and sisters are watching. Influence them well."

Except she wasn't speaking of my one brother who sat silently beside me with his eyes transfixed on our father. What she meant was that the dozens of people in this open, yet unifying place were watching, and I was to be the perfect example that they molded me into. My brothers and sisters weren't only watching—they were waiting for just one wrong move. One sign that told them that these seemingly perfect men and women of God weren't as flawless as they appeared to be. Just one, small, *anything* that assured them we fell short from time to time just as they do.

Anything to remind them that we're only human.

"Yes, mother," I whispered with the briefest smile, and met the eyes of the man behind the pulpit.

The brow of a man who feels every conviction in the words he bellows rested upon my father's face, drawing the image of a person possessed. His demeanor left no room for doubt that he believed every lesson he read and taught, and every person sitting in their seat could see it. I knew that each of them felt the exact way I did now, just as well as I had many times before—that his message was directed specifically towards them and their soul.

My father had the unique ability to address each person individually while speaking to an entire room. While stern in his features and equally so in his beliefs, he had an air about him that made him seem so approachable, as if he held every answer to every problem you needed a solution for. I guess that's why he made the perfect preacher. He had all the information that needed to be taught and shared with the masses.

"'Everyone who does evil hates the light," he recited passionately from the book of John, "and will not come into the light for fear that their deeds will be exposed.'"

He didn't have to refer to his bible to quote the verse, and neither did I to know exactly where it was found within that tome of life's guided lessons. Chapter three, verse twenty. I'd heard it before, I'd read it before, and I had felt this same sensation under its condemning spell enough times in my life to engrain the message to memory.

No sin goes undiscovered and unpunished.

Though my gaze rested upon him, my mind wandered through the dull and lifeless events of my existence, ensuring that there were no such deeds that hid inside my transparent self. Empty guilt was a tiring and confusing thing, but it's the thing that was most familiar to me in my endless efforts to strive for perfection in the eyes of those watching; which I knew from the incessant reminders did not just amount to my parents, but every other soul around me.

The sermon continued to fade in and out of my focus, and I caught the concluding verse that my father shared as he closed the leather cover of his ancient book— "Whoever is pregnant with evil conceives trouble and gives birth to disillusionment."

I could recall the hundreds of sermons taught on evil and all of the frenzied warnings to avoid it at all costs, to let not your guard slip and expose your fragile, human soul to the darkness; but for the life of me, I couldn't remember a single lesson that spoke on nothing but the good. Of the pure, and the whole; of the soul that's spotless and its reward that I could only assume is held to higher significance than that of the stained. My father never spoke on such things. Every memory that I could grasp onto was of a lesson inciting fear of the dangers of the wicked.

A sudden shake of my body brought me out of my nervous trance, and my father's face brightened with a smile as he stepped down from his elevated position above us all, slowly taking the steps of the stage towards his devoted family.

Mother rose from her seat and my brother and I followed suit as Father kissed the cheek of his doting wife.

"Well done, dear," she assured him with a gentle pat on his chest, and he looked down upon her face much like he was accustomed to from his stance behind his pulpit.

"Thank you, Lauren." His words were gentler than his expression, despite the smile that remained on his lips. I could tell by the taut skin of his brow that his mind was still catching up to his feet, not having left the words he had just been speaking to the church. He had two modes: father and preacher. The only real difference between the two was that my father's eyes didn't always pierce into my soul as harshly as the preacher's did.

"Glad to have you back in these seats, Gene," he told me, hiking up the massive bible he carried against his side. The tabbed pages and scraps of paper that served as placeholders nearly doubled the size of the already giant book. Though well-loved, it was holding up just fine considering the many years and heated readings it had seen. Indestructible nor invincible, I only wished that I could feel as sturdy as it was in such close proximity to my father. The ribs encasing my fluttering heart felt as though they were made of paper even thinner than the bible's. I felt certain that my father knew that I hadn't been giving him the attention that I should have while he preached. I was a grown woman about to be lectured for my lack of respect, and my body trembled with mixed frustration and uneasiness. "Did you get anything out of today's message?"

It wasn't the accusation I'd been expecting, but my nerves didn't diminish immediately. I was to make sure that I not only had the right answer at the ready, but the information needed to back it up if he decided to question me further. It was a tense back-and-forth that he and I often endured.

"I did." Would it necessarily be a lie if I provided an evasive answer rather than the one he wants? Not a lie, no. I had to reassure myself that I wasn't sinning right before the stare of a man that could detect such a thing with his eyes closed. "You gave a memorable sermon, Father. A lesson that stays upon the heart."

It wasn't a lie because it would stay with me. My heart would remain heavy with the knowledge that I spent nearly the entirety of it focused less on the words he spoke and more on the man speaking and his overwhelming intimidation. I don't know why I bothered worrying about being called out for it when he was able to flood me with guilt without even trying.

Never the one to speak unless spoken to, my brother stood beside me with one hand clutching a bible in an obvious reflection of our father. He wasn't being a try-hard, he wasn't going out of his way to show the world that he was his father's son; he was just being his beautiful, gentle self—the soul that always longed to be the generous one that saved the souls of others. That's how he had always seen our father.

I wish I had the luxury of having his point of view.

"Nice to have your sister back beside you for Sunday services, isn't it, Son?"

I've always been convinced that my parents named my little brother Grayson just for the sole purpose of being able to shorten his name to sound so formal. I've also wondered if they were disappointed that they couldn't find a name that would make just calling me 'Daughter' suitable.

Father, Mother, Gene, and Son. You tell me why I tend to feel like I don't belong.

"It really is," Grayson answered with a gentle squeeze of my shoulder. His eyes were unmistakably kind, and his life of only ever letting truth pass his lips made for the most honest eyes ever seen on a young man. There was no doubting that Grayson was nothing but good and everything that sincere purity is.

I wondered briefly if I appeared to the world as bitter purity.

"I've really missed you, Gray." And there was the first, complete truth that I've told since arriving in this church. It wouldn't make up for all the guilt of tuning out the sermon, but it was a start to feeling like I wasn't making only wrong moves now that I was back on this schedule. Back to this former life, really.

Those four years I spent away from my uniform life and family were only an illusion of freedom. A single ploy that my parents held the strings to that gave me the ignorant idea that I was ever allowed to make decisions for myself, or even be on my own. Getting a business degree through a Baptist college may not sound like liberty to most, but it was the most I had ever known. And despite having always come home for breaks, holidays, and occasional visits, knowing that I was back for good was a new experience to my brain entirely.

I couldn't help but feel like I really missed my chance to run. But there's no running on legs so unsteady and unsure. All I'd ever experienced was whatever my parents permitted. That amounts to next to nothing.

I hadn't realized that I'd still been staring at Gray until he tightly squeezed my shoulder again briefly and his blue puppy eyes jumped back into my glossed vision. He gave me a small smile and my arms went around his neck without thought. I could feel his chest catch with surprise before his arms went around me in return, the bible still held in his hand weighing on my back.

"I've missed you too, Vieve." I knew that he was smiling through the soft-spoken words, and felt the love in the very sound of my name.

Fond recollection of all the time we'd spent together throughout our close lives came to mind. I was given the fortunate stability of having a friend in a brother, someone that I never fought to have approval from. I never second-guessed the authenticity of his love because he always showed me in more ways than it even mattered to most. I may have been the older one, but he was the stronger one. I was the fallen seven-year-old in the dirt, and he was the five-year-old illuminated above me by the sun behind him, offering his outstretched hand. He wasn't my rock, because I never sturdily stood upon his strength nor rested upon his surety. He was always above me, like the moon that promised not to burn out and leave me to be alone when all was bleak and dark.

He was younger, but he was better. In every way.

"I still love that you're the only one that calls me that, even though I much prefer it to *Gene*," I told him with a smile, pulling away to find the last touch of peace from his eyes that I'd be needing to face the after-church chaos.

"You mean you didn't have all your friends at college call you Vieve? Why wouldn't you?" The scrunch of his nose made him look even younger than just a playfully confused twenty-year-old. I don't know if he'll ever manage to age to me when my eyes hang on to the mental picture of him as my five-year-old brother.

"I wouldn't dream of it. That's our thing," I told him, picking up my purse from the pew where I'd sat. "You're the world's Son, but you're only *my* Gray. So I'll live with being Gene, even if I don't like it."

"Fair enough," he said with a forced nod and a smile pulling at the corner of his mouth. "Why wouldn't you just have everyone call you Genevieve, then? Is that not a happy medium?"

"Somehow that seems even worse than Gene. Something about 'Genevieve' makes it feel like there's a lot of expectation to be entirely proper behind the name."

"You are entirely proper," he told me, gesturing for me to take the lead as we walked out of the sanctuary, "and your name *is* Genevieve."

"I'm really glad that you think so," I said, but I couldn't manage to even force a grin in response to his compliment. It didn't feel right between the doubt I constantly had with myself and the realization that not even my *name* sounded right or even felt like it belonged to me anymore. "And I guess sometimes it's easy to forget who I am."

Our parents were standing by the main doors, saying their goodbyes to each and every person as they left the church and met the too-bright summer sun upon their exit. This was routine, and it was custom for Grayson and me to also be by their side, showing our appreciation to our fellow brothers and sisters for attending service as well. During all the Sundays that I was away at university, I have no doubt that Grayson didn't miss this part of our responsibilities as the pastor's children, and the only reason that he was arriving late now was because of me. He didn't seem to either notice nor care, but it bothered me to feel like I kept him from promptly performing a duty that I knew he enjoyed.

It bothered me to feel like, because of me, he briefly fell short in the eyes of our parents.

As we took our positions by their sides, I was the only one to notice the look in our father's eye. It was brief and easy to miss, but I had been waiting to receive that small gesture of warning, of disappointment. I only hoped that he solely blamed me for our tardy arrival to something this important to him. Knowing Gray well enough, surely he did.

"It's so lovely to have you back for good, doll! How we've missed your pretty face being here every Sunday these past years. It just wasn't the same without you always up there between Son and your momma," Mrs. Hannigan cooed as she held my hand in both of hers, cupping it with warmth and a firm grasp.

"It's so nice to finally be back," I told her with my best fake smile. Maybe it was a stretched truth, but it was still the truth. There were a few things that made it nice to be back. Familiar faces and getting to be with my brother again were a couple of them. Mrs. Hannigan may have been overly enthusiastic at times, but she always meant well. Her and her family, which each stood at the opposite end of the hands of my family, were all kind and generous people. With a son near my age and a daughter the age of Grayson, it didn't escape me that my parents were always excessively happy and eager to accept every invitation for our families to dine together. There was no surprise when I heard Father and Mr. Hannigan already discussing and deciding on the eight of us getting together at the Hannigan's home for lunch.

"We'll be over just as soon as I get everything locked up here, John," my father said, giving Mr. Hannigan a friendly nod before moving on to shake the hand of Mr. Guffin and his wife.

"Son, why don't you and Gene head out after we finish up here and go pick up a dessert to take with us? Your mother and I will make the walk over to their house after we're done, then we should all be getting there about the same time," Father said in the few free moments between the elderly couple finally making their way down the steps and the last of the stragglers snailing their way to bid us farewell.

Not that it's ever quite been a problem since we're a family that's expected to stick together, but we've always only taken one car to and from church so that we gave the appearance of a united family. Not that we weren't, but it did make for having to plan out logistics like this from time to time, and the occasional one or two hours that Gray and I would have to spend stranded here waiting for Father to finish up one of his ever-lasting conversations with a member of the church in need of guidance.

"Sounds great, we'll get it done" Gray assured dad with his picture-perfect smile. I don't believe that anyone in history has ever had a better, more obedient kid in their life than my parents do with Grayson. Even with me never having broken a single rule or order of theirs, he was still the ideal child to have out of the two of us.

But he wasn't my competition—he was my inspiration.

Within minutes, the two of us were done doing our part seeing everyone out and were pushing open the doors for ourselves and meeting the pleasant warmth the sun kissed upon our skin. I never understood why the church was always one of the coldest places, but I never bothered—or dared—to ask. Who am I to question such a trivial thing?

"Let me drive," I told Gray with an open palm as we walked out to the parking lot together.

"Are you pulling a 'big sister is boss' move right now, or did you just forget to say please?" He jingled the keys between us with two fingers, and I grinned knowing that if I reached for them he would pull away.

"Pretty please, may I drive?"

"See, I told you that you were proper, *Genevieve.*"

Keys relinquished with a smile, he passed in front of me toward the passenger side and I got into the driver's seat. It felt good to have my hands on the wheel, a small but real symbol of control that I gripped tightly.

I let Gray control the radio as I pulled onto the street, windows down and hair being tossed about on both sides of the car. I stole glances at him while he quietly sang along to the hymn on the radio, strawberry-tinted-blonde mane in adorable disarray. I took that moment to thank God for giving him to me, for putting someone like him permanently by my side for our lives. It was a special thing to have an abundance of love for a sibling, and I knew that I was fortunate to have been given the gift of Gray. For all the things that I found myself questioning about my life, there was no doubt that I was blessed—with him.

"Do you miss it yet?" He asked me as my hands turned one over the other along the wheel, bringing us around the corner onto Main Street.

"University?" I don't know why I asked, I knew exactly what he meant. There was nothing else about my life *to* miss. "Honestly, not really. It was all work, and I only did what I was there to do; pass all my classes and please Mother and Father. I didn't really make any friends, unless you count my roommate. Which I don't, she wasn't ever around much, anyway." I could hear the words spill in my own ears and felt like everything I was saying was coming across as complaints. I sounded bitter, and I didn't want to sound that way, even if I was. "Anyway, no. I don't miss it."

"Then are you excited to be back?" He asked with his head turned to me, elbow propped on the open window and hand cradling his soft-featured face. If the questions were coming from anyone else, it would feel like an interrogation and like there were, in fact, right and wrong answers. But with Gray, I knew it was all polite and genuine curiosity. I had no reason to feel as guarded as I did.

"Truthfully?" I asked him, hoping maybe that in itself would imply a negative answer.

He nodded once, drawing his brows down as his smile lifted. It was an exaggerated expression that had me grinning. "You know that you never have to lie for me, and you never have to lie to me. Give it to me straight."

"I know," I assured him. "I just don't want it to sound as bad as I feel it does. But the thing is, I'm not excited to be back. Not as much as I thought I would be. Spending those years away, and yearning to be in familiar company like I was, made me think that I would want to drop to my knees and kiss the very ground that I returned to once I came back for good. But when I pulled into our driveway last night with all of my belongings piled up in the car, ready to plant myself back home, I noticed it. The lack of excitement, the lack of joy. I didn't even feel relieved, I felt. . .off. Like I left one life that's all wrong for me to come back to a life that's also all wrong for me."

A shrug of my shoulders was all I could offer in conclusion, because the brief silence kept me from wanting to look at his expression. I wasn't sure if what I said even made sense to anyone but me. Only I knew exactly how I felt. Trying to explain it didn't mean that it would be understood.

"I understand."

Or maybe I'm just always wrong.

"You do?" I exhaled relief. "I didn't know if I could actually express to you how this place doesn't feel right for me when you love your life here so much."

"What's best for me isn't what's best for everyone else. I'm one man meant to guide many lives, not live them all for them." There was that smile again, accompanying wisdom from the mouth of a babe. He was too young to know everything, and yet, he always had an answer. "I'm happy because I've embraced my calling. I've always known what I was meant to do, and I'm doing it. It has nothing to do with the place I'm in physically, but the place I'm in mentally and spiritually." He ran a hand through his hair, failing to put any wild strands into order. "Maybe you've just not met up with your purpose in life, yet."

"What if I don't have one?" I argued. And though it may have sounded more stubborn to him, the reality was that it was scary for me. To be this age, to have all these doubts and concerns, and to feel like there were no corners to even turn to look for answers. What would a lousy business degree bring me in terms of fulfillment? A job that I was meant to answer to day in and day out until I was old and gray or simply dead? I hadn't even gotten a job yet and here I was thinking of how death would one day release me from it.

There had to be more to life. I had to know why I was feeling so empty when I knew all too well that I was full of questions.

"Everyone has a purpose, Vieve." He wasn't belittling me in the confidence behind his answer. He was reassuring me.

I pulled into the market's parking lot, eyes catching the dim N on the Winston's sign hanging above the doors while I found a place right up front to park.

Just because everyone had a purpose, it didn't mean that everyone found it and pursued it, did it?

"Are you coming?" he asked with an open door and one foot already on the ground.

I needed a moment alone. Not that he wasn't always who I wanted to be around, but I wanted to get to shut my eyes and breathe without having him, or anyone for that matter, concerned about what was going through my head. I needed to align my loose thoughts.

"I really don't feel like running into anyone we know in there right now," I told him, realizing in the moment how much I really meant it. "We'll get stuck here longer than we should be, you know how that goes."

"All right," he relented easily, "but what should I get? Are we thinking cake? Pie? You name it."

"Oh, get a key lime pie," I said with enthusiasm. "It's been ages since I've had one of those."

"Key lime pie, it is. I'll be right back."

The closing door brought a jolt to the car, and I became aware of every second I was losing against the clock. I wanted to control myself, I wanted to regain my peace.

I wanted to stop feeling this way.

I wanted to know my purpose.

The soft air coming in through the windows embraced me, and I drew as much as I could into my lungs. I turned up the radio until I could feel the music in the soles of my feet. I closed my eyes against the tune of the hymn, allowing its comfort to soothe the muscles pulled taught in me. I leaned my head back against the seat, but kept my hands on the wheel. The relaxed hold I had on it felt like it grounded me.

"*And sings my soul*," I carried along with the hymn, each familiar word leaving my tongue without required thought.

I could sing along just as I had a thousand times before, but it didn't remove the weight from my chest. I could feel the frustration in me mounting up like setting bricks, and behind my closed lids I felt the tears pooling. It didn't feel right that I didn't feel right. There was nothing for me to not be happy about and satisfied with and appreciative for, yet here I was struggling to even understand why I couldn't force one second of serenity upon my heart.

One hand let go of the wheel and clutched my aching chest as one drop of water escaped the dam, falling from the corner of my eye and slowly traveling down my cheek. Its presence made me feel weak, and my voice grew in volume as it matched the words of the song in retaliation to my brokenness until I couldn't even catch my struggling breath.

My panting forced my eyes open, a few tears breaking free from the hold I had on them as I willed myself to calm down between heavy gasps. When my vision cleared and my chest rose and fell under my control, I saw him. Standing with his back against the concrete wall, directly in front of me with his eyes clearly on mine.

I couldn't bring myself to feel humiliated. It wasn't only that I was caught up in trying to possess myself, but because there was no humor in his gaze. He wasn't watching me with malicious intent—he was studying me.

Much like I was studying him now.

He had a lit cigarette between the fingers of the hand that rested over the top of the ice machine he stood by. The end of it continuously put out tendrils of smoke, but he never brought it between his lips. Such a strikingly pretty face, one that I couldn't tear my eyes from. We watched each other with nothing but the windshield and the new hymn coming through the speakers that carried loudly through the air. I sat in the driver's seat in my Sunday best, and he stood like a king who makes every location he graces sacred ground, robed in a suit of dark, tattered denim and cloth adorned with a band that I'd never even heard of.

While I felt like I was trying to figure him out, he looked like he already had me solved. As the sliding doors beside him opened to reveal Gray exiting with a pie in hand and a gleeful whistle from his lips, the man didn't spare a glance in his direction. His eyes remained on mine as a smile transformed his face.

I never knew that a face so pretty could possibly hide a smile that menacing.

Gray opened the car door at the same time the sliding doors revealed a small group of three that immediately cut me from my fixation on the man as they stood before him. One guy with hair as black as sin plucked the cigarette from the still visible hand, wasting no time bringing it to his mouth for an impressive drag as he smoothed back the top of his slick hair with his palm.

"Are you okay?"

I could barely hear him through the cloud-like state I drifted upon. A distant voice, but enough to pull my attention away from the mingling group in front of me.

"Huh?"

"Are you okay? You've been crying," Gray said with a single swipe of his finger along my jaw, wiping away the remnants of the episode that I'd temporarily forgotten.

"Oh yeah." I wiped at my own cheeks with hurried hands, clearing the already seen evidence. With wet lashes and a smile, I wasn't sure how convincing I actually looked. "I'm just fine."

"Okay, if you say so." So he wasn't convinced, but he wasn't going to push it, either. That, I was okay with.

I pulled the car into reverse, and as I backed away I watched the three people start to make their way down the sidewalk, one woman holding the neck of a burgundy wine bottle in each hand.

He took a step forward, breaking free from the wall. His steps were slow, the intent of it made evident as our eyes met one last time before he turned away and followed behind the others.

I stole one last look as I drove past him, his nearly-white curls catching the light of the sun like a halo.

FRAILTY

Everyone was waiting patiently and distracted by multiple conversations when Gray and I arrived at the Hannigans'. Father was accepting the praise that Mr. Hannigan was giving him for that morning's sermon, and Mrs. Hannigan was speaking to Mother with a hushed tone and raised brows which told me everything I needed to know about the gossip she was sharing. My mother would never initiate such a thing, but she felt no wrong in listening to others when it came to scandalous talk; it wasn't her lips that were being brushed with sin. And my mother liked to always know everything she could when it came to the town—and especially our church family.

Luke and Amelia sat across from each other, occupied in simple conversation with an empty seat beside each of them. Gray set the pie on the kitchen counter and I took the seat beside Amelia, Luke's eyes leaving his sister to acknowledge my presence.

"Hi, Gene."

The smile I returned was less enthusiastic than his. It wasn't that he wasn't a nice-looking guy who had always been kind to me, because he was. He just always suffered for the fact that I resented that my parents set it in their mind a long time ago that he and I belonged together. A match made in heaven—the pastor's daughter and the son of a deacon. We were brought up by like-minded parents, taught the same set of commandments to abide by, and told how to live by people that felt that what was best for us was to dictate our every move.

I bit my tongue against these thoughts, feeling like the hostility behind them was nearly audible. I had no right to be this angry. I was given a good life, and though I didn't know every little thing about Luke's, I knew enough about the similarities between Father and John Hannigan. Surely our lives couldn't be that different aside from me being a highly-protected female and him having the freedom of being a male.

I wasn't actually fooling myself. That made everything different.

"Hey, Luke. How've you been?" What was expected of me and the pressure put on the two of us wasn't his fault. I could swallow my feelings and be polite. It wouldn't be the first time.

"Great, now that summer break is finally here. I'm ready to get this last year over with. It feels good to be on the final lap, you know?"

"I do know. As exciting as it is to go to college, it's funny to realize that you're just as eager to leave it once you've spent a few years there. The last year is a breeze, you'll be done before you know it."

Mrs. Hannigan was placing dish after dish on the table, lining the middle with enough food to feed at least ten people. If it weren't already apparent, that was enough to tell me that she'd been expecting us to be here today. I'd no doubt that it was my parents' intended plan, too. They'd waste no time ensuring that they occupied any spare moment of my schedule now that I was entirely back under their control.

There had to be something wrong with me to have been both frustrated and comforted by that.

"I've enjoyed it for the most part, I'm just ready to really get life started. Ready to be done with this step and move on to the next," he said as he grabbed a roll from the platter in front of Gray and added it to his full plate. "But I'm grateful for the opportunities and experiences that all this provides, of course. Aren't you?"

"Experiences?" What experiences? "Yeah, of course."

"Surely you've had enough college talk to last you a lifetime," Mrs. Hannigan cut in with a dab of her napkin to each corner of her mouth. "You've done your time, now let's go 'head and move on to the present. What are you going to do with that big ole degree now that you're back?"

That was a good question. One that made my heart race because I knew there was probably a right answer that I didn't particularly know, and because every set of eyes was on me, waiting for me to provide it. I was going to say the wrong thing. Whatever I said, it wasn't going to be what my parents wanted to hear.

What did my parents want to hear?

"She just got back, mom," Luke intervened with eyes locked onto my face. "She hasn't even been here a whole day, I'm sure it takes more time than that to find a fitting job."

I silently thanked him with multiple anxious blinks. I doubted that he understood the message.

"Your mom asked for her plan, Luke. Not for a job she's already acquired." Mr. Hannigan brought his fork up to fill his mouth, and I thought about doing the same if only to give me more time to think of what to say.

How did I not know that these were the types of questions that I'd be asked? I should have known. I should have been prepared.

I was floundering. I was stuck pursing my lips with a blank mind, no random answer to grab on to. For having spent my entire life with constant pressure from everyone I know, why in the world did I still struggle under it?

"It's a business degree, so the plan is to go somewhere that there's business. Right?" Amelia chimed in with a gentle smile, awarding her a laugh from both Gray and Luke.

I returned her expression the best I could. I'm sure her face looked sweeter than mine.

"Well, you aren't wrong," Gray told her with a humored shrug. He knew exactly what she'd just done. Surely it was just as obvious to everyone at the table.

"So nothing specific in mind then, Gene?" Mrs. Hannigan insisted.

All I had to offer was the truth. Hopefully even my parents could appreciate that.

"No. Nothing yet, Mrs. Hannigan." I couldn't bring myself to gauge my parents' reaction. I'd done the best I could, I would no doubt suffer the consequences later on if they had any disapproval.

"That's perfect!"

What I didn't miss was the curious look on Mother's face when she finally decided to speak. "It is?"

"It is. I've been looking for someone to help with one of my patients now that Sara is on maternity leave, and I think that Gene would be just perfect for the job. It will be long hours, four days a week, but she's the type of good person needed for a job like this. What do you think? Do you want to think it over for a couple of days?"

The proposal caught me off guard; but although I wasn't entirely sure of what I wanted, I knew it wasn't this.

"Thank you, but—"

"It's exactly what she needs. You would love that, wouldn't you, Gene?" If my mother's tone didn't relay the message not to argue, Father's facial expression would have. One brow rose sternly as he took a drink from his glass. The thing is, I don't even know if they realize that they sound and look this way. Ensuring that they get what they want just comes naturally to them.

"Yes, of course. I'd love that. Thank you, Mrs. Hannigan."

I never felt like saying the opposite of what I felt was a lie if it meant I pleased my parents. Because the bigger truth was that I'd always strived to be as perfect for them as possible.

And apparently that meant that my own feelings weren't always right.

"Tell them about that dream you had the other night, Henry dear," my mother insisted with eager eyes. The conversation shifted as Father took over with a detailed story of demons crawling the earth, transitioning into a sermon of how in reality demons hide in plain sight and how we must constantly be on guard.

I caught bits and pieces as I managed to feed myself a few bites off my poorly filled plate. A throat cleared across the table pulled me out of my thoughts about demons, disappointment, and my attempt to face the fact that I will never know what I'm supposed to do with my life unless my hand is held each step of the way. I looked up to Luke, knowing that he'd been watching me sulk for some time now.

His hands were clasped in front of his mouth with his thumbs tucked under his chin. His improper-elbows on the table propped him up as he watched me, the only other one not transfixed by or engaging in the heavy conversation.

He winked, one brown eye disappearing behind slowly-closing lashes. Somehow I knew that this gesture wasn't intended to be flirtatious.

It was a show of comradery.

CURIOSITY

The job gave me an opportunity to escape. That was the bright side that I was focused on. That, and the fact that I really did enjoy my time with Ms. Owden. She was young for a seventy-four-year-old woman. She had high spirits and a sense of humor that would make a man much like my father blush. It was a minuscule form of freedom, and I was quickly able to overlook the matter of having been volunteered to be here.

She set another shoebox of memories on her lap. "You know what will set you up for life? Marrying a rich man. And an old one, so that you're rid of him sooner and you have nothing but money and time ahead of you."

I separated the papers and photographs on the coffee table that I sat beside while she poured out the contents of the new box. I didn't bother to hide my smile—something I would have done if I were in any other company. Here, I was safe. Being in this apartment with Ms. Owden felt like neutral territory. She could say no wrong, and I could do no wrong. It was interesting, the mutual understanding we immediately had with each other. I needed to be here with her just as much as she needed me to be here, too.

"Getting married isn't a bad idea. As for him needing to be rich and old. . .I don't know. I'd be happy with someone who's patient, and kind, and understanding." I picked up one of the photographs, looking into the eyes of a teenage Nancy Owden as she smiled an award-winning smile, sash placed across her shoulders to let all the world know that she was the winner. She was the beautiful one, the worthy one, the very idea of the young lady that should represent Miss Kansas.

I liked the idea of winning such a competition, if only to feel accomplished. Maybe I'd feel worthy if I convinced so many other people that I was worthy with my awards, crowns, and sashes. But what I really wanted was to be wanted for my talent, for my intelligence. And even those things I was unsure of. What did I really have to offer aside from a face that's pretty enough to get me a husband, just like my parents wanted?

"I just want a little more experience with the world. I thought maybe going to college would offer me that, but apparently it just isn't in the cards for me."

Nancy unfolded a certificate, the date 1922 in big bold letters heading one of the many awards she had from her pageant days. That would have only made her fourteen at the time. As much pride as I knew she had for those exciting years, I couldn't help but wonder as she folded the thick paper back up if she resented the fact that she was only rewarded for her physical attributes for all those years. It's how I felt, and I wasn't the woman being paraded around. Or maybe she just resented the fact that those years were over.

Life is harsh, either way. You either hate the years that you're given, or you love the years and they leave you.

"The funny thing about those cards you're dealt is that you're able to put them down and leave the table at any time. Go play golf or something if card games aren't for you."

I laughed as I pulled myself to my feet. "The thing is, I don't know which of life's games I'm good at. What if I pick the wrong one and spend my life failing?" I asked her, sobering quickly to the reality of the conversation as I grabbed her 8 o'clock pills from the cabinet.

"That's why you've got to try them all," she hollered back from her spot on the couch. "These hypothetical games, careers, men—whatever it is, that's always been my motto. You don't know what's out there for you until you take all the chances you can. It took me three kids and five husbands to get it right. My youngest daughter is flawless, and my fifth husband was perfectly good to me. You don't get what you want until *you* get what you want. Practice makes perfect, or whatever it is they say."

"My mother had no idea what she was signing me up for, here," I mumbled to myself with a grin.

Humorous thoughts on how my mother would faint to hear a woman condoning loose morals aside, I reflected over each of Nancy's points as I brought her the pill and a glass of water. It was the first time my opinions or desires were not only listened to, but respected. It felt wrong. It was so different that I felt like I messed up by being so open about what I wanted in my life.

Who was I to question all the plans that my parents had set for me? It was my responsibility to honor their wishes. It wasn't about taking chances; it was about doing what I was told. I needed to come to terms with that.

"Who's this?" The newspaper folded showed a young woman that looked just like Nancy, but the date on it was printed twenty years ago, 1962.

"That's Bridget, my youngest. My pride and joy, that one. She followed in her dear mother's footsteps, but damn if she didn't do it wearing prettier shoes." Nancy laughed, throwing herself into a coughing fit and taking a drink as she held a finger up to me. "If I live with any regrets, it's all those damn cigarettes. Do everything you want in life, but promise me you won't pick up smoking."

"I promise," I said without thought, caught up in the newspaper article. "Miss Ohio?"

"Oh yeah, that's where she grew up. Her father's family was there, so that's where we called home until she was old enough to set off on her own. Once she left for bright lights and big cities, I made my way back here to live out the rest of my days where I'm reminded that I was really, truly somebody. I may be an old and forgetful woman now whose daughter insists on having her babysat, but by George, I was who all the ladies wanted to be and who all the lads wanted to be with. And these are memories that I'm happy to die surrounded by."

She lost herself to the photo between her fingers, recalling a better time when she wasn't constantly reminded of the existence of life's clock. The dreadful ticking that grows louder as the years go by, the ticking you're deaf to when you're young and confident that the years you're experiencing are your best ones.

I was young, but I wasn't deaf. I could hear that clock, and I knew my life was passing me by as I lived without confidence.

The newspaper article praised Bridget for her many years of pageantry, telling the world of how all her hard work had led her to this and how they were sure that she would only continue to move on to even bigger things. Which I didn't even need to ask about to know that she did. With someone as supportive as Nancy for a mother, I'm sure Bridget was living out exactly the life she wanted because she knew that she was capable of having anything and everything her heart desired—no matter how big or small.

Clipped away as though someone cut the paper to fit into a frame, the back of Bridget's front-page article had bits and pieces of other stories that were relevant at the time. It was crazy to feel like I held a piece of history in my hands, even if that history was insignificant. These bits of news were important enough to be immortalized by this city in Ohio, and now they'd made the travel over two decades and several states.

"Such a sad story to be on the back of such a happy article about Bridget," I told her as my eyes locked onto the section almost entirely cut off at the bottom.

"What story would that be?"

"*Children Still Missing, No New Leads*," I read off to her.

"Oh, yeah, that. It's been ages since I've even thought about it, I'd entirely forgotten. It blurred together with all those years of Ohio scandal, I suppose."

"Do you remember if they were ever found?" I read the one available line that was left: *With the children of the recently deceased woman still unfound, the police are quickly losing ho—*.

"You know, I don't remember. I don't recall seeing much more about that whole thing a few months after the news first broke," she told me as she put the newly organized photographs into one of the shoeboxes. "Their mother was a user, you know. Just terrible, doing that kind of stuff around those kids. But the drugs killed her, and when they found the body, the little ones weren't around. It was all over the front pages at first, but then it became back page news. It's a sad thing for sure, but the world quickly loses interest in the problems of people like that drugged-up woman. I hate to be the one to say it, but it's true."

"That's so awful." I tucked away the newspaper clipping, adding it to the pile of others before setting them all into their own box. "Is there anything else you need me to do before Jane gets here in a few minutes?"

"No, you've done plenty. Thank you, sweetheart," she said as she pushed herself up off the couch. I rushed to her side, ready to catch her if she lost her balance.

"You're much more enjoyable to have around than that *Jane*," she said as she carried her glass to the kitchen. "I would complain about how she has it easy, getting to make money for doing nothing. I mean, why would I need someone to be here overnight? What trouble could I get into while I'm sleeping?" She pulled a pitcher out of the fridge and filled her glass with tea. Her strict diet called for watching her sugar intake, but I didn't bother asking if the tea was sweet. She would probably lie to me, anyway, and Jane was going to be here any minute. She could be the bad guy. "But I suppose I won't complain since it's Bridget's money and not mine. I think her claims that I need to be watched are a bit exaggerated, but nobody cares about an old lady's opinion." She rolled her eyes and took a drink just as the front door opened and Jane walked in.

Immediately, she honed in on the glass and set her best serious face. "Is that sweet tea, Ms. Owden?"

"*Is that sweet tea, Ms. Owden?*" Nancy mimicked in her best Jane-voice and I covered my mouth to keep myself from laughing as I backed away toward the door. "Goodbye, Gene!" She called as Jane took the glass from her and poured it down the sink.

"See you tomorrow, Nancy."

The night was wrapped in summer's humidity, the moisture in the air kissing its way up my exposed arms. It was a pleasant and mostly quiet walk down the few blocks to my car, nothing but my thoughts and the sounds of the city preparing to sleep as company. I'd begun parking farther and farther away from Ms. Owden's home as the first couple weeks went on because I enjoyed this part of the job; getting to spend time with myself before inevitably having to go home. The farther away I parked, the more time I had.

The sounds of the night began to crescendo as I reached the last block before getting to my car. My steps on the sidewalk slowed as I neared the lot containing all the noise, music inside the home so loud that I could barely make out all the profanity-laced lyrics. The familiar shape of the house had my attention, the large building having all but a steeple as proof of what I was seeing.

And I recognized the back of the person walking inside through the open front door.

"Luke?"

Curiosity and fear are a sickening combination. My stomach twisted as I made my way up the long sidewalk to the front door, entering the welcoming opening that had already greeted at least one hundred others. There were bodies everywhere, all conversations covered by the blaring instruments within the music.

I stepped around a man propped up against the wall. His head hung awkwardly to the side and his shirt was torn open to reveal the words *lying asshole* in what I hoped was lipstick. My fingers clung to the cross on my necklace, a nervous and comforting habit. I pulled the pendant back and forth across the thin gold chain, keeping as much distance as I could between the bodies inhabiting the giant room. It wasn't the same atmosphere that I was used to, but it was a place that I knew well.

The sanctuary was littered with people dancing, some sitting on small clusters of worn-down furniture and consumed with conversation and cigarettes, and others entirely passed out and laying in inconvenient places across the floor. My fear and focus to find Luke kept me from realizing how out of place I must have looked among the tattered clothes and extreme hairstyles until I brushed up against a woman who stared me down starting from my knee-length skirt and up to my long brown hair. She wore a skirt that formed to her body and her hair was short, wild, and pink beneath the flickering lights above us. It was clear that I wasn't the one that was normal, here.

"Excuse me," I said politely, brushing my sweating palms down my skirt.

"Are you lost or something, girl?"

Despite the fact that we were probably about the same age, I did what I could to force a smile at the comment. As different as she was to me, she wasn't someone to be afraid of. "No, I'm just looking for a friend of mine."

She laughed, looking me over once again. "I doubt who you're looking for is around here. I don't think this is the place a *friend* of yours would be. What's their name?"

"His name is—" Luke appeared at the far end of the room, leaving through an open side door. "Actually, I just saw him. Thank you for your help."

I took off in his direction, rushing and ready to get out of here. I didn't even know exactly what to say to him when I did catch up to him. As curious as I was about why he was here, was it actually any of my business? Wasn't I the one who often silently complained about not having a life of my own? Whatever the reason was, he was here living his own life. I, of all people, should respect that. There were many reasons why I should leave this place, and his privacy was one of the important ones to me.

As I walked through the door he'd gone through, I turned down the hall toward the direction of the front entrance. I wanted to leave, I wanted to be out of this place that had my neck perspiring more than the outside heat did. I wanted to go and to forget about my curiosity and listen to my fear or my instinct—whatever it was that told me to get out of there in that moment.

But it was too late.

Luke was leaned against the wall, lips embracing those of the man he held onto passionately.

My heartbeat became louder than the music. My fingers clutched at my necklace. My mind told me to leave and never let him know that I invaded his privacy.

I turned back to go through the side door again, running to avoid him seeing me and knowing that I was ever even here. Colliding with a body in my hurry sent me falling backward onto the hallway floor, my hands catching my fall as I twisted and pushed myself back up quickly to rush away through the door. The body still blocked my way, the man's pierced and angry face preventing my escape.

"Watch where the fuck you're going, bitch," he practically yelled as his hands shoved against my shoulders, pushing me back against the wall.

My back pressed tightly up against the wall as he stepped closer to me, pushing at my shoulders again just to prove a point. I couldn't move. I was trapped. I was petrified.

"Gene?" Luke's voice called from what sounded like miles away.

"What, are you too good to say sorr—"

The furious face was torn back from my sight as he was pulled down by one of the spikes atop his head.

A man with a cigarette between his lips kept a tight grip on the guy's hair, aggressively holding him captive. I immediately recognized the man restraining my aggressor as his free hand pushed back his dark hair before plucking the cigarette from his mouth.

"Now, Axel. You can't go around treating our guests that way."

A wide space around us cleared. People gathered on both ends of the hallway watched from a safe distance— one that I was envious of. I saw Luke watching from the frontline, and I wasn't sure if the worry on his face was because I was here or because I was in the middle of something like this.

I was too busy trying to find comfort in the one soul that I knew to realize that it wasn't just the three of us that were the center of attention anymore.

"You owe the lady an apology." His bright hair no longer had the halo of the sun, but held the shadows of the dim hallway in between his white curls. It possessed both the dark and the light—like his beautiful face with its wicked smile.

Axel's eyes promised violence unto my face as he was held down by one man and confronted by the other. "She owes me one and she knows it."

"I recall her stumbling into you being an accident. You pushing her around wasn't. Doesn't seem to me that you're the one with the right to be upset about this." The chilling smile wasn't on his face as he dropped down to Axel's eyeline. It didn't make his presence any less terrifying. "Apologize. Now."

"She can fuck right o—"

All it took was one tilt of his head to summon the woman from the group of bystanders. She broke free of the crowd with a sprint just as quickly as the man holding Axel shoved his head down to the floor. It was a matter of seconds that stretched into an eternity for me as I watched her speed and the force of her booted foot meet with Axel's floor-pressed face.

There were cheers, there were laughs, and there was a guttural yell that left Axel as the man released his head and left his busted face bleeding on the floor. He coughed and grunted while he pulled himself up onto his hands and knees.

The man knelt before him and patted him forcefully on his abused cheek, his crouched form blocking most of the damage done from my view. "You should always know to take the second chances I offer. I rarely give them."

He put a hand to the floor and pushed himself up. He turned to me, and his smile appeared as he saw my head flinch in turn to his approach. He stopped a foot away, close enough for me to hear him over the chaos that now continued after everyone had had enough of the show, but far enough to let me know he wasn't intending to be a threat.

"Hello, Dove."

I was confused. I was in shock. I was sick with emotion.

"Sometimes you need to bare your teeth. And sometimes, that means you need to break some."

He extended his closed hand, and the fingers around my necklace unraveled to fall into place beneath it. He dropped the contents into my palm and then closed my fingers with his.

"Is she a friend of yours?" he asked, but my mind was turning too quickly from all the events to focus on any one thing. The contents in my hand felt like they weighed more than me—or at least more than I could handle.

"She is," Luke said from beside me. How long had he been there?

He was probably wondering the same thing about me.

"Take her home," he directed Luke. "She's sick with shock, but she'll be all right."

My brain registered enough of what was going on around me to watch as the man left.

"Get the fuck out of my house." He pushed Axel's still-bent head aside roughly as he walked by him and caught up with the other man and woman. They all left the hallway through the side door that started this entire thing, and my body began to shake.

I felt Luke's grip on my arm and I knew that I was being pulled and led away by him, but everything that my eyes took in was a blur. All I was really seeing was the last twenty minutes played over and over again in my mind. Never in my twenty-two years had I seen such violence, nor such a joyful response to it. The sound of the heavy boot meeting such a fragile face looped in my ears as the scene insisted on commandeering my thoughts.

The change in the air greeted the sweat on my skin, and by the time I was able to pull myself out of my own head, Luke had already brought us next to my car.

"Get in, Gene." He held the passenger door open, waiting for me to comply. I opened my hand to grab the key from my pocket so that he could drive, and the contents I'd been clutching scattered on the concrete.

Two whole teeth and several small pieces finally stopped rolling around our feet. The sight of them and the blood marking my hand forced an involuntary reaction, and I vomited all the built-up fear and curiosity that had been twisting my stomach so much. The shakes were shock, the growing headache was guilt. Somewhere buried in my alive and wired nerves was the excitement of the experience. I felt sick in more ways than one.

Luke held my hair back until I was done. The second that I was able to catch my breath, I focused on the concrete that wasn't marred with bloody teeth or vomit and willed the world to stop spinning.

"I'm so sorry."

"Don't be. I'm sorry that you had to see that." Luke gently pulled on my hair, silently asking me to stand up and face him. "Are you okay?"

"I'm fine. I'm not the one with a broken face." I didn't bother to look back down at the evidence on the ground. I would never get rid of the mental image or the feel of the bloody bones that I'd hung onto for so long.

"Yeah, but he shouldn't have been shoving you. He could have apologized."

"And I shouldn't have even been there. I could have avoided all of this in the first place."

Luke stared into my eyes long enough to tell me that he could argue for as long as I could, but that he wouldn't. He nodded his head toward the seat and I obeyed, glad to have my shaking legs out from underneath me.

We pulled away from the teeth on the sidewalk, away from the house that held the only horrors that I knew; away from the Luke and Gene that existed before tonight. I knew too much. I knew his secrets, and I knew the reality of the world.

"What were you doing there, anyway?" Luke asked me, breaking the silent tension in the car. I knew what answers he was wanting, and I wasn't going to withhold them.

"I was walking to my car from Ms. Owden's house when I saw you going in there. I didn't think about it. I just followed in behind you. I wanted to see you and why you were in a place like that."

My thumbs fought each other as my bloody hand clasped my clean one. Though, I supposed neither of my hands were clean. So many things were now upon my conscience, including how uncomfortable I knew that Luke was right then.

"Did you happen to see anyth—"

"I saw."

His jaw clenched, and his hold on the steering wheel tightened. I could see the whites of his knuckles catch the streetlights we passed by. "I know that you've been through a lot tonight, Gene. I don't want to ask too much of you, but you have to understand what I'm saying when I say that you *cannot* tell anyone. You can't, Gene. Please tell me that you understand."

"I understand. I'm not going to tell anyone, Luke. I never was."

"I mean it. Nobody can know." His voice was steady, but his worried eyes were pleading.

I wanted to turn up the radio, I wanted comfort in the hymn that I knew would come through the speakers. The security of a song that I knew I'd heard my entire life; one that reminded me of the life I'd had only a couple of hours ago.

I'd longed for change in my sheltered life. I never thought that just wanting it would ignite it.

"I mean it, too. Nobody will." I wiped my hand down my skirt, mentally reminding myself to wash it before anyone could notice the small traces of blood. "I wish you knew that you could have told me, though."

He laughed, a bitterly humored and sarcastic sound that had me looking at him to try to gauge his expression. I wanted to see inside his head and get out of mine.

"Tell you? How? Just say, 'Hey, I'm actually gay' at one of the family dates, surrounded by our *very* strict parents that have obviously been trying to set the two of us up for our entire lives?" He rolled his eyes toward me briefly, offering a sad smile. "It wasn't you that I was worried about disappointing, Gene."

"And I'm not," I assured him. I hadn't ever considered whether he felt the way our parents wanted him to.

Knowing that he didn't was a relief for one reason, but concerning for another. "Just promise me that you'll be careful. I don't want anything to. . .happen to you."

We both knew what wasn't said. The implication itself hurt. I could see it in his eyes that strayed from the road and looked into mine, and I could feel it in my heart as I thought about the danger that society posed to him. Luke was good. Luke was generous. Luke was the guy that held back your hair when you were sick from witnessing violence for the first time. I cared about him; he was one of the very few people my age that I was ever able to be around growing up because of who his parents are. His secret wasn't a burden to me. It was something I would hold onto because it mattered—because he mattered.

"I will be. I promise."

I rolled down my window, hoping the wind whipping in would strip my hair of all the smells of smoke and blood and change. Cigarettes and other unidentifiable scents lingered on my clothes, and I knew that I would need to wash them twice to hide it all.

"Hey, did I hear Othello call you 'Love'?"

I pulled away from the window and looked at Luke, my brows drawn as I tried to process his question. "Who?"

"Othello. The one that gave you the teeth." The shudder that ran through him was nearly invisible to me, but it reassured me that I wasn't the only one that found that so unsettling. Luke being affected by it, even a fraction of the amount that I was, calmed me down enough to make me think that I was on the verge of feeling normal again.

Whatever normal was, now.

"No," I told him, my index finger tracing the metal of the cross hanging from my neck. "He called me Dove."

ANONYMITY

I sleepwalked through two days of my life. Every morning that I sat at the table for breakfast with my family, I couldn't feel the difference between being asleep and being awake. My nightmares blended with my daydreams. I was consumed by foreign feelings of unnatural excitement, my system holding onto the only thrill it had ever known. I couldn't pry myself away from this new state of mind.

Inciting pain wasn't always the same as violence. I knew the difference. I vividly remembered the time that Gray broke his arm when he fell out of the rope swing we played on in our backyard—the cracking sound, the scream, the tears that I watched pour from both his eyes and Mother's as our father set the bone back into place. I remember holding onto Gray as he cried with his head upon my shoulder while Father wrapped and casted his arm. Of all the painful memories, all the times that we were hurt and had to endure such things while Father did what he could to fix us, it wasn't the same as this. There wasn't the same intrigue that there was behind the incident that kept me so consumed with trying to hide my thoughts about it from Gray and Mother and Father as we dined together.

"I ran into Peter Handish just yesterday, Son." Father addressed Gray with eyes on a newspaper and coffee in hand. "He had a few things to say about your work ethic and your quality as a student."

"Good things, I hope." Gray's spoon hovered in his hand above his bowl of oatmeal, a slight flush to his boyish, round cheeks. I don't know how he could actually worry about something such as talk of his character; he was perfect. There was never an ill thing that could be said in honesty.

"Oh, I'm sure they were," Mother translated my thoughts aloud. "We all know how hard you work to prove yourself worthy of your father's insistence that Peter reserve you a spot."

Grayson would have a degree and be a minister himself in just one more semester. Father had personally asked Mr. Handish to allow Gray in when the classes were already full, because Gray was last to make the decision that we all knew he would inevitably make. It wasn't surprising that Gray took so long to finalize our assumptions, though. He never did anything that he wasn't certain of.

"He said you're one of the brightest, most driven students he's ever seen. That you excel in every course, and that I should be proud." Father looked at Mother, sharing a parental exchange before looking at Gray with what could be considered a smile.

Our father was never the man to say that he was proud. But there was no denying the pride he had in a son that wanted to walk in his sacred shoes.

I wasn't a disappointment. I knew that I had never given them any reason not to be just as proud of me, but it was different than with Gray. I was the daughter that begged to be let go so that she could go to college almost an hour away. Gray was the son that wanted to become a minister, stay close to home, and never leave our parents' sight. I question every move I make after I make it. Gray doesn't make any move that hasn't been calculated thoroughly. He was more than okay with his life here, and my very core was being shaken by mine.

The phone rang on the wall behind my seat, startling only me with its chime through the silent room.

"I'll get that," Mother said enthusiastically, folding the corner of the page in the catalog that she'd been happily perusing.

I'd never noticed how happy we'd all always been to just sit in silence like this, my parents satisfied with just having us in their sight. They would quietly settle for knowing exactly where we were, though, too.

"Hello? Hi, Sandy!"

My body stilled as I waited to hear what Mrs. Hannigan called for. I knew better than to think that Luke would utter a single word about where we had both been the other night, but it didn't stop my heart from racing. It made no sense to be this on edge. Nobody was going to know everything I saw—nobody could hear my thoughts.

"Of course! We would love to. Thursday night, it is!" Mother nodded against the phone held between her head and shoulder as she wrote her plans down on the calendar hanging next to her. "But next time we'll host, deal?" She pointed to the phone as if Mrs. Hannigan could see her playful face. How was everyone in this house so happy and content—and why wasn't I? "All right, we will see you then! Bu-bye."

"I've got to run to Winston's and grab several things. Does anyone want to go with me?" Mother asked the three of us, grabbing her purse off the counter.

"I'm going to head to the church in a few minutes to fine-tune tomorrow night's sermon. I'll be home in time for dinner," Father said. He got up to give her a kiss goodbye, just as he always does, and she smiled in return, just as she always did.

Something in me was becoming too conscious of what was normal in this family. The small details, the routine. Why was I no longer blind to it all?

Father disappeared down the hallway and returned with his bible and a messy stack of papers tucked under his arm.

"Are you working tonight, Gene?"

"Yes. I should be home around ten-ish," I told him, giving the answer to the question that he didn't have to ask.

"Ten-ish?" he repeated with a raise of his brow as he held the front door open.

"I'll be home before ten," I corrected.

He nodded a quick approval and left the house, not needing to ask Gray the same questions. Not because Gray didn't work at the moment, but because it was never custom for him to question Gray.

I was becoming aware of everyone else's normal while I was losing the hold on mine.

"Gene?" Gray called from across the table for what could have been the twentieth time for all I knew from my oblivious focus on the front door.

"Yeah?" A shake of the head brought me enough clarity to realize that I didn't notice him leave from his seat beside me.

He shuffled the deck of cards fluttering skillfully in his hands. We'd played often, and he would always win. "Do you want to play?"

Cards just wasn't the game for me.

"Sure, I've got time to kill before work."

But I would do anything to keep pretending like it could be, for as long as possible.

There were many factors that could have been what made me stop on the sidewalk in front of that reformed church, that dark home that housed violence and all the things I'd always been shielded from. I'd been told before that curiosity is what killed the cat, but my curiosity didn't feel like it was going to lead me to death.

It felt like it was leading me to life.

"Take care," Ms. Owden had told me as I left her house. I said that I would, but now, not even ten minutes later, I found myself standing before the place that I had been careless for the first time.

The silence of the house was so strange compared to the music and state of mayhem that emanated from it last time. My feet inched their way closer, my ears straining to hear just a semblance of the noise from my memory. This still and quiet place couldn't be the same one that held the people and events that now plagued me; but I knew scary smiles and anarchy lived somewhere inside. The part of me that wouldn't let myself ignore the excitement from it is what had me standing three feet from the door.

"Hello, Dove."

My hand clutched my chest instead of covering the startled noise that escaped my mouth. I stared at the man I now knew as Othello while my heart pattered beneath my palm. I didn't expect to be caught lurking by the vehement man himself. I didn't expect that I'd return here in the first place either, though.

"I'm sorry, I don't know what I'm do—"

"Don't be," he cut in, brown eyes exuding a fire that the summer heat could only be envious of. It was amazing, how so many threatening features were molded into a face that deserved to be immortalized. "I knew that you'd be back."

"You did?" My mouth ran dry, my voice betraying every ounce of fear I attempted to disguise.

He leaned back against the wall, setting a scene that resembled the first time I saw him. Only this time, the moon was high and the sun wasn't there to keep me exposed. This time, there was no boundary of a windshield between us.

"I could tell by the look on your face that what you saw was new to you. New things lead to further curiosity, don't they?"

I didn't want to tell him he was right. I knew better than to lie, too. The smile that grew on his face told me that he already knew that he was right, and that he didn't need an answer from me. He was proving to me over again just how well he could read me.

"What more do you want to learn from me, Dove?"

I couldn't tell him my name. The intrigue behind what he called me and the safety behind him not entirely knowing me prevented it. "Nothing," I said instead. "I don't know why I'm here.

His head rested back against the white siding of the church—the house. I'd spent many years inside a building built with the same purpose as this one. I looked up and down the height of it, wondering if it were just the structure that had drawn me in. Just the way my instinct recognized the building as a place of surety and refuge. I looked down from its great height and back to Othello's waiting expression. He knew just as well as I did that that wasn't why I was here, even if I was confused about the truth of it.

"I've got to go. I'm sorry for showing up like this. It won't happen again." I turned around quickly, my head telling me to just get in my car and drive home like I should have. There was still enough time to escape whatever destructive path I was subconsciously on. I could still change course. I could still get away.

But I couldn't ignore the strong voice that stopped me in my tracks.

"Wait," he said with no softness. He knew that the second he ordered, I would obey. "Why don't we start with something easier than that." I turned around to face him again. He was trying not to smile now that he got what he wanted. He knew that his smile could send me running. "Why don't you ask me that question you have, instead."

"What question?" He looked down at me from his elevated stance, and I felt smaller than I already was beneath his stare.

"The one that you just had in your eyes before you tried to leave." He told me as he shoved his hands into his pockets. "Ask it."

I didn't like that I had to be guided through my own thoughts and emotions by him. I didn't like that he knew me this well already when we were still perfect strangers. I also didn't like that I had to lie to myself about not liking it.

"Why do you live in a church?" A fraction of the weight that rested on my chest lifted as the question left my lips. It made me aware of how often I hung onto all of the thoughts and questions that I had all the time. It made me appreciate him in a way just for forcing me to notice.

He nodded his head in approval, apparently pleased that I gave in. There wasn't anything smug about his satisfied expression, though. "To prove to the world that I'm just a man with the fact that I don't burst into flames the very second I step inside," he said, a trace of his smile visible. "Or maybe because it was abandoned around the same time I was and it's just the way things worked out. Maybe not everything is as complex or as simple as it initially seems."

"How old are you?" I asked the very second the thought came to mind. The age and life behind his words didn't match the face my gaze was latched upon.

He smiled his full smile, and I instinctively took a step back. "Allowing you to ask one question was all it took for you to be comfortable asking more?"

"I'm sorry. I didn't mean to pry." I felt the embarrassment and the heat of the predatory glare rush through my face.

"Stop apologizing to me." It felt like an order as he took a larger step toward me than the one I took away from him. "You need to learn what is and isn't worth being sorry for."

My focus shifted to the dwindling space on the ground between us as he continued to approach me. As active as my nerves were, I couldn't move. Whatever brought me there in the first place—curiosity, suspicion, naïvety— whatever it was, it's what kept me there now.

"Where's that unaffected woman that could stare me down while tears fell from her eyes the first time she saw me?" He asked when he stood close enough for me to hear the authority in his lowered voice. "Who's this little girl that's now flinching and shying away from the same man?"

I looked up to see his smile gone and a disappointed expression replacing it. I had had enough of disappointment, and feeling like it's all I gave anyone. If he was the first person that would let me freely ask, then he could be the first to hear me freely speak.

"I'm not a little girl," I corrected with more malice than I had intended.

His brow raised in response, and though there was humor in his eye from my clearly surprising retort, he watched me steadily as he replied to me seriously. "You are so long as you allow the world to treat you like one."

The front door opened and colliding voices walked through it, letting it slam shut behind them while I stood with my lips tightly sealed in a silent standoff with Othello. I wouldn't know what to reply to something as honest and hurtful as that even if I wanted to.

"If it isn't my favorite party favor," someone said, tearing me away from my wounded trance.

A group of four had emerged from the house. The man who always had a cigarette, the woman who'd disfigured Axel's face with the boots that she wore right now, another woman in a short, skin-tight dress with hair that was curled and twice the size of her head, and a tall man between the women whose smile held all the gentleness that Othello's lacked as it dazzled against his skin, which matched his dark brown leather jacket perfectly. All of them wore clothes with signs of wear and tear that my mother would mistake for trash, let alone ever allow me to have or wear in the first place. All of them, especially Othello before me, were the vision of exactly who Father would insist we cross to the other side of the street to avoid. He would draw a clear line between *them* and *us*.

But here I was, alone amongst them. It wasn't my body or my life that felt physically threatened. It was my entire world that was threatening to change by my being here.

HELLO, DOVE

"Party favor, huh?" the woman with the painted-on dress said as she leaned into the tall man. Even with her hair as large as it was, she barely reached his shoulder as he wrapped his arm around hers and pulled her into him.

"Because she came to the party, and did me the favor of bringing some bloodshed along with her," the man with the cigarette clarified, pulling the stick from his mouth and letting the smoke escape from between his grinning lips. "Shit was awfully boring before you arrived. It's been a few days now since I've got to knock someone around a bit. Did you bring some more trouble along with you this time that you wanna share?"

The woman with the boots laughed, her voice a light twinkle in the void space of a dark conversation. Despite how sick I was with guilt about that incident, I refused to let them all know exactly how it affected me. I forced my face to remain blank and scolded myself to control my stomach as it turned with the thought of that bloodshed, that trouble. I held back the apology on my tongue, too, for fear of Othello admonishing me for being sorry about an act that I didn't even commit. I was trying to catch on to how to act here, but I still wasn't any less confused and out of place.

"No trouble," I told him, my arms crossed over my stomach, the only thing hiding my fists that I kept clenching in nervousness. "I was on my way home from work. Just passing by."

"Why don't you stick around a while?" he asked as he leaned against one of the pillars of the front awning of the church. House. "You didn't bring trouble to us, but we can take you with us to find some, *Genevieve*."

My pulsing fists stilled, as did my heart and sense of control that I had in my anonymity. The shock must have shown on my face, because I wasn't great at guarding my reactions and the four of them standing together all laughed as I involuntarily took a few steps back. Othello's smile was present again when I looked to him, grappling with whether I should be running or asking more questions.

"That's Adam," he said, nodding his head toward the man who traded his laughter for smoke. "Then there's Nora, and the ones hanging all over each other are Michael and Rachelle."

"Nice to meet you," I said to them all, and smiles, nods, and brief waves answered.

"And you already know my name," Othello stated. I looked from him, to Adam and his almost finished cigarette, to Michael and Rachelle as they displayed their affection openly, and back to him, finding no proper reply in between.

What is there to be said to someone who knows your every thought?

"As I assumed," he said, finding whatever confirmation he needed in my silence.

Apparently nothing was required to be said. Unsettled, I forced in a breath and with it the strength to make my escape. "I've got to be getting home," I told Othello, sparing a quick look at the others to be polite. "Sorry for. . ." I stopped myself, but shrugged because it was too late and already said. "showing up like this. I don't know."

He stepped closer to me, speaking quietly enough so that the others couldn't hear. His light-colored curls draped the sides of his face as he looked down at me, the dark irises contrasted by the whites of his eyes just as his hair was against the black sheet of the night sky.

"I do know," he said, keeping my focus held prisoner by the seriousness on his face. His purely beautiful face. "I knew that you'd be back, and I know why you're here. You're here because you're in search of something." He pulled back, straightening and keeping his gaze on me with downcast eyes. "Maybe it's more than something. Maybe it's everything."

My feet were rooted into the grass as he left me. He walked away from all of us, but the others immediately followed behind him as he made his way down the sidewalk. They disappeared together into the night, and I finally found the capability to flee from the empty church that I'd been left alone with.

TEMPTATION

Let's let Gene have that seat, Amelia," Mrs. Hannigan had called from the doorway of the kitchen as she removed her apron and hung it on the hook in the wall beside the fridge. Amelia stopped behind the chair beside Luke, then smiled as she saw the only other available one beside Gray. Our parents were no longer going out of their way to solely play matchmaker behind the scenes. They were making it just as obvious now as it had always been to us. Or at least to me.

The purpose of the dinner together wasn't just about forcing the four of us to spend time with our intended partners, though. As tiring as it was to have my strings pulled around by Mother and Father, it was clear that our parents really did just enjoy the company of John and Sandy Hannigan. It was especially apparent during times like these, when the four of them would be caught up in their own conversations over an hour after dinner was over.

The four of us had moved into the living room to play board games together some time ago, and after two rounds of Gray and I losing to the most competitive siblings in existence, we called it quits and opted to put on a movie and wait out our social parents.

Gray and Amelia sat on opposite ends of the couch. I watched her watch Gray more than the movie, and I wondered if I had ever missed the times when Gray had been the one watching her. I'd never seen him show her the attention that she paid him, and even in that case, our parents were going to have an easier time pairing those two than they would Luke and me. For more reasons than just the obvious.

I looked at Luke, who like Gray, was glued to the screen. We sat on separate seats entirely. The distance wasn't put in place by just one of us. It was always an amicable thing that kept us apart like this. While I knew now that he had no desire for me, I thought about why it was that I had never felt any for him. He had always been as close to me as a male friend would be allowed by parents like mine, he was inarguably handsome, and he was consistently respectful. I'd never thought about how I wanted more than all that. More than *just* that.

He caught me looking at him, and I didn't bother to try to hide it. He gave me a friendly smile, but his creased brows held concern. I didn't know why I was studying him, using him as an example to myself of how to evaluate every aspect of my life. That's all I ever seemed to do anymore.

"Excuse me," I said to nobody in particular.

There was no way to get a grip on myself. As I cupped cold water from the bathroom sink into my hands and submerged my face into it, I promised myself to adjust. To accept that I felt different now than I did before, and that that was okay. I didn't want to continue to fight myself like this constantly anymore. I had to make a promise, because the only thing that I still knew about myself, without a doubt, was that I kept my promises.

I let my mind run free as I began to make my way back to the living room. I told myself to take the short walk to accept everything new, everything different, and return to feeling like Gene again by the time I sat back down.

Children went missing, people kept huge secrets; there was violence, and those that didn't follow any rules. This was just the reality of the world that existed outside of my own. As quickly as I had to learn of it all, I had to digest it. I didn't have to be entirely over it; I would have forced myself to be already if I could. I just had to come to terms with it. I was slowly swallowing that bitter pill.

I took my time thinking through everything, inching my way down the hall back toward the living room. My eyes saw the framed photos along the wall that I would appear to anyone else to be studying, but my mind was lightyears away. Until I saw one of the Hannigans' family photos, and caught myself involuntarily grinning at the exaggerated smile on Luke's face in one of the pictures. It was such a classy photo, aside from the kid staring at the camera with eyes opened too-wide and that smile that seemed to take up half his face.

"My mom was so upset with me about that picture that she refused to hang it up for nearly four years after we took it," Luke said from beside me, and my grin turned into a short laugh as he shook his head with a smile.

"I don't see why," I told him. "This is my favorite one, by far. I don't know how I've never noticed it before. How old were you in that one? I've known you our whole lives, basically, and I can't gauge it."

"I was nine in the picture, and thirteen when she finally displayed it. Thirteen-year-old Luke found it just as funny as nine-year-old Luke did. To be honest, twenty-one-year-old Luke thinks it's pretty great, too," he said with a vigorous nod of approval and a pleased expression. "But you've probably never noticed it because mom tried to hide it in plain sight. That's why it's above eye-level and surrounded by several others. Apparently to her, it isn't worthy of having its own place to stand out."

I pointed to it, gesturing to the two people that I didn't recognize that stood on separate ends. "And who are they?" The man stood by Mr. Hannigan, and the woman stood by

Mrs. Hannigan. Luke and Amelia were in the middle together, his arm around her shoulder in the only acceptable pose that he was offering for the picture. I got caught on his contagious smile once again.

"Those are my grandparents. My father's mom and dad. Getting the picture taken was their idea, and they weren't even upset about my face. My mom was being a little dramatic about the whole thing, if you ask me."

His subtle sense of humor made me smile. He'd always been this way—himself, I guess—but it felt like I knew more about Luke now. It wasn't just knowing more about who he was because of what secrets he kept, but also because I felt closer to him now because of it all. It took one night of his secrecy and my mistakes to bring us together after all those years of knowing each other.

Nothing was as complex or as simple as it initially seemed.

The echo of Othello's words sent a shiver up my back. One that jolted me with a realization.

"I forgot that most people have those," I thought aloud.

"Have what?" Luke asked as he took the framed picture down off the wall.

"Grandparents. I forget that they're a normal thing to have," I said as I put my back against the wall and watched him walk farther away from me. He paused whatever he was doing to turn around and face me fully.

"How do you forget about grandparents?" The judgmental shock on his face could have been feigned or real; he was skilled enough at schooling his expression to never let his audience know the difference. Either way, I didn't feel embarrassed to further clarify.

"You forget by not having any, that's how," I told him with a grin as I watched him replace the photo that had hung by itself with the one of his ridiculous face. "I mean, I guess I do, technically. I've just never known them."

"Any of them?" He took a couple steps backward and appreciated his work before coming back over to me to hang the other picture up in its new spot. "Usually people have at least one of them around."

"Not me and Gray. I guess that makes us the unusual ones."

"I know a thing or two about being unusual," he said as he put the finishing touches on his mischievous photo-swap. "Which kind of brings me to something that I've wanted to ask you." He took a last look at the new picture in front of us before turning to me, closing in on me and dropping his voice down to a whisper. "How would you feel about dating me?"

"Dating you?" I felt the surprise show on my face, and I tried to reign it in. The expression felt as loud as my voice did, so I gentled both of them before speaking again. "Why would you want me to date you? I thought that you were. . .n't interested in me."

His lips pulled up into a grin at my uncertain slip, relieving me of my worry of offending him. "Yes, as you know, I'm *not* interested in you," he said, putting up his hand to halt his statement. "Not that you aren't lovely, of course."

I shook my head, unable to keep myself from snickering at the compliment. The first time I was told that I was lovely, and it came from the unobtainable man that my parents wanted me to be with. My life was once a clear picture, but was now a complicated puzzle. I was having to figure myself out by fitting together all of the pieces that were being thrown at me left and right.

"So you aren't interested in me, but you want us to date?" I asked, letting my confusion show plainly. Maybe this was the way that it worked? For all I knew, this is what relationships were. A mutual agreement to participate and an understanding of one another. My parents never set an example of romance, nor was it condoned by their strict standards. This was the man they wanted me to be with, and here he was pursuing their wishes. Was I meant to overlook the details, despite how major they were?

"In a way, I do," he said, tossing his head slowly side to side. "What I want is for everyone to *think* we're dating. Know what I mean?"

"Oh." Somehow, actually dating a man who wasn't interested in me felt far less difficult than this. "So, you want me to lie for you?"

"I don't want you to do anything that you don't want to do," he clarified. "But realistically, yes. You'd be lying for me. For us, really."

"Us?"

"Yes." He checked over his shoulder to make sure nobody was still around. I'd been watching for the same thing for the last several minutes, feeling on edge by the conversation alone. "If everyone thinks we're together, it helps me hide what I want to keep hidden. And the times that we "go out together"," he emphasized the lie by making quotes with his fingers, "you can feel free to go do whatever it is that you want to go do."

"Like what?" I asked without hesitation. The guilt of planning out a lie and the intrigue of freedom were both taking precedence in my mind. The nail that I brought up to my teeth to bite at did little to calm my nerves. I was afraid and excited of something that I hadn't yet agreed to. My nervous system wasn't used to this much activity.

"Like anything," he told me, clearly taken aback by the question. "You're twenty-two, Gene. You can be out doing whatever you want to. There's a world full of wonders out there. You should let yourself get out and find a few."

"I don't know." It all sounded so easy when he explained it, but I knew it was bigger than how he made it seem. He may have been used to going out and doing what he wanted, and I was sure that he was only asking this of me because this was the one thing that he didn't feel that he could do openly. But I had never gone out and just done what I wanted to. I didn't know how to begin. I didn't know if I wanted to start, for fear of not being able to stop.

"Just think about it. I know it's a lot to ask of you when it comes to covering for me, but, I honestly don't think it's too much to ask of yourself. You're letting other people deprive you of living your life." He was trying to be respectful by not directly naming my parents. I was trying to be respectful by following my parents' wishes. There were so many ways to look at a person's life, and I was becoming familiar with the existence of perspectives. The black and white filter that I'd always seen through was slowly filling with color. "I'll bet there's a version of Genevieve Rowlen that you've yet to find."

"Okay. I'll think about it." Thinking about it and making a decision were different things. Thinking was going to be the easy part for me, given that it was all that I could do lately. "I'll let you know."

"Thanks, Gene. Even if your answer is no, I really appreciate everything that you're already doing for me." That reassurance took a small amount of the weight from off my shoulders. "And if your answer is yes, just find me after work on Saturday. I'll be at the Sarris party."

"Sarris party? Where's that?"

"Othello's place. Othello Sarris," he smiled as he gestured between us with a circular motion of his finger. "The place where this all began."

And now that weight that he'd removed was back. Everything kept leading me back to that house, and I didn't like the feeling of the unknown. The mystery of why.

"Why do you go there?" I asked. One of the first times I had asked one of the many questions on my mind. It took one person persuading me to spit out my thoughts, and now I felt a little more free to do so. It only felt right that the question had something to do with the person that was the one to push me to start asking what I wanted.

"Because it's one of the few places where anything goes," he said. "And it's important to have somewhere that you don't have to hide."

I broke away from the defeated look in his eyes. For how happy he always was, it's clear that he was positive by choice and not because he didn't live a life of difficulty. The part of me that felt ashamed for thinking of my internal situation as tough couldn't look into the face of someone who clearly had it harder. Of all the things I had to figure out with myself, knowing how to keep my self-pity in check was one of them.

"Just try to be careful if you do decide to show up this time, all right? Causing a scene the first time you came can't be a good sign of what to expect from you in the future."

"I didn't mean to—" I stopped trying to explain myself when he winked at me and the mischievous smile made an appearance on his face again. "It's not funny, Luke. I'm still not over that night."

"I'm sure you aren't," he said. "Something like that is hard to stomach for the first time."

"And does it get easier?" I didn't know what answer I wanted. Becoming accustomed to violence and staying this affected by it both sounded wrong to me.

He thought on it for a moment before giving me an answer.

"I think that everything gets easier. Even the tough things."

That rang in my head, a hopeful chant as I sat in the back of the car on the way home, my forehead pressed against the chill of the window. I could barely hear Gray beside me singing along to the song coming through the radio. The silence coming from Mother and Father was typical, the way it usually was when the four of us were alone together. There was minimal conversation, just Mother's "that was nice" acknowledgment as we got into the car.

I saw in the passenger side mirror that there remained a smile on her face; her signature look. Was she actually this happy? Was she so happy with her life that there was something to be smiling about all the time, or was this smile one that was just placed upon her face long ago that she's forgotten how to remove? I wanted to know more about what it was like to always have something to smile about. I wanted to know more about everything.

My breath caught in my throat as my brain prepared the question to vocalize, my endless curiosity about all the things I didn't know thinking of a simple place to start. Just when I found the nerve to ask Mother and Father to tell me something about the grandparents that I would never get to know, my bravado buckled. I was reminded of my place, how it was impolite for me to pry, how I knew better than to speak unless spoken to.

There was nowhere here for me to direct the questions that I'd been taught to ask.

PERSUASION

"For as smart as she thinks she is, she's yet to find the stash I keep under my mattress," Nancy said of her ongoing war with Jane over sweets. "Everything's a little smashed, sure, but it all still tastes good. Tastes even better knowing that I'm getting away with something, if you know what I mean."

"Afraid I don't," I said to myself as I smoothed out the striped blouse that Nancy had handed me to iron. Its puffed sleeves held their shape as it laid on the board, and I looked between them and the ones that she wore now. Anyone with eyes could see that Nancy was a beautiful older woman, with better taste and sense of modern fashion than I ever had. My long denim dress over my white shirt was nothing to take a second glance at, while Ms. Owden had been stealing hearts with her appearance for practically her entire life.

"May I ask you something?" I asked her, thinking maybe I would feel better about asking more questions if I preluded them with polite warning.

"I wish you would," she said before drinking from the glass of iced tea in her hand. No sugar. "I'll be dying any minute now, and I'd prefer to go in the middle of a stimulating conversation rather than silence." She smiled at my wide eyes from behind her transparent glass. "Anyway, dear, ask me anything."

I took a moment to reel in my surprise at her comment, gliding the iron over the shirt. Not that she would likely die any time *too* soon, but her words made a fair point to me. All lives were too short to be spent in silence. I was hoping that her long, adventurous life would make for an open mind to the private inquiry I had.

"What's the toughest decision you've ever had to make?"

Her glass stilled in front of her pink-painted lips, her penciled eyebrows raising in response. "That's a very good question," she said, setting her tea down on the table beside her chair. "And by that, I mean a hard one, because I've made so many big decisions in my life." She sat back in her seat, her eyes finding a place or some memory on the right side of the room that they halted on.

The silence grew on as I waited for her answer. Each second that ticked by had me second-guessing whether I should have asked or not, or if it was too big of a thing to ask of someone at all.

"You don't have to answer if you don't want to," I told her.

"It would have to be the decision to leave my second husband," she replied, removing her far gaze from the side of the room and looking back to me again.

I didn't know if I should ask why or not. Her answer was far more significant than the decision of my own that I was weighing in comparison, and I didn't want to push my luck of trying to find out even more when she'd already offered enough.

"And I'll tell you why," she continued, and I halted my hand that had returned to maneuvering the iron around the puffed sleeves of the blouse. I didn't want to miss a word, and I wanted to hear everything she said in response to my unspoken thoughts. "That was the only time I had other people to think about that would be affected by my decision. The kids that he and I had together, they were involved in the life that my husband, Dan, and I had. It wasn't just my life that would be changing. It was theirs, too."

I turned off the iron, setting it up and aside on the edge of the board. I placed my palms on the warmed fabric, focused on the woman before me that watched me but thought of the time when the decision mattered. The emotions that came with it. I could see what she was reliving in her million-mile stare.

"So do you regret it at all? Because the decision you made for yourself, you also made for them?"

"No," she said as she shook her head vigorously. She shook herself out of her stupor in the process, bringing her expression back to the present. "Not at all. Because though their life changed, it was for the better." She shrugged and picked back up her glass. "They still had their father around, and they gained their loving step-father soon after, too. As well as another sister, whom everyone adores. So I don't regret it. I don't regret much at all. Everything has a way of working out. The decision was only difficult while I was making it. Once it was made, that was it. Everything was fine."

"What about everyone else in your life?" I asked. I walked around the ironing board to sit on the couch, placing myself as close to her as I felt to the conversation. "What did they think about the decision you made to leave him?"

"I wouldn't know anything about that," she said with a careless wave of her hand. "I never bother to collect the opinions of those that don't matter. If they aren't involved in the decision I make, then what's it to them?"

"You never cared about what they thought of you for leaving a husband for a second time?" My cheeks flushed with the shame of my phrasing. She laughed as I apologized quickly. "I just meant that, for having made these decisions that were out of the norm for society's standards, there were surely outspoken opinions from plenty of people. Weren't there?"

"Sure there was," she said as I began placing some of the already ironed clothes on the couch beside me onto hangers. "Lots of people had a whole lot to say about me and their fierce disapproval of my choices. Dan's family, and my own family being some of them."

My ears caught on that, my actions slowing as they creased her khaki skirt to rest on a hanger. I was stunned by her ability to disregard the thoughts of people that close. It was more than a strange concept to me. It was impossible. "But?"

"But they weren't the ones married to these men, so they didn't get a say so. They could waste their breath all they wanted, but I was the only one living that life. Me and the kids, and the man who didn't know how to keep his paws off other women or show respect to his wife. If they cared so much about the marriage, then they were welcome to try their hand at it. I couldn't care less about them, what they do, or their thoughts."

"How do you get to that point?" I asked. I turned my attention to her fully, putting the clothes and the feigned distraction of them aside.

"To two divorces or to not caring?" She leaned forward a little closer to me. It looked like we were conspiring, our focus absorbed in our conversation that our thoughts and bodies had turned to. I smiled at her easy sense of humor about something that felt so serious to me, and the fact that nobody had ever been this open with me. The first friendship that I had with another woman, and she was more than three times my age.

"To where you don't care so much," I clarified. Here I was, the one asking all of the questions, and yet my asking gave away just as much about me as her answers did about her. But for once, I didn't try to hide my face and the open book it held that displayed everything I felt. I let my expressions remain as free to her as she was with me.

"You get there by accepting the role that you have here on Earth," she told me, pointing a perfectly manicured fingernail in my direction, "and that's to live the life you're given. Nobody is going to do it for you, no matter how good, or how *loud* their directions are as they're shouting at you from the passenger seat."

I nodded my understanding. She sat back in her seat again, breaking our fixed-connection to down the last of her drink. "Whatever decision it is that you're trying to make, make it for yourself. Do something that's going to benefit you for the first time in your life. You're old enough to be doing what you want, and still young enough that making a few mistakes won't be the end of the world. Enjoy that while it lasts," she said as she stood up with her empty glass in hand. She headed to the kitchen to get a refill for the fifth time since my shift began. "Because the older you get, the less time you have to fix the mistakes that you can and get over the ones that you can't. And then before you know it," she said, taking a sip from her freshly-filled glass, "you're my age, and being babysat by a young woman who has the potential to live a full life but isn't utilizing it. Imagine how terribly annoying that is."

Her smile reached me on my seat on the couch, touching me with its care and good-intent. I managed a grin before I grabbed the shirt from off the ironing board, slipped a hanger into it, and added it to the pile of others before picking them all up.

"I'm sure the young woman finds your annoyance endearing," I replied belatedly as I walked past her with the clothes in hand.

Her answering laughter followed me into her bedroom, where I hung up each article of clothing in her closet— according to color, just as she preferred. I stopped in the doorway as I was fixing to leave, turning back to do her one more favor.

Jane was coming in the door as I made it into the living room, speaking to Nancy in a chipper tone that I was sure was annoying her. And not in a caring way, as was her annoyance of me.

"Hey, Gene!" she said to me as I put my back to the door.

"Hey, Jane." I gave her a forced smile as I opened the door and backed out of it. "See you on Monday, Ms. Owden," I called, shutting the door on my exit as she said her goodbye.

I stopped at the end of the sidewalk when I left, picking up the metal lid of the trashcan to put the bag of flattened sweets inside.

The music had returned, and with it the pounding of my heart that accompanied my close proximity to this house. To another Sarris party.

There were more people this time, the overflow of them making themselves at home on the front lawn. The group that loitered by the front door let me through without much more than their obvious disapproval of my appearance. Theirs was made up of form-fitting and statement clothing, big hair that was spiked or colored, and skin that was pierced and tattooed.

I felt less intimidated this time, despite my apparent lack of belonging and my unsteady heartbeat. I was making use of Nancy's advice, and finding Luke to give him the answer that I knew he would be glad to hear. I was looking forward to making someone happy. I was ready to play a role in making someone else's life easier, even if it meant I was muddling mine to an extent.

I had enough simplicity to spare, and a lack of life lived.

"You're back," said the lady with the pink hair from the last time I was here, stopping me as I worked my way through the room of endless bodies. She was wearing what could only be called a net over small amounts of clothing that covered her most intimate parts. She was perfectly comfortable with how she looked, and I was blushing at the sight of her. I tried not to stare, but I couldn't help but find her. . .fascinating. There was something about her that I admired.

"Yeah, I am," I spoke over the music. "And I'm actually looking for the same friend as last time, too."

"And are you planning on finding yourself some trouble again, also?" She smiled, her teeth nearly glowing in the dark room lined with blacklights. The sudden show of teeth was slightly frightening, and I noticed too late that I flinched. "What, are you trying to fool everyone with this whole getup of yours?" She asked, gesturing up and down the length of me. "Because it works. You definitely fooled me."

"I'm not trying to fool anyone," I told her, looking briefly around the room to see if I could spot Luke. I wished his sudden appearance would get me out of this conversation with her like it did the last time. "I'm just here to find someone and give them a message. That's all. I didn't mean to cause all the stuff that happened last time, believe me. I wish it didn't."

"Whatever you say," she said with hands up in mock surrender, one of them hanging onto the plastic cup she had. "I'm not trying to argue my way into getting the shit kicked out of me because of you."

"I'm not trying to argue," I started. When I saw her smile before she took a drink, I knew that I was wasting my breath. She would keep me here all night just to argue for the fun of it. I could just drop it, and this could be the first time that I learned how to live with letting people think whatever they want. I told myself that she was likely kidding, but that it shouldn't matter regardless. I could let it go. I could live with this misconception. "I'm just trying to find a guy named Luke. Do you happen to know him or where he is?"

"Luke Hannigan? Roman's boyfriend?"

That was the first time that I'd heard the acknowledgement of Luke's preference spoken aloud by someone other than me and him. I found myself smiling not only because she knew exactly who I meant, but because she spoke of him and Roman with no judgment in her tone. It reminded me of exactly why Luke came here, to this place where anything goes.

"That's him, that's who I'm looking for," I answered eagerly.

"I saw them leave through the doors over there just a little while ago," she said, pointing to the side door on the opposite wall that I went through last time. "If they're not in the hallway, they're probably in one of the rooms. Be sure to knock when you go searching there," she added before rolling her eyes. "I'm sure that's another thing you're just pretending to have never seen, too."

She walked off with a smirk, leaving me no chance to assure her that all of her assumptions were wrong. I let go of my desire to defend myself and my reputation, carefully moving through the throng of people in that giant middle room. Despite my efforts, I could only be as careful as the bodies around me would let me be. Before I reached the door, someone turned around and collided with me, their drink in hand spilling down the top of my white shirt and the front of my denim dress.

Nora looked just as stunned as me as we quickly traded apologies that muddled together. "No, I really am sorry. I can go get you some new clothes really quick, I'll be right back," she said as she turned to go in a hurry.

"It's okay, really," I told her, catching her before she disappeared. It was amazing to see the same woman that I once saw ruthlessly break the face of a man with one solid kick, now being this considerate and going out of her way to be so polite. I'd never known someone with that kind of balance. I'd never even known violence until I met her in the first place. Everything and everyone in this house was new to me.

"Are you sure? Because it's no problem at all," she said before giving my stained, wet clothes a second glance.

"Except maybe that I don't have anything that will likely be suitable for you."

"I'm sure," I told her. I smiled at the apologetic look on her face that continued to roam over my outfit. "I'm just here to see someone really quick, and then I'm leaving. I don't need a change of clothes for that. Really. I'm fine," I said as I made my way to the door. "Thank you, anyway."

The hallway had more people than the last time, making it hard to tell if Luke was amongst them. There was no middle of the hall to walk through, as there were people standing in it as well as lining the walls. He must have noticed me before I found him, because he was already smiling at me when our eyes met. I made my way over to him, and who I could only assume to be Roman, where they stood together against the wall.

"I can't believe you showed up," he said, hugging me in spite of the wet fabric I wore that was sure to transfer to him. His arms around my shoulders squeezed, and my arms circled his torso as I realized this was the first embrace I'd had like this from someone other than Gray. Not even my parents showed affection for us to this degree. The last time I was held onto this tightly, it was while my mother held onto me as I cried, holding me back from rushing to Gray as he received punishment for the church window that we had accidentally broken.

I removed myself from the memory of rogue rocks and the tears that silently fell from my brother's face when Luke released me, pulling back to grab onto my shoulders and shake me in his excitement.

"You have no idea how much this means to me, Gene," Luke said. "No idea."

"And I should be thanking you, too," Roman said from beside him, green eyes full of sincerity. He looked to Luke, and back to me with a smile that showed his infatuated heart in it. "It means a lot that you would go through the trouble for Luke." Roman took the hand that left my shoulder, twining his fingers between Luke's. "For us."

"It's no trouble at all." At least I hoped not. My guilt and instinct reached up to my throat, wanting to suffocate me for putting myself in this position. "Just, nobody can know except the three of us." I knew that it was too late to back out of the decision. I wouldn't dare take away the joy that the both of them felt. It wouldn't be worth it just to save my own conscience on this one thing, but at the very least, I just wanted reassurance. I could live with this one colorful lie, as long as I knew it wasn't going anywhere outside of our knowledge.

"Of course, we won't say a word," Luke nodded in agreement. Roman's moved in sync with his. "Nobody's in on it but us."

"Great," I told him, letting the pressure seep out of my chest. "I've got to get home and wash these clothes before the stain sets in. I'll see you tomorrow at church?" I asked Luke, itching to get away from there and the foreign adrenaline that coursed my veins with the completion of this decision. I was ready to be home to reflect—and likely regret. I wanted to get that part over with.

"I'll be there." He and Roman waved their happy goodbyes before I turned away.

The maze of people had grown denser in the span of our discussion. Four feet down the hall was about all that I was able to make it before a body stood solidly in my way.

"It's a pleasure to see you again, Genevieve." Adam had a cigarette tucked behind his ear instead of his mouth. It made the cunning smile that he gave me all the more suspicious without the distraction of it. His intent eyes kept me in my place in addition to him blocking my way. There was a spark of interest in his eye that magnified the atmosphere of trouble.

"It's nice to see you too, Adam," I said politely.

The scar that ran from his temple to the corner of his eye stood out as we remained so close. It was the first time I noticed it, though his hair was always pushed back away from his face. I'd not paid him as much attention before, but now I took a full look from an unwilling stance.

The denim he wore over his white shirt was cut off at the sleeves, frayed bits perfectly disheveled. His jeans were cuffed at the bottom over his black and white sneakers, and I put together the pieces of his appearance from his hair to his shoes that gave him the air of decades past. In the hallway of clothes of all colors and hair that was unkempt and forced to be wild, he was an old-fashioned picture of confidence. Hair styled to leave proudly-worn scars on display and clothes that told the world he wasn't changing just because they were.

He watched me look him over those several seconds, silently waiting until my eyes reached his again. Once they did, he raised a single brow that temporarily shortened his scar. I didn't know by his face what question he wasn't asking, but I didn't want to wait here any longer to find out.

"I was just leaving," I told him, pointing at the door that led back to the middle room. "If you'll excuse me."

"Don't be in such a hurry. The night is just getting started." He pulled the cigarette from behind his ear, holding it in front of his mouth. "Come with me."

He put the unlit stick between his lips before he turned around and started walking. I looked back over my shoulder to see if Luke could see the begging that my eyes were doing for someone to intervene, to keep me from following orders like I knew I would. Like I always did.

Luke and Roman were gone, and I was on my own as I followed behind Adam's lead. The hallway seemed to part for him, none of the messy, moving around people every foot of the way like usual. His walk was graceful, his body guided by purpose as he brought us to a stop before a shut door at the end of the hall.

He opened the door and leaned against its frame. I was displayed in the open space to the room full of people. To Othello sitting on the edge of an antique desk, arms crossed over his chest.

He looked at me, to Adam standing beside me with a roguish smile, and then removed himself from his position above the people in the room.

"Everybody get out," he told the entire room. I stood aside as people left, only a few daring to take the time to look at me—the thing that forced their exit.

Adam gestured me inside once the room was cleared, and I stepped into the gray-walled study. I knew the feel of the room just as I knew the feel of the church, recognizing it as an old pastor's office. It held the same impression of solitude, somewhere that was often used for a single soul to study themselves, study the world, study others. There were more books lining the wall than what I was used to, as well as oddities and jars of things that I didn't immediately recognize but stopped trying to figure out once I saw one near the far edge filled with teeth. Only a fool couldn't deduce that the rest of them were continued collections.

Othello took a chair and backed it against the wall. He looked at me as he nodded toward it, and I sat down with my fingers fidgeting with my necklace. I didn't know why I was here. I didn't know why I'd followed.

Othello pulled a lighter out of his pocket and tossed it to Adam. He stood back against the adjoining wall, watching me from the side of his eyes as he lit his waiting cigarette. Othello stood in front of me, watching with practiced patience. I didn't know if they were waiting on me, but I was waiting on them. My nervous pulling of my necklace was propelled by the lack of direction I was being given.

"Tell me what you have to say, Adam," Othello broke through the silence. The tension that only I was feeling.

"How about you do the honor of sharing the exciting news with the room, Genevieve?" Adam said after a hefty drag. His smile broke free from behind his breath of smoke.

"I don't know what you're talking about," I told him, looking into Othello's analyzing eyes to convey my confusion. His face of stone lent me no assistance.

"Another lie? You're already becoming an expert," Adam replied, reaching across to an ashtray resting on the bookshelf behind him. "Tell Othello about the secret that you're keeping. The first one you've ever had, guessing from your worried pleas to your friends to not say a word about it. We're just so proud of you," he said in preamble to Othello's laughter.

His voice carried through the room, knocking the breath from my lungs along with the fear that came with other people knowing about something that I hoped would never come to light. Something that wasn't any of their business. Something that would ruin an entire life of following the rules, not because I chose to lie for someone, but because the information fell into the wrong hands.

"How do you know that?" The question fell from my mouth hastily. Painfully. The knowledge of the decision made had been given to Luke only minutes ago, and already I was facing consequences. The reality that a secret can only remain secret when it belongs to a single person.

"Gathering information is what I do," Adam said with a shrug. There was no care for my distress, no remorse for his prying. He was telling me the truth about sharing my first lie. This was just what he does.

Othello's smiling face studied me; the scary image of that insidious mouth stirred into my existing panic. "You can't say anything to anyone about this. Please," I begged the humored faces of two men I knew as ruthless. Two men whose way of life was as foreign to me as my fear of a single lie likely was to them. They didn't know me. They didn't owe me anything, not even something as simple as their silence.

"What is it that you're so afraid of?" Othello asked. His smile was receding, his eyes focused on watching me. I knew the expressions that I displayed were scattered, but his look told me that he was catching every one of them. From my attempts to calmly examine the situation to my fierce self-rebuke.

They were both invested in my answer. They both wanted to know exactly what it was that made someone squirm this much over what they'd consider just a simple lie. They were interested in finding out more about something that they couldn't understand.

"I'm afraid of my father finding out." There was shame attached to the admission. I couldn't even consider lying to them about the answer, the new-found result of lying fresh in the exhaustion of my heart.

Adam huffed as he reached for the ashtray again. He and Othello shared a look before Othello stepped closer to me. He put his hands into his pocket, waiting for me to look up to his face. "Are you not a grown woman?" he asked when my eyes finally surrendered to the connection. "I recall you insisting to me that you're *not* a little girl. And in only the literal sense, you aren't. Your father is not your keeper." His brown eyes never gave me a chance to look away. They weren't just holding me, I was chained. To them, the voice sharing intimate wisdom, and the consistent effect of the smile that reappeared. Outwardly, my body was still. Inside, I was battling chaos.

"But if it's lying you're going to resort to," he continued, "don't bother being afraid of it. We all lie to get to where we want." He traded a conspiratorial look with Adam, their enjoyment of this situation evident. "Or to get *what* we want."

"Not all of us," I argued quietly. "I've never lied to get what I want."

"You're doing it now, aren't you?" He pointed out.

"From my understanding," Adam interjected as he put out his cigarette entirely, "this lie benefits your friend Luke and his guy Roman because you're agreeing to cover for them. You lie about being with Luke so that they can be together, and you're left on your own. That's your end of the secret. I don't see why you feel so bad." He turned his body to face me where he leaned against the shelf. Both of them now watching me intently. Their watching and waiting put all the more pressure on my answers.

"Because I've never done something this selfish before." I looked down to avoid their reaction. The thumb of my right hand stroked the palm of my left where it rested on my lap, beneath the drying stain on my denim dress. It was too late to salvage my clothes. It was too late to look back. I was longing for my own past for once in my life.

"It's not selfish," Othello said. His voice was one that commanded attention. One that struck the masses and certified himself as a leader. Looking back up at him wasn't an option—his voice demanded it.

"It is when I'm lying to people who've never lied to me." I was weighing out the downfalls of my decision more now than I had before I made it. I'd lived this long avoiding missteps, avoiding mistakes in order to follow the perfect path guided by my father.

"Everybody lies, Dove."

Where Adam stood dressed to defy conforming to modernity, Othello represented the current appeal of the outcast. His natural hair wild, his clothes dark and tattered, his skin displaying permanent statements that peeked out on his upper arm below the rolled-up sleeves of his black shirt. The shirt with a tear beneath its collar that allowed me to see only a piece of the ink embedded beneath the skin of his chest.

I looked down to my shoes, the dull and worn loafers with my toes hidden inside turned toward each other. I knew how different I appeared to them; my drink-stained coverings more modest than any of the clothes worn by a single woman in this place. Yet I was the one that felt exposed. My dirty laundry aired—in every sense of the term. I wanted to be as comfortable as every other woman here was.

And since I wasn't, I would just have to pretend.

"I don't know you. I don't know how much is too much to ask of you, but you can't tell anyone about this agreement.

Luke and I were supposed to be the only ones who knew about this."

Othello backed away as Adam took a step toward me. Their synchronicities and balance of power kept them in agreement without having to say a word to each other. I was already on edge, but their shift forced me back further against my seat.

"Genevieve," Adam started, smirking at my flinch of my full name, "it's my job to know these things, remember?" He reached out and stilled my hand that was pulling my cross back and forth on my chain. The physical contact stilled my breath along with my movements. "Now, you want us to do you a favor—albeit, a small one," he said with a shrug as he palmed back the side of his hair. "But the thing is, we don't do any favors for free. That's just how business works." He looked at my hand as it began to pull on my necklace again, and only smiled before looking back to my eyes. "Surely you, with an impressive and unutilized degree in that very thing, could understand that."

It was his job to know information. It was his job to know everything about me that I knew about myself.

It didn't make it any easier as I repeated that to myself before I forced a reply.

"But you've done a favor for me before."

"And what was that?" He appeared surprised—the calm raise of brows that was calculated and possibly fake. He was waiting for an already expected answer.

"You saved me from Axel." I looked past Adam to watch Othello's reaction. There wasn't one; every feature guarded his thoughts on the conversation he observed. "There's no way to know how far his anger would have taken things if you guys hadn't intervened."

Bile rose in my throat reflexively. Of all the time I'd spent thinking about that night and the effect it had on my life, the toll it took on my perspective, I'd never thought about the dangerous direction it could have gone for me had they not interrupted Axel's unnecessary fury the way they did. I was too consumed with the image of violence bestowed upon him to think of the violence that could have potentially found me.

"But that came at an unsettling price for you, too. Did it not?"

The question was rhetorical. Othello asked it, knowing that I wouldn't lie when he was already watching the memory play out on my face. Knowing that I wouldn't lie when I was already distressed in the midst of another.

Their knowledge exceeded mine. They held the cards in this game that I'd never been taught how to play. My only option was to rely on their direction.

"Then what do I owe you in exchange for your silence?" I followed Adam's movements as he backed away from me, no longer needing his nearness for coercion. His smile was satisfied, his job done for probably the thousandth time. "I'll give you whatever money I can."

"I don't want your money for such a miniscule thing." My focus left Adam to follow Othello's voice. I was surprised by my lack of a racing heart as I met his stare, but realized that my heart was in fact racing. It had been the whole time I was here, and I'd adjusted to the feeling of my natural state while I'm with them. When I'm near them. When I see them.

"Then what do you want?" My question came out with the absence of breath. An unintentional whisper of the last amount of suspense I could take from this situation. If I couldn't leave soon with sworn secrecy and clarity of this deal made in desperation, I would likely faint.

Othello held his hand out in front of me. I looked to his open palm, unsure of what he wanted me to give him if it weren't money. My own hand slowly rose, hoping he would correct me and save me from further humiliation if my action was wrong. No correction came, and my hand covered his in a handshake of an agreement for a payment I didn't know I was making.

His grip tightened as he backed away, bringing me off of my seat to rise before him. Adam remained still, watching as Othello guided me between the two of them. Adam stood behind me against the bookshelf as I faced Othello, his hand holding mine with refusal to let me go.

"Pay a favor for a favor," he said. His voice was even more unnerving this close. The seriousness that never took no for an answer cut deeper when the lips that commanded what they wanted were only a foot away. "Give me something that you've never given anyone else before, and your secret won't be shared with any other unknowing souls."

What if there was a wrong answer? What if along with everything they knew about me, they knew exactly every something I had and had not shared? I panicked before his patience, knowing not to lie to the eyes that already knew how to read my face. I couldn't leave without giving nothing, and I grappled with what I had that was worthy of being given. There was no way to be sure of what was worth giving someone who knew how to get exactly what he wanted.

My chest clenched as my gaze settled on his lips, held firmly in a line as he waited on my offering to him. He was unrushed, and I knew that he found joy in watching me drown in worry. I knew it by the scarce blinks that came from brown eyes that forced themselves to remain open so as not to miss a single second of the show.

If I didn't get it over with, I would be sick. If I did it now, the sooner I could leave and purge my fear in privacy.

I took in a breath of the small amount of air between us, holding it as I timidly moved my face in toward his. My eyes slowly closed as I felt that I was unable to watch myself give in the closer I became to him. I couldn't watch myself fold through my reflection in his eyes.

A hand rested on my shoulder as my intent lips never met with their receiver. I opened my eyes to no pretty face before me, but a gentle exhale by my ear that preceded his affecting words.

"If your lips ever rest upon mine, it will happen with lack of condition, Dove." His mouth remained by my ear, our hands still gripped between our almost touching bodies. "Give me what you're just now giving yourself. Share your newfound freedom with me. Come back, when you're alone with your lie and spending time on your end of this simple secret. I want to be there for every step of your acceptance of your humanity."

My head nodded the answer that my voice couldn't make, the movements sending his lips briefly grazing against the sensitive curve of my ear. My skin rippled with chills as he pulled back and brought his unfazed expression before me again, shaking our joined hands in a final stamp of agreement.

Our hands separated as the door opened without a knock, Nora stepping in with a couple of folded clothes in her hand.

"Someone said you were in here," she addressed to me, "I know you said you didn't need these, but I figured if you were going to stay for a while then you might wan—"

"I'm leaving now, sorry for putting you through the trouble," I said hurriedly as I reached her by the door. I rushed out of the room without a goodbye, without looking back, without seeing if I were supposed to ask for permission before even making my exit.

For the first time, I didn't slowly make my way through the house to avoid everyone else because they avoided me in my hurry.

For the first time, I realized I didn't care about not having asked for permission to make my next move.

For the first time, I drove home with a twisted sense of independence.

ASSUMPTION

'"Do not judge by appearances, but judge with right judgment."'

It was one of the first scriptures read off on that next morning during the day's first sermon. I held onto it, rolling it silently over my tongue and ingraining it into my head as a sign—as I did with all the words that always felt directed toward me.

I thought of how the appearance of certain people terrified me, the forced perception of the bad or unacceptable in the world involuntarily taking precedence of my actions. Of my judgments. Then I acknowledged the opposite, and thought of how I'd always allowed myself to feel unquestionably safe in the presence of all who appeared to be good. Appeared to be acceptable.

I lost half of the lesson taught to these ideas, losing myself to the shame of it and doubting my own translation of the words. I never knew if I was right until it was confirmed for me. I didn't know what to think for myself until someone supplied me with the thought.

I'd looked upon Gray's undistracted face and saw the good. The good he exuded to the world by action and appearance, and for a brief moment, I wondered if I was wrong in my judgment of him. I wondered if he'd ever done wrong by the standards we were held to, ever fallen short in the eyes of all who watched—all who mattered.

Guilt tore through my soul at the very thought. To dare to question a man like Gray was below the line of wrong. It had my mouth tasting the overflowing amount of disgust that I had with myself. Gray's good nature went past the shell that was his appearance. His every move done in goodness and every word was said in good intent. Gray was good.

I was the one that was deflecting, being eaten alive by my current confusion of what was and wasn't bad.

"Stand up, Gene," Mother harshly whispered through my thoughts. It alerted me to my Father descending his stage, Gray and Mother already upright and awaiting him.

I stood up, nestled between them as Father came to greet Mother first as he always did.

The routine my eyes were now open to.

She congratulated him on another successful service, her hand resting on its usual spot on his chest as he sternly beamed with the praise she was doting upon him. Gray shook father's hand, and for the first time I felt it to be odd. The show of this repeated cycle of a supportive family toward a man that made a point of not gloating, but couldn't hide his eager reception of admiration.

Was this only for appearances? Such things that I wasn't meant to judge, but couldn't help but notice? I questioned things more now than ever before. I was spiraling down this aware state of everything, blinding film slowly being removed from my eyes day by day.

"Was today's teaching not to your liking, Gene?" Father asked upon my silence amidst the others glorifying the job he'd done.

I'd been looking at him with eyes unfocused, my sight having a hard time staying alert to what I saw when I was lost in thought. I was more alert to what was real and what seemed forced, forced like my reply was as I recited an answer often before given.

"It was great, Father. You shared something memorable with all of us."

His arm remained around Mother's shoulder, as did the forced look of satisfaction on his face as he listened to me. All eyes that looked upon him would see him as being perfectly content, just as he wanted them to. But I could see in the eyes that didn't crease from his fake smile that he wasn't happy, and the sinking feeling I felt told me that it was because of me.

"I'm glad you spared enough time to listen to it when you weren't busy studying Gray, then," he said with malice in his tone that only the four of us could hear. I kept my half-hearted attempt of displayed content on my face as best as I could. Our family affair would remain between us, this family meant to set an example. "Gray is the one to set your sights on if you're going to ignore the lesson I give you, though. At least he's a proper influence."

Father turned away from us, leading Mother away with him by the gentle hold he had on her. They offered smiles and accepted handshakes as they walked down the middle aisle toward the front doors, where Gray and I would soon be expected to stand beside them.

I turned to my brother, needing the sight of a face I knew never looked upon another person with disappointment. A soul that shared empathy with any other that was hurting. And by the smile he offered me when I looked to him, he knew that I was hurt. He knew the effect of having disappointed a man like our father. He knew that I was counting on that smile.

"He's just overworked, is all," he said in Father's defense, remaining on middle ground as he gave me reassurance. "I've heard him rehearsing his notes in his office at home for the past two days. He just put a lot of effort into this one," he said of the service. It didn't relieve the sting of Father's passive-aggression much. "Don't take it personally."

"'Personally' is the only way to take a complaint directed solely toward me, Gray. I think what you mean to say is don't take it "too hard"?" The humor he found in my weak attempt at a jest had the start of a smile blooming on my own face.

"And I think what you mean, Vieve, is don't take it "to heart"? Which, when you think about it, really means the same thing as taking it personally. I think that I'm right, either way?" he asked instead of stated. And just like that, with the brother I'd always known to count on, my spirits lifted from their flattened place beneath my feet. "What I mean is, don't let it bother you. You always learn what you need to, and you're doing just fine."

He moved to start toward the main doors, and I followed behind with a lighter heart. For all the talk of how becoming older made you wiser, it was ironic to know just how clueless and naïve I was compared to my younger brother that never failed to know exactly what to say in every situation. Call it wisdom or call it his birth-given gift, but it proved to me that you were never too young to be right and never too old to be wrong—or at least unsure.

Father's face was entirely clear of the hidden bitterness he'd left with, and it made falling into place next to him a little easier as I showed my gratitude and shook the hands of my eager brothers and sisters that slowly filtered out of the church.

It was easy to fall back into the motions. To forget about all of the people and places that my mind constantly wandered to. With each pleasant exchange with the cheery souls that stopped for a handshake, or extended a kind compliment about the service as they took those final steps back to their own lives, I took a step mentally back. I reevaluated each decision that I'd made that left me experiencing such new emotions. The entire morning was a struggle that I battled on my own, and being here next to

Father after he'd shown his observation of how out of line I was, I was longing for the feeling of being in my comfort zone again.

"Hey, Gene," Luke said as he walked out of the doors before his family. He pulled me into him with a hug, and after my arms wrapped around him reflexively, I remembered my surroundings at the last moment. I wanted to pull back and correct what I'm sure looked inappropriate to Father and maybe Mother, but the excited faces bearing smiles behind him were my reassurance. This was what they all wanted. This is what I had agreed to, and my end of the agreement was already being applied.

He let go of me, his face more than content with our exaggerated exchange. He reached over and shook the hand of my father, whose eyes held all the approval that his mouth wouldn't give. They were alight with satisfaction, the spark of a man who always enjoyed seeing things go his way.

"Wonderful sermon, Mr. Rowlen." Luke said as his hand fell away from Father's. "I especially appreciated the part about not basing judgments off of appearances. You really drove that one home."

My eyes widened at his choice of words, and his same takeaway of the service. For how unsure I was moments before I saw him, I was brought back to the present with the feelings that led me here. I felt more sure of myself as he unwittingly voiced how I wasn't alone. He didn't even know how much he said by saying so little.

Everyone around us was exchanging their own thoughts, caught up in small conversations. I heard Amelia asking Gray about a movie, and I thought about how mistakenly thrilled my parents would be if those two ended up together just as Luke and I had. The facade was becoming an emotional trap the further I ventured into it.

"I'll call you later," Luke said as his family began to walk away from mine. "I'd love to take you out soon." I cut my eyes toward my father in silent defense, hating the way my nerves were eating at me even if this was the plan. This was the initiating statement. Undoing what we've done would feel just as painful as it did to go through it. All I could manage to do was watch

"If that's all right with you, Mr. Rowlen?" Luke added politely. His acting was spotless, no holes in this cover of ours for anyone to see through. For now. The glee on my mother's face at what she was finally hearing made for one more thing that I felt guilty about.

"That sounds like an acceptable idea to me," Father said. His ability to play off his pride in watching the tables turn in his favor was almost as flawless as Luke's performance, but I was catching on to subtle tells in people's character around me. I was catching on to a lot of things quicker than I was able to process them all.

"Then you'll be hearing from me tonight, Gene."

Luke's charming way of smiling his way through a lie remained on my mind long after I watched him depart upon his place on cloud nine. He was so happy with himself, happy with the way that everything was working out, and I was still waiting for my happiness to kick in. I'd made the decision, I'd found myself placed within two agreements now, and my path was more unclear now than it was before I became so tangled. While I was already caught in the initial spinning of this web of lies, everyone else involved remained free of the strands that I felt trapped in.

Maybe freedom was just a state of mind, and this web was my own illusion.

I dwelled on it, willing my mind to detach me from the snare of my design. It consumed me for hours, my focus keeping me just out of touch from the world that I drifted through. I wanted to do more while feeling less. I wanted to learn how to cease being my own captive.

"What did you think of it?" Gray asked as we left the theater, its shelter giving us no time to adjust to the immediate blaze of the sun. My eyes squinted against the overwhelming light, and my hand raised to shield my sight as I tried to see through the bright haze and focus on Gray. With my eyes, if not my mind.

"What?" I asked him for what had to be the dozenth time. He'd tried to hold conversation with me on our drive here, and I could never pull myself away from my thoughts long enough to give him all of my attention. He deserved better than the distracted sister that he was with. I shouldn't have agreed to come out with him if I knew I couldn't mentally handle interaction with someone right now. I should have known even a simple task such as going somewhere that's meant to be enjoyed would be too much for me.

"The movie," he said, providing me again with more from his never-ending supply of patience. "Did you like it?"

"Oh. Yeah, it was great," I answered too quickly. I watched our matched steps as they carried us down the sidewalk. It was becoming too easy to lie, now. I'd done it once, and despite the ache it had permanently given me and my conscience, more lies followed already. One so small required little to no thought, when used to, there was never a doubt about telling the truth. But if I told him the truth now, I would tell him I didn't pay attention to the movie. When he would ask why, I would tell him the truth about where my mind was. And the truth behind the devising of this lie was not my truth to give.

"What did you think of it?" I asked him after he left his response to my answer as only a shrug. He looked at me, and I could see the honest answer already forming behind his blue eyes.

"I thought that it was too violent. I've never actually enjoyed that kind of thing."

"Then why did we watch that one?" I asked as we stopped at the end of the sidewalk before crossing the street to the next block. I didn't remember the lot that we left the car in feeling this far away.

"Because you picked it," Gray said with a curious grin as our feet hit the road before the next sidewalk.

My forehead tightened in confusion, and the strain sent a jolt of pain through my skull. I'd worried myself into a headache. "I did?"

"When we got here, you said that you wanted to watch that one because you heard Amelia mention it to me. Remember?"

"No, I actually don't," I admitted with a short, bitter laugh. It was a small redemption for myself to have not lied about something insignificant again, but it still didn't feel good to acknowledge my mental absence. I'd lost a precious moment in my life with my brother to my state of internal stress. The regret in that alone was enough to make me loosen the wrenching hold I had on myself. Our relationship was suffering over something he knew nothing of.

"I'm sorry I'm not the best of company to have watched it with," I told him. He wouldn't tell me that he didn't enjoy himself. Actually, I don't think that Gray ever let others factor into what he enjoyed. "Maybe you should have brought Amelia with you instead."

"Not you, too," he said with a roll of his eyes. It was something that we had in common, the lack of discretion when it came to our facial expressions.

"What?" I couldn't help the smile on my face just like he couldn't help the exasperation that came with knowing people had plans picked out for you. "I'm just saying that she would have enjoyed coming with you, is all. She would have made for a good movie partner. You probably would have liked it better if you came with her instead of me."

"I still wouldn't have liked the movie no matter who I was watching it with, Vieve. Having Amelia next to me instead of you wouldn't have changed that."

He stopped in front of one of the stores lining the street, its window displaying jewelry that reflected the sun off its giant clear stones, some colored ones accenting certain pieces. His focus seemed to be on a silver bracelet that had a single ruby in it. It was simple. It was pretty. It looked like something Mother would wear.

"Do you think Mother would like that one?" he asked with a finger pressed against the glass in its direction. It felt good to know that I hadn't lost this type of connection that I had with Gray. I was happy that I still knew him better than I knew myself.

"I think she would love it."

He nodded before proceeding down the sidewalk, his content with walking in silence no longer what I wanted now that he had my attention.

"So," I cut through our quiet stroll, "why did you agree to watch a violent movie with me if you know that you don't enjoy them?"

"Because sometimes, things can surprise you and end up being exactly what you needed in order to have a change of mind about something." He bent down and grabbed a rock from the sidewalk, smoothly maneuvering and not breaking the rhythm of our strides. "So I took the chance on that movie. It just turned out not to be anything profound enough to sway me."

He tossed the rock up in the air, watching it flip over itself again and again before it landed back in his palm. He repeated the trick three times before I found the courage to ask him what was on my mind.

"Do you ever think violence is okay?" I looked ahead at the lot we were finally nearing. We'd used this lot to avoid the cluttered parking by the theater, and now I was using it to avoid letting him see into my eyes. With how apparent my expressions were, I just knew that he would be able to know exactly why I was asking. I didn't want him to have to see the violence I'd seen if he looked through the window of my eyes. "Do you ever think it's necessary, I mean?"

The rock stilled in his hand, his fingers laying over it in a closed fist. I saw out of the corner of my eye that he was thinking it over. He would give me a calculated-Gray-answer.

"I think everything has its exceptions," he said after he began flipping the rock into the air again. "Even violence. There's likely situations when it's an only and last resort."

And was it the last resort with Axel? Was there another way to handle a situation with a man like him, or could force only stop someone so forceful? Could violence be the only thing that made an impact on the violent?

I was asking myself questions that could only be answered by someone who was there, someone who knew the situation. You had to know details to make a decision about worthy exceptions, and I couldn't divulge details to Gray.

"Is your aversion to violence your way of saying that you just don't like the sight of bloodshed?" The quick change in my line of questioning let my mind move on. I quirked a playful brow at Gray over the roof of the car as he walked around to his side.

"I feel no shame in admitting that I don't like the sight of blood," he said with an over-the-top, matter-of-fact face that made me laugh aloud. The happy sound felt strange to my own ears as it rang through the nearly empty parking lot. Only Gray could make one forget their woes.

The smile lingered on my face as I got into the car. I turned over the engine while Gray adjusted the temperature and the volume of the radio, as was the agreement we always made for riding in the passenger seat. My hand settled onto the gear shift to pull into reverse when the sight across the street stood out to me.

Othello was leaning back on the hood of a car, watching me through my windshield as he was one to do. His relaxed seat on the tan metal exuded his confidence. He was displayed to the world with indifference, anyone that looked at him was doing so by his allowance. Adam was on the sidewalk, talking to a man that stood too close for a typical conversation. My initial thought was that the violence that Gray hated to see was about to erupt before our eyes—until

I saw the man pull his hand out of his jacket and with it a stack of cash.

Adam grabbed it from him, replacing the money in his hand with something that had been small enough for him to conceal in his grip. The exchange felt so private despite them standing out in the open, beneath the light of the sun that they didn't seem to care exposed their every move.

I backed away, knowing that Othello knew what I saw. I knew that I saw something that I wasn't meant to see by the smile on his face as I pulled onto the street he was on. I knew as I passed him, that he was fearless in my observation of their suspicious doings. He had no uncertainties about anything that they did, and I was now full of questions regarding *everything* they did.

"Will you roll down your window? There's not enough air coming through here," Gray asked me as he continued to fidget with the vents.

I waited until I was past the stoplight that removed me from the street that Othello was on. I waited until I was sure that he wouldn't take an open window as an invitation to stop me while I wasn't prepared.

Because I would be prepared. I would answer Luke's eminent call, and agree to see him tomorrow night. And while I held up my end of both agreements, giving Luke his freedom and paying Othello with mine, I would learn more of the secrets that belonged to my secret-keepers.

Until then, I would gather all the courage that I could in order to do so.

My anxiety burned. It was a pyre in my belly that gave off the flames of expected doom to the rest of my body. My neck remained covered with a nervous film as I dragged my feet through the hours of my shift.

Nancy took no particular notice of my spaced-out condition, but remained a welcome distraction as the night stretched on to the final curve of my race to new places. To a new experience for an almost twenty-three-year-old that couldn't retain possession of her own courage. Every ounce of what I had when I ended that phone call with Luke and relayed false information about what I would be doing after I left Ms. Owden's was being filtered from my system by the minute.

What replaced it was fearful anticipation of facing Othello again. Shame of being as old as I was and living out a lie for the first time. Guilt. Uncertainty. A sense of doom that I couldn't shake.

The surprising part of the mixture was the excitement. The piece of me that kept me from making the decision to forget it all and just go straight home. It was the same feeling I had the night that I found myself standing before the door of a quiet, converted church. It was the remnant of the thrill I experienced any time I was near to Othello.

It was my craving for exploration that grew with each small taste that was supplied by our interactions.

"Are you ever going to tell me what you're fretting about, or are you going to make me carry the conversation up until the very second you leave?" Nancy interrupted my inner-analysis, and I stopped pretending like I was watching the news that she had playing on the television.

"What are you talking about? I'm fine." I gave her a quick smile and locked back onto the news. Now that I was watching, it was showing reports of only upsetting events. Knowledge of things that I wondered why they would want to subject their viewers to not long before we're meant to try to sleep. And if we surrender, all the bad we were told of would find us in our dreams.

What did it say of me that I could feel this way, and yet pursue the bad that I'd been warned of all my life? The line between reckless and brave was one that I couldn't find. All I knew was that I'd set off on the road of experience. The thing I'd not long ago longed for, and fought with now that I had it.

"Don't lie to me," she said as she reached up to secure one of the rollers in her hair. Another detail of feminine appearance that she paid more attention to than I did. My long hair reached right past my chest in waves that came with no styling, no effort. It wasn't the wild or outrageous look that everyone else my age was going for, nor was it the sculpted style that those older than me kept up with. I wondered if I appeared as fashionably lazy to her as I felt.

Her superiority didn't only exist in her appearance, wisdom, and life experience. She was also the best at locating the exact subject I didn't want to visit.

"You've been pulling on that damn necklace of yours for the past half hour. And that's not to mention all the times tonight that I've looked at you and saw that you're no longer here. You're somewhere else entirely." She used the clicker to turn off the news and eliminate interference. She was going to get what she wanted out of me—I knew that. "So, wherever it is you're running off to in that young mind of yours, why don't you take this old lady with you? It's the only escape I'm likely to have before I'm put in the dirt."

"Nancy!" I admonished with my eyes, but couldn't refrain the laugh of surprise that left me. "You can't manipulate me by saying stuff like that."

"Shouldn't, or can't?" She emphasized each beat of the question with a tilt of her head. "Because maybe I shouldn't do it, but that doesn't keep it from working each time I pull out the death card. So I *can*. And I did. Now, talk to me about this something you've got going on,"

I couldn't give her the secret. But I could give her my concerns.

"Is lying always wrong?" I could hear the echo of Othello's voice in my head, assuring me that everyone lies. But did it make it okay? What was new to me was this thing I knew to be a sin, but one that each individual inevitably committed. If we were all lying, then what defined which of us were in the wrong? I needed more direction for this course untraveled.

"Well there's an interesting conversation starter," she said as she turned her body in her seat and directed it toward me. One question and she was invested. "There's a whole lot of details that go into deciding something like that. But if you ask me, the simple answer is no. It's not *always* wrong, but it definitely can be."

And just like that, I was loosened. I was awakened from a slumbering state within my own body that kept me from being alert to the rest of the world that could provide heartening insight. If only I would have just spoken up hours ago and spared myself the trouble of agonizing. Like all other things for me, it was something that I learned too late.

"Then what makes lying right?" I asked. "When it isn't wrong, I mean. What makes up the difference?"

She nestled her shoulder into the back of her chair, settling in for the discussion. She was prepared for depth. "Like I said, many factors play into what makes lying okay. Or right, or acceptable. For instance, is this lie benefiting someone you care about? Is the purpose behind the lie for the greater good, the bigger picture?" I remained mute, not wanting to divulge anything about the lie that pertained to me and the situation that I was in. I'd wanted this exchange to remain vague, and was relieved when she continued without my reply. "Look at it this way; it would be hard for me to be upset about someone deceiving me when it was done in my best interest."

My father. He was my biggest concern, and he wasn't being lied to for any reason other than my need to keep him from knowing that I'd fallen short. A lie that did begin by only benefiting someone that I cared about, would be used tonight for my own sake as I remained beneath the cover of a lie, with people he didn't know of, in a place he didn't know about. And that's what made it feel wrong.

"And what if the lie isn't for you?" I asked in search of further comfort. "What if only the people involved in the lie are the ones benefiting, and you're being lied to and don't know the truth only because it doesn't include you, and it's better if you're left not knowing?"

The roll of her eyes confused me. For a moment I felt foolish, and thought over what I must have said incorrectly. But she gave me what I was looking for.

"Then you said it yourself," she said as if she couldn't believe that it wasn't just as obvious to me. "If it doesn't include *me*, then *I* don't need to know." Her emphasis on the pronouns told me that she knew this line of questioning wasn't hypothetical. "A person can live a life of their own while the rest of the world remains blissfully ignorant to it. As long as there's no harm done, then what's it matter to anyone else?"

Blissfully ignorant. The very thing that I was before I stepped into this stage of my life.

Before I stepped foot into the House of Sarris.

"So, then, you would be okay with being lied to for another person's sake?"

She nodded her head easily. While Nancy Owden wasn't my father, my mother, or the ones that I hated lying to, she was the only substitute I had to ease my persistent state of doubt.

She wasn't the person that I was terrified of sinning against.

"Do you think you could subconsciously forgive someone for something like that?" My hand reached up to find my comfort chain, but I stopped myself, knowing better than to reach for a gift my father had given me when it was his disapproval that I was hiding from. "Without ever even knowing about it?"

"Of course I can." She turned back in her seat, her body leaving the conversation before her words. "I forgive everyone for all the instances I don't know about. I'll forgive any person for anything that they could never admit to me—or that they can't admit to anyone. I'll forgive without being asked for forgiveness."

Smiling lips graced her face as she closed her eyes amidst her closing words.

"Just like I forgive you for taking my mattress-stash from me."

MERCY

It was the first time that my knuckles had rapped upon the door. Any other time I was here it was either open or I was distracted by the face of an Adonis with a serpent's smile. But now, I was here by my own volition. I was here willingly, invited by the inhabitants that were behind this closed door. I was here to share my new-found freedom.

A serpent smile wasn't what greeted me as the door opened. Instead, Rachelle with the copious amounts of frizzed, blond hair was the first face to meet me.

"Well, well," she said with an open perusal of my lacking style. "Looks like the cat dragged in Othello's little bird."

"It's nice to see you, Rachelle." It wasn't another lie. She left her judgments in the open, but her demeanor was welcoming. It was clear she thought me to be strange, but I was beginning to find solace in strangeness. I hoped mine offered her the same. "I'm here to—" I didn't know. I was just here because I said I would be, and now I realized that I hadn't thought about what to expect past my worries of my own lies. "I'm here to visit, I guess."

"You're an interesting visitor," she told me as she moved from in front of me and gestured inside. "Come in. It's going to be fun having you around."

An implication that I would be here more. At least I was being given small expectations.

The massive room typically filled with bodies under heavy influence and music capable of starting a stilled heart was void of both. There were no large groups, no individuals dancing, no people lying on the floor having surpassed their own limits. It was eerily quiet in the vast room that showed its origins—altar and serenity intact.

I continued to follow behind Rachelle as she wordlessly led me around. She didn't waste her time with a tour or showing me around, and I figured it was more because she didn't care to rather than the fact that I'd been here before. But there was so much I'd missed in the distractions of a packed party, such as the altar that set before a stage that I'd never seen anyone stand upon.

She walked us through the hallway door that I'd last gone through. When she turned right down the hall, I knew where this was leading. I rubbed the fabric of my pants discreetly between my thumb and forefinger as my hands rested at my sides. It's what it took to keep me from clutching my necklace while I stood behind Rachelle as she knocked on the door of Othello's office.

"Come in," called a voice from within. Adam's, maybe, I thought as she opened the door to many waiting faces. Each of them were trained on me as Rachelle walked inside, displaying the arrival of their visitor—the reason she bothered to knock before we entered, I assumed.

Othello, Adam, Nora, Michael, and Rachelle all occupied the office as I stood in the doorway. With the door still open, there was the chance for me to turn back. A chance that I passed on as I closed the door and put myself within this group, where I was now the outsider.

"Nice to see you again so soon, Genevieve," Adam said from the back wall that he stood against—behind Othello who sat at his regal desk. Everyone here exuded importance, as if they were all in on a meeting that I had interrupted. Nora was sat in a seat against the wall-to-wall bookshelf, and Rachelle was sat in the lap of Michael on the opposite side of the room. I was the disrupting center of attention, forced to the middle. "Did you enjoy your movie yesterday?"

There's no way to get used to someone knowing so much about you. All the information he gathered was unnerving, telling me that I was always being monitored. If there was anyone that I couldn't get away with lying to, it was Adam with his devious ways of gathering the truth and Othello that could read through any lie told. Honesty was something that I wasn't sure they lived by, but it was what they had their ways of acquiring.

Adam's teeth displayed with a grin, satisfaction of my surprised face shown on his. There were a few things that I could read about him, and his ability to unsettle a person was one of them. He thrived on shock.

"Did you enjoy conducting shady business yesterday?" I didn't know where the nerve behind a question like that came from. There was something about the pressure in the room that pushed at me, and told me that if my limits were here to be explored, then test them. I only wish that I could have known that I was going to say it before I did so that the shock on my face wouldn't have been as apparent.

Othello's smile answered my inappropriate question. Nora, Rachelle, and Michael all laughed while I was caught between the pleasantly surprised look on Adam's face and the proud smile on Othello's.

"I did. Thanks for asking," he replied easily.

"So much fun," Rachelle reiterated with a smile from her reclined position in Michael's lap. I quickly looked away from her fingers gently stroking up and down his thigh. My face flushed at the sight, the burn in them growing as I tried to maintain the same focus on Othello that he was giving me.

"Any more questions for the room, Dove?" Othello asked as he wrote something down on the paper sitting on the desk. It looked so professional, like he was piecing together the terms of an agreement. Our agreement was verbal, the shake of our hands negating the need of a signature. Or maybe I was wrong, and I would end up signing that very paper. Signing my freedom over to him would be binding. I don't know if I could bring myself to do it—or if it were actually any different than the commitment I'd already made.

"What am I supposed to ask?" My fingers rotated between tapping on my thighs and busying themselves with the grappling of the fabric covering them. I clasped my hands in front of me to stop my fidgeting entirely. I would force my way into learning composure.

He looked up from the paper and capped his pen. "Anything."

I was given permission, but even that didn't feel like enough to ensure that the questions on my mind were okay. I was the one standing in the center of the room for them to laugh at when I made a show of my mistakes. Or my inexperience. Or my naïvety. But maybe silence was exactly what they were expecting of me. Or maybe they had no expectations, and I was the only one in my head. Not them.

"What is it that you guys do?" Maybe here, I could think less and speak more. It made sense, given that they represented the opposite of everything that was familiar to me. Everything but my usual.

"Whatever we have to," was his prepared reply. It was said so quickly, so coolly, and without thought. I knew that his was the lead that everyone else in this room followed, so in this part of my world, I would do the same.

"Is that your way of evading telling me the truth?" I asked quickly. One of my thumbs was stroking the other as I stood as tall as I could in the storm of my nerves, and it was all the proof that I would allow myself to show.

"It's the entire truth." He sat back in his seat, each hand lightly resting upon the wooden ends of its armrests. I couldn't see through him the same way that he could me, but the truth is what he was giving me. Simplistic answers and explanations were two different things, and I would have to be more direct if I wanted anything more.

"What were you doing when I saw you from across the street yesterday?" My peripheral vision was filled with the watching faces of those that moved back and forth between Othello and me. They were watching us dance circles around a point, and I only knew what point I was trying to make—which was that he was mistaken in wanting me to be here. The only watcher that didn't follow each movement between the two of us was Adam. He watched only me.

"Business," Othello answered simply once more. I was being defeated in a game that I didn't want to be playing.

"If you don't want to tell me the truth, then why don't you just lie to me? Why do you even let me ask anything in the first place?" My hands unclasped before me. They hung back to my sides weakly. It was a reflection of the strength to fight that I was giving up on.

He stood up from his seat. My eyes followed him, feeling like they pulsed with every beat of my heart as he rounded his desk and came to stand in front of me. He left space between us, but not enough to be sure that he couldn't touch me. If I reacted to his touch the way that I did last time, I'd humiliate myself in front of more people than just Adam again. I took a step back for my own good, and to my relief, he didn't match it.

"I'll never lie to you. I don't need to, and you've been lied to enough." His hands went into his pockets, relaxing the air between us, but the ease that he displayed couldn't retract from his power. The eyes that captured my gaze wouldn't let go once they'd found mine. They demanded my focus. "Remove the idea in your head that you need permission to ask your questions. There's a whole world to figure out in your lifetime, and you're only going to accomplish it by asking what you need to. I don't *let* you ask me anything. You're doing what everyone else does freely."

He walked past me toward the door. When I turned to watch him leave, he stopped my movement as he stood behind me. I froze, my back against him with my sight set on Adam. He wouldn't console my erratic nerves even if he could.

"But if it's better answers you want, Dove," he said, loud enough for all to hear, "then by all means, let me show you."

He pulled away from my body, leaving chills that replaced his warmth while he addressed the rest of the room. "Let's go."

Everyone jumped at his command, eager to follow behind him with smiles and mysterious glee as he led them out. I was stuck to the ground, my feet holding steel that kept me from falling in line. My instinct knew that I didn't like the promise in his words.

"You're going to miss the show, Genevieve," Adam said from the doorway. "I can hold your hand through it, since that's what you're used to."

For as vulnerable and unsure as I was, there was strength in my step that came with his implication. Not an implication, an observation that was accurate. If being here wasn't my choice, then I would endure what I had to—but I wouldn't hide my thoughts from them. If the only freedom that I had leftover from that which I'd surrendered to Othello was my freedom of speech, then I would use it whenever I could. I would push myself to be clear.

"I don't need anything from you," I replied as I walked past him, forcing myself to catch up with the others to get this thorough answer I was going to be given over with.

"'Atta girl," he said behind me.

I could tell by the mumble of his words that they were said around another cigarette.

We'd divided into two cars. The journey to finding out whatever it was that I would be shown was growing more nerve-wracking by the mile. I sat in the backseat of the car that Adam drove, Othello sitting in the front seat. There was no good idea of what they were bringing me to at this time of night, because there were only bad ideas.

My foot thumped against the floorboard as my knee bounced up and down. The speed of my shaking picked up the longer we drove. I was being taken farther and farther away from my own car, and my own means of escape. And in the black night of the inside of that car, I was too afraid to mention it.

Asking questions is what led me here. I didn't want to know what would come of asking more.

Adam pulled the car over on the side of a dim street lined with mostly closed shops. Some light was given off by the few that remained open, their awake businesses offering glow to the dead road and empty sidewalks.

The car turning onto our road briefly illuminated the entire block before its headlights shut off as it pulled to a stop on the other side of the street. When my sight readjusted to the dark, I could make out the silhouette of Nora in the driver's seat. She'd parked their car facing the opposite way of ours.

There was no time for me to wonder why we were split up or what I was to expect anymore, because the answers began to unfold.

Michael and Rachelle both left the car, walking up the sidewalk together before going their separate ways. He ducked into an alley before the last building sitting on the corner of the block, and she continued on until she reached the outer edge of that building where she leaned back against the brick, waiting, preparing.

Her short dress and the heels she wore were all that covered her delicately curved body. She was displayed to the night in ways that would encourage ill assumptions, but the position she placed herself in must have been exactly what she wanted. This all seemed too random to me to have not been well thought out by them.

Michael was shielded by the void of the alley, his skin and leather jacket concealing his station to any passerby. Only those that knew who hid in the shadows could possibly be aware, and barely able to make out the outline of the right side of his body as his left was hidden by its lean against the brick.

Othello left the car, his closing door making me jump out of my invested view of the scene being set up across the street. He walked slowly to cross the street, taking his time as he did with all things. Life wasn't rushed for him—it knew to wait for his arrival.

My palms pushed against my knees that had yet to cease bouncing. With the car sitting idle, I felt the shake that I couldn't be sure was caused by me or was only felt by me. Anticipation, along with all other things that were heightened by this picture of what I saw lurking in the dark, was vibrating through my muscles.

"Do you need a drag?" Adam asked as he pulled the cigarette from behind his ear and lit with the car's built-in lighter. He took a drag of his own before offering it back to me as he watched the unchanged scene outside his window. "It might help you calm the fuck down."

Then he probably could feel my shaking. Or my errant breathing that switched between holding my breath and pulsing air into my lungs. Or maybe he knew my every feeling like he knew my every move.

"No, thank you." I said as I lifted a hand that he couldn't see, politely declining. "I made a promise that I'd never start that."

The explanation wasn't intended, but the sound of voices, even my own, was bringing its own degree of calm. And even the sound of his chuckle settled better with me than the silence.

"And I'm sure you keep all your promises. Don't you, Genevieve?" His head didn't have to turn to look at me for the question to sound so direct. Accusatory, the sound of my name said softly with a tone that had bite. My effort to do good, and be good, offended him. Regret momentarily turned over the fear in me. If something I'd said made the implication that I'd thought less of him for anything, that was never my intention.

But when I opened my mouth to state my regret, I couldn't bring myself to apologize. If one thought little of promises, then they likely thought little of the word sorry. I didn't know the right way to learn exactly how he felt.

"Why are you still in here?" I asked instead, still needing the comfort of words. "Aren't you a part of all this, too?"

"I'm an important part." His fingers lightly tapped on the steering wheel. The movements were inaudible, and I wondered if it was his way of letting out his own tension as he never took his eyes away from the scene across the road. "The getaway driver never leaves the car."

Clarification in an answer like that is jolting. My head snapped to look back across the street, spotting the proof of the statement of Nora's place still in her driver's seat. Othello's slow pace up the sidewalk he was now on had him moving in Michael and Rachelle's direction. The light in the windows of the shop Rachelle stood by shut off, and she pushed off the wall just as a man emerged from inside, turning to lock the door behind him.

Rachelle took graceful steps that had to have been accentuated by each click of her heels, and the man was quick to take notice. He followed behind her as she continued down the sidewalk, leading the man in Othello's approaching direction. I didn't have to see the man's face to be sure of where his eyes were trained, and I didn't have to know the details of this plan to know that he couldn't possibly imagine what he'd be led to.

Rachelle and Othello met opposite ends of the alley that Michael was beneath the cover of. As they passed each other in the middle, the man closing in on the distance that was between he and Rachelle, Othello turned around.

One agreement leads to watching your life turn on its axis. In two large steps, Othello caught up to the man. In his third move, Othello's arm wrapped around the man's throat. Within four seconds, the yell that couldn't be pushed through crushed vocal cords was silently given to the empty street. Five beats of my defeated, slowing heart, and the man was on the ground in his spreading puddle of crimson.

No breathing. My lack of air was painless as I numbly watched Michael step out of the shadows and follow Rachelle back to their car, his job to intervene if anything went wrong excused by lack of incident. It all happened too quickly for there to have been any mistakes.

Othello turned back to continue his slow walk away from everyone down the sidewalk. Adam pulled the car into drive, moving us onto the street and putting me closer to the end scene. My ears rang with the static of disbelief. Fright had deafened me, affecting my senses as if a gunshot had torn through the night. But I'd seen the glimmer of the knife. I watched the soundless crime. I was a witness to the extreme lengths that men with no care for law went to.

And my seat in the back of the getaway car could make me an accomplice.

My ears couldn't even register the sound of the car door shutting when Othello slipped back inside. I didn't know when we'd caught up to him. I'd been so consumed with the sight of the man barely moving on the ground, the tragedy shrinking the farther away we drove on. But the aftermath only magnified.

He was turned around in his seat to watch me as Adam continued to put distance between us and the recent past. He waited like he knew that I wouldn't be able to hear a word he said if he were to speak. Minutes, or maybe just seconds ticked by as the wheels carried us from the bleeding man on the sidewalk.

"Do you have anything left to ask?" The indifference in his voice cut right through the static barrier. He was visibly unaffected. As cold as the fatal blade that I knew he must still have concealed somewhere. I didn't know how to exist in the same restricted place as him. The space in the car continued to feel smaller, and I felt too close to the man that showed me he could end another.

"Is he going to die?" I was indirectly involved. I knew in my quivering heart that I was more concerned for the soul that was on the brink of meeting its eternal fate, but I had concern for myself in the involuntary role I played. I had to know if what I witnessed was terminal, and if I would have to live with this until I died, too.

"If he doesn't stop the bleeding," he replied. No nod, no remorseful eyes, just an answer to the visual answer he'd given me tonight. "He'll need someone to come save him," he said as he turned back around in his seat. He set his sight on the road before us, his stoic profile shown by each streetlight we passed. "But there aren't many people who want to save a man like him."

I had more questions. I wanted to know if it was all justified. I wanted to know what it was a man 'like him' did that resulted in him bleeding out on the sidewalk. I wanted to know if Othello, Adam, Nora, Michael, and Rachelle would all lose sleep tonight the same way that I knew I would. I wanted to know if it were my existence of a conscience that set me apart here, or if they all had one as well that was set with different terms. Was I weak? Was that what made me the one that felt sick when she watched others do sick things? Was it just that I was learning late of corruption? Did I just not know the rules that warranted it?

How was I to know what things were wrong, when the things were done by those that thought themselves right?

The whole car was spinning, even after it stopped. Everything in sight twisted along with my thoughts. I sat on a seat that was cold with a body that burned.

"Do you want me to hold your hand now, Genevieve?" Adam asked. I turned to him and his grin as he ducked down to watch me while he held the backdoor open.

I slowly pulled myself across the seat, and he backed away and leaned against the car as I brought myself out into what should have been fresh air. But my mind was focused on death, and the blood that was shed on a sidewalk much like the one I stepped onto, and my legs gave out beneath me. I was caught by Adam's hands that held onto each side of me, standing me back up onto the ground that shook beneath me. To my assistance, he didn't let go.

Othello walked toward us, leaving the others he'd been speaking to that remained by the other car. The closer he got, the more detail I remembered. That same slow walk before he turned on a man, knife in hand and put to use. His approach made me instinctively back away, which pushed me back into Adam whose hold was still on my throbbing ribcage. The pressure of him against me was as comforting as it was uncomfortable. He wasn't the one that I watched stab a man tonight, but I didn't know boundaries anymore. I didn't like feeling so safe being pressed up against someone I barely knew. Nothing about anything made sense to me anymore.

Othello leaned against the car in front of me, taking his time in observing my current state. His eyes slowly roamed over my frightened face, my hand that had found its way back to my necklace, Adam's hands on my sides, my unstable body that was nestled against him. He studied the strange things that I did and felt, only to smile at my distress.

"How can you even smile?"

His brow rose in the only proof that he'd not expected me to say such a thing. He thought my shock had silenced me. I was just as surprised that it hadn't.

"How can you not?" he asked instead of answered. "One more blackened soul is rotting in Hell right now, and the Earth is free of his terrors."

"What about your terrors?" I asked. My shoulders stiffened with Adam's tightening fingers that nearly crushed my bones. If it were meant as a warning, it came too late.

"What of them?" Othello's expression remained careless. The hint of the smile of a snake was all the feeling he would show. I was right to think that the only one bothered was me.

"Are your terrors not the same?" I was unable to pull the hatefulness from my voice. It seeped from me, eager to flee the hold I'd kept on it for my entire life. But here was a person that wasn't polite, whom I didn't care to be polite to. If he wanted me to be here, if he wanted me to witness the things that I had, then he could accept my disdain for the things that I saw in him. My inability to understand whatever it was that he wanted me to. If he expected change, this was all I knew to give. "And what of your soul? Will it not see Hell for the crimes that you commit?"

"Genevieve," Adam cut in, punishing me with my own name. His hands slipped further around the bottom of my ribcage, shielding the front of me with his hands as he held me back when Othello took a step toward me.

He drew closer, knowing that I had nowhere to retract to. I was exactly where he wanted me—unable to run, and forced to watch and listen. He stopped before he was close enough to put his body against mine, forcing me to look up into his leering eyes. Eyes that would show fire within them if they weren't under the control of their master.

"It sees Hell every day," he told me. The restraint behind his words was visible by the tension of his neck. It was the only indication he'd give me that he was holding himself back. "I walk the Earth that you know nothing of, because you've allowed all those you claim to love to blind you to what really goes on outside of supposedly pristine doors."

His lips pressed together as he drew in a breath to continue peacefully. "The world is full of knives that are illusions, and the ones that are real. The only difference is that the real ones spare you a lifetime of suffering. If anything, I'm merciful." He took a step back, allowing my head to lower from its place pushed back against Adam's chest.

"And I am merciful, Dove."

FEELING

I managed to find my way into my own bed that night. Adam had to drive me home in my own car while Michael and Rachelle followed behind us. I was incapable of everything. I was either thinking too much, or couldn't think at all. Adam's hands around me had guided me to the car, and sat me inside before forcing me to sit in silence. There was nothing that could make anything better or worse. I was just below the surface of in over my head.

Father had been sitting in the living room, leaving to go to his own bed after he'd ensured that I'd come home. The crime that I'd seen replayed through my eyes, the guilt that I felt emanated from my pores. I waited for him to question me before he left me standing in the living room without a single word, and I wasn't even okay enough to be comforted by that. It only showed me that everything that I thought, expected, and *knew* was wrong.

There were no nightmares to terrorize my sleep for the next days, because I hardly slept. I forced myself to lay in bed and get out of it all the same. Only when I had the distraction of others' innocent questions that didn't lead to death did I find escape for blissful, brief moments.

"Luke hasn't called you in several days. Is everything okay?" Mother asked me as we all sat together in the dining room for lunch—one normal, non-murderous family. A family with terribly unnerving predictability.

Father sat in his usual spot with a paper in his hand as always, finishing the parts of it that he didn't get to at breakfast. The front of the paper displaying the news of a man slain not far from his place of business kept me from touching any of the food sitting on my plate. It was the third day of the black and white claims of a suspected robbery attempt gone wrong, and for the misguided, I was grateful. But the taste of the even worse truth didn't taste good in my mouth.

"Everything is fine," I assured her. I didn't bother to force my usual smile. There was only so much that I could expect of myself at this point. "He's just been really busy lately."

Busy being safe from the knowledge I'd acquired from my end of the deal. I'd wanted experience, I'd wanted desperately to learn more—and I'd learned that there were also things that I desperately didn't want to experience or learn. I now wanted to know how to move past things that I'd learned. And I didn't know where to begin, when I couldn't even forgive myself for things I didn't do.

"Do you want to go watch another movie this weekend? Some of the new ones look like they might be pretty good." Gray pushed away his empty plate from in front of him. I replaced it with my full one, and he took a bite without question. He had plenty of room to grow, and he should have his fill. I only hoped for him that growing didn't come at the same cost as it was for me, and that he was full of nothing but the good in life. Our sheltered life that I used to know no longer seemed so terrible.

"Yeah. Just, you pick the movie this time," I told him. Last, I'd chosen violence, and violence followed. I wouldn't trust myself again.

"Or we could let Amelia pick," he replied before busying his mouth with another bite. He was looking at his new, full plate instead of at me. He was avoiding a reaction. But reactions are what you should expect from parents like ours.

"Amelia will be going with you?" Mother asked. She was more eager than Father, who just looked over the top of his newspaper at Gray. The fact that he spared his attention was what said he was pleased. "Since when did this start?"

"Nothing has started," Gray clarified before wiping his mouth with his napkin. "She's just been insinuating that she wants me to take her for a while now. It would be rude if I keep ignoring it. So, I'll let her tag along with Vieve and me."

"Well that's lov—"

"Wouldn't it be rude to also lead her on?" I said at the same time Mother voiced her approval. "Can't you just tell her you aren't interested?"

"Genevieve Wren," Mother chastised. I knew better than to be so outspoken. All that I'd gained from outside of my life here had trampled over my self-preservation. I'd forgotten to think before I spoke. I forgot that I wasn't meant to be so direct about things that weren't my concern. "What's rude is you implying such a thing. He's not leading her on. It's just one movie."

But it did feel like my concern to protect Gray from making a potential mistake for the sake of pleasing others. "Why give her the hope that comes with that movie when he can just tell her the truth?"

"Because taking the girl to a movie with you both will be harmless, Gene. I won't hear any more about it. Let him invite her. You'll all enjoy yourselves just fine."

That and Father's displeased glare were the only warning that I was going to get. I tried to turn my attention to Gray, who was studying the embroidery on his napkin. He appeared more lost in thought rather than avoiding the tense air of the outburst. I looked away when I couldn't get his attention, and my eyes met with Father's again.

I knew what he was noticing in his study of me. I'd never acted in such a way before, or ever spoke out of line. It wasn't just something that wasn't tolerated in this house—it was something that wasn't taught by those he permitted association with. He was looking through me for answers that I was doing my best to hide. But if I remained beneath his watch much longer, I feared my shield of silence would break.

"May I be excused?" I asked to anyone and everyone.

"Yes, you may," Mother answered as she continued to pen the lengthy grocery list she'd been working on throughout lunch.

I left the table and made for my bedroom. My feet dragged through the hall, not wanting to return to the chamber of thoughts and dangerous solitude. Nothing good came of being left alone with my mind. I hated having questions that either couldn't be asked or couldn't be answered. Here, I couldn't ask. And it wasn't by anyone here that they could be answered.

I stopped in front of my door, hand on the handle as chilled as the dreadful room within. The door down the hall to Father's home office was barely ajar. It either never was before, or I'd never noticed because I knew the rule was to not step foot inside. It was made clear to us from a young age that that room was off limits to anyone but Father for his studies and service preparations. Not even the curiosities of childhood had lured me in before, but now I found myself pushing the door open wider.

It resembled nearly every aspect of his office at the church. The white walls, the bookcase that sat beneath the window behind his desk, the daunting atmosphere that I found less welcoming than that of Othello's. It was a strange difference, the comparisons between Othello's office and Father's. In Othello's there were no empty spaces because everything he had was out in the open, displayed proudly. In here, there wasn't enough of anything to convince someone that it had been used for over twenty years. Where were the marks of a human, the traces left behind of a man that I knew spent so much of his time in here? Was it just a forbidden, pristine room that existed behind a pristine door?

I supposed that we weren't allowed inside for fear of leaving our own traces. As I stepped in, I wondered more if my defiance would leave its remnants than if it would leave me scolded.

My fingers traced along the edge of the wooden desk. Men with power sat behind these, placing them between themselves and the rest of the world. They were the symbol of a barrier placed with that intent—that's what I thought of them.

I could picture Father sat behind here as well, Bible placed in front of him for hours at a time. When he was in solitude, I doubted that he despised it as I did. He could be alone in here for days without needing the distraction of other people. Is that because he wasn't scared of being alone with his conscience?

And Othello. He could sit at the seat behind his own desk, writing the terms to deals made and souls bought without needing the comfort of anyone else. There was separation of leader to followers, important to common. Men who sat in such seats knew their place.

"You're somewhere you shouldn't be, Gene," Father voiced from the doorway. I jumped, my fingers pulling away from the smooth surface that they longed to feel the significance of. It was too small and harmless of a mistake for me to feel so bad about.

"I know," I admitted. My hand fell to my side, grabbing at my skirt to keep my hands from places they shouldn't be. Such a desk wasn't meant for me—someone so weak, someone so common. They should have burned at the touch, but instead they burned to explore more. "The door was open, and I just wanted to see what—"

"An open door is not always an invitation, Genevieve," Father cut in with fervor. He walked inside with steps that were forced to remain slow. He was a man who could hide his thoughts and intentions behind his face, but he couldn't match the degree of invisible emotion that Othello could. His face showed the light red flush of his anger in his cheeks despite the control he had over the rest of his features. I wondered if perhaps the inability to hide the fire of feeling was the only trait that I got from him.

He walked around the desk to his seat. Even sat beneath my standing height, he was still above me. He made me want to apologize, but I knew that it wasn't enough to make up for falling short. Nothing but perfection was good enough. And I knew too well how imperfect I was.

"I'm sorry." My hands clasped behind my back. My head fell, unable to bear the weight of his condemning gaze.

"And what exactly are you sorry for?" The question did hold assessment. It struck through me like he had answers. Like he knew everything that I'd done wrong, everything I'd seen or heard or lied about. Everything that was impossible for the world to know. Everything that only a man who knows everything could know.

"For being here?" It had to be a question if I didn't know what was right. I barely knew what was real.

"You're forgiven," Father said. "What else?"

"What else?" My head looked up to find all the help that it could. I didn't want to admit anything more. I could ask for forgiveness for so many things, but each of them would kill my father the way that they were slowly killing me. He was the reason that I was suffering alone, and in a large way, he was the reason that I was suffering at all. I shut down that blaming thought before he had the chance to reach into my mind and see it.

"Is there anything more that you need to tell me?" he asked as he placed his clasped hands on the desk, absorbing all the power it projected. "Because I'm not a man of change, Genevieve. So I know it when I see it." His words sped up along with my worried pulse. "And I've seen the change in you. You seem to have forgotten the duty bestowed upon you, and that's to obey and respect. You're disobeying me by being here. You're disrespecting important people around you by speaking your unsolicited thoughts. I may not know what it is," he said as he leaned back into his seat, "but I know it's nothing good that's brought this on."

I could give him what he wanted. I could spill my soul that had been tugged on and chipped at, not only for these past weeks, but for my entire life. As I thought over every detail that he wanted me to admit, I thought longer on all the details of the life that I didn't long to return to. All the questions that brought me through the things that I'd now been through were given answers. I didn't want to go back to living without the option of answers. I didn't want to tell him of the wrong I'd done only for him to tell me that he was right in never letting me learn.

"It won't happen again," I told him with a beaten, strained voice. The uncertainty came from not knowing whether I meant I wouldn't break his rules again, or if he wouldn't find out a second time. Did I want to find an uneventful life once more now that I'd found more than I'd bargained for, or did I want to be more careful in letting its effect on me show?

I knew I was changed. As I left without a final reply spared by him, I knew that there was even more changing to come.

My back stayed against the closed door of an office forbidden. A room that reminded me that there were things I wasn't meant to know, power I wasn't meant to have. I couldn't pull myself away from the remaining curiosity that brought me to that room. Curiosity that sent me to places most men had never seen, and that controlled and guarded girls like me weren't meant to.

I'm not a little girl.

I'd felt so sure of myself when I first said it to a face more intimidating than any other. But now I felt like one. I was little in the presence of my father with his unclear

110

accusation and his ability to make me hate myself for living my life. A life I wasn't given, because it was never handed over. A life that I wasn't allowed my own control of without the freedom of a lie, which had taken me in circles through men that continued to steer my life how they pleased. I'd seen the safe by the control of one and I'd seen the dangerous by the influence of another.

And I couldn't turn around to direct the anger I'd never before felt to the one behind that office door.

It wasn't me that dialed the phone, but the blame in me begging to be redirected. It needed to be dispersed, it needed more than just the one host that wasn't resilient enough to bear it.

Luke being home to answer that call convinced me that I was right to come here in the light of day. My anger grew with the burning of the sun against the skin of my exposed arms. I'd asked Luke to drop me off a distance away from Othello's for the chance that I might find the intelligence to change my mind and save myself on the walk there, but all the walk did was spur me on. I wanted someone else to admit responsibility for my unraveling. I wanted someone to tell me I was right to think it unfair, even though I allowed it. I never knew how much I'd agreed to allow.

The police car parked in front of the house stopped my determined steps. It faced away from me, but I moved behind hedges lining the sidewalk in the yard of some stranger. I couldn't show my face to an officer that would read my guilt right off the words of my expressions. It was more than just anger now that shook my clenched fists. I knew my deserved place was in the backseat of that car for having watched a crime from the backseat of another.

The right thing to do would be to step out from behind my self-preservation and be free of having control. If I were taken away in that car, I'd no longer have to make my own decisions. I wouldn't have to hate what I went through anymore because there'd be no other choice but to remain caged, and sure, and safe. But as I focused through the dense branches, I watched Adam approach the car fearlessly. He stood before the open window of its driver, and looked down upon him as if he wouldn't allow the law to ruin his life. He wouldn't allow another to control him the way that I had.

He took a lighter from his pocket and leisurely lit the cigarette in his mouth. Adam could breathe the air better than I could, even with all of the smoke he filled his lungs with. His breaths were calm and unstrained, and mine were frantic from behind a covering that he didn't feel the need for. He stood there, lips unmoving aside from the drags he pulled from his cigarette. He did nothing but that until the hand of the driver reached out the window. The palm was upturned with expectation, and Adam reached into his back pocket to retrieve a large amount of folded bills that he handed over.

Adam's nod after payment was the only other thing given before the officer drove off. He remained on the curb, finishing the last inhales of smoke alone. The way that his eyes remained on the ground, trained on the street where the cop car had been made me think he was still reliving whatever the officer had been here for. Whatever it was that was said or done that deserved to be rewarded with money that I knew was acquired by disreputable means.

I stepped out from behind the hedges. I wanted to let him know that I'd seen it all as I took myself out of hiding and stood on the sidewalk. I wanted him to see me and know that I knew just how deep their scandals went. And as I watched him watch the street where the crooked cop had been parked, I was horrified with the question of who there was left to trust in the world if everyone was doing wrong. It was the reason why I was still unable to trust myself. Nobody was entirely honest.

"For as good as the dark looks on you, you look even better in the light," Adam said without looking my direction. He stomped out what remained of his cigarette beneath his shoe before turning to me. "It suits you. That innocent, angelic glow of the sun."

I wanted to ask him how someone who only dealt in corruption could even recognize innocence. But I wanted even more to know how he always knew so much. How he knew I was here without having to look, how he always knew how to be one step ahead.

"How did you know I was here?"

"Because I saw you standing behind those hedges when I walked out the front door." The first direct answer any of them had ever given me, and it was terrifying. If I wasn't hidden the way that I thought I was, then I would have looked just as suspicious to the officer as I knew I was. "Don't worry," he said in reply to my thoughts, "only I saw you. Officer Kephum is clueless where it matters."

"What does that mean?" I knew I was pushing my luck as I approached him as well as more answers than he was obligated to give me.

He waited for me to approach him before he decided to answer again. "That he has important information, but he doesn't know everything."

"What information did he give you?" I asked quietly, my morbid curiosity under my control for once. It didn't sound as desperate as I was.

He looked back and forth between both of my eyes as if he would find a suitable answer there. He was the one with the answers to give, but there was something in my face that he was looking for. I was beginning to learn how to read the signs that he was silently giving me, and it meant something to me. It meant that I was finding connection with the unspoken language of the world that had always been lost on me.

"You don't want to know."

"Tell me the truth," I tried to demand, but for lack of experience I didn't know how. It was said with begging, a beg for him to not give up the slack he'd been giving me with his answers. He was reeling back in the leash.

"That is the truth, Genevieve," he told me. There was a controlled amount of anger in the pressed set of his lips. But there was concern pulling over his eyes that he'd never shown before. Every bit of it was unforced. He was showing me that he was telling all the truth that he could—but it wasn't enough.

I took off toward the front door. I could hear him following behind me, but I didn't bother holding the door open for him after I walked in without announcement. I walked into the large middle room where I found Othello, Michael, and Nora sat together on a small group of furniture on the right side of the room. Othello sat alone on a seat across from the couch that Michael and Nora were on, and his set-apart position urged me on. It was all this intangible power that was boasted in front of me that brought me here, and it was what kept my feet marching in his direction.

I wouldn't be weak anymore, I promised myself as I stood between the couch and his seat, facing one of my surmounting problems head-on. I always kept my promises.

"I can see everything that you've forced me to watch, but I can't know anything more than what you *painfully* show me?" My words spilled out of a body built up with too much. Too much everything. I'd known I was reaching the point of what I could handle, but I didn't know that passing that point meant losing control. Words that felt as bruised as those did couldn't be held back.

Othello set the bottle that had been in his hand onto the floor beside his chair. He leaned forward, looking up at me from beneath lashes that were too dark to belong to the bright hair atop his head. It was another puzzle of the man resting his elbows on his knees as he watched the girl before him break. He was used to seeing things come unraveled.

"What are you trying to say?" he asked. His search for clarity when I was angry over the way he both did and didn't give it to me infuriated me further.

"That because of you, I've seen horrible, *horrible* things. You tell me that I can ask you questions, but you only answer the ones that ruin me." I forced myself to capture my voice as it nearly broke. Two breaths in and the pain was only in my conscience where it always was, no longer in my throat. "I see Adam outside paying off a police officer only days after I watched you ki—" I couldn't say the word out loud. "Do what you did, yet I'm not capable of knowing what that's all about? Was I not involved by watching you do it? Am I not included? Or am I just some *thing* you're having too much fun with through this life that you admitted to be hell?"

Othello didn't move to answer. He watched me drip my hatred, and anger, and animosity from the once sewn seems that he'd ripped apart. Seems that before, held back a tongue so sharp and careless. The only reaction he bothered showing was the tapping of his steepled fingers that pointed at the floor I'd taken center-stage of.

"Maybe it wasn't such a good idea for her to have gone with us," Nora said from behind me. "She seems too shaken up. She might end up spilling her guts to the wrong person, and we'll all pay for it."

"She won't," Othello replied without a second's hesitation. "That's exactly why she's here right now. Isn't it?" His fingers continued to tap, and my focus of his every move noticed that it had sped up to match each quick beat of my heart. "Because as scared as you are of everything you've seen, and as afraid as you are of me, there's something else that you're even more afraid of. Isn't there?" He stood to his feet, and I shrank beneath the truth. "You're here showing me all your hatred, because you can. You won't breathe a word of anything you've seen, because you can't. Not because of me, but because you can't handle disappointing that father of yours, can you?"

"You don't know anything," I lied. He knew everything and more about me, but he didn't know what it was like. He didn't know what it was like to live beneath the same expectations that I did, or live with the same conscience that I did, or even care. He especially didn't know what that was like.

"Don't I?" He said as he lowered his head to peer through my eyes and into my soul. "Then why have you come back? Tell me what it is I don't know. Tell me what it is that makes you angry about the life that you've had since you met me that's so much worse than the life you had before that had you crying and alone. Then tell me why you'd be here with me, so angry and full of feeling, when you could be sad and all by yourself."

"You might know enough about how I feel, but you damn sure don't care about it or else you would have spared me from it all."

The inappropriate language left my mouth for the first time, and it stunned me into silence. It forced me to slow down. I realized that my anger was being replaced by building amounts of something that I was used to: jealousy. I was jealous of him for knowing me better than I did. I was jealous of him for being stronger than I was. I was jealous of him the way that I'd been jealous many times before of anyone who appeared to have all the answers, or a life that was lived without insecurity, or a life of real freedom.

"Everyone, leave," Othello commanded the room, leaving his eyes on mine. Mine stayed on his because I didn't want to see everyone leave me alone with him. His stayed on mine to watch my reactions like they always did. "Adam, stay."

I could feel Adam stop close behind me. I knew his limitless loyalty to Othello, I knew that he owed me nothing and gave him everything, yet I felt safe with him here. I didn't understand it, but in the face of the situation, I didn't bother trying to.

"You're here telling me how angry you are and how much you don't like me," Othello spoke again when the sound of the side door announced the exit of the others. "How much you don't like the things you've seen because of me, and how much you despise that I've asked you to even be here. Tell me, Dove." His voice gentled the storm I'd brought in through the doors with me. The air in the room changed with every accurate acknowledgement. "Tell me about how I'm the first person that's shown you that you have the freedom to do so. I told you that I wanted you to share your freedom with me—not just your time."

He was right. I'd never before been led by my anger. I'd never before let it spill before the eyes of anyone else for fear of the consequences. I'd always been afraid to let anyone know that I wasn't simply satisfied with something. But my purge of anger did bring satisfaction. He was right about freeing me to show how I felt, but it didn't prove that he cared.

"I've given you everything you've asked of me. You've muddled my freedom in return with the things you've shown me."

"Just because they weren't answers that you liked, it doesn't mean that they weren't the answers that you asked for. I gave you what you wanted," he said with conviction. His words were too sure for me not to fight them.

"You don't know what I want," I said with conviction of my own.

He waited for me to say more, to tell him how I was sure of what I said. He smiled when I didn't, a fraction of the usual appearance of terror that I knew. He could detect all the holes in the fight left in me, and he knew that his superiority could fill them.

"I know what you want, because I watch," he told me as he let his threatening smile fade. "I pay attention to what makes you shrink back, and what makes you feel secure." He took a step forward, and I unconsciously took a step back, meeting with Adam's silent form. My startled hands that had hung at my sides grabbed the front of his legs for stability, and his hands that found my arms kept me from shamefully pulling away. The quickening of my heart fell back into step at the unexplainable relief of his touch.

"You think I don't notice that you feel safer with Adam giving you his body for support?" Othello pointed out with a gesture of his hand, and I knew then that he'd predicted my reaction to his approach. "I see you ease at his touch. I watch your every reaction. The blush on your face tells me everything I need to know, and I've no doubt that I know more about it than you. I know the things that you want that you don't even understand."

He took a small step closer as I fought myself between wanting to be embarrassed and wanting to be difficult. I didn't want to admit that he was right, and that I didn't understand why I felt the way I did. Why I blushed a deep shade of scandalous red with Adam's body standing still against mine, my hands still pressed against his thighs burning at the touch.

"What are you talking about?" I pressed, trying my best to feign ignorance. I couldn't hide the heat of my cheeks just as I couldn't hide the hesitant interest building in me. And I knew I couldn't get away with lying to him the way I'd lied to myself for years.

"Do you really want more of my answers, Dove?" he asked, closing in on the last of the space between us. He was a breath away, giving me the intimacy of the question without touching me. "Do you want to discover more than just the parts of reality that terrify you and make you angry?"

I remembered this secure feeling of my head leaned back against Adam's chest as I looked into Othello's eyes. Without the shock that distracted from it, I was more aware of just how reactive my body was to this contact. Othello was telling me that it was right to feel this way after I'd been told all my life that it was wrong—but it didn't feel wrong. For how much my body trembled, it didn't feel like this was something that I was supposed to be this scared of.

My head nodded my assent. My throat felt as though it would swell from the heat that was burning up through my body. I knew if I used my voice that it would be weak, and I didn't want him to know just how weak I really was and suddenly refuse.

"Show her, Adam," Othello ordered with his words and his intent eyes. They came back to mine as Adam's right hand on my arm began to patiently slide down. To watch Othello's guarded face as I felt Adam's every move stimulated the reaction on the surface of my skin beneath his hand. "If it's Adam that makes you want, then he can be your answer."

Adam's hand rested over the top of mine before his left hand traveled down to the fabric of my skirt over my thigh. I shut my eyes as the ache of my center began to pulse. I wanted to hide every new sensation from the eyes of the experienced, but I didn't want it to stop.

"Open your eyes, Genevieve," Adam instructed, the order in his voice forcing me to comply instantly. I shivered at the echo of his words near my ear as he began pulling up my skirt.

Othello didn't dare smile, but the satisfaction of watching me was clear in his focused look at my involvement. His slightly raised brows were all that told me that he was enjoying watching me unfold—watching me learn.

Adam's hand that had my skirt held up to my hip paused at Othello's raised palm. "Do you want to continue?" Othello asked me, sincerity laced in an authoritative voice. "I'll be the person to let you know that you have the power to say no."

I wanted more. I was on the brink of learning something that felt so off limits, and worth learning. For the first time, I was given the option to say no, and I knew that I didn't want to use it. With his assurance of my control given, I wanted it to continue with every ounce of my quivering being.

My left hand covered Adam's, holding a fistful of my skirt, just as his right hand covered mine. "I want more," I admitted. My shaking found its way to my voice, but it didn't shadow my certainty.

Adam's hand over mine continued, guiding my hand over to my panties. The first time that my hand slipped into them, and it wasn't alone. There was forbiddance and thrill that made me suck in air between my teeth as he pushed two of my fingers gently between the top of my slick folds. His fingers remained on top of mine as he pushed them slowly back and forth over nerves that tore out of me to greet our touch.

"You said I didn't care about how you feel," Othello said directly, pulling my attention away from Adam's encouraging hand. "But I not only care about how you feel," he told me with intensity in his eyes that watched me begin panting, "I care to *see* you feel."

I whimpered in response to his suggestive words and the building push of Adam's fingers over mine. Adam's groan grabbed my focus as his grip on me tightened, pressing him harder into the back of me. I felt his body's reaction growing against me. I closed my eyes at the feel of him as I whimpered again.

"Do you like being watched?" Adam spoke into my ear as he began rubbing our fingers in circles. He was pushing me closer to an edge that I wasn't sure of where it led to. I nodded as I looked into Othello's dark eyes. They were endless pits that didn't show me if he found the same pleasure in watching me as I did in being watched. "Then tell him."

My face flushed with more fire as I wanted to both writhe and tense up. Adam's fingers were doing all the work with the comfort of my own touch, and he was going to work me until I shattered. I stole from this temporary confidence to obey him.

"I like it when you watch me," I confessed to Othello, in a voice so out of breath and struggling that it didn't sound like my own.

"I like watching you, Dove." His brows gently lowered as he watched my mouth snap shut.

My mind couldn't wrap around everything I felt. His words, the overwhelming build-up that Adam was making me stir. My breath caught on the heightening of all the sensations they coaxed, and I didn't know how to allow air into my lungs when my body was so full of all they were giving me. I didn't know what I was being given.

"Breathe," Adam said at the very moment I met the peak of the unknown, and my exhale escaped with an uncontrollable cry pleading for him to let me down from a high I didn't know if I could handle.

"Adam, I—"

"Feel it while it lasts," he instructed me, his movements steady as I held tightly onto his hand and my diminishing stability that was slipping from my control.

Every panting breath came out with a clipped scream of ecstasy. Whatever I felt was both too much and not enough, my tensed and trembling body undoing itself as it came apart beneath our touch—beneath Othello's watch.

My hand that held Adam's to my hip found solidity on Othello's chest while Adam's control worked out the last ounces of bliss that my body would give me. My lids had forced themselves closed against the elation, but they opened as Adam slid our fingers slowly up and down between the wet walls that had found a way to force me to willingly touch Othello for the first time.

My fist was clutching the front of his shirt, tightening with the shift back to reality. Back to my surroundings. Adam removed his hand from atop mine, and mine limply followed out from my exposed panties. He let go of his hold on my skirt, and it slowly fell. A growl emanated from his chest while his body was still held against mine.

"Fuck," he said with audible restraint, and his warmth abandoned me before his heavy steps and the sound of the side door closing.

My hand still had a hold on Othello's shirt, and the pads of my fingers still had the slick proof of what felt like a dream. Only it wasn't, and now my shaking legs relied on the grip I had on a man that I'd seen kill someone. He'd taken someone's life, and given me a taste of nirvana. It was only one of the things that kept screaming at me that I was wrong as I descended from the highpoint to which he'd shown me.

I released my hold on him at the protest of my shuddering legs. If I didn't move, I wouldn't fall. And falling was what I was already doing from the confidence I'd had for only those few fleeting moments.

I'd found strength in my vulnerability. My thoughts traced back over what Othello had seen, what Adam had felt, and everything I'd said and given and shown. Now that it was over, I was left grappling for that strength. I knew how certain I had been of my desires, how right it felt to be so open and honest with both of them to bear witness to my acceptance of them, but the aftermath was riddled with regret that began to seep back in.

All my life I'd heard the lectures of harlotry. I'd heard the lectures of sins that one could commit against others, but how the sins committed against one's self were the most damaging. I was meant to feel damaged, but as I looked at the dark hair and metaphorically opened eyes of the woman that was reflected in Othello's brown irises, I saw myself as whole. There were pieces inevitably missing within, a life that had yet been filled—but it was being filled. It was being provided with the good, the bad, and the real that is the epitome of a life lived.

This was the first answer that he'd given me that didn't come at the cost of suffering. The lesson learned was enjoyable, and the only suffering that was occurring was due to my own doubts. Was I now undesirable for having my own desires? Was I now damaged by the generous touch of another? Would the red of my face in all my growing shame for having known pleasure permanently mark me as unacceptable, as a failure to the watchful eye of my father?

"And just as easily as it was given, it's being taken away," Othello said with studious eyes. "You couldn't let yourself have one simple thing that nobody is supposed to be able to steal from you. The knowledge is only yours, and you're letting it leave by the thieving hand of someone else. Whoever told you that you should be feeling as guilty as you are is a liar."

"How do you know? How do you know that I even feel guilty? What makes you so sure that you're always the one that's right?" All of the quiet questions were asked in desperation. I wanted him to be able to tell me that I wasn't meant to hold myself to the standard always set one step above me. I wanted him to tell me how everything I felt was so clear to him when so many things were unclear to me. I wanted him to tell me something that proved to me that I should be trusting his word over the others.

He gestured with his hand for me to sit down on the couch. My left hand was clutching and unclutching the place of my skirt where Adam's hand had held it up and left me open to the encounter. I sat down to the relief of my unstable body, and watched him return to his chair across from me.

"I know because no man has the right to tell you how to feel when they feel nothing. They don't live with even the smallest amount of regret or remorse that you do, and their actions actually warrant it. I don't sulk over all the things you've seen me do, so it isn't my place to tell you that anything you do is wrong. I go to great lengths, great *pains* to crush the spirits of other men, and you're crushing your own for no reason other than your need for approval." He leaned forward and grabbed his bottle from its place on the ground. "As for knowing how guilty you feel," he said with the neck of the bottle hanging from the grip of two fingers,

"I see it in your face just as I do everything else. All the answers that you don't find the courage to ask for, you look for in my eyes. It's why I'm always watching. I don't want to miss all the questions that you deserve to have answered."

The bottle held loosely in his fingers was brought up to his lips, and he finished what remained inside the tinted glass container before setting it back down on the floor between his feet. His eyes remained down on the empty bottle as he rested his forearms on his knees, sitting on the edge of his seat as he had been when I came in here angry, clueless as to where my anger could lead me.

Unhurried seconds passed before he looked back up to me. "And I know when I'm right, because I did a hell of a lot of being wrong to figure things out. Your idea of failure and mistakes are flawed because they weren't labeled by you, they were labeled by everyone else's standards that they can't even meet, themselves. I'll spare you all the misconceptions that everyone has of the world, and I'll answer all your questions so that you don't have to figure them out on your own. I'll keep you from finding out the hard way."

My mind pulled out the image of the man on the ground, bleeding out the last painful moments of his life as Othello walked away with the weapon hidden in his hand. "Watching you kill that man wasn't 'finding out the hard way'?"

He tilted his head as I asked the question, the sideways look he gave me making me think that the answer should have been obvious. He shook his head, and his smile appeared to accentuate the intensity of the topic.

"No. You asked what it was that we do. If you hadn't asked me, if you'd found out the hard way, then that would mean that it could have been you having your guts spilled onto the sidewalk. Watching was the easy answer."

My eyes grew with his smile. The humor he found in my fear of his words was disconcerting, and he shook his head again at my reversion back to being afraid. Being terrified of the implication only felt natural.

"I'll never hurt you, Dove." His smile began to slip as the mood turned. He didn't toy with the remaining fear on my face. He showed sincerity with few words and a lack of expression.

But I'd been told many things. I'd been controlled in the disguise of guidance, I'd been manipulated by opinions, and I'd been lied to in the form of comforting words. He'd given me every answer I'd asked for, no matter the cost to my innocence. His honesty was always raw and brutal and left a mark with its weight. But the trust that was being formed was provided by his terms, and I finally realized that I needed the reassurance of mine. I wanted his words to be the truth, and I wanted him to know how much I needed them to be. If I'd been lied to, deceived, and betrayed by everyone else, I didn't want to be by him.

"Do you promise?"

He peered into my question with thoughts of his own that I was yet to be able to read on the clean slate of his face. "Does a promise really mean more to you than a man's word?"

"A man's word means nothing," I told him, knowing that I'd surprised even myself with my capability to lie. "You told me that *everybody* lies." And a promise was something that I trusted myself to never break, so it was all I could place my trust in with him when it came to such important words.

His hands clasped together in front of him, and I thought of how we joined our hands to finalize the agreement that led me to this moment in time. The sight of his hands coming together was like an agreement he was making with himself, and I wondered if this was the first time he was giving someone more than just his 'word'. I wondered if he internally made an agreement to make such a small change for someone else's peace of mind. Someone as fragile as me.

"I promise."

Adam entered through the side door, breaking our connection. I looked away from Othello, searching for somewhere neutral to turn my focus. I didn't want to look at Adam's face. It wasn't the shame that still lingered; I didn't know how to act around someone that had had their hands on me in such an intimate way. Could we continue as normal? Would I blush like this any time he was near me? Would I think about the feelings he incited every time I saw him?

He sat down beside me, languidly leaning back and extending his arm along the back of the couch. From the corner of my vision that I had set on Othello's empty bottle, I could see Adam's ease. He pulled a cigarette and a lighter from the front pocket of his cut-off denim vest, pausing before he took his first puff.

"Genevieve." I left my eyes on the bottle, reading the brand's letters for the eleventh time. A brief flicker to the corner of my safety zone assured me that he wasn't looking at me either. "I got you off," he said after his first fogged exhale, "I didn't murder your entire family. It's still safe to look me in the eye."

He got me off. It sounded so straightforward, a term given to the ledge he took me to and over. Off. It was an answer that I didn't have to ask for, saving me from further embarrassment. I did turn to look at him then.

"So this doesn't change anything? I didn't mess everything up?" I looked between Adam and Othello, who were trading silent glances. Whether it was a good or bad thing that I was left out of their soundless conversation was unclear.

Adam turned to look at me, giving me a grin with lips extended on each side of his cigarette. He turned away for a moment to discard the smoke toward the back of the couch. "Nothing's changed. My fingers smell of sex and smoke; all is right with the world."

I turned scarlet with the word. They were both so poised and unaffected by the fact that sexual things were done and that sexual things were being said. I didn't know if it was the difference in me because I was a woman, or because I was inexperienced. Could I learn to be as unbothered? Why was I the only one with shame?

"You're fine," Adam insisted with a tap on my shoulder. I gave him my attention again, willing to tear them from my thoughts. "Nobody is going to know."

"But I know," I countered. We were already the only ones that knew, and the problem was that I was fighting myself.

"And aren't you glad you do?" he asked with a devious smile.

I turned away from the way his implication made me feel. Because above my worry, there sat the truth. I was more than satisfied with the knowledge he'd given me. That they'd both given me. I looked for the answer in Othello's eyes to the question that I kept asking myself now that I was reflecting.

Could I be content with the fact that I took pleasure in the things I'd been taught to be wrong?

"Yes," I answered simply—to more than just him. Othello's brows raised slightly, relaxing with satisfaction as he sat back in his chair.

"Could you tell me what time it is?" I asked Othello amidst the comfortable silence. A million things had happened since I left my house with so much hatred ready to be directed at the person willing to listen, and I couldn't give myself a good idea of how much time had passed since then.

"It's almost four," he told me after a quick glance at his watch, his head remaining rested back against the seat. This silence wasn't full of neglect like I was used to. It was patient, not forced due to lack of event or the hesitance of possibly saying the wrong thing. I wasn't ready to return to that pressure, that neglect.

"Then Luke should be here soon," I said, my guess confirmed by the honk of a horn outside. His choice to not come up to the door of the Sarris house was a natural one, but my feet dragged as I stood to them and made to exit through it. I was drastically overcome by how much I suddenly didn't want to leave.

"Dove," Othello called as I reached the front doorway of that room. He looked through me, and I knew he saw the dread of my departure. Returning to the house that birthed my anger was a difficult thing that I wished I didn't have to do.

"Deal's off," he told me as he stood from his chair, and Adam followed suit. "If you return, it will be because you want to."

They walked off together to the side doors, leaving the experience of the big room behind. They'd stayed with me and sat in the silence as they let me sit with my thoughts, but didn't make me sit with them alone. I took that comfort with me as I walked out the front door, nearing Luke's car under the high-risen sun.

I'd forgotten all about the officer that had greedily taken the money until I thought of how Luke's car was parked in its place. My questions had been unanswered, and I had lost them in the avalanche of distraction before they were crushed and smothered by more selfish things.

He got out to open my door for me, smiling with joy that coerced my own lips and halted my sullen thinking. "You seem awfully happy," I told him as I sunk into my seat. "More so than usual."

"I'm incredibly happy," he replied before shutting the door. His smile was stuck with him as he rounded the front of the car and got inside. He was far away from being here in the present with me, but I enjoyed seeing his delighted wandering. "And you don't seem as upset as you did when I dropped you off. Feeling better now?" he asked as he put us in drive and dragged me closer to home.

"I don't know how I'm feeling," I told him honestly. My head rested back against the seat as I watched the road before us roll away under our tires. The end of my hours of freedom were coming to a close, and this time I wasn't eager for it.

"And I don't know why you'd want to spend so much time beneath the same roof as Othello Sarris, but that's a detail I won't question, as well."

I laughed at the big eyes and shrug he ended with, reveling in the light and warmth of the car ride with him. I'd hang onto this small pleasure while it lasted, because I knew now just how quickly the pleasure slipped away.

"It isn't all that bad," I said with confidence stolen from what Othello and Adam had given me.

I knew not all things that happened behind dark doors were as iniquitous as they appeared.

COGNITION

The only thing keeping the living room from being drowned in the neglectful silence was the noise of the movie Father and Gray were watching. The sounds of horses and gunshots from the black and white western they were honed in on occasionally cut through my attempt to read.

The book in my hand was worn and hanging on by fine threads from constant repetition of turning pages. I'd stopped keeping track of how many times I'd read it around the time that I realized I could practically quote the entire thing. I'd dismissed the effect of routine entirely, but now it was back as I couldn't concentrate on a story that I didn't even need to read to relive.

Sounds weren't the only thing that disturbed my peace. The sight of my mother in her usual spot, with her usual needle and thread in her hand was somehow grabbing my attention. She even worked with a smile as she completed a task that seemed so unstimulating, so mundane. How was she more than just content? Was she not in the same room with me, living in this same moment that the four of us had already lived in a million times before?

The page I tried for the seventh time to read was one of death, and one of mercy. As I watched the scene unfold in my head without the assistance of the words, I allowed my mind to gently transfer over to memory. One of death, and one of talk of mercy.

For the past week I'd forced myself not to think of the people and the events from a deal dissolved. I knew if I allowed the recollection, the physical reaction would appear on my face. But now, I willingly thought of Othello. I thought of his claim of mercy, and all that I could now acknowledge that I didn't know of the death I saw.

His confidence in his actions, in something as permanent as the execution of a man, made me think through the factors that I didn't see at play. As much as he let me know on that night, he kept just as much from me. He let me watch, but he didn't give me the details.

All the horrible possibilities of what type of man Othello's victim could have been ran through my mind. When I felt reassured that there was a chance that Othello could have been the merciful one, that the man could have deserved a fate worse than the release of death, I was able to live without the answers. I was able to comfort myself with the things I searched for on my own, and I didn't feel the need for confirmation.

The confidence that came with the release of the hold that the memory had had on me for so long was engulfing. I wanted to search for more details in all the other answers I wanted to ask for. As I looked at my father, contentedly watching the moving images of the screen, I reached for details before any hesitations could stop me.

"What were your parents like, Father?"

Mother's hands paused in her needlework. Piercing the bubble of our quiet family time was something rarely done. I could see the subtle movement of Father's lips as he pursed them, mulling over the disturbance. I looked to Gray to see if he had been as bothered by it, but he looked at our father as well, waiting for the answer that also concerned him. I hadn't considered that I'd be asking for the both of us.

After nothing but silence, and Mother's quick return to busy hands, I counted myself lucky for not being reprimanded if I wasn't going to get a reply at all. It was better to be given nothing than the reminder of how impolite it was to pry.

Gray and I shared a brief look before he returned to the movie and I returned to my decaying book. I continued my duty to pretend—pretend to read, pretend that I didn't care about being ignored, pretend that I didn't long to know what the generation that led to these four dull lives was like. I cowered back into my place, and threw the confidence that had forced me to step out away.

I was finally learning how to fall back into the seasoned ability to escape into a story when Father's reply came.

"They were good, God-fearing people," he said with his gaze still on the screen, unseen film rolling along in his vision. "But they didn't see the world clearly. Their beliefs weren't always in line, and they suffered for it." He spared me a harsh look, breaking the concentration on his answer. "As all do when they choose to fight the way of the righteous."

I turned my attention to Gray, only to remove myself from the pressure of the guilt forming beneath Father's stare. There was implication that seemed to only be felt by me, the suspect that questioned the ways taught by the righteous. Gray was unbothered by the warning, watching Father's generous reply with information that we didn't deserve, didn't need. I found a small amount of peace in watching the light of Gray's face as he turned back to the screen with answers he didn't have to discover the painful process of asking for.

"You're lucky to have us, and the correct guidance needed in life," Father reminded us—or maybe just me, but I couldn't bring myself to look at him anymore. I'd never admitted my faults to him, but the judgment in words that he spoke to me made me think that he somehow knew. I was more than just 'out of line' to him—I was walking along an entirely different path. The wrong path. "It's a shame they weren't around to see the proper way that you were raised."

A pat on his own back, not on ours. It wasn't a shame for them to have not seen the kind and smart and *good* people we'd turned out to be, but instead it was a shame that they didn't get to see how the raising of us was done. It was a shame that they weren't shown the right way to shape a human into an ideal of perfection.

I knew I wasn't perfect. As I sat my book aside and watched my blessedly unaware brother focus his attention at a movie he was forced to sit through for the countless time, I counted my imperfections. I ticked off each instance, each thought, each unknown mistake I'd made that could warrant my father dismissing my self-achievements in such a way. I was slipping off the pedestal that we'd been placed upon, but Gray didn't deserve to be pulled down with me. His place held high above the murk of the world—above the rest of us flawed humans—was secure.

My anger grew on his behalf. Whatever grandparents we could have had would have been just as proud of him as our parents were. In my defensive need to protect the dismissal of Gray's goodness any further, I discarded the desire to ask Mother about her parents, too. I would never care to again hear of people who missed the opportunity to give praise where it *wasn't* due. Because I knew that a parent's perfect guidance didn't always result in perfection. I was proof of that.

"Would anybody like some tea?" Mother asked in passing as she stood and walked out of the room. Her neglect to wait for an answer betrayed her intention to disguise her escape from the poisoned air of the room.

I got up and silently made mine. No excuses needed, and none deserved.

Amelia's hand on Gray's shoulder as she laughed about something he'd said was the most physical contact I'd seen between them. His grin at her pure, uninhibited laugh showed more connection between them than anything. Things were slowly changing between the two of them, and Luke and I were watching it happen before our very eyes as we sat on his back porch.

"You know he's called her three times in the past two weeks?" Luke questioned with a nudge on my arm with his elbow.

I looked away from our younger siblings that played darts on the ancient board nailed against the biggest tree in the backyard. The slack of my jaw as I looked away from the reserved Gray that I knew said everything there was to say about my disbelief.

"Grayson? Called Amelia? Three times?" It sounded even more impossible the second time I heard it.

Luke laughed at the look I couldn't remove. "Yes, Grayson. Who the hell else would I be talking about?" He looked back out to the two of them. Gray was removing the darts from the board, and one from the tree that was thrown by, most likely, whoever was losing. "It's surprising, I know. But at least our parents' disappointment will be consoled by the grandchildren that they give them after you and I don't end up giving them any."

It was easy to smile at his joke, but it couldn't remain long. That brought up so many questions about what we were doing here, and if there was even an end to this plan. I couldn't live the rest of my life through a lie. I would have to give myself closure at some point, and it didn't have to be soon for Luke's sake, but it's something that I needed. Something I looked forward to.

When I looked at Luke and couldn't see the lie we lived together, I hoped that that was how everyone else saw us. I hoped it was as believable as it seemed, because the joy on his face with his current life lived was obvious. It was joy that I didn't want to remove, but I was beginning to accept the fact that I was capable of doing selfish things. And I had to know; I had to jeopardize his joy.

"We can't keep this up for that long, can we?" I asked him, turning in the plastic chair of the set we sat in. I angled my body to him, investing as much into the question as I had into our agreement. "Can a lie last a lifetime?"

He sat his cup of water on the table between us. I watched the effects of the movement ripple from the center of the cup. How far from the center of our decision was I, and how many more rippled effects were to come?

"Can it last a lifetime? That, I'll likely need the rest of my life to figure out. It's a theory I'm willing to test." He looked away from his sister and Gray, who'd given up their game and were leaning against the fence in conversation. "But no, we won't keep this up for that long. After the summer, I'll be leaving for my final year before I'm out of this town for good. And you'll be—"

"Here." Interjection preceded any assumptions or speculations that I didn't want to hear. It was easier to fall back on the reality that I was certain of. "I'll be here until I'm told where to go next."

I wanted his time at college to give him more than mine gave me. I wanted his accomplishments to lead to success and propel him forward. My time away gave me false hope for a different future, and my accomplishments amounted to nothing. Everything I earned was proving to be useless.

"Do you want me to come back for you after I finish school?" Luke grabbed onto my hand that mindlessly traced the pattern of the table, stilling my thoughts of failure. "Because I'll come back, and we can say goodbye to this place together." He moved his hand up onto mine, giving it a gentle squeeze. "Or, I can come back, we can get married, and we can both settle for giving everyone what they want."

"I'm growing tired of settling," I admitted, looking at my hand that was shielded by his. He was giving any seeing eyes simple things that they expected, but the gesture would be taken out of context. It wasn't faked, but it was friendly. "And I couldn't let you settle for marrying me."

I knew the suggestion hadn't been made sincerely, but my response had. I'd felt stuck, lost, and confused enough to know that I didn't want Luke to feel that way. I didn't know how he expected his life to work out, and his shrug told me that maybe he didn't know as much as I thought he did, either.

"I don't know," he confirmed, "marrying you would make life quite a bit easier. It would make sense, make everyone happy."

"But are we supposed to settle just because it's easier?" I turned my hand over beneath his, grabbing on to him and the conversation he had risen. "Things that start out making sense don't always stay that way. And what will it matter if everyone else is happy, but you aren't? If everyone used that logic, then nobody would be happy. Maybe nobody really is."

His fingers laced into mine easily. It was the first time I'd held the hand of a man outside of prayer, and knowing that it wasn't intimate let me feel the safety of contact he was sharing with me without guilt.

"Plenty of people are happy," he assured me. He nodded his head toward Gray and Amelia who still stood against the fence, content with simple conversation and shared smiles. "You can't tell me that those two aren't happy. They're happy, and I don't think they're settling. Technically, I wouldn't be settling if I married you." He returned his eyes to me, sadder than the smile he had. "You'd be settling for me."

"Why do you think that?" I didn't want to entertain this idea any more than he probably did. But if this were going to be the first option clearly given to me for a look into my future, then I would look at it no matter how hard it was.

And I could feel by the grip of his hand that it was hard for the both of us.

"Because you already know me. You know my secrets, and that's the hardest thing that I'm going to have to carry through my life. Alone. But if I married you, then we would be sharing my secret just like we are now, and life would be easy for me. Easy for me, but not fair to you."

I sat looking at our hands, wondering if it did make sense to have this for the rest of my life. Transparency was one of the things that I wanted for my future; I was so worn down by going through life blindly.

"Do you think about all the things you'd be missing out on if you did things the easy way?" I asked, hoping to hear something reassuring. "Is going through all the trouble actually worth it?"

"It's worth it. I wouldn't want to have missed out on all the things I know about now. Memories are better than living a life of 'what-ifs'. Don't you think it's worth it?"

Memories did last forever. The things that I had seen would follow me through the rest of my life, plaguing me until my own death released them. But did the bad outweigh the good? Would I trade the enjoyed experience just to erase the terrible mental pictures in my mind?

"I don't know." I wanted to be able to say yes, that it was worth it and that one blissful moment diminished the rest of my internal anguish. But there was the feeling in my gut that told me that it wasn't over, that reminded me that I wasn't done living behind a lie. I wasn't through living the hard way, yet. I wouldn't know if it was worth it until it was over.

"You don't know a lot of things, Gene," Luke said with a tap of his thumb against my hand.

One look at his brown eyes told me that it was meant in observation, not offense. I shouldn't be offended by the truth, anyway. I should want to change it, and in the most real way, I was.

"I know," I acknowledged as I pulled my hand from under his, "but I'm learning."

"And how's that going for you?" He picked up the seat beneath him and turned it to face me, sitting back down to pick his cup up off the table. "What kind of things do you learn when we're *supposedly* together?"

There was too much that could go wrong in an answer to that. I opted to be evasive, not trusting my face to hide the lie that I would have to give him.

"I don't know," I said quickly, inadvertently reaffirming his observation about how much I knew. "What do *you* learn?"

His cup paused before his lips, his smile greeting the corners of his eyes. "Do you really want me to answer that?"

"I don't think I do," I said with a shake of my head. A small laugh escaped me at the awkward implication. It said just as much to me as an answer would.

"You don't know enough, and you think too much," Luke replied before setting the cup on the table with an empty thud. The playful smile lingered, giving his words tenderness. "That's a very destructive combination."

Destructive. He wasn't incorrect, though he couldn't begin to imagine the extent of it.

"Would I be better off knowing too much and thinking too little?"

The air he blew through his lips relayed his answer before he gave it. "You'd be better off asking fewer questions. Or at least directing them toward someone with the right answers."

It was alarming to see how right he could be in giving me answers without knowing the context. Almost like he could see through me the way that Father did, saying the things that touched too close to my own secrets. Only, with Luke, his statements lacked judgment. They didn't hold the same malice as they did when they came from Father. Luke didn't hold his better understanding of the world over my head.

"I didn't think that what I said was nearly as thought-provoking as what you said, but you sure are stuck in your own head over there," he said, pulling my fingers away from my bottom lip. It was a habit that had taken the place of my urge to hold my necklace. I didn't even notice the change until I woke up with a bruise on my lip one morning from rubbing it back and forth between my fingers so much. It was apparently more harmful, but it didn't make me want to force myself to turn back. "You're abusing the hell out of those perfect lips."

My hand dropped to my lap when he let go of it. I didn't voice my confusion. I didn't have to when my face said enough.

"Yes, I said your lips are perfect. My eyes do work, Gene." He leaned forward on the table, and I remained frozen and unaffected in my seat. He wasn't the type of man that made me shrink away. "I'm not asking for you to share them with me. I'll leave the pleasure to Othello."

"Othello?" The name left my mouth eagerly. It was the first time I'd said it aloud in weeks. I lowered my voice to ensure that I wasn't overheard. "Why Othello?"

The heat was slowly rising to my face, more potent than the current feel of the summer day. I'd once intended to kiss the lips that spoke passionately of the world of the outcasts. The lips that declared justice be carried out with violence, that demanded respect. Respect that was inevitably given by will or by force. I once tried to kiss those lips and they slipped past me, telling me that my lips were mine to give. His lips had assured me that I didn't have to surrender myself to another just to please them. His lips were on my mind for the first time, pictured against mine.

"I just assumed, I guess." His shrug made the idea seem so reasonable. I didn't know normal the way that he did. "You haven't kissed anyone over there?"

"I haven't." In the truth, I found the realization that I'd done something much more intimate before I'd had my first kiss. Did I do something normal the wrong way? I hadn't waited for order; I'd stolen the chance and reveled in the opportunity. Maybe being momentarily selfish caused me to ruin the chance of future intimacy. If I told someone that I'd never been kissed, they wouldn't expect that I'd done more than that instead. And I knew that I couldn't confess the deeds done to anyone else. Did I sabotage everything by not saving myself entirely the way that I'd been directed to do? Being a woman and being the woman accepted by those that groomed her life were very different, and I was feeling so far away from being either.

"Don't you want to?" Did his smile mean that I was wrong to think of these things as mistakes? "At least a little bit?"

I did want to. I wanted to find out for myself what it was like to have lips that made promises—lips that kept the world in place with daunting smiles—pressed upon mine. Would the answer come by simply asking, or should I expect more from such a daring thought, just like every time before?

"I guess I do. It's just hard to know who to trust enough to give it to." The blush on my face was thought of secret touches, confessions of impure thought, and shame of admitting that I was clueless. "What if I do it wrong? What if I give my first kiss to the wrong person and make a fool of myself?"

He hid his smile for my benefit. He couldn't dim the eyes that found my superficial worries to be satirical. Though I appreciated the effort, it didn't do much to make me feel better.

"It's pretty hard to do it wrong, so don't worry so much about that. Maybe you should start using your free time better, Gene. Learn to kiss. Do the fun, wrong things that you can before we die or the world ends—whichever comes first." He watched Grayson and Amelia making their way toward us. Our time to speak of such improper things was closing with their approach. "Because according to your dad, we don't have much longer."

Gray and Amelia walked close together, and I watched her hand in curiosity of whether it longed to be held by his. Did she struggle with the same trivial uncertainties that I did? Were all women scared of how they felt or what others would perceive?

When I'd let mother know that I would be coming here to see Luke, her immediate suggestion that Gray tag along should have been expected. What was surprising was his quick agreement, and the way he didn't put space between him and Amelia—all the signs I'd missed along with their maturing connection.

Things would be so much easier if I found the same happiness in the things that were wanted for me. Gray was remaining on the path desired for him, *and* finding joy along the way.

"We were just thinking about going to eat before maybe catching a movie. Do you guys want to come along?"

And there was the major difference. Gray knew how to play it safe and enforce boundaries. He'd yet to be alone with Amelia, and that's why he was better at this than me. He knew how to naturally save himself from making mistakes. There was no need for Luke and me to infringe upon their time away other than him wanting us there. Or maybe they both did, and Amelia was more capable of staying on her preferred path, too.

"Sure," Luke said as he got to his feet and held out a hand to pull me up with him. "We can all ride together; I'll drive."

I followed behind Luke, the last one to reach the doorway that was leading to a double-date to make our parents proud. He stopped short, bracing his hands on both sides of the door before turning around and whispering to me despite the lead that Amelia and Gray already had away from us inside.

"You know, it's almost too bad that this thing with you and me can't be real. We would make much cuter babies than them, and it could be one more thing to add to the list of things I'm the best at."

And with that, he left me behind.

He and Amelia grew up being competitive; Gray and I grew up being taught to please others instead of ourselves.

REASON

Nancy's hands removing the rollers from my hair were soothing, expertly pulling away the plastic pieces from the absurd length that she was attempting to style. There was nothing special about my simple locks, so I didn't quite understand her excitement when I agreed to let her fix them.

"You're wasting all of its potential if you say no," she'd said after asking if she could 'just show me what it could look like with a little assistance'. So I'd said yes, and an hour later I was still sitting on the floor in front of her chair. I had too much hair, and I'd never considered cutting it all off until now.

"Now, flip your head over," she directed as she put the last roller from my hair away.

I did so, pulling over the mass of warm curls and their surprising weight. Nancy pushed what I missed over my shoulders and began weaving her fingers into the hair near my scalp, shaking it out. I could have fallen asleep with all the gentle attention paid to my hair, and nearly had a few times. But when she told me to sit back up and held the small handheld mirror before me, I was alert to the stranger that took up my reflection.

Just one change, and I looked like I could possibly belong to the modern world. My hair was big, purposely wild just like the appearances and personalities of others my age. I couldn't deny how much I loved the way it looked and how good it made me feel to not see myself as set apart, but I didn't know if it was meant for me. Then again, neither was feeling plain. I recognized that it would take more than just the confidence in my appearance to find belonging.

I'd ruined her fun by declining to have my lips colored.

"I'm an old woman, let me have my fun while I still can," she'd said in her own way of begging.

I laughed at her persistence. "It's almost nine, Nancy. I'm fixing to leave; I don't have another hour to spare."

Truthfully, I did. I had hours to kill, given that I was supposedly going to be with Luke, while in reality he and Roman were spending our date together at a party across town. What really kept me from caving to her wishes was that I didn't want to forget about my painted lips before I finally did go home. My waiting father would already be disappointed to see my hair done the way it was. I was mentally preparing myself for the silent lectures against vanity that he would give in a single look.

"Fine, I suppose they're perfect as is," she relented with a dismissive wave of her hand.

Her echo of Luke's opinion rang in my ears as Jane walked in the front door. I didn't see my lips the way that they did, and perhaps it was because I'd never considered the purpose behind lips. Their shape, their sensitivity to touch, all designed to fit against the embrace of others. It had never crossed my mind until I was finally asked about a kiss.

"Take these with you," Nancy intruded into my impure notions. I hoped the distracting hair would keep her from noticing the colored effect of my thoughts.

She handed me the set of hot rollers, and I wanted to decline but her smile said that she knew that I was going to. "I have another set, and these are perfect for you. Don't let your beautiful years and great hair go to waste."

"It does look amazing," Jane called from the kitchen, turning her head toward me over her shoulder as she stocked the cabinet with groceries she'd brought in. "I'd kill for hair like that."

I returned her generous smile, distracting her from Nancy's mumbling. "I'd kill to never have to hear such an annoying voice again."

I said my goodbyes after the roll of Nancy's eyes, eager to leave before the mumbling turned to their usual bickering. The set of rollers tucked beneath my arm still had heat to it that penetrated through my shirt, caressing the skin of my side. I did away with the warmth as I put it in the passenger seat, turning on the car to find a place to be for a while.

My reflection in the rearview mirror kept me from driving away. In a few hours, I would be rid of this gifted confidence. I would wash it from my hair, whether it belonged to me or not. I could predict the regret due to how familiar I was with the emotion now. I would put my head to rest, and live through the hours of what-ifs before I finally fell asleep. This wasn't death, this wasn't violence, this wasn't tragedy, and still I was terrified. Being terrified was tiring. Being scared of opportunity was growing repetitive.

I already knew that I would be ashamed of myself, of my appearance, of my life outside the lines once I returned home. If I couldn't escape it, then I could immerse myself to a fault in the meantime. I could steal the hours until then and borrow this short time of self-assurance, and find out what it's like to fit in with the colorful society that I paled against.

The key beneath my hand turned toward me, shutting off the car. I began the walk down the next couple of blocks.

Giving in was a learned habit, and I was setting it apart from giving up. Giving up would have been spending the next hours on my own. Giving up would have been going home without attempting to find some sort of happiness that I needed to hide.

I knocked on the dark wooden door, waiting to see which face would be my welcome. My fingers pulled at the ends of my hair, circling the inside of a loose coil. My hands dropped to my sides when the door opened and Adam's face took in the strange image of me.

"I didn't think you'd ever come back," he said as he gestured me inside. "Turns out, you can be surprising."

His eyes kept returning to my hair. It made me self-conscious, and my hand found its way up to try to smooth it out, force it down. He reached out and caught my wrist before the damage could be done.

"It looks good," he assured me, shaking his head twice before letting me go. "You just look different."

"I thought I looked more different before." I didn't expect him to understand what I meant. But then I looked at his clothes, his hair, his appearance compared to all that was current, and knew that he understood perfectly well.

"Different is acceptable," he told me with a grin. "It's weakness that isn't."

He walked past me and into the big room, where there sat Nora and Rachelle. The seats they occupied sat on the opposite side of the room from where everyone last sat. The room could hold the same furnishings of at least five normal living rooms. It was dwarfing.

I continued to follow behind him, unsure of where to go or where I even wanted to be. All I'd told myself was to be here, and now I was. We passed the elevated section at the front of the room on the way to the right side door. Void of any proof of use, the stage sat neglected.

"I've never seen anyone up there," I pointed to the neglected area as he turned against the door to push it open with his back. "Even during parties when the house is full of people doing whatever they want."

He spared a glance in its direction, and grinned. "I guess nobody who comes around here has ever met a preacher worth imitating."

So much insinuation was packed into that one sentence. Adam had all the information. He knew exactly who I was—he knew exactly who my father was. My mind told me that I was supposed to be offended, but my heart reminded me that I would be being hypocritical. Was I not, myself, learning of things that I questioned, or couldn't force myself to understand or agree with? Was Father not the man who relied on his strength in intimidation instead of inspiration? There was so much I was still learning—I would say nothing about the things that others had learned for themselves.

He led me to Othello's office door. He leaned against the wall beside it, and tilted his head in the door's direction. I looked at the knob, deciding against going in unannounced whether Adam was here or not. I rapped my knuckles against the door, much to Adam's entertainment.

"Come in, Dove," Othello's voice called from within. I looked to Adam in confusion, my arrival having yet to be announced. He shrugged an uninterested shoulder, and opened the door for me impatiently.

I stepped in and Othello pushed the book in his hand into its place on the shelf. He looked over at me and then to Adam still lingering in the doorway. Othello issued a single nod of his head, and Adam shut the door and left.

"You're the only one that bothers to knock when it's just us here," he said in reply to the worried crease of my brow.

I turned my attention to the contents of the top shelf on the side of the room. His twisted collection wasn't where I'd intended to direct my focus, but I couldn't take my eyes off of all the translucent jars and the boxes that concealed their contents. I walked closer to them, craning my head as I neared the out of reach oddities. I stood beneath the jar of teeth, blood stained and nearly three-fourths full.

The feel of another's broken and splintered teeth was singed upon my palm as I revisited the memory. It burned the shape of violence's consequences along my skin, which I traced with the nail of my left thumb. Were the ones I dropped on the sidewalk that night the only pieces of his collection that he was missing?

"Do you always keep the things you take from people as trophies?" I turned to ask him.

He sat against the front side of his desk, content to silently watch me with crossed arms and no care. I was invading privacy and territory that didn't belong to me, but he'd yet to tell me my limits. I braced myself for him to say so now.

"Is that how you see them?" There were no nervous movements of his body, no ticking of impatience or anxious thought. To learn to wait for life to hand its next moments to you was a skill that I was envious of.

"Is that not what they're meant to be?"

"There's no definitive answer, because they can mean whatever the mind that sees them wants them to mean," he said. "But they're just reminders. Reminders that people are given things that they don't deserve, and sometimes the right—or wrong—people come along and take them."

I looked back up to the shelf, looking at the yellowing liquid of another large container that held the fingers of dainty and masculine hands alike. I could see the blurred and toxic remains of polish on some nails, and the fading tattoos on the knuckles of another. I averted my eyes to the floor before I took in more than my stomach could handle.

"And are you the right, or the wrong person?" My voice was surprisingly strong for how weak I felt. I was beginning to understand how to hide the signs that informed others of too much.

I looked up in time to see his smile materialize. It took over his face before he looked at the pieces taken from other humans for himself.

"I'm both. If I take the undeserved things from people who took them for granted, then I'm the wrong person for them to have encountered. But sometimes, people are given unfortunate things that they don't deserve. And if I take those, then I'm the right person."

It was disturbing that such a gruesome thing could be said by the same voice that spoke with so much sense. Wicked thoughts were hidden by wisdom, and sparked the question of my own sense. What left of it did I have if I were here, alone with the man that collected the pieces of people that they took for granted? What deceived me into feeling so safe when he displayed the evidence of his capabilities so freely?

"The teeth you placed in my hand were meant to be my own reminder, then?" I placed my back against the wall, the contents of the shelf out of sight above me.

"Exactly."

"A reminder of what you're capable of inciting, or a reminder of how I froze in the face of violence?" My fingers were winding themselves in the curls that rested upon my back. My fidgeting hands were hidden behind me, busied by my hair's length.

"A reminder of exactly what I told you."

Sometimes you need to bare your teeth.

To be brave in the face of uncertainty. To be willing to face the unknown, the way I had been for weeks now. I'd willingly walked through all the differences between this life and the one I was given, but I was still full of fear. I feared my father. I feared deviating from a path that I could never return to. I feared the things that couldn't be unseen, that couldn't be controlled, that couldn't be corrected.

And I feared Othello.

I feared the man that could leave so many things open and so many things hidden at the same time. Feelings, experiences, the expressive evidence of internal thoughts were all vaulted, yet he would let the dangers of those things be known. The proof of anger, rage, bloodlust, any form of fury that could force a man to take pieces from another was sat on the shelf above me. The proof of a past, a path leading to violence and destruction, business done behind closed doors was sat on the shelf above me. The proof of terrible truths, the acceptance of the existence of evil, the wisdom that came with knowing that the world was full of wrongs that men took upon themselves to rectify was sat on the shelf above me.

With all the reasons that he laid out in the open for me to know to keep my distance, I still stood only feet away. I placed my soul close to one that rid itself of all the inconveniences of good. No regret to wear him down, no care to stop him from making the same morbid moves again and again. My soul was full of all that he lacked, and his lacked all the weary weight of mine.

My soul feared what it couldn't find in the places where his should be; and it feared the attraction of its void.

"Tell me what you're thinking." It wasn't a request. There was no room left in his words to believe in an option to refuse. No way around providing anything but the truth.

The truth was I'd questioned my trust. I trusted him too much. He'd always given me exactly what I asked for, and reminded me that my place in the world was wherever I chose to make it. I trusted him for being consistent, for never refusing the constant inquiring of a wondering soul. He'd given me turmoil, and he'd given me bliss, but he'd never given me a reason to doubt his underserved loyalty.

And as my gaze was set upon the mouth that demanded so much of me, I admitted to myself that he was the one I trusted the most. The one whose lips should be set upon my inexperienced ones. The one that should show me the things I don't know just as he had been since the first time I set foot in this place.

I'd longed to know of the secrets his lips would tell mine, and now that I was in their presence, my fear outweighed my longing. I couldn't be so vulnerable, naïve, and direct with him. I would be a fool to ask him to show me what such a thing is like, and all the trust that was built would be crushed if he were to refuse. My lips weren't meant for his; they were meant to ask of his ways, not feel them.

"I'm thinking that I should leave," I admitted. I would leave now with the unanswered question on my face, or I would fold and potentially ruin all that we'd acquired. All the confidence I'd walked here with was fading. I was too afraid of rejection.

There was a brief moment where his eyes roamed over me, down to my worn-out loafers and back up to the intended mess of hair on my head, when I waited for him to tell me I was lying. For him to call me out for the truth that I was withholding, where I knew that I would cave. You can't stand beneath such intense scrutiny, with trembling hands hidden behind your back, and not give in to the commands of those knowing eyes.

But a command for the truth never came. He showed me his mercy.

"Then I won't stop you."

It was a gift given by lips I didn't dare look at again before I left the room. I tried to pace myself on the way to the door, but I was propelled by a rush of relief. I leaned back against the door after it was shut, separating me from Othello's eyes that had burned against my hurried departure. My own eyes were shut as I tried to gain possession over my flushed skin and the familiar sensation that formed in the pit of my stomach.

"You didn't last nearly as long in there as I thought you would." Adam's unsuspected voice forced my eyes open and my hand to clutch my heaving chest. "Why the rush?"

He stood against the wall across from me, foot kicked back against the gray plaster. I should have seen him the second I came through the door, but my vision was clouded by emotion. Or he was too still and too secretive to have been noticed, regardless.

"I'm not rushing." But I did rush away. I just wasn't rushing to find the answers I was in search of inside that room. "I'm just ready to le—"

"To run from your fragile feelings?" His foot came off the wall as he put his hands into his pockets. His stout arms were displayed by his cutoff black shirt, highlighted against the backdrop of the gray wall.

"I don't know what you mean." It was a pointless thing to deflect. I was glued to this door until Adam got whatever information he wanted, as Adam always did.

"You don't know what I mean, or you don't know what you're feeling?" He took two steps that put him in the center of the hallway. "Because you're either lying to me, or you're lying to yourself. I know what you're feeling. I can see it in the rise of your face's color and the rise of your labored breathing. And you should know what you're feeling, because it's already been explained to you before."

I looked down at his black and white shoes, focusing away from his spot-on observation. It felt like I was exposed, my emotions naked to anyone that looked at me. Or maybe it came with him having walked me through these emotions the first time, and recognizing the signs that only he knew? He, and Othello. Othello knew what dignity I was trying to escape with just as well as Adam did. I was the only one playing the fool. My heartbeat picked up as my already hungry thoughts turned over to this similar feeling that I'd already explored.

"So you do remember your first lesson on the subject," Adam observed. My hand still held against the doorknob came up to gently cover my cheek, though it was too late to hide what was already seen. "What's the hold up, then? Are you too afraid to ask for it yourself?"

I wanted to tell him how often I'd thought of that day, and how I wasn't scared of what I knew. I felt defensive of what I'd learned, and that it had been the first selfish secret that felt good instead of destructive. What came out instead was the truth that I wasn't prepared to give him.

"I'm afraid that I don't know how to kiss."

His answering grin quickly turned into a laugh. It was demeaning, and humiliating, and I wanted to shrink back farther though there was no place for me to go. I wanted the heat of my desires to ignite into flames and turn me to ash. This is the response I'd been afraid of. This was a way of being reminded that I was fatuous.

"That's an issue too simply solved for you to be *afraid* of it, Genevieve," he replied as he pushed his fingers through the top of his hair. The laughter had disappeared from his voice, but he wasn't ready to part with the grin. "You wanted to kiss Othello, and you ran away instead?" He shook his lowered head as he raised his obsidian brows. "You're proving to be helpless."

"No I'm not," I countered with a rush of heated breath. He was coaxing the anger in me to come join the desire and the longing, creating a rush in me that was trying to preserve my pride against the embarrassment and the shame.

"You are," he insisted. "Because you're too scared, too often. You're given freedom, given answers, and you keep reverting back to relying on the version of you that only keeps you ignorant, not safe." He took another step toward me, his eyes charged with determination. "You can't save yourself from a man that puts his hands on you. You let someone push you around, allowing yourself to be disrespected." Flashbacks of Axel standing just as close as Adam was now intruding my vision. Adam's face began to drift away in small blurs, Axel's furious image replacing it. "And you don't even have it in you to find out for yourself what it's like to let another's lips touch yours. You're scared to ask, but I'll fucking teach you."

His head dropped closer to mine, and my hand instinctively found his shoulders to push him away. There was the fleeting return of Adam's grin that pulled at the corner of his mouth, and the sight of it enraged me further. My heart was ferociously alive and unsure how to process it all.

"It's a push and pull of what you can dish, and what you can take." His hands sturdily dropped into place against the door, my head trapped between them. "You show what you want, what you won't settle for. What you're demanding— just like you would in a fight. It's unspoken ferocity and desire to *own* another." His face neared mine again, and his body refused to be moved against my shoving hands. "So let's fight, because I'll *own* you, Genevieve."

"Get away from me," I seethed between clenched teeth, the burning of my body beginning to spill from the corners of my eyes. I pushed against his shoulders, his chest, angry with myself for being smaller and not having control.

He brought his eyes down to level them with mine, his hair escaping its form around his face with every pointless push I made against him

"I can have you if I want to. And you want to know why?" he asked with terrifying intent in the intensity of his expression. "Because you're fucking weak. You're weak. You're just as weak now as you were when you let me put my fingers between that pure, sweet cun—"

My shoving hand was balled and fisted, connecting up to his mouth before I could hear him punctuate our experience. His head was held up, his face looking toward the top of the door frame that we still stood beneath. One of his hands against the door slowly removed itself, his middle finger greeting the bottom of his lower lip before coming away colored.

He tilted his head back down, showing me the damage that dripped from his split lip the way that my hurt still dripped from my lashes.

"You're fucking capable, Genevieve," he said to my shocked face, still reeling from the lengths that he pushed me too. "You're capable of fighting back, and you're capable of figuring out what you want for yourself." He stepped back from me, wiping the blood that slid down his chin. "And for fuck's sake, you can ask for a damn kiss." He reached forward and grabbed the wrist connected to my still-balled fist, bringing it up to be displayed between us. "Remember this the next time you feel weak. You have more options than just surrendering."

He walked away, stained hand reaching for the mouth I'd marred. I wiped the tears from my eyes, the thin carpet of the floor catching and soaking up the remnants of the difficult lesson learned.

I wanted to be mad at him. I wanted to follow him and tell him that he couldn't just push me that far, that he couldn't expect me to be okay with being terrified and trapped by a person that I had somehow trusted. But the same part of me that searched for days or weeks for the clarity in all the other answers that I'd been given before found it here quickly.

He wanted me to realize that he couldn't just push me around. He wanted me to not *surrender* to the terror of feeling trapped. He wanted me to face my fears, and fight them. It was the worst way to learn, coated in blood and tears. It was efficient. I was growing to know the approach of my adrenaline, the purpose behind such a physical response. While I hated Adam in that moment for forcing my hand, I hated the thought that it could have been someone else. I could have found myself in the same situation, with someone who wouldn't have spared me the consequences of cowards. Because as good as Adam was at leaving the evil upon his face, he never would have carried out his provocative threats. The proof was in the blood he forced me to spill— and the blood he didn't seek.

I knew better than to think that he'd let another take his blood without cost.

As I walked back to the big room, I thought of how Othello sat behind the door that held the commotion. He must have heard every word, every thud of the force used to teach me, every plea that prefaced the way I tried to push it away. He didn't bother interfering, and I wondered if it were only because he sat behind the situation, waiting.

Waiting for the end that he expected; because if I knew that Adam wouldn't follow through, then he did too.

"Looking a little roughed up," Rachelle called from the seats that she and Nora still occupied. "Why don't you come give us the dirty details?"

I walked to the cluster of couches, all mismatched and belonging to lost sets. Nora sat on the dark blue piece that showed its dark stains, Rachelle sat on the center one with rips and a missing back cushion, and I took my seat on the only couch that looked to be entirely intact and hardly abused. The couch beneath me had seen fewer wild gatherings than the others, as new to this place as I was.

"I don't have anything to tell," I answered honestly. The details that I could give them weren't the ones they'd want to hear, and I wasn't eager to share something so humiliating. I doubted that they had to be taught the same things the way that I had to be taught. I doubted Nora ever hesitated to throw her fists—or deal a kick. And I'd seen Rachelle put her body on the line to lure a man to his death. The details behind my flushed face, tangled hair, and heavy eyes were beneath them. It didn't amount to anything worth sharing, anyway.

"You can't just keep all the fun under wraps, little bird," Rachelle told me as she pulled her feet up to the side of her, beautifully tucked back. She was an ideally created woman, flawlessly disguising her fatal abilities. She was a nightmare in a goddess' body. "Were you here for Othello? Or Adam?" Her eyes lit up beneath her thickly coated lashes. "Both?"

"I only came here to visit because I had nowhere else to go," I told her, my fingers busying themselves with the edge seam of the cushion. "I wasn't here for *that*."

The existing interest in her eyes multiplied by tenfold. She was eating up every uncomfortable second of this conversation, and Nora sat with a smile as she silently watched the exchange between Rachelle and me.

"So you aren't having sex with Othello?" Rachelle pushed.

"No," I answered. The subject brought my heart to a light race again. I almost fell apart under the idea of simply kissing him. She overestimated me.

"Then I don't get it," she said as she leaned back on the couch, spreading her arms across its back. "You're either a good liar, or the first person to come here without some price to pay."

"I'm definitely not a good liar," I admitted. But I had paid. My initial debt was paid in full, and hidden costs kept finding their way to me. I was making my payments one change of myself at a time.

"And this is where you go when you have nowhere else to be?" Rachelle continued. Her face slightly clenched in confusion, and I didn't know how to give her answers that would make sense when my decision to be here hardly made sense to me. It was one of my few moments of impulse.

"I'm supposed to be on a date with a friend, whom I'm not actually dating," I tried to explain briefly. She wouldn't be interested in the whole story. She probably wouldn't be interested, regardless. "But he's at a party across town with his actual date. I don't know of anywhere else to go, and I have a couple of hours to kill before I can go home. My father would be suspicious if I showed up too soon. He waits up to make sure that I come home."

She didn't seem as uninterested as I thought. Instead, an eyeroll prepared me for her unexpected opinion.

"Why should you care about that? Go wherever, home if you want to. Your dad is the suspicious one."

I mulled over her response for a minute. Maybe the clear disdain I'd sensed was imagined, and what she meant was just her general opinion of men like my father. But the smile that escaped Nora's face hinted at more as she quickly looked to Rachelle, staring at her in controlled anger or disbelief until Rachelle shrugged.

"Why do you think that?" I managed to work out of my mouth. My lips felt tight, pressed against each other as I watched Nora try to silence Rachelle with her own charged silence, and Adam walk into the side doors across the room.

"Because only suspicious people have their name changed and pay cops to let them know when their identity is looked into. Must be hiding something pretty serious, and you're worried about going home too early."

I wanted to believe that her smile was because she was doing something horrible, and not because she found humor in the comparison. It would be too real if she were smiling at the drastic difference, and information like that couldn't be real. I wanted her to be lying, trying to sway me into believing that I could do whatever I wanted to because she'd given me a reason. But the reason was too specific. The way that Nora didn't want her to tell me, the way that Rachelle dripped venom from her tongue as she told me, the way that Adam stopped walking entirely and watched me intently upon the reason's release.

The reason was enough to let me know that I wasn't going to like anything more that came from the wisdom that this house had.

"I've got to go," I said as I sprang up from the couch and ran toward the door.

I could hear my name being called as I broke into the night and forced my feet to reach my car as quickly as possible, to put space between me and the life I thought I knew before it was too late.

Did I know nothing of the man I chased perfection for? The one I hid my defiance from to spare his own pride, and the soul of mine that he would claim to be damned?

I knew enough to drive away, farther from home and the House of Sarris and toward somewhere I knew there to be people that didn't hold lies or expose them.

KNOWLEDGE

There's no preparation for having the veil torn from your eyes so abruptly.

I drove by the light of the moon and the few lights of the town that remained on. My focus wasn't on the road, but the hollow feeling I had beneath my heart. It was the type of pain that couldn't force tears, because it couldn't force anything. I didn't know how to think properly, or what to think of such a blatantly shattering reveal. I knew better than to find my father and ask him directly, the way a small part of me wanted to. I knew that I didn't want to turn around and demand to know the reasons why one group of people wanted to uproot my former life entirely.

I knew that I wanted the only person that wasn't directly involved to help remove this weight that was crushing me. I didn't know if I would be able to utter a single word of the truth once I saw him, but I knew that I needed to see someone that had yet to hold me down or hold onto a truth that didn't belong to them.

The street where Luke had said he would be was packed with people sitting atop the hoods of cars that were in rough shape, and others that were too luxurious to be used in such a way. He'd told me where he'd be in case any instance arose where I needed to find him, but I'd never intended to need him for a reason like this. I couldn't have predicted a situation where I'd need the sight of Luke's face to remind me that some things in my life were still the same.

He'd only given me the name of the street and not a specific address; but chaos was easily pinpointed. I saw Luke's car as I sought out a place to park, and walked the three blocks back to the small house of sound that reverberated through the yard once I reached its overgrown lawn.

My mind kept falling back with each step I took forward. What would I do with what I knew? It was a bomb shoved down my throat that was counting down to detonation. It would destroy everything inside me if I kept it down, but if I painfully coughed the intrusion back up, it's appearance would put the next person at risk. I could sacrifice myself to its damage. Hold onto it just to keep others safe from its effect. But was it more dangerous to be this fatally aware, or to not know of its existence?

Would Gray be better off never knowing that the man he looked up to was hiding behind an illusion? Was I right to want to spare him from something that could break his spirit? Something he didn't deserve? And how could a woman not know the liar she lies with night after night? Could she be just as unaware as he'd forced Gray and me to be, living our days being looked down upon and kept right beneath his nose?

I stopped suffocating myself with the questions breathed into existence with the air of a life I no longer knew. I'd taken the first steps away from it all on my own, and now I was pushed away by the secrets of those who I'd kept my secrets from. Being blinded felt no better than seeing the world too clearly.

The house couldn't hold the amount of people that it had gathered, explaining the abundance of bodies that lined the yard or opted to sit on parked vehicles. While I found my way through the packed rooms, I concluded that I wouldn't tell Luke anything. I confirmed it to myself as I looked for his image in every face that I passed, knowing that passing it to him would be like sharing poison. I wanted his face before my eyes just to know that the world hadn't forsaken me and that the simply good things that I knew weren't lost.

It was the simple laugh behind a good-natured smile that I knew, shining a light on what I was in search of. My face had turned to his direction the second he unknowingly called to me. When his eyes reopened from his joyful moment, they found mine full of relief.

He waved me over to the couch that he and Roman sat on across from two others, a long and wooden table between them holding coins and drinks. I managed a smile for the happy faces that surrounded me, masking the desolate haze that I drifted upon.

"Is everything all right, Gene?" Luke asked me as he held out his hand to me, guiding me to sit on the arm of the couch beside him. I held onto him longer than I should have, not willing to forfeit his grasp. "You never come and find me on your nights away."

"Everything's fine," I told him, with the acidic taste of the lie on my tongue. The bomb in me had left its traces. "I just didn't have anywhere to go, and nearly two hours left until I should go home."

Home. I would have to return and face my father no matter what the situation. It's where I lived, it's the only home I'd ever known, and his deceit was stripping it of its comfort more than his strict ways already had. I would have to hide what I knew better than he hid the man that he really was.

"Do you want to play, then?" He pointed to the table in front of us, and I easily shook my head.

"I'll just watch." Watch more things happen before me that I didn't understand.

"What did you do to your hair? It looks great," he said before he bounced a quarter against the table's surface. The soft splash of liquid and answering laughs and groans were all I could register as I looked behind me out the window. The neighbors could surely hear all the commotion, the music muffled by distance and the boisterous noises of the people on the street. But maybe the world knew when to stay out of affairs that weren't their own, and how to look away from something bigger than them. The world still had lessons to teach me.

"Nancy did it before I left work," I answered mindlessly as I watched a couple tangled together on the hood of a car outside. They displayed their desires to any who watched, no hesitation in their melding mouths. "It took an hour of too much fun for her, and too much waiting for me."

He laughed before leaning back against the couch, reaching up to pull on the end of the styled strands. "Does that mean this look won't be seen on you again?"

"Well, she gave me the rollers, so I have the option," I told him as I watched the hair slip away from his fingers. "It's just the practice that I don't have. It wouldn't look like this if I did it."

"If you gave it a shot, I'm sure you'd have it figured out in no time," he said before he leaned back up toward the game. "You're good at being good." He left me with a wink before he turned away from me.

"At being good for the wrong people," I corrected under my breath. His tug on my hair pulled my attention back to him from the window.

"Tell me what's going on, Gene." His hand patted mine that sat on the edge of my skirt at my knee. "It's not like you to be at a place like this, not for no reason."

He wouldn't understand if I told him that I was there for comfort. That would be a lie to him until I told him the truth of it. I promised myself that I wouldn't, despite the want I had for someone else to hear of it. To tell me that it couldn't be true, that the information couldn't be attached to a man like Henry Rowlen. He was my father, but he was Luke's pastor. Luke had grown up knowing him, his parents were close to him, and Luke could have been the person to put my mind at ease. Or I could be the person that gives his mind and his heart my strain. That, I couldn't do.

"I'm just pushing myself to do things a little differently," I said. Because different was the only option that I was being given as my life around me changed.

He smiled as he handed me his cup from off the table. "Like learn a little more, think a little less?"

I stared into the half-full drink. My reflection was unstable in the deep amber pool, jostled by the waves of its journey to my hands. An accurate representation of my current existence, and a sign that I believed in as I put the cups to my lips and opened my throat to the rest of its contents.

His laughter and Roman's slow clapping brought me back down with a smile. If I was going to lose myself, then I would have a part in it. I wouldn't sit by and miss out on the scenery that I passed before I was finally stranded. I handed the cup back to him, feeling the contents trickling into my stomach and being introduced to my system.

"I'll get a refill and get you your own," Luke said as he stood up with the emptied plastic in hand. He looked at me with a grin, pointing his finger back and forth between the two of us. "Mr. Rowlen wouldn't think as highly of me as he does if he knew that I had this kind of influence on you. Our secrets keep getting bigger, and more fun."

My father. Secrets. Not but a few minutes into my search for distraction and I was being reminded of what I had to be distracted from. It would take more drinks than my system could handle. I would have to drown myself in every cup he could hand me, and consume until all of my blood was toxic and I wouldn't know where the problem inside me was. It would take the grave to put my head and suffering body to rest. Death would replace all the damage that this amount of life had brought me, and I wouldn't know peace until I met it. I was brave enough to face my end—not enough to face my father. It was an issue that made me feel insane, and I'd drink enough to dissolve that, too.

The hand that tangled itself into my hair and pulled me out of my solemn pit pushed the back of my head onto the couch. My body torn from its seat, I was forced down against the open cushion of the couch, my head colliding with Roman's leg before he jumped away. My hands were both grabbing at the wrist that held my hair, keeping me tethered down. My eyes opened against the stinging pain of my scalp, taking in the broken smile too close to me.

"You aren't fucking welcome here," Axel seethed. What teeth he had clenched together against every yank of my hair. "Let me show you how we treat unwelcome guests in this house."

The pain blurred my senses, dulling the shouts that I knew I could hear but could only recognize as Roman. I couldn't hear anything being said over Axel's mouth directly in front of my face.

"Let's see how you like it when that pretty face of yours is broken," he said with his deformed smile and too much pleasure that filled the spaces of his missing teeth.

"Let me go!" I yelled over the noise that had turned white to me, my vision sparking with black around the edges.

His free hand tore its way across my face, leaving a stinging print of itself on my cheek. I kicked at him, the pain propelling the urge to fight my way out of his impossible grip. One movement of his knee was all it took as he drove it between my legs, into the opening of my skirt. The agony tore from my throat upon its impact, stilling my body beneath his weight and hold.

It was all too quick, with no time to know how to get myself away. I was stuck beneath him, in a too-crowded room where everyone inside either didn't know or didn't care. Luke would be back, but the chance that he'd be too late was heavier on my mind than the signals of pain that my body was enduring.

I let go of his hand in my hair, pushing against his shoulders the way that I pushed Adam. My hand began beating against his chest, pushing against his face until a searing tear on my arm froze my movements. The knife in his hand was all I could see; all my body was alerted to as it told me that he had the control.

"It's your fucking fault that I look like this!" His rage consumed the inches of space between our faces as he brutally shoved my head with every irate word. "And I hoped that I would be the one that made you pay for it. I'll leave my mark on you the way that you left yours on me, you little bitch."

He set the blade flush against my cheek, the dark pleasure he took in my fear oozing from his face. He turned the blade and his attention to its light push against my skin before digging its edge through the surface.

And I knew that I was marred. I knew that I would lose this fight and be left with its marks. But I looked at my fists frozen against his chest, and knew that I didn't have to surrender.

My cries of pain slid into a screech, the blood that leaked around his blade exiting my body with my conjured strength. My hands clawed his face, my feet fought against him, and my face turned away from his knife, ripping my hair held in his clenched fist. One push was all I had in me, my arms and legs meeting with his body to no avail.

Another breath led to another scream as my nails dug into his arms, braced against the being that set his blade back to my face, settling it into the already open cut.

"One wrong move, and it's your throat that gets slit open." His hideous expression of sick emotion and focus was what I directed my hate at, forcing myself to hold onto my adrenaline before my consciousness slipped away.

He slowly carved his knife back along its intended path as my lungs expelled their only defense left. I could hear a shout from somewhere in the room, Luke's voice sounding angrier and almost unfamiliar. But before he could have reached me, Axel's body was torn away from mine. The grip he had in my hair was unprepared, taking chunks and tangled strands with it. I knew that it should hurt, that I should be feeling the exposed flesh of my scalp, but I felt nothing but the release of his weight and the warmth falling from my cheek into my ear.

I was pulled up, my hands held by soft ones that led me to sit against the back of the couch. I was a little dizzy, but held upright by the dainty arm around my shoulder. I looked next to me at Rachelle, who was tearing apart the bottom of her already short, red dress. She ripped up the edge seam before pulling a small pocket knife from between her breasts, flipping it open to cut down from the split at a thick angle.

I stopped watching her, unable to handle the sight of the knife. She grabbed my arm, pulled it over to her lap, and I felt the fabric she wrapped around the cut of my forearm. So much hurt all over, that I'd forgotten about that injury.

Stay awake, stay awake, I told myself until my eyes found their desire to focus. Axel was sprawled out on the playing table, held down by Adam, Michael, and Nora. The sight began to become clear, just in time for me to see Othello stab the already blood-stained knife through Axel's hand, nailing it to the table. I was going to be sick; from pain, the sight of the remnants of my blood mixing with Axel's, or both. Axel's yell of pain was echoing all of mine until Adam cut him off, grabbing a cup that sat on the floor by the couch and pouring it in his open mouth. There was struggling, and heaving, and I thought that maybe he would drown in the drink that I'd wished to drown in until he started coughing.

"You see that fucking mark on her face?" Othello pointed to me. His question was for Axel, but his eyes were on me. I could feel the blood that he was focused on, puddling into my ear and finding its way down my neck.

Axel didn't answer, his coughs dying down but still controlling him. Othello fisted his hand into Axel's hair—the way that Axel had done mine—and turned his head toward me. "Tell me you see it right now," he demanded, voice even and possessing all the control that Axel had had only moments ago. The tables turned quickly, and his back was now laid upon it.

"I fucking see it," Axel hissed, his forced words leaving spit across the table and down his turned cheek.

"Good, because you'll never see the full result of your work again." Othello's blade was pulled from his pocket and held above Axel's head just as quickly as he'd turned it. The tip of the blade met with Axel's eye, Othello's movements deliberately slow.

I don't know if the music was silenced or if I just couldn't hear it anymore. All my ears registered were the blood one held and the guttural cries of a tortured man. I thought my vision had slowed in shock, but it was Othello's purpose to make each nauseating second as long as possible. Adam held his weight down on Axel's, the unpinned arm held firmly in his grasp. Michael held down one leg, the first I'd ever seen him without a bright smile, and Nora held down the other. Rachelle held tight to my shoulders, unfazed by the bloody work being done in this room full of people.

The blade came just as slowly out of his eye, and Axel's body had gone limp. There were no more screams, and the music was back. I looked past the table, capturing Luke's disturbed expression as he hid Roman's face against his chest and saw only the mutilated body on the table. Jaw slack to show his shattered smile, blood and gore bursting from his useless right eye, hand held in place by the piercing of his own blade—Othello was the wrong person for Axel to have encountered. His ways were outdone by Othello, his work incomparable.

The lesser work was performed on my flesh.

My shaking fingers reached up to remember the pain. The sting of my own touch forced air through my teeth. I looked at the blood on my fingers, my unsteady hand held in front of my face. Gentle fingers wrapped around my wrist, and I looked up to Othello's face of stone.

"Come on," he said as he pulled me to my feet. "This is his house, leave him where he is," Othello told the others as he passed by Axel's unconscious form, towing me behind him.

The others parted easily from the body. Rachelle rose to her feet, her cut dress showing her hip in a flattering way. I stopped looking back at the damage we were leaving behind when I saw Adam gesture for Luke to follow us. I was done thinking for myself. I was done thinking at all. I would let Othello guide me to whatever came next.

The air we stepped out to was sticky, making the rest of my body feel like it was covered in my blood. I touched the skin of the arm that Othello led me by, making sure that my blood wasn't actually seeping from my pores. I could see my clean fingers beneath the moonlight as Othello led us to the car parked in the middle of the street.

He opened the back door for me, leading me around and into its seat. I could see the couple still on the hood of the car, bodies held against each other like their surroundings didn't exist. They hadn't stopped for the screaming, or cared for the bloodshed. They would suffocate together before sparing the world any attention. It must be some kiss.

"Keys," Othello said with an outstretched hand. I looked at his empty palm, not seeing what he was offering. I looked around the backseat and to the ground before I looked up at him again with no answer. "I need your keys, Dove," he clarified.

I reached into my skirt pocket, retrieving my ring of keys for him. He handed them over to Adam before circling to the other side of the car and getting in the backseat beside me. Michael got in the driver's seat, Rachelle in the passenger, and Othello moved in close to me and took my bandaged arm into his lap.

He held the tight knot of the red wrap in his fingers and pulled back out his knife. I flinched away, and his eyes looked into mine as he silently reached for my arm again.

"Do you think I'm a man that would break his promise?" he asked as he looked back down to the knot he held and swiftly cut through the fabric beneath it.

His promise to never hurt me was one of the furthest things from my mind. I was still feeling the throb of being kneed somewhere so sensitive and reliving the memory of having my skin slashed open. I'd forgotten about the torn hair from my head until I rested it against the window and the glass shot a pulse through my ravaged scalp. And I was too aware that I was right back with the people I'd run from an hour ago.

"You bandage just as well as you keep your mouth shut," Othello said to Rachelle as he folded the bloodied scrap of dress in his hand and held it against my steadily bleeding cut. The pressure he put on it made me reach for his hand, wanting the ease of release. But when my hand grabbed the top of his, he only looked at me and shook his head. Pressure to the wound was excruciating.

"She deserves to know," Rachelle argued as she turned around in her seat. "The guy's her father, not yours."

It was my father. It was information that belonged to me more than it belonged to them, but I was honest enough with myself to know that I still couldn't say if not knowing were any better than knowing. I couldn't say anything to the subject at all, other than that the reality of it scared me.

"So he is." He peered up at me from his focus on my arm. "But look where your loose lips landed her. It could have been handled better if it came from someone else."

"I would have run from you, too," I assured him. I let go of his arm and braced it against the back of Rachelle's seat. My urge to be sick was returning. "And I would have landed in this same situation. It's everyone's fault. Even mine."

"Not yours," he corrected quickly. His white curls stood out in the back of the dark car, shielding the face that watched his own grip on my arm. "But it's acceptable to blame everyone else."

"And pointless," I added as I rested my head near my hand against the seat. It felt as though my heart were in my arm beneath his hold, beating away the last of the management I had over my pain. "Could you please just let me go?"

"No." The word came too easily. It killed me along with the rest of my suffering, and I grunted behind clenched teeth. "Focus on something else."

"There's nothing to focus on but the pain." It was everywhere, my entire body giving out to the strength it'd surrendered to my fight. Not even the cut of another blade would register against my body that already felt too much.

"Why don't you tell me why you cried when Adam forced himself on you, but not when Axel did?"

I wasn't wanting any suggestion, and especially not that one. Rachelle had turned back around in her seat, but that didn't mean that she and Michael weren't paying attention. They could hear my answers if I gave them, just as they'd heard the embarrassing question. I sat back against my seat and Othello's eyes followed.

"You heard all that?" I asked his shadowed face. He nodded his head, and a slow smile matched the light of his hair. "Then why didn't you do anything to stop him?"

"Because I didn't have to," he said through exposed teeth. "You know as well as I do that he wouldn't have taken things that far. You handled it yourself."

"But I didn't know that at the time." My blood pressure surged, and I wondered if the rag he held against me was being drenched with the anger I couldn't control. He was no stranger to having blood on his hands, and mine wouldn't faze him.

"Is that why you cried? Because you felt betrayed by someone you trusted?" He gripped my arm tighter, the pain spreading up to the tips of my fingers. I hadn't noticed that they'd gone numb until they hurt so much.

Adam had gripped my fear and forced it to come out to face him. He reached inside to where it always stayed, and pulled it out with everything he knew it would take for me to strip down to my instincts. He used against me everything he knew would hurt, and it amounted to Othello's words. I'd felt used, betrayed by, and afraid of someone that I'd grown to trust.

"Yes." The quiet admission could have stayed between us. It was small enough for it to have only reached its asker, the one that demanded transparency. But he couldn't leave it there.

"And no tears when you're beneath a senseless man's blade?

My cries for help weren't accompanied by weeping eyes. The difference in the type of fear I felt from Adam and from Axel could only be evaluated now that it was all over. Doing it so openly was ripping my composure apart, and I couldn't sit still under the pain and exposure.

"I don't know what it matters," I nearly yelled. Unaffected, he sat back against the seat, giving me nothing but the assistance to my arm.

"It matters to know your weaknesses, and how they play into your ability to survive. It takes you being emotionally attached to a person for you to unleash yourself entirely. It takes them breaking you for you to become unrestrained. Because the more you care, the harder you fight."

I stared at the outline of his profile. The features that always remained at rest until they were adjusted by rare emotion, almost always a disturbing smile. They were all at rest now, looking ahead and seeing moves that he calculated before he ever met them. Observative, patient, and ruthless.

"That's stupid and unfair." I didn't want to have to care. It hurt too much, and there were only so many times that I could be broken before I wouldn't be able to be whole again. "There's something wrong with me to have to feel to fight."

His smile answered my complaint, or maybe it was the answer to his eyes resting on the church that the car pulled in next to and faced. He either enjoyed my own observation, or the sight of his own home.

"There's something wrong with all of us," he replied before he reached across me and opened my door. Adam appeared in the open space with an offered hand. Othello held onto my arm, keeping me sat down as I put my free hand in Adam's. "You're fucked up because you care." His eyes caught the moon that snuck its light past Adam, making his eyes glow their black and white. "I'm fucked up because I don't."

Needles and thread are only so gentle when repeatedly pushed through skin. It wasn't the same relaxing pastime as my mother's as Adam's fingers nimbly moved through the motions. It wasn't as rewarding to have stitched flesh as it was to see a finished garment or embroidered cloth. It was just painful, despite the strong drink in my hand.

"Loosen up," Adam spoke to me and my stiff arm that kept tensing with each new puncture. "We're almost done with this one. Drink what you can before I start on your cheek."

"It's almost as painful as you stabbing me like that," I said of the swallow of burning liquid I took to comply. He was the only one in the room grinning as everyone else sat, tiredly watching me be amateurly doctored.

"Strange how the pain can lead to the desired numbness, isn't it?" He pulled the final stitch through at the end of the cut before tying and cutting it off.

All the supplies were laid out on the small side-table beside me and Luke as I sat between his legs on the couch, leaned back against the only body that could calm me through the procedure. His arm circled my waist, pulling me to him while Adam did the dirty work. With the way he was hanging onto me so tightly, the sight of the blood and needles could have been making him uneasy. Or maybe it was the memory of Axel's undoing that we shared.

"Did you stitch up your own lip?" I asked Adam, pointing to the closed cut that I'd issued him earlier. The drink in my hand sloshed over the side, landing on my tan skirt before it dissolved into a dark circle. I was more unsteady than I'd thought. Luke's arm around me was maybe just as much for me as it was for him.

"Yeah, I did," he said as he leaned toward the table and grabbed the alcohol and washcloth. "But I only needed one. You're a bit unlucky." His eyes went to the eleven stitches on my arm and glanced at my still-opened cheek. "Maybe finish off whatever you have left."

I groaned before setting the plastic to my lips. I avoided inhaling the stinging scent before throwing it back, two last large gulps to an empty cup. I lost my breath to the scorched skin of my throat, and gagged on my first pull of air. This wasn't the same drink that I thought I could drown myself in. It provided the burn of hell's flames to ensure that you'd never want to witness them.

I wondered if other people thought of hell the more drunk that they became.

Othello had refused all the other methods of managing my pain that Rachelle had kindly offered. There were pills and a small vial in her hand, which he looked at with disdain.

"Those aren't an option," he'd said. "The idea is to ease her, not send her away with an addiction. Go grab the decanter from off my shelf." She'd turned away and made towards the door, taking one of the pills for herself.

Now she looked more relaxed than I was, nestled into Michael's side as he stroked the blonde hair against her back while he talked to Nora in hushed tones. Whatever she had was more effective than drinking was for me, because I could still feel every ounce of pain in Adam's suturing. It just felt like my body was swimming instead of sitting.

"Better," Adam stated, alerting me to his presence at my side. He was already pressing a cloth against my cheek, unnoticed in my slight inebriation. "You didn't tense up at all." I could feel the swiping on the side of my face, soft work that felt like caresses. I closed my eyes until it stopped, opening them to see him reaching for another rag.

"Quite a bit of blood for someone who's still standing." He wiped the rag against my ear, taking his time around and beneath it. He delicately cleaned off my neck before grabbing the alcohol I'd already learned the torture of. "Look ahead. Keep still. Focus on Othello," he directed as he doused the cleanest area of the cloth with its potency.

"Do I have to?" I asked as my eyes found Othello across the way, my lips loosened with the rest of me. He watched Adam work, intently set upon each move he made. If he was waiting for a wrong move, I hoped it wouldn't come.

Adam pressed the rag against the angry cut, eliciting a hiss from my set teeth. "You don't have to look at him, but you do have to sit still," he answered before picking up his needle and first piece of thread. "No talking once I start."

"When do you start?" If I was going to be silenced, I was ready to use my last seconds of freedom with the courage I found in my cup.

"About ten seconds," Adam said as he pulled the thread through the eye of the needle.

I set my eyes on Othello, bracing myself for an answer that I wouldn't be able to reply to. I would be forced to sit with whatever he gave me, and maybe that's the only way I was able to bring myself to ask.

"Why didn't you tell me what you knew?"

The lack of anxiety was replaced with a sharp pain as Adam held together the sides of my cut before placing the first stitch through its center.

Othello removed his focus from Adam's hands and set it on my waiting eyes. He could have ignored the question, knowing that it wouldn't be asked again. For my inability to speak and the meaning I would take from his refusal to answer. But he waited just long enough for me to think he wouldn't say anything—right when the second suture made its way through.

"I didn't know until you'd left; the day that Officer Kephum told Adam." His eyes watched for my silent reactions, seeking out the questions only he could answer that came from my eyes.

I'd thought the officer was there that day to ruin my life for having watched the life being taken from someone else. I'd asked Adam why the man was there, and he told me that I wouldn't want to know. Turns out, we were both right. He was there to ruin my life, and I now wished I didn't know how.

Now that I did, a piece of my life was closed off, and I couldn't see back into the time when it was open. When I was open to believing that my fear and my secrets were the only ones that existed and that I was fumbling into a world that scared me because I didn't know anything about it. Now, I sat here in a room with the people that I had feared. The marks upon my body from the violence I'd feared. Held by the arm of a friend whose request for a shared lie I'd feared. What I now feared most wasn't what I didn't know, but what I did.

My father harbored the deception of the world that I'd first been so afraid of. I'd trusted in the wrong thing all along.

Why this came out now, and by their assistance, was a part that I didn't understand. How could they learn something of my father that he'd hidden from me for almost twenty-three years?

"Why?" Othello asked aloud, repeating the question so easily read in my gaze. "We learned about your father, because information is what gives us what we want," he answered. He leaned back in his chair, momentarily watching Adam perform another stitch before looking back to me with the start of a smile. "Just like we used your own information against you. Blackmail, Dove. Your secret made you give me your freedom, and that came with the risk of upsetting your father." His hand rested on his leg, still and unhurried movement. For the first time, I sat as still as he did. "If your father found out, it wouldn't just be you that he'd be upset with. It's always important to look into a potential enemy. Remain one step ahead."

If so much was attached to having me around, then why bother? A timid soul like me didn't belong to their home, and it came with such great pains to have my company. I wasn't worth the effort or the money spent. Remaining in my old world would have come at no cost other than oblivion.

"I paid Kephum to find something that I could hold over your father in case it ever came to that. If your father found out and chose to show up here, upset and with angry threats, I would have needed to have already found out more. So I did." His eyes bounced from Adam, to my lips, and back to my eyes. "And while you're forced to sit and think, I'll tell you the rest since you can't run."

I couldn't blink the growing sting of my focused eyes. They remained wide, worried they'd miss the lips that said the words that my ears possibly wouldn't hear. I was too influenced by drink, too encompassed by pain, and all that kept me wanting to stay alert was the omission I waited for and Luke's arm tightening around my waist. I didn't break my own promise not to tell him of my father, because he wasn't hearing it from me. He was learning of the details through the same, dangerous source that I was.

"Kephum let us know of your father having his name changed, excluding the name belonging to his prior identity. All we needed to know was that there was something he was hiding. That's enough for us to get what we would need out of him. But what more Kephum found, was that your father was informed of his record being looked into by another cop that had been alerted to it. Turns out, Kephum isn't the only shady officer in this town," he said too easily for the drastic news he was sharing. "And I guess we aren't the only ones with a dirty cop on our payroll."

It wasn't thoughtful or cruel that he'd told me so much when I had no choice but to remain silent under his watch. It was just wrong, all of it. It didn't make sense that I was hearing these things that were meant to be speaking of my father. In a single night, the strict and saintly man that I knew was turned into a stranger by someone who had actually been one only months ago. Nothing felt right about the needle through my skin being the only thing that I could feel. I was helpless, I was numb, and I was clueless as to what anything meant. I'd learned too much, and asked too many questions. The price of knowledge and answers had found me.

"That can't be Mr. Rowlen," Luke voiced from behind me. His rumbled voice vibrated against my back, bringing his quick heartbeat to my focus. I shut my eyes and focused on it instead of Othello. There was only so much destruction from something beautiful that I could take.

"The very one," Othello confirmed. With my sight unused, his words only cut deeper. It was easier to look at him while he assisted my life's end. It was comforting to see the image that would be my downfall. "A pastor who hides his sin from the world. Who would have guessed?"

"Then what's he hiding? Just his real name?" Luke asked. I couldn't turn to see his face, and by his tone I didn't know if he was asking incredulously or not. If Othello knew so much more about my father than even I did, then why couldn't he tell us the extent of it? What more existed behind the man with an unknown name?

"I don't know," Othello said. I believed that it was honest despite my inclination to begin questioning everyone I thought I knew. I was too tired to start now. The fact that he would answer at all would have to suffice. "I didn't bother looking into it. A man that goes to the lengths of changing his identity will go to greater lengths to ensure that his past isn't found. I sought a single detail that would prepare me. Not the entire story that leads to unnecessary danger and work."

Unnecessary. It was enough for him to know that my father was a liar, but I'm the one that had to pretend to live like I didn't know the lie existed. I would have to go home soon, and face the man that would be expecting me to be as respectful and subservient to his rules as normal.

The passing of time was a concept that I'd stopped keeping track of over the course of the night. He could be expecting me right now for all I knew.

"What time is it?" I asked against Adam's orders. The hold he had on my cut tightened when my speaking movements disturbed his work.

"Fucking dammit, Genevieve." His words were nearly a growl as he finished pulling the needle through. "You're lucky that I'm good at this. I'm trying to make sure you end up with the smallest scar possible."

"Scar?"

He grunted again at the single word uttered. "Yes, the scar that you're going to have because you had your face sliced open by a fucking idiot. The scar that's going to end up being bigger than it has to be if you don't let me do my job right. Now shut the hell up. Not another word."

I was so caught up in the sickening rush of my violent encounter that I hadn't thought about the evidence of it left behind that I wouldn't be able to hide. I was so concerned about facing my father because of what he hid, that I hadn't considered how I would hide my own secrets from him. They were carved upon my face. It was something I wouldn't be able to do.

"It's half-past midnight," Othello finally answered. All I could do was shut my eyes and press my lips against the trouble I was in. There was too much going wrong for me to know what to do about any of it.

"Should she even go back to that house if we don't know what sort of secret life he's hiding in it?" Luke's point only kindled the out-of-control fire that was my dilemma.

"She's a twenty-two-year-old woman. She can make that decision for herself."

It was such a simple thing said to have had such a big effect on my thought process. I was used to having things decided for me, or my movements controlled by the wants or expectations of others. But the expectations that I'd always tried to meet came from someone who now didn't even meet my own. Luke's concern for my well-being came from a place of caring, and Othello's reply was empowering. It was a small reminder that I had control although I'd always been guided as if I didn't. The few decisions I made for myself had led me here, to mutilation and treachery, but I also had encouragement and reassurance.

"Done," Adam said as he brought the scissors near my face for the final cut of thread. "You're free to speak now. Just try not to overdo it and pop your stitches. This is some of my best work."

"Will my scar be as subtle as yours is?" I pointed to the faded mark that ran down his temple toward his eye. It was only noticeable when you were close enough to analyze every inch of his face, which I was as he cleaned his equipment with alcohol and set it back into his black case.

"Fortunately for you, I'm even better at this than Othello is," he said before grinning at the serious face across from us. "So your scar will end up even better looking than mine. If you care for it correctly."

"Is it supposed to be an L?" Nora asked. Her head was tilted, studying the stitches along my cheek from her seat on the end of the couch that Othello sat on.

"Maybe," Adam said while he finished packing up. "His intent was likely to carve his name across her face. The L was easiest to start with since his right hand is dominant."

"That's a disgusting thing to want to do with someone." Luke's arm remained around me. He pulled some of my hair back to get a better look at my finished cheek, and I could feel the clumps of it dried by blood pulled with it.

"Not as disgusting to *want* to do to someone as it is to actually do it," Adam said as he put the full case on the side-table. "Regardless, he ended up looking worse. Or rather, barely looking."

The room filled with smiles and laughs aside from Othello, me, and Luke. I could hear Luke's gag at the forced memory of Axel on the table. I was too fixated on the thought of the mark I'd yet to see as I stared blankly at Othello. I would already be forced to relive the trauma any time that I saw the scar on my face, but now I knew that I would have to bear the brand of a piece of my attacker's name.

"It looks more like a V at the angle he put it," Michael added. "Kind of like a set of wings etched into your face." He shrugged the shoulder that wouldn't disturb Rachelle's place against him. "Not so terrible."

"That's pretty fitting, little bird," Rachelle chimed in as she turned beneath Michael's arm, leaning back against him. I'd thought she'd been asleep for how quiet she'd been, but apparently whatever she took just made her the calmest of us all.

I was more comfortable with the thought of brandishing that shape. A name that had been given to me, generous and unexplained. I'd found a lot in my short time as Dove, and I could live with knowing that she'd stay with me one way or another. If I didn't know the reason behind it, nor know if I were really the person that lived by that name, then at least I would keep the faded memory. A faint scar to ensure that I'd never forget this part of my life. It was better than remembering it as just the work of the man who didn't get a chance to finish signing his name.

Othello didn't look like a man who'd not long ago stolen the sight of my attacker. His appearance was a disguise, beautiful and at peace, with no mind giving in to the guilt that most would feel from his actions. His charcoal-colored shirt either had no blood that he'd spilled, or hid it all. All I cared to know was that his darkness devoured my trouble. If he and the others hadn't come when they did, I would look and feel even worse than I did.

"Thank you," I told them all, my eyes ending back on Othello, "for showing up. For saving me."

"You're thanking us instead of finding our fault for the things he'd already done before we got there?" Rachelle asked.

"Not our fault, but yours," Othello corrected her. "She wouldn't have been there had you not sent her running with information that wasn't yours to give."

"Information that wasn't yours to hold onto," she retorted. "You're just as much to blame as I am. If you're going to care for your little pet bird, you have to feed her what's hers."

He said everything with his eyes that he didn't through sealed lips. He was daring her to say more. His anger with her wouldn't budge just as her belief that she'd done no wrong wouldn't either. Both and neither of them were right. There were too many ways to see how tonight went wrong. Fixating on one way wouldn't make it right. Othello blamed her for her divulgence, and she blamed him for caring. Neither thought was accurate.

"It doesn't matter," I told them. I could feel the subtle pull of the stitches in my cheek, telling me to speak less for now. "I'm the one that went there. I'm through dwelling on the things that have already been done. It won't change anything." I'd worried for weeks over violence, a lie, witnessing death. Life didn't care if I worried, it just continued on and dragged me along beaten and exhausted. Worrying had been a waste, because I was still in the midst of an uncontrollable life. "I'm just grateful that you knew where to find me."

"You'd told us that your friend was at a party across town," Nora said as she began unlacing her boots. "You'd told us where to find you and you didn't even know it. We knew about Jason's get-together, and that you were likely running right into the mouth of a beast with a vendetta. Jason is Axel's roommate." She pushed off her boot with her other foot, then pulled her legs up and crossed them. "We found you because I paid attention."

"What if I'd gone home? Finding Luke wasn't my only option." I wasn't sure what I was trying to prove. There was a small part of me that was tired of being predictable. Tired of being figured out by a single look from someone. Emotions showed on my face, intentions told by my words, insecurity displayed by all my timid actions. I was too open for someone that wanted to hide so much.

"Yes, it was," Adam said. He sat on the floor beside Luke and me, leaning back against the couch with a retrieved drink in hand. The bottle hung in his grip over the knee he had pulled up, and his black hair was in disarray. Stalking, saving, and stitching me must be grueling. "If you ran from being told about your father, then you wouldn't run *to* your father. Being scared can make you do stupid things, but it doesn't mean that you're suddenly illogical. You wouldn't know how to face him after hearing that."

"I still don't," I said quietly, cautious not to strain Adam's work.

"Then don't." He turned the bottle around in his hand, looking at the details of his drink written on the bottle. He could have just grabbed the first thing he saw and was only now wondering what he was consuming. "You're the only person thinking that you have to go back."

"I do," I insisted. It was weak; I was weak. I was too tired to force the emotion I felt into my words. "If I don't go home, he will know that something is going on with me. And if he already knows that someone has looked into him, then I don't know what further problems that would cause. The safest thing for me to do is go home and somehow explain away these stitched-up gashes and the reason why I'm so late."

"That's the safe option, not the only option," Othello corrected. His fingers raked through the loose curls of his hair before they slipped through when he rested his hands behind his head. His hair was frizzed apart by the motions, the most disheveled I'd seen it. It made him look more like a man than an austere entity. "Nothing is really safe. You live with a man who's hiding something. There's always been risk that you were never aware of. You can play safe to please him, or you can do what you want. Anything you want."

"What I want is to hang onto my ability to remain free. If I go home, then things can possibly continue as they are. If I don't, then he'll come searching. I may be just prolonging the inevitable, but I want what I have while I have it. Because if finding out about my father tells me anything, it's that a secret can't last forever." I felt Luke's arm loosen against me. I wasn't the only one affected by the truth. "Things can't change before I know what I'm meant to do."

"Then you're going to need a good story," Michael told me. His hand on Rachelle's hip traced the open space where she'd spared me her dress. She was still, and serene, and definitely asleep now. I was almost upset that I couldn't have been given the artificial peace that she'd taken. "Something believable to explain away two knife wounds. The stitches you can always say you got at the hospital."

"No, she can't." Othello's insistence was enlightened. He'd already thought it through, and as he looked at me, I knew that he would go over the steps that he'd already beat us through. "Not only would that raise the question of a bill to be paid in the future, but your father is a man with a hidden identity. To remain unnoticed and in plain sight, he lives a normal life, but I'm willing to bet that one of the things he does without are doctors."

It was a detail that never meant anything, but screamed at me now. I thought of all the childhood injuries that seemed so insignificant, small scrapes and cuts never needing to be cared for to the extent that Adam had cared for me. But the cries of Gray's pain as Father set his broken arm, the tears that poured down a hurting and scared face, they couldn't be dismissed now that I knew better. They couldn't be explained away by faith that was put in more than the facilities of modern man the way that I'd grown to believe they could.

I didn't have to confirm aloud what Othello could see to be true.

"Here's how you lie, Dove," he continued. "You keep things simple. Explain too much, you'll say too much. The less you say, the less room there is for you to make mistakes. From there, you take questions as they come, and be selective with which ones you bother to answer. Nobody has to know everything, they just need to know enough, even if what they know is false. Like the simple life you've lived that's covered for your father all these years." His hands fell away from behind his head. He reached into his back pocket, pulled out his knife, and opened it. The sight of it made my cuts sting, and my eye sympathetically throb.

"Tell your father that you both were out with a couple of others, doing something that he would find acceptable. Movies, dinner, that's up to you. You simply tripped, but right through a window in one of your friends' cars. The glass shattered on the impact of your hands and face, leaving your arm and cheek ripped by the collapsing shards. You were out, had a bad fall, and wound up with those wounds. That's it."

He began wiping the open blade of his knife with the bottom of his shirt. On the small part of his exposed stomach, I could see the tracings of ink leading over to the side of his hip. The only clear mark of the tattoo that I could make out was the letter V. A letter that I now wore, too.

"And the stitches?" Luke asked from behind me. I was glad to have him there to gain the information that I spaced on. He would be my rock when it came time to use it. All the holes that my uncertainty would cause could be filled by him. For once, I wouldn't have to face my father alone.

"You're a college kid, makes sense that your friends likely would be, too. One of them is studying medicine, and they fixed you themself." He looked away from his glinting blade, right to me. "He'll be so relieved by that part that he won't bother to question you further. All he'll care about was that all your damage didn't damage his own life." Back down to the knife, he ran the cloth of his shirt back over the polished steel. "This all happened as you were leaving, and that's why you're late. Luke, you say all this to him. Say the friend gave her something for the pain and that she should get some sleep. She shouldn't bother trying to speak to her father after the alcohol she's had."

"Feeling nice and loose over there?" Nora asked me after a drink of her own. "Your first experience with the drink is going to be a memorable one."

One drink led to the knife; the other drink led me through stitches. I would never be rid of the taste. Bloody bitter.

"I'm not feeling much of anything, except anxious," I admitted. "Maybe I don't even know how to drink right."

"Sounds like you just haven't had the right amount," Adam said below me. He held up his bottle to me, gripped by his steady hand. "Have some more."

I turned my head to look up at Luke, not knowing for myself what to do. I didn't want to feel this way when I approached my father with more lies. But I didn't want to make the wrong decision, and I didn't currently feel that I was capable of making a good one on my own.

"I'll be the one doing all the talking," he assured me. "You may as well take the drink. Just enough to make you tired, it will play better into the story that I have to give Henry."

No longer was he perceived as Mr. Rowlen to the soul that had always liked him. Being called by his first name was an insult to my father. He had a title and a place of power that he was proud of. One that Luke wasn't going to acknowledge anymore. Now, he was just a man who was as human as he'd always denied being.

And to that, I drank.

I finished the bottle without a second thought, hoping to be oblivious to the man I met when I got home. It poured into me easier than before, less painful than the medicinal drink I'd been given, and I handed the empty bottle back to Adam.

He stood from the floor and held out his hand for me to take. "We'll go get you another."

"And one for me," Nora added as I let Adam pull me to my feet.

"Me too," Michael's voice called as my light head attempted to steady myself with shut eyes.

"You good?" Adam asked, and I opened my eyes intending to give a dishonest answer.

"Yeah," Luke told him. The question luckily wasn't mine. "I need to be as clear as possible when I take her home. I'll pass."

Adam led me to stand in front of him before he let go of my hand to have me walk on my own. I managed to make it to the side doors without stumbling, pushing through them as if my system weren't compromised. I felt alert as I walked into the hallway, too aware of all I felt and had endured. Was that normal for a first-time drinker? Wasn't I meant to be forgetting the things that I wanted to hide beneath the alcohol? There was no forgetting the newly formed memories that I would carry with me forever. What the drinks had done was cut the ties to the fear that was attached to them. My mind could see things clearly, it'd just stopped feeling. Maybe that was the appeal.

I stopped walking in the middle of the hall, and Adam noticed and stopped without a missed beat.

"I don't know where we're going," I realized openly.

"To get more drinks from the kitchen." His answer was patient, catering to the unfiltered thoughts of an influenced woman. That could become troubling, quickly.

"I know that," I said. "I just don't know where the kitchen is."

"I do." The roll of his eyes was too slow to be serious. Was drinking what it took to be able to read past people's faces? "That's why we're going together."

And maybe it made you look past the obvious, just the same.

He led me down the dark hallway, the large lights overhead dimmed by use or preferred setting. The halls had always been eerie, but usually because I was finding my way to trouble within them. Now it was empty, with only two bodies occupying it instead of the masses that flocked here during other nights. Eerie was just the natural state of church halls.

"Thank you for stitching me up," I said. The silence was begging for words, and my loosening mind had plenty. "It feels better already."

The chuckle that followed was unexpected, but it made my relenting lips smile in response. I didn't know why it was funny, I just knew that it was.

"It only feels better because you aren't sober enough to feel it entirely," he told me. His feet directed us at an angle toward a door we were approaching, and he grabbed the knob and opened it. "It's going to hurt like hell in the morning. All of it."

He turned on the light, the brightness overhead far more intense than the hallway. I shielded my eyes with my forearm, forgetting about the threads and wound that it now had. I grunted at the pain of pressing it against my forehead, and the severity of the white room that I was forced to look at.

"More like that." He walked toward the fridge after pointing out my discomfort. It wasn't going to be easy to feel this all over when the numbness I had wore off.

The kitchen was huge. The counter space expanded from one wall and cut across to the middle of the room in one open section. Cabinets overhead doubled the amount that were in my home, and equaled the amount that I knew to be in our own church's kitchen. The purpose of ours was to make grateful preparations for the man that led us to a life of light. Deceit lived in that light.

"Do they look similar?" Adam asked as he leaned back against the counter next to the fridge.

"Strikingly similar. Like walking into a parallel universe. Or maybe my mind is just picturing what it's used to because that's easiest for it right now."

I forced myself to look for the differences to ensure that I could still see correctly. The color of the tile, the size of the fridge, the countertops themselves that had a lighter surface than the ones that I was used to. The differences were there, reassuring me that I hadn't walked through the door right back into the other side of my life.

"Well you're the only one out of the two of us that would know," he said as he opened the fridge. "You're the one that's ventured into both. But chances are, they're probably just similar. From what I know, all churches are the same."

"Do you think all preachers are the same?" His hand halted at the question, two bottles sitting alone on the counter before he added another to them.

"I haven't met enough to give you a good answer." The five bottles lined the counter, and he turned back around to lean against the fridge, in no hurry to deliver them. "With what I know of one, I would hope not. But if they're anything like preachers' daughters, then apparently they aren't all the same."

"And what do you know about preachers' daughters?" I watched him line the cap of the bottle against the edge of the counter before quickly popping it off. His eyes watched me observe as he reached for the next one.

"That they tend to find us much sooner than you did."

"What other preachers' daughters come around here?" It was a rude thing to ask. I knew it the moment that it was said, and I wanted to apologize for gossiping, but the apology didn't come as easily as the prying did. Failure liked company, and if I was here finding all the ways that I'd missed and failed, then I was comforted to know that I wasn't the only one.

"Ones that don't stick around once they get what they come for." The voice behind me sent shivers down my back. I was slower to react to something so startling, no jump or scream leaving my calmed body. I didn't realize that I'd left the door open or that I was still standing in the way until Othello placed his hands on my shoulders. I made to move over, but he kept me still.

"Because they're smarter than I am?" Smart enough to know that the longer you were around here, the more you found. Smart enough to have learned the things that I was learning before they had to resort to this place for answers. I faced Adam as I asked the question, but I was asking something of all of us. I didn't care if the answer came from myself or them. I was growing used to finding things out for myself.

"Because they weren't in search of as much as you are," he replied behind me.

I tilted my head up and back, threaded cheek showing to the eyes that looked down upon me. "That makes them smarter."

He removed his left hand from my shoulder, tediously bringing his fingers to my face. Everything was slowed in my unwound vision, relaxed enough to catch every millisecond that passed through the closing space between us. He set his thumb onto my cheek, his fingers folding themselves around my chin. He made one gentle stroke beneath a line of my cut, showing me that where there was pleasure there was pain. I would have gladly accepted the feel of his touch against my hurting flesh again, but once was all that he gave me.

"That makes them less curious. And curiosity is a delightful thing to venture." His hand left my face as he forced me farther into the room. "Now," he said as he shut the door behind him. "I have something for you."

His hand reached into his pocket and pulled back out his knife. He flipped it open with a stealthy flick of his finger, and I stepped back into Adam. The spot of safety that my body reflexively found. The person that hours ago had me crying and forcing me to physically harm him. Now I was looking at the knife that blinded the man who'd used his knife against me. Safety was as deceiving as righteousness.

"This is yours," Othello said as he flipped the knife around in his hand, holding it by the blade. "And before you drink too much, before you go home to a man that you don't really know, I want to see you use it. You're going to have to know how to save yourself when no one else can."

"You want me to use that?" I pointed to the smoothed handle that he was offering me instead of taking it. Would I be able to see the violence it had seen the moment I touched it?

"Yes," he said as he took a step toward me with another offered motion of his hand. "The blade's already seen blood, so it knows its purpose."

The smile that followed his guilty words sent my stomach tumbling and my hand reaching. I grabbed it, wanting to give him what he wanted. I turned the steel around in my hand, running a steady finger slowly along the edge of the blade. Sharp against the soft pad of my finger, I lightened my touch as I pulled it along. I was a stranger to the knife, but it felt like it belonged to me.

"You're going to show me that you're willing to use it," Othello demanded. He took a step back and my eyes followed, tentative to leave the sight of the knife. "I'll be the one to attack you, and you use that to stop me and ensure that you can get away."

"You? Why do I have to fight you?" Why would he willingly want to be put in that position, weaponless in a fight against a knife? I knew that I knew nothing of what I wielded, but I knew enough about what it was capable of.

"You're fighting me because apparently Adam sutures better than I do," he said with a flick of his eyes in Adam's direction. I turned around to look at their receiver, the grin on his face out of place in the midst of what was being proposed. How were they both okay with what was being asked of me? And why wasn't my own heart beating furiously against something I knew I should feel nervous about?

"I don't want to." I closed the knife in my hand, finger lingering over the lever that would trigger the blade's return. I reached out to hand it back to Othello. "I can't."

He looked down at the offering, eyes lingering on the weapon he knew well before he reached out to take it from me. His hand slipped past mine, grabbing my wrist and pulling me into him with one harsh yank. My hand met with his chest, the injured arm attached throbbing at the sudden contact. His hand released mine as he grabbed my shoulders, turning me around to haul me onto the open counter.

As the back of my head met the hard surface, the image in my brain showed me the last time I was forced down. The last time I was held beneath the weight of a man crawling onto me the way that one was now. I could see the beautiful face before me, the terrifying man who'd shown me what horrors he could issue. The terror he was forcing me to relive was steadily breaking through my thoughts and out of my lips.

"I don't want to, I don't want to, I don't want to," I kept repeating to the face that didn't move. His brow held firm over his fierce eyes, focused on my every movement that he would deflect.

"Did Axel stop pulling his knife through your skin just because you didn't want him to do it?" His hand left my shoulder and held my face firmly in his hand. "It takes more than just telling someone to stop. You have to make them."

His palm covered my mouth as he forced his knee between my legs. My eyes went wide at the recollection of pain that the movement had last caused me, the tenderness that lingered made aware in my growing alertness.

I shook my head beneath his hold, muffled begs being ignored as he began dragging his hand down my arm. My inability to breathe became more severe with every forced inhale. My scalp hurt, my face hurt, and my heart was hurting from all the exertion. He wouldn't give me the breath I needed until I gave him what he wanted.

He was too rough, too serious in his steps to make me hurt him. I didn't want to hurt him. I didn't want him to hurt the way that I'd been hurt. If I looked at his face, I saw the man that'd given me all that I'd asked for and saved me when I couldn't ask for his help. I had to close my eyes, and imagine that the feel of the hand that began pushing up my skirt wasn't his. I had to push away the thought of what he was doing and make myself think of it as unwanted. It was confusing and sick to transition the image behind my closed eyes to recreate Axel and the feel of his hands pressing against my shoulders, pushing me down and holding me there. To imagine that his deformed, smiling face was the one that was above me and enjoying seeing me writhe. Hearing my labored breaths and silenced begs.

Then it was unwanted. The hand that met my hip with all the material of my skirt was one that wasn't welcome. The hand over my mouth tasted of abuse instead of savored sin. The image in my closed eyes was one that had my finger finding the lever on the knife in my hand. The wail that issued behind a heavy palm directed my hand as it slashed down at the arm that crept over to between my legs.

My eyes sprang back open at the unmistakable feel of contact. Othello watched me look down at the gash in his arm, not bothering to look for himself. His brow loosened as his hand peeled away from my mouth. I was panting from the exertion, and from the sight of the blood that I was responsible for spilling. He remained hovering over me, his hair falling in various tendrils around his face. I was more affected than he was, and he was now the one with blood running down his arm.

"And if that doesn't make them stop, you continue until stopping is the only option they have. A body that's dead can't fight. Understood?"

I nodded my head, catching my breath as I ran a hand through my hair. I couldn't bring myself to get off the counter after he did. I sat there thinking of how all the blood that I'd seen in a single night amounted to more than I'd seen in my entire life. I'd hit someone for the first time, fought against an accidentally made enemy, and used a weapon for the first—and hopefully last—time.

My head turned to the side, my unmarred cheek resting against the cool surface of the counter. Adam was still leaned back against the fridge, drink in hand. Othello was standing before an open drawer, wrapping a dish towel around his arm. He tied the towel off, one piece pulled with his hand and the other grasped between teeth as they tightened the knot he made. He grabbed one of the opened bottles from the counter by him before turning around and leaning back against it.

They shared a silent look, one not meant for me to know the message behind. My lips were currently more dependable than my mind would be in an effort to decipher it. I couldn't stop my thoughts from spilling out through them.

"How do you two talk with your eyes like that?" I asked. They looked to me where I laid on the counter with a used knife in hand.

"Practice," Adam answered.

My skirt still sat at my hip, leaving me exposed and on display. The thought registered without shame, and I pushed it back down without the heat that would typically show on my face from my indecency. As I sat up, slowly adjusting myself to work my way off the counter, Adam came forward and put his hand around my waist. Before he could pull me off, I put my hand on his shoulder to brace myself.

"How long did you have to practice before you could entirely understand?"

He waited, leaving me up on the counter with his hand gripped on my side. How long did you have to do anything before it became easier? How much practice made for total control and capability? It wasn't just skilled silence that they were good at.

"Six years and counting," he said, looking up at the brutalized side of my face.

"Do you ever misunderstand each other that way? Does your mind ever translate his incorrectly?" I rubbed the flat surface of the blade in my hand across my skirt. A thin line of blood was left from its edge, forcing my eyes to look for its supplier. The white towel around his arm had a growing stain of crimson that he paid no attention to as he used the wounded limb to put his bottle to his lips. With the silence and stoic face that he directed towards me, I wondered if I'd ever failed to uphold my end of a silent conversation with him. There's so much I could have missed.

"It's hard to get wrong at this point, but it's happened before," Adam loosened his hand against me, letting it slide down to my hip as he turned and faced Othello. "See if you can read into him. Find what your senses are telling you."

"I can't," I admitted as I watched the bottle in Othello's hand tip up, spilling itself into his mouth again. "My senses always tell me not to look too closely."

Othello's venomous smile surfaced. His reaction would have been unsettling had I not been tranquil, but now I was only interested in the joy he found in my admittance. The smile was fascinating to a mind that temporarily set aside fear.

"Then you're already tuned in pretty well," Adam said, smiling as he watched Othello watch me. My eyes kept darting between them both, trying not to miss anything that they were giving away. "That's instinct. That's a guarded observation. You need to be more open to receive thoughts instead of signals."

"I'm nothing but open right now," I told him. No overthinking, no worries, no hesitations about what I was doing. It was the least myself that I'd ever been, melted away to just an existing being by doses of alcohol.

"Then now's the perfect time to try. Let's hear what his thoughts make you think."

Othello sat his bottle on the counter and crossed his arms over his chest. I watched his movements until he became still, and then focused on the face that I was meant to see past. It was hard to see anything but his features, etched and flawless. No small reactions gave me any hints that I was looking for.

"Come closer," I said, needing the space that I studied to be nearer to my hunting eyes.

He came and stood in front of me, close enough that I could have reached out and placed my hand on his shoulder. I nearly did, assuming that touch would enhance my connection, but didn't because I knew I shouldn't need it. Adam and Othello could communicate from afar, and I already had him right in front of me.

My eyes began at the top of his head, scanning down every attractive inch that housed his mind. His hair was perfectly tousled, just a distraction that would hinder my search. His brows were aligned, untensed and giving me nothing. I moved down to his eyes that latched onto mine, drawing them like wind that was felt and not heard. I was pushed into the murky waters being charted for the first time, allowing myself to drift away. I was afloat, feeling the easy direction being given to my search. A gentle push of an abrupt wave told me that I was where I needed to be, but that I hadn't found what I was looking for yet.

I pulled myself out of those depths, moving my gaze down along his nose. Centered in a chiseled face, the timeless standard of beauty, it wasn't the alluring sight that I was meant to stop at. I moved on to the lip that sat atop the other, its curved and full shape capturing my attention. My eyes lingered, tracing the edges of the sharp shapes of his mouth. The slow path I took along its outline brought me closer to a warm feeling, the heat of my answer drawing near.

My eyes flicked back up to his, confirming the thought where I'd been reeled in.

"What's on his mind, Genevieve?" Adam's hand on my hip tightened. I knew that he was watching the two of us, but I couldn't break my focus on Othello.

"The things that happened between me and you in the hallway earlier." It was only a detail of what Othello had been telling me. I didn't want to be wrong out loud—but I knew I wasn't wrong.

"What about what happened with us in the hallway? What's he telling you?" Adam's fingers tapped one at a time along their grip on me. He was waiting to hear what he already knew.

I held onto my sight of Othello, secure in what I knew was his thought and not just my assumptions. "That he heard everything. He heard me say that I'd wanted to kiss him. He already knew it when I rushed away from him." Othello's lips tugged at the side, telling me that I was right.

"Now give him your thoughts," Adam instructed. I could hear him take a drink by the slosh of the bottle that he still held onto.

"If you're already thinking about it then why don't you just teach me like I want?" After it was said I realized that he'd meant for me to give him my thoughts silently. I'd said it louder than I would have thought it, immediately boldened by my success of reading into him and the absence of hesitation that I no longer had tonight.

Othello stepped into the space between my legs. My skirt was pushed up by his approach, and he placed his hands on my thighs. My hands rested on his shoulders as he brought his face before mine.

"What do you want me to teach you, Dove?" The feel of his words caressed my lips, and they parted to consume them.

"Everything. Show me how to kiss, show me how everything that I'm supposed to already know is meant to work." My hands tightened on his shoulders in reaction to his grip on my thighs.

"Showing you how to kiss and showing you all the things that you've yet to learn aren't the same thing. My kiss won't be what teaches you everything you're wanting to know." His face remained in place as mine slowly fell forward, eager to close the last remaining space between my lips and the knowledge they craved.

"I don't have to know everything right now. Just teach me this one last thing tonight." My lips slowly touched his, electrified by the rush that the contact sent through me. Tingles spread from the place where mine grazed his until his hands around my thighs moved to my sides, abruptly pulling me off of the counter to stand before him.

The fading feel of his lips was all I had left as he looked down at me, his hands steadying my disoriented body. The sudden switch in the simple emotions I had was what had me swaying, finding the ability to remain still on my feet again. I went from hungry for his touch to hating the lack of it too quickly.

"You've learned more than one person should in a single night." He looked into my eyes as he spoke, the connection I'd found moments before returning to inform me of all he said that wasn't spoken. "I'll teach you if you're still brave enough to ask me when you're sober." *Refusal isn't the same thing as rejection.*

"I thought you said you didn't care? Why should a detail like my sobriety stop you?" Just tumbling from my mouth. Every thought and question that I wouldn't dare ask otherwise for the chance it'd be heard as complaint or insolence. I couldn't be stopped, the way that my crumbling life couldn't.

"I don't care," he said as he let me go and fetched his drink. "But you do. And if you're wanting to be taught something, then be taught when there's no doubt that you'll remember every detail of the lesson." He swallowed another pull from the bottle before he grabbed another and started towards the door.

"One more wound to stitch," Adam said as he handed me a bottle before grabbing the last one left on the counter. "What a fucking eventful night."

"How could you just stand there and watch him force me to cut him open like that?" I asked as we followed Othello out the door, back into the dim hallway.

"I could do it easily. I watched him give you the opportunity that other people have died fighting for."

"Cutting him open?" I watched Othello push through the side doors ahead of us and go back into the big room.

"Seeing if a man like Othello Sarris bleeds like a human." He clarified as we reached the doors. "And I enjoyed every second of watching you find out for yourself what few others ever will."

Luke was sat where Nora had last been, wrapped up in conversation with Michael who still held a sleeping Rachelle. Nora was moved over to where Othello had sat, and I thought he might ask her to move as he handed her the extra bottle that he held. Instead, he sat on the end seat of the only empty couch, and began untying the towel around his arm with quick fingers and his teeth.

"Should we all be expecting to find ourselves bleeding before the night is over?" Nora asked as she watched him expose the blood trickling from his cut.

I sat down on the other end of the couch he was on, watching him smile as he used the towel to wipe away running droplets.

"Only if you want to," he said as he waited for Adam to open his full case from the table beside him and begin unpacking it again.

Only if she wanted to expect it? Only if she wanted to be bleeding? He'd both expected and wanted me to draw blood when he put that knife in my hands; the knife that was tucked away in my pocket, ensured in its familiarity with violence. He was telling her that he'd been bled willingly and she likely didn't even know it. From her serene state across the way, I doubted that she cared. I wondered if she'd also taken whatever Rachelle had.

The drink in my hand was growing warm with the rest of my body. As I sat there watching Adam prepare the cut to be sutured, I thought of how much easier it would be to stay here. To drift off to sleep on this couch, surrounded by people that were mellow and having relaxed conversations. Even the sight of opened flesh and blood beside me was more enticing than going home.

It was fascinating, seeing the mark on his arm made by a woman who had a similar one on hers. Opposite arms, different knives wielded, but the same-colored blood escaping from the same-sized cut. I was entranced instead of repulsed by the sight. Pulled in instead of put off. Violence and blood and gore had all been things I'd averted my eyes to and found sickness in seeing. But now, the gentle motions of assisted healing being performed was exactly what my eyes wanted to be set on.

"What, now you want to watch since it's not your body being stitched together?" Adam asked as he glanced up from disinfecting the wound.

"It's the first time that I'm not terrified of seeing it," I said in my defense.

"Then come closer."

I looked at Othello, wondering if he even wanted me that close to him while he was being worked on. He saw me seeking his permission and beckoned me over with his head. I sat my drink on the ground and crawled across the couch, hands stopping near his leg as I peered over the gash, held together by two of Adam's fingers as he pushed the first stitch through the center.

"Does that not hurt?" I asked Othello as I turned to him and away from the painful process.

"Did it not hurt you?" he asked in reply.

I didn't think about how ridiculous my question would sound coming from someone who'd just sat through the process. It was just that he sat so still, not being told to 'loosen up' and relax as it was being done like I had been. Then again, he didn't react to receiving the cut, either.

"I know that it did, but I can't remember what it was like now that it's over." I settled back onto the seat next to him. I tried to keep my space, but my interest in the wound and Adam's careful movements lulled me, lured me in.

"That's the easiest thing about pain," he said, and I realized how close my head was to him as I heard the deep vibrations of his chest. "It's only temporary."

My ears were attracted to the rumbling sound, my head falling against the shoulder that it was near as I watched the sutures continue to be placed through heavy eyes. I was drifting again, only now I was being pulled beneath my exhaustion as I watched the disturbingly peaceful pattern of patched wounds.

I'd never experienced pain like I had that night, introduced to the world where it runs rampant by the man who now sat and endured it without sound nor grimace. I'd fallen into the hands that guided me through the darkness, who'd made a life and dwelling in its severe and vicious shadows.

And that man remained in his preferred silence as his dove found the gift of sleep upon his shoulder.

SIMILARITY

The only thing different about this service was the seating arrangement. Mother had insisted on sitting on my right side, unable to bear the look of my ruined face. She hadn't claimed that it pained her to see her child hurt, the way that a mother might. She'd not said that she couldn't handle the sight of my face's imperfection, either. But over the past days, because of each cringe and quick aversion of her eyes when she caught an unintended look at my colored, hideous, swollen cheek that bore the consequences of what she knew to be a clumsy accident, I knew that's what she was thinking. That she was devastated that my face was no longer an image she could flaunt as pristine.

Only an accident to them, and there was still shame to the scar sealing itself on my face. I was made to feel unworthy by the lingering looks of my father and the lack of them from my mother. Only Gray, who sat beside me, in view of my hurting and healing cheek, had asked about how I felt. Didn't care to know the false details of how it occurred or force me to feel that the mark I wore was a brand of dishonor, but cared to know that I was okay and forced me to remember that, even in this seemingly faultless family, my well-being was worthy of being cared about.

But the seemingly faultless was coming undone at their seams. The family around me felt unraveled now that I knew what I did. I knew that I had reason to doubt my father and grow suspicious of my own mother as well. I knew of a lie that was hidden so well, but that I didn't believe could remain silent in the confines of a marriage. Only Gray was consistent, the good that the world had and didn't deserve. Hand around the shoulder of the battered, and sat upon the side of a face that wore the scores of darkness's talons.

Father left his podium, nearly every word now finished unheard by my ears. It's hard to focus on the words of a man whom you can't trust. Every meal spent at the table together, he was a man I didn't know. Every day spent appearing to the world as a man who lived by truth, he was a man they didn't know. The father that I knew was strict and abrasive and kept me tightly tucked away from the world that held secrets just like his. The father that I knew was a man that was living the life of another. The life of a lie.

Mother met him with outstretched arms as Gray and I stood, his arm around my shoulders. Father watched us standing together, silent and obedient, as Mother lingered in her hug of pride and appreciation. Her face shielded by his, I watched his eyes settle onto my cheek. What she was saying was not her usual praise.

"Gene, go ahead to the kitchen and get yourself a glass of water. We'll let those that ask know that you aren't feeling well," Father instructed as Mother pulled away from their embrace, their quiet conspiring.

I felt just fine. I was fine enough to be here, sat in the front row to hear the service that I didn't dare ask to be excused from. But I was being hidden by subtleties; mother directing me to Luke as she and Gray shook the hands of the congregation without me, and now being excused from the duty of saying our thanks and goodbyes as a family. A task that they deemed significant, crucial for our image as the grateful family that we were. But my image now wasn't one that they wanted stood beside them. My damaged face at such a close look would cause concern, speculations, or questions. And I knew that my father was in no position to be questioned. Sending me away was the simplest avoidance that would spare their image from being sullied the way that I was.

Gray squeezed my shoulder, and when I looked to him his eyes were upon our father. They lingered, just as surprised by his directions as I was. Gray didn't see the scheme the same way that I did. Gray didn't know all the intricate details that had to be strung to keep a web of lies intact. Gray saw no harm in the world seeing the face of a woman who suffered from human flaws, because Gray didn't condemn flaws or suffering. Only our parents did.

He looked to me with a smile that cared about the woman behind the inconvenient wound. "I'll come get you when we're ready to go."

He would come save me after being isolated and set apart for the wrong reasons.

I nodded to him with a weary smile, the best I could manage under the tired circumstances. It was overdone and not worth the trouble, chasing after the illusion of perfection. It's one of the things I was falling back from in this family; in the ideals of my parents. Perfection wasn't the same as goodness, nobody had both aside from Gray. They'd done right by having him, and he would have to suffice in their endeavors to have birthed and raised excellence. I was born to find my way here, walking this hall alone due to failure. If an accident could make them feel this way about my flawed face, then the truth would break all the respect they had left for me.

The kitchen light turned on by the switch beneath my finger, the lights overhead shifting into use with a buzz. I could hear the call of electricity through the silence, a room filled with nothing but the dismissed soul that awakened it. Just me and the familiar scene that I'd visited in another universe only days ago.

I retrieved a glass from the cabinet, not needing it but inclined to follow the simple orders that I'd been given. It was done on instinct, my mind trained to do as I was told and internalize my own opinions. My opinion now was that I shouldn't be listening to someone who didn't listen to their own words. I'd been so scared of lying, so scared of my feet tracing the outline of the path of sin, and for what? The man who'd fashioned me to feel so was doing those things himself. And if his own warnings were meant to be guidance given through experience of his own troubles, then his troubles wouldn't be hidden. I would know what they were.

But I knew nothing except there existed a name that I didn't know. A name that belonged to my father and was cast aside for buried reasons. Reasons important enough to be guarded by cops who broke their own rules in exchange for pretty pennies. I couldn't trust anyone that I should be able to expect to trust.

I sat my water down, drawn to the counter space in the center of the room. I put my hands on its surface, cold to the touch and the wrong color to properly replicate the one that I'd last laid upon. But I climbed up in my Sunday dress and put my back against the chill that seeped through the fabric. No knife in my hand and no man hovering over me, but I could close my eyes to imagine. I relived the memory as closely as possible, vague in its sober recollection. Something I shouldn't be comforted by, lessons in violence from a fierce man and a bloodied blade, but I was. All that used to be wrong was what made me feel right.

A knock against the open door snapped me out of my sadistic haze. My head twisted to see who was witnessing me in this strange state, lying on the counter in the church's kitchen. The sideways image of a sweet face and hands being wrung together in nervousness was a relief.

"I'm sorry to bother you," Amelia said as she moved into the room from the doorway. "I saw that you didn't go outside with Gray and your parents." She looked at the vicious marks on the cheek that was exposed to her. "Luke told me about what happened to you the other night. Are you doing all right?"

I sat up on the counter, turning to hang my legs off before I slid down and corrected my dress. "I'm doing just fine. I appreciate you asking, Amelia. I'm sorry that I've raised so much concern."

I turned my back to her as I took an unwanted drink from the glass I left by the sink. I felt like an inconvenience to all that needed to check on me. I felt even worse knowing that I was hiding a lot behind this mark.

"Oh, don't be. I'm just glad that you're doing okay. Honestly, checking on you isn't the only reason why I'm here," she said.

I turned around to the hesitation in her voice. I was in tune with the signals that I was familiar with, and she sounded like someone I knew. She sounded like me, curious and uncertain.

"Is there something that I can help you with?" I couldn't imagine anything that I could help another wondering soul with. I, myself, was full of questions, and dark answers were all that I'd found. I still knew very little, but I knew myself well enough to know that I wanted to help if I could. I couldn't force another person as nervous about learning as I was to settle for just not knowing. What I knew, I could share.

"Maybe," she said. Her hands found the sides of her dress and crumpled them between her fingers. I was barely past the terrified position she stood in. In this room, she was me, and I was able to see how helpless I appeared to those who watched me falter in this same way.

"Hopefully," she continued. "It's just that we've known each other for basically our entire lives. And I know that you've always been better friends with Luke, and now you two are more than that," I flinched at her incorrect belief, "and I guess that's why I'm hoping that it's okay that I come to you about this. And that you won't think less of me, because you know me."

Think less of someone else than I already thought of myself? Her anxiety over what she'd yet to reveal to me was tugging at my heart. Physically paining me to see myself in her. The worry of being belittled, judged, shunned—it was all too much. I wanted to give her all the comfort I'd found, the comfort I'd never been given from anyone from this version of life before aside from Gray.

But she had Gray. What was forming between them was real, and not the façade that Luke and I put on. She had the perfect person to give her comfort and be at her side with no judgments. Why come to me when she'd already found someone better? What could I give her that someone as all-around good as Gray couldn't?

"Amelia, is everything all right? I don't know what's bothering you, but I'll help you however I can. I promise." An unbreakable word of trust was the most I had to offer, because the answers she was looking for in me might fall short.

"Everything is okay," she assured me, "I just don't really know who else to talk to about this. And you're older, and Luke is older, and I'm not stupid enough to think that you guys don't—"

She cut herself off and my brows hitched up in confusion. I was trying my hardest to follow, but she was speaking in circles.

"I just think that maybe I—"

"Amelia!" Luke called from the hallway. Her words were swallowed again, and I could see the painful red of her cheeks as her concerns were trapped in her throat. I wanted to tell her to spit it back out, beg her to let me help to not leave her silent the way that I was always left to be. But when Luke appeared in the doorway, I knew her lips were sealed. What words she held onto were going to remain hers.

"Amelia, what are you doing? I've been looking for you for like four whole minutes," he said with a smile before he realized I was in the room, and that she and I both stood in silence. "Is everything okay?"

"Everything is okay," she said for the second time. It didn't sound as believable as it initially had. She was becoming less convinced. "I was just checking on Gene."

Half of a truth. I knew what it was like to tell one, and I hoped she didn't suffer for supplying half a lie like that the way that I did. I watched her face as Luke approached me, and couldn't find it in me to return the small smile that she put on. Smiles didn't have to be worn over the wrong feelings.

"How are you doing?" Luke asked as he put his hand to my cheek below the barely healing cuts. "Not too swollen. Still pretty sore?"

"I think I'm becoming so used to it that I don't even register it as hurting anymore," I told him. He looked down to my arm, the wound less bothersome and more discreet. "I forget that that one is even there. So, I'd say I'm doing all right. Just numb and looking like a monster."

He blew air through his lips that caressed the top of my head as he pulled me to him for a hug, putting my unharmed cheek against his chest. "The most angelic monster." He rubbed his fingers gently across my back before he pulled away. "Do you want to go out tomorrow? Try to have a better time than we did the other night?"

"What can be better than being ripped to shreds?" The sarcasm came out monotonous, making the statement dark. The severity made me smile, and he grinned back after forcing his brows together.

"Not having to deliver your unconscious and ripped body to your father at the end of the night, that's what."

He'd faced my father alone, holding me in his arms as he relayed a practiced story to the man who'd waited until after two in the morning for his daughter to arrive home in an unacceptable state. I knew it went okay for him and that the incident was forgiven due to the crafted excuses that he supplied. But I recalled the fear that I saw through exhausted eyes when I was awakened by the car's sudden stop in front of my house. My own heart had raced,

207

knowing that my stranger of a father was fixing to see me in the worst state I'd ever been.

"How do I look?" I'd asked Luke, *my voice strained by sleep and my eyes begging me to close them once more.*

"You look like hell," *he'd told me honestly. Honesty is the most that he and I had between us, the thing that kept us as close as we were now. He knew just as much about the secrets of my life as I did about his.*

"You haven't seen hell yet," *I'd said as my head lolled to the other side, looking at the house's front door that loomed through the night. "It's through there, and I don't think that I can face it."*

"Then go back to sleep and you won't have to." *He'd turned off the car and him opening his door was the last thing that I'd seen. Him opening mine was the last thing that I'd heard. Him cradling me in his arms was the last thing that I'd felt.*

Now, I couldn't even say that the worst was over. I was still paying for a lie that was meant to make things easier and stuck in the silence that I couldn't break about the things I knew. Life was different, but it was resuming. It was heading in a direction that couldn't be braced for. There was nothing I could do but hang onto the seat I'd been given.

"If I'm an angelic monster, then you're a saint for doing so," I assured him. I'd had the easier task of being woken to the gentle knock on my bedroom door the next morning, and having my brother ask me how I was feeling after hearing our father tell our mother everything that had happened. "Thank you, again."

"It doesn't quite feel right to accept thanks when you're the one suffering," he replied as he looked down at my cheek, then to my eyes. It wasn't just about the physical pain, but the things that he now knew that I lived with. The lies, the wondering, the insecurities behind not understanding my own reality. He'd done the hard part of immediately facing my father after what we'd learned of him, but he was able to turn around and leave after he delivered me to that house. Where I would stay and continue to live, constantly on guard.

"It doesn't feel right to accept anything. It's all hard." He knew the meaning behind every word, nodding as I looked back over to Amelia who patiently waited for her brother. I'd forgotten where she stood, able to watch the exchange that she'd perceive as affectionate. I hadn't forgotten about her worry, still lingering as shown by the hands that clutched her skirt. My concern for her had my fingers at my lip, squeezing the sensitive skin as I tried desperately to look into the thoughts that she'd been stopped from giving me.

"This again?" Luke said as he grabbed my hand and pulled it away from my mouth. "You've got to quit that. There's got to be a better habit that you can replace this with."

"This is already a habit that I've replaced another with," I told him as my finger caught on my necklace's chain before easily falling away. "And I don't choose them, they choose themselves."

"Luke? Amelia?" Mrs. Hannigan called from down the hallway. Luke backed away from me before pointing a finger to hold onto my attention.

"Tomorrow? What do you say?"

"I say I'll see you after work," I agreed with a smile. I shared the momentary happiness that I could with Amelia's retrieving form. "And I'll see you again soon, too," I assured her. I didn't know what she wanted from me, but if another chance to reveal what she needed was what I could give her, then I would.

"Thanks, Gene." She left before Luke, who waited for her to leave before he turned back to me.

"Is everything still okay?" he asked, wanting to know more than just about the marks on my body and my pain. He was assuring that the struggles that he knew I was enduring weren't becoming too much.

"Everything is okay," I told him, borrowing Amelia's lie and speaking it to this bright room for the third time.

He winked at me before he left the room, and I stood alone against the counter with a half-finished glass of water and the buzzing sound that returned to the silence. I closed my eyes and listened to it, emptying my mind to all that I thought and felt and let my body just hum along to the noise.

I was one with the emptiness, complete and hollow until my name was called and I opened my eyes again to Gray's pure face in the doorway. Bright and pure like everything in the room. I was the only darkened and defeated thing within it.

PERMANENCE

Do you think it will be a pretty noticeable scar?" Nancy asked as she reached out and swiped a gentle thumb beneath my stitches. Anyone who looked was alarmed by its appearance, the already fading colors of the bruised flesh around it not dimming the severity of the wound itself. Its noticeable size and place on my cheek attracted any and every eye. She'd been questioning me since the moment she saw me, distraught by the thought of me bearing this hideous thing for life.

She was an aged beauty queen with standards of appearance that I would never reach and never had. I knew now more than ever that I wasn't meant to know perfection, I was only meant to see it in others. Unattainable, and always just out of reach.

"The person that stitched it said that the scar shouldn't be too bad," I assured her. "But I'm sure there's no escaping one entirely. It's definitely just a part of me now."

"What a shame," she said as she leaned back in her seat across from me, done hovering over the board as I sat and debated on my next move. "Doesn't that devastate you?"

"Should it?" I said as I sat my fingers lightly on a pawn, but removed them before I committed to the move. I wasn't yet sure that there wasn't a better option.

"Not if it doesn't already."

She coughed, the rough sound of a smoker's lungs. I wondered if one day Adam's would sound the same, and if he'd regret touching cigarettes the way that Nancy did. I wondered if he had any existing regrets. It was hard to assume with someone as self-assured as him.

"But I think a face like yours being permanently scarred like that is just about as bad as it gets. There isn't much worse than that," she said before she drank from her glass to soothe her hacking spell.

"Sure there is," I told her as I settled for the pawn, moving its location on the board. I looked up to her smiling face, elegant and strong for all the exciting years it had seen.

"And what could possibly be worse than ruining the gift of beauty like that?" She didn't bother leaning forward as she glanced at the board. Her turn would wait for my answer.

"It'd be worse to have a broken spirit, a broken soul from all the terrible things that life can bring." She kept her sight off my cheek and on my eyes and I answered her. "A scar on the flesh is healed. A reminder of what you survived. It doesn't compare to the damages that a person internally endures."

She looked at me with a hand tucked beneath her chin, arm rested against the side of her seat. It wasn't often that she was the one asking the questions and I was the one answering them so openly. We'd come a long way—she'd brought me a long way. She assisted me in finding what I knew and where I was now. And despite my own damages, internal and otherwise, I was grateful to her.

"I'm glad you see it that way," she said. It wasn't an agreement, and I smiled knowing that what came next was likely to assure me that it wasn't. "But I think that beautiful face having to bear an atrocious scar is just as real of a catastrophe. Also," she leaned forward and quickly made her move on the board, "checkmate. The old lady wins again."

"Is it really something to be proud of when you keep beating someone that you just taught the game to a little over two hours ago?" I asked with a grin as I began to reset the board. "And *catastrophe* is a strong term. It might be unfortunate, but I really don't mind it. Fate could hold worse things. A man meeting his end on the sidewalk as he walks to his car at night, that's worse," I said, knowing that she would know of the story that had been on the front page of the paper for nearly a week not long ago. "A woman dying and leaving her two kids behind who vanish in her absence," I added, thinking of the article that I'd read in the paper from her boxed of cherished belongings, *"that's* a catastrophe. Tragedies happen constantly. Over the past decades, centuries, there have been far worse things to have happened than my face being altered by a non-fatal wound."

I'd seen so much of the bad, that I was learning how to see the good in it. You had to find the light that you could in all the desolation. Otherwise, everything was hopeless. My scar was the least of my concerns as I waded through the mess and confusion of life. It bothered others more than it bothered me, but I refused to be selfish enough to think that I couldn't have been given worse. I didn't want life to prove to me what it possessed—not any more than it already had. The fact that I wasn't dead from finding myself beneath an enraged man with a knife was the light that I was determined to hang onto. I'd escaped with my life, and with scars.

I'd been saved by the walking image of destruction that life could deliver.

"Fine," she relented as she watched me pointlessly arrange the board. She knew there was no time for another game—and we both knew that she wouldn't play with Jane. "Perhaps it isn't a catastrophe. But you know what is?"

I quirked a brow at her as I set both queens back to their starting positions. "What is?"

"That hair that you didn't even *attempt* to fix with the rollers I gave you. That's a catastrophe. All that potential, just wasted. You're wasteful," she affectionately admonished as she reached for her glass again, draining it just in time for Jane to walk in the door.

I laughed at her persistence and the fact that she held her glass above her head for Jane to take notice of and grab to refill—which she did. "I suppose we'll have to consider this a stalemate. I don't see either of us changing our minds about what classifies as a catastrophe."

"When you get to be my age, you don't bother to do much more changing. You're the young and beautiful one that still has plenty of time to do all the changing she wants to; change your mind, change your hair, or change nothing and stay the same. The option becomes futile the closer it comes to expiring."

I stared where I stood, looking down at the face that had lived a long life that she'd loved. And when she broke into a smile, I knew that she was still spending every moment she could doing something she loved.

"Are you manipulating me into fixing my hair? And smiling because you know it's working?" I asked as I grabbed my keys from beside the door.

"The best thing about being this old is that I can use the death card as much as I want to. That's another thing that won't change. So, get used to it, and have that hair done the next time I see you!" she called as I opened the door and stepped out.

"For you, it will be," I agreed before closing the door.

I walked to my car, the aging Ford reflecting all the light that the stars and moon were supplying. I didn't notice the person sitting on the back of it until they jumped off as I approached, my heart lurching before I could make out who it was.

"Luke? What are you doing here?" I asked as I propped a hand against the top of the car, the other clutching my racing chest.

"It's date night," he said as if that explained everything. I scowled at his smile that caught the same glint of the night's light.

"I know, but that means that you're going out with Roman. Doesn't it?"

I put my back against the passenger window. The last time the car was parked here, it remained overnight. I had to come get it the day after Luke had delivered me home. Gray hadn't asked questions as he drove me to the car, but instead let me control the temperature and radio and talked along the drive as if everything were usual. I didn't want that experience to become the usual. I shouldn't have parked the car in the same spot.

"Not tonight. I thought we might do something together, instead. I didn't feel right having you cover for me again after what happened last time."

I could barely see the eyes that I was looking up into through the dark. My keys stopped spinning around my finger as I tried to capture the eyes that I could feel searching for my battered cheek.

"Nobody is to blame for what happened except for one person," I replied. Then I thought about how my choice to go there was my own. "Or two. But regardless, it's fine. You're free to go do something that you actually want to. Have fun. You don't have to entertain me out of pity," I said with a smile that I wasn't sure he could see.

"It isn't pity, and it could be fun," he clarified. I could hear the contained excitement in his voice, and both my curiosity and reservations spiked. "So why don't we go find the fun together?"

I hesitated with my answer. I knew that I had hours that I'd intended to waste without him. I was happy to not be lonely and to spend my time with what I knew was good, entertaining company. But agreeing to whatever it was that he wasn't telling me was my only qualm. One that I could get past, knowing that nothing he could plan would be worse than the time I've spent in my own suspicious house the last few days.

"Okay," I decided, stuffing my keys into the front pocket of my pants that also held my knife. "You drive."

He grabbed my hand, immediately setting us toward the destination only he knew. "We don't have to drive," he said as he laced his fingers into mine. It felt more like he was assuring that I couldn't get away rather than a comforting, friendly action. "We're only going a couple of blocks away."

"Back to—"

"The House of Sarris? Exactly," he said as he continued to easily drag me along.

I didn't want to put up a fight about it. I was drawn to the house, my curious soul always in search of the answers it knew to live there. I was interested to know what gave him the idea to go where it was that I'd always gone on these nights that I was left with too much time and secrets to hide for him.

"Why there?" I asked as I squeezed his hand in return, letting him know that I wasn't planning to stop or run. He loosened his hold, leaving our fingers interlocked as we crossed the road to the block where the transformed church was.

"Why not? Don't you go there all the time?" I could hear the smile behind his question; the insinuations behind what he wasn't saying. My face grew red, shielded by the dark that we were nearing the end of as we walked the sidewalk.

"Not all the time," I said defensively. "I came here when I had nowhere else to go, or no other choice." Forced by lack of option or lack of control, those were the times I'd found myself at the House of Sarris.

"Well tonight, we're here by choice, choosing the experiences that this place provides over all the others," he said as he turned us to the sidewalk toward the front door. "Doing something fun together."

I watched him as he knocked on the door, still not letting go of my hand as we waited together for an answer.

"And what are we meant to be doing in there together that's so fun?" I asked. My heart remembered to beat quickly in the vicinity of this house. It picked up its pace now that I was entirely sober and alert, recalling all it had learned and endured behind that closed door. It knew to prepare itself for anything. Everything.

I could make out the motion of his brows as he responded to my question with an exaggeration of its meaning. The red that returned to my face was as uncontrollable as the fact that I was facing another night of unknowns.

The door opened and Nora's face appeared, darker than its usual shade of light brown from the night's shadows that she looked toward.

"Michael said that you'd be coming," she said to Luke. An interested smile grew on her face, one side of her lips pulling up and raising her left brow. "You're a welcome surprise, though," she directed toward me before she stepped out of the way and let us through.

Why was I the surprise when I was here more often than Luke, usually alone? They all knew me by now, had saved me from the same man twice and brought me along to witness their debauchery. Had pieced me back together in this very house, and knew of my father just as they knew of me. I was no stranger even if I didn't belong. I was wedged into this circle as a sharp and jagged piece, unfitting and sticking out. But I didn't think of my presence here as surprising at this point.

Then I saw that it wasn't a surprise that I'd shown up— it was a surprise because of *when* I'd shown up.

The sound came first, the loud buzzing of machinery that felt like it vibrated and charged the air. It was foreign, a noise I couldn't put an image to, until we walked into the big room and saw the source in Michael's hand.

A man sat backwards on a metal folding chair, facing us and the rest of the room's inhabitants as Michael tattooed ink into the skin of his shoulder. Michael smiled as he worked, focused but keeping conversation with the man he worked on. I turned to Luke, worried and surprised now for myself.

"Tattoos?" I said as quietly as I could beneath the loud, electric sound. I pulled my hand away from his, sticking my hands into my pockets to hide the anxious movements of my fingers. "This is what you had in mind for us to do together?"

"Fun, isn't it?" He said with an uncontrollable grin. He had more excitement than I did doubts, looking to Michael and his machine with longing.

"No, not fun," I admonished as I shook my head and looked around to ensure nobody else was watching us. A room full of familiar faces and some strangers, and the only person watching us was Adam. "You didn't expect me to actually get one, did you?"

"I don't know." He shrugged as he pulled his attention away from the tattooing and settled it on me. "I thought maybe since you're going to wear those scars permanently, that you might want to have the option to choose something that you'll have for the rest of your life. Willingly, since those scars didn't come by choice."

My body now had marks that I'd never wanted, and his guilt over it had brought us here. It was a feeling and obligation to compensate that I wished he didn't have. I reached forward, putting my hands around his neck as I embraced the body of a sympathetic soul.

"I promise you that I'm okay with the scars," I told him, my tender cheek pressed against his shoulder. "I don't need anything more. My choice is to move on from it. And I've had my fill of needles for a little while."

"Are you sure?" he asked as he put his hand to the top of my head, lightly rubbing his fingers into my hair. The pain of my scalp was dull, forgotten in the midst of the other injuries I'd had to acknowledge and keep up with. "Because we can get matching ones. I'll even let you pick what we get. I'll just put it somewhere it will remain hidden."

"I'm sure," I told him as I pulled away and patted his chest. I was growing used to how it felt to be held by trusted arms. Our friendship had given me more comfort than he knew. Something so needed born of something I'd avoided. "So, pick whatever you want. It's your body that you're going to wear it on forever. Better make it something good."

"Your name? Just right across my chest?" he teased, gesturing to his heart with a finger as he walked backwards away from me, toward the seats where Nora and Rachelle sat with two other men.

"No evidence that I was involved," I said with a grin, pointing back at him. "Your mother will kill the both of us."

He winked before he turned, finding his seat beside Nora and slipping into easy conversation. He was more comfortable here than I was, not concerned about the impression he'd make on the people he didn't know that were mixed with the people he barely knew. Luke was unreserved. Luke knew who he was, and liked it.

I was still searching, unsure of what I should do or where I should go as I stood there watching Michael place permanent pictures into the man's skin. The only thing the lost woman that I was knew for certain was that I didn't want to be the person in that chair as I watched the burly man attempt to hide his grimace beneath the work of the needles.

I looked away from the stranger, knowing that it was rude to stare at the pain he tried to hide. I'd give him what privacy he could find in this large, open room. My eyes found Adam instead, beckoning me over with a single gesture of the hand that was reached across the back of the couch he sat on. I complied, my steps leading me farther away from Luke and the ones that sat on the other side of the room.

Three strange men sat with Adam, taking up the couches around him. The only open seats were beside Adam and someone that I didn't know, so I settled into the former. He turned to me, placing a finger beneath my chin to tilt my head the way he wanted to as he looked carefully at his and Axel's work.

"How does it feel?" he asked as he inspected the sutures he'd placed, gently pressing his thumb around the sensitive wound.

"Better than it did." My eyes caught one of the men across from us watching, and I quickly averted my eyes from his and rested them on Adam's close face. I looked at his scar—one like I would soon be left with. His added to his ferocity. Mine would add to all the proof of the ways that I was weak.

"It's healing well. Nothing ripped or infected. Your inclination to follow all the orders that you're given is paying off," he said as he pulled back from my face, letting his finger fall from my chin and to my arm. He grabbed my wrist, setting my arm on his leg as he repeated the process. "Did you keep them both covered for the first twenty-four hours?"

"All day long on Saturday," I answered. I hissed as he touched on a spot near the end of the cut, the flesh there more sore than the rest. My hand reached for his and halted his prodding.

"Does that spot hurt the worst?" he asked. I nodded my head as I watched him tentatively touch it again. "It's more red there than anywhere else. I'll clean it and give you something else to put on it."

"What happened?" the man asked. He put his lips around what I thought to be a cigarette, but the smell of it told me that it wasn't. I scrunched my nose at the unexpected scent before trying to compose myself, not wanting to be insulting.

"Knife fight," Adam said curtly as he looked up from the white imprint of his thumb on my arm that kept fading back to red upon release. "The other guy lost."

It was a short version of the truth without all the details in between. It wasn't a fight, because I could hardly fight back. The other guy lost because I was saved and he had his strength—and sight—taken from him. The answers that Adam gave painted a simple picture that made me out to seem stronger than I was. That left out the many images in the real scene that would have shown the man how weak I was.

"He must be in rough shape if he ended up having it worse than you," he said as his laxed and red-rimmed eyes focused on my cheek. Of all the people I'd seen since I'd acquired these cuts and these stitches, he was the one who stared the most openly. No discomfort in knowing that he was looking right at the evidence of an obviously painful memory. I felt more bashful beneath his eyes than he did at his own impropriety.

"I'll go get my things," Adam said as he placed my arm on my lap. He left me waiting, sitting in a group of people that I didn't know and wasn't sure of. The two men having their own conversation weren't of concern, but the one with his eyes fixed on my torn face was content with the silent discomfort he was giving me. I adjusted in my seat, trying to turn my face away from his sight. I remained beneath his watch, the weight of a stare too invested in its target, until I finally stood and left.

An easy enough situation to escape, I followed the direction I'd seen Adam go through the side doors. I walked down the hall toward where the kitchen was, not sure of which of the closed doors lining the walls he could have disappeared behind. I looked into the kitchen, the only room that I knew I could peer into without prying, and the dark assured his absence. As I shut the door, the one across the hall from me opened.

"I didn't want to wait there. I didn't like the way he was staring at me," I admitted as Adam looked at me from his doorway with his case in hand. It was an excuse he hadn't asked for, and one I probably didn't have to give. But the sight of me looking into a closed door was one that I felt the need to explain.

"Battered women seem like easy targets to men who look for that type of shit," he said as he put the case on what I assumed was a table behind the wall in the room I couldn't see in. "Come on."

He turned back around and moved behind the wall, and I followed to stand in the doorway. It was a dark room with a bed, a table beside it, a chair in the corner with a small bookshelf beside it, and a desk near the window. Everything was too tidy, appearing untouched aside from the unmade bed, the book atop the bookshelf, and the full ashtray with a lighter next to it. As grateful as I was to be away from impolite eyes, I was very aware of the amount of privacy we had in here. My heart thudded against the reminders of what transpired in intimate spaces.

"In your bedroom? Just to clean my arm?" I asked. I could hear the subtle shake in my attempt at a quiet voice, and his head turned to me at the sound of it.

"Unless you have something else in mind." There was no smile to tell me if it was a joke or not. No quirk of a brow or indication that I could reign in my thunderous pulse at the suggestion. My hands were clasped together, showing him all my hesitations as they rubbed nervously back and forth against each other. He looked to where they fumbled and back to my eyes.

"Don't be nervous," he said as he guided me into the room by the shoulder, shutting the door behind me. My back was pressed to it as he grabbed my hands and looked into my concerned eyes. "All we're in here for is to clean your arm. Unless you change your mind."

He pulled me by the hand and sat me on the edge of the bed. I moved back until my legs hung against the sides, my feet not touching the floor. My heart was still sputtering as he retrieved the brown bottle from his case and pulled out a folded cloth. My insides were turning on me, making me feel the excitement of the forbidden feelings he'd once shown me. The familiar warmth of desire that pooled at his insinuation.

"Change my mind?" I asked as he pressed the saturated cloth to my arm. I could feel the sting, the pain mixing with the wanting that I knew I shouldn't pursue. It was hard to turn away when the pleasure that I knew was achievable was trying to piece itself together within me. All I could manage were questions that I knew would lead to more.

"Yes. Change your mind," he repeated as he stood up to put the cloth away and grab a salve. "You're allowed to suddenly decide that you want something that you thought you didn't."

I watched him rub a portion of it over my healing cut and aging stitches. The back and forth of the light touch of his finger made me suck in air at the slight soreness and the vivid recollection of his fingers guiding mine much the same. I couldn't push the memory from my head, couldn't force myself to understand that I shouldn't want what I did in the midst of other problems. There was too much going on outside these walls, outside this house, for me to be so fixated on wanting something so selfish. My own feelings were adding to all the confusion.

"Genevieve," he said as he sat beside me, turning my body to him as he taped a temporary covering over the finished cut he'd cared for. "You don't get what you want unless you ask for it."

It was on my tongue as he smoothed his palm over my bandaged arm. To ask him for just one more taste of the euphoria that he'd shown me, that all I would need to get past this muddled moment was just a few more minutes that showed me that good and pleasurable things existed on this same earth as the dark and the violent. I could feel the heat of my face melting into every other corner of my body. He could see it, and he was waiting.

"Adam, I need you to find out if Ste—" the voice said that barged in the door, making me jump beneath Adam's hold on my arm. Othello looked between the two of us, silenced by the sight as he rested his gaze on my face. My red, guilty face.

"I'm sorry, I—" Cut off by the hand Othello held up, my words remained trapped by the lips that couldn't confess their longings, but only their desperate apologies.

"I've told you to stop being sorry," he said as he shut the door. I swallowed, trying to remove the lump in my throat. Its only useful purpose was blocking another apology of the guilt I felt. I looked at Adam, his face unfazed as he watched every move I made in this delicate situation.

"He doesn't care," Adam said as he moved his hand down my arm, fingers stopping over mine. "You're the only one here that's bothered by what you want. And we can easily see what it is you want."

I closed my eyes, breathing heavily in and out with the building heat of the room. I was the only one affected by the sweltering of the space, and I knew exactly what thoughts I was walking into when I stepped inside. I knew that I could give in—I knew that I would. I was only prolonging it the longer I fought it.

I opened my eyes that felt heavy with the hold my body had over them. They focused on Othello as my hand turned over beneath Adam's and laced his fingers into mine. The world outside was selfish at the expense of others. Here, I could be selfish without cost.

"Teach me." The only two words I could manage to expel from the vessel that was my body, consumed by emotion. The only two words it took for Othello to come and lift me from the bed, and stand me before him. My hand dragged Adam to stand behind me, our interlaced fingers hanging at my side.

"Tell me what you want to be taught," Othello said as he lifted my chin up to look at him. My breathing was labored, the space that I stood in between the two of them small and familiar. The heat that my body felt burnt nearly as much as Othello's gaze did.

"Teach me what it's like to feel this with someone else." The breathless words escaped my lips, the very things I so desperately wanted him to place his upon. I wanted the pleasure they'd shown me, and I wanted it to be shared. My desires were to give as well as receive. "Show me that it can't be wrong to feel this, to want this so much. Because I'm afraid that it is."

"I'll give you what your fear is forcing you to miss out on," he said as he lowered his lips in front of mine. "Take the leap, Dove, and I'll guide your fall."

I pulled Adam's arm around me as I pressed my mouth to Othello's. The soft touch of lips that moved against mine for the first time brought a moan from my throat, and Othello's fingers gripped my chin in response. He deepened the kiss, pushing our lips to wrap around the open spaces of each other and feel every rough movement. He halted the action of our mouths, capturing my bottom lip between his teeth. I melted into the sudden pain, my free hand reaching around his head to lock my fingers in his hair. I didn't want him to move, or the ache that he was stirring to end.

He released my lip and held onto my chin as he spoke to me, his voice steadier than my heart would likely ever be again. "You tell me what you want by returning what you like."

Reactive, hungry, my mouth found his again and took his lip between my teeth, biting to share the pain that spurred me on. The groan he emitted traveled through me, lips to feet that lost their solid grip. My legs buckled, and I was caught by his hands on my hips. Solidified, and reminded that this was real. What I'd always been taught to avoid was being taught to me in seductive steps.

My tongue darted out, licking the marks that I'd left beneath his lip. He let me caress him tenderly before his own tongue caught mine, bringing it into his mouth and tangling us together in a second that set my patience ablaze. My hands wrapped around his neck, pulling him into me as I greedily absorbed all that he was showing me.

His hands left my hips and pushed my shoulders back, breaking us apart and pressing my body back against Adam. "Now show him what you've learned."

My eyes searched his, lips opened in loss of breath and the weight of the abuse they weren't accustomed to. It felt wrong to want what he was telling me I could have. I searched for reassurance in his expression, and when he offered me nothing more than that one direction, Adam tilted my face back to him, raised by his fingers beneath my chin.

"Do you want this, Genevieve?" he asked, his hand across my stomach splaying its fingers over the warmth I gave off. "Tell me that you want to share." He put his mouth next to my ear, and my hand on Othello's neck dug its fingernails into his flesh. "Tell me you're wet with the thought of tasting us both."

I turned around and set my mouth on his, the rush of improper words fueling the desires that I was giving up fighting. Nothing seemed okay about wanting to share the experience with them both, the first time that I was sharing my lips with another. But my thoughts were fading as my feelings grew, being muted by the permission to have what I want. Take what I was offered. Forget what I was told I shouldn't know.

Our lips fought, the back and forth of giving everything we could to show how badly we each wanted to win. I took his lip between mine, showing him what winning was to me—feeling him give me what I craved. He raveled his hand into my hair and yanked my head away from him, setting his lips on my neck. The sting of my hair being pulled sent a jolt through me, making me press myself against his leg in response. The noise that came from my throat wasn't me, but the ravenous creature they were freeing.

His teeth bit the flesh of my neck, and I reached out and captured Othello's arm. He held onto me, his hand over my bandaged wound tightly squeezing and showing me just how good it could feel to drown myself in the delights of pain.

"Have you learned what you wanted?" Othello asked as he pulled my face toward him while Adam placed his tongue and lips on the base of my neck, sucking on the sensitive skin above my collarbone. The sharp pull that was centered beneath his mouth made the breath hiss from my lips and forced my grip on both of them to tighten.

"Yes." I was satisfied with what he'd given, what they'd shown me, what we'd all shared. I knew there was more to have, the throbbing between my legs that pressed against Adam's thigh begged me to seek it out.

"Then take what you've been given, and use it for yourself," he said as he released my arm and Adam pulled away from his place on my neck. They both let me go and walked to the door, leaving me alone in the room that they shut me in. My legs shook, missing the stability that their bodies had offered me. I sat on the edge of the bed, my head spinning from the quick succession of emotions and the sudden abandonment. The longing lingered, and Othello's words repeated themselves to me.

I wasn't abandoned. I was told to be selfish.

I was given the opportunity to use all the desire they'd built, take all they'd shown me, and keep it for myself. My fingers traced over the area that Adam's mouth had been, pressing into the bruised skin he'd left me with. The pain propelled my fingers to travel down my body as I laid back on the bed, shutting my eyes to recall every immoral step that had been shown to me by the experienced—the ones who knew their way through selfish sin.

As the fingers of my right hand reached the path Adam had once shown me, my left hand came up to my mouth to touch my tender lips. I pictured Othello's mouth upon me, seducing the building pleasure in my body to break free and spill over. The dampened fingers between my legs slid back and forth, remembering every indelicate movement that Adam had guided me with.

I could smell the smoke of the room, embedded in the sheets, like poison that my body craved. It wanted a pleasured end, to wither here in the scent of Adam and to let all that Othello had taught me bring finality. My closed eyes imagined the release I was building up to, wanting it to be the last thing my body ever felt. Covered in pain, holding on to what I had left of my tortured soul, I wanted this feeling to set me free entirely. To leave me lying here in the dangerous place where I'd found corruption, and I'd found safety.

My fingers squeezed my lips as my quickening hand forced a cry from my mouth. I didn't want the pleasure without the pain that made it real, and my voice carried the sound of both throughout the empty room. I met the height of bliss, and the edge I leapt over made my body arch and my left hand grip the bed. The wound on my arm throbbed as it was pressed into the mattress, the ache and the euphoria tearing an uncontrollable scream from my throat.

The fingers lingering in the wet traces of desire slowed as my body trembled and twitched, my muscles untensing themselves and my system attempting to regain its composure. I laid there, still alive and not taken by the ideal escape. I'd leapt, and the iniquitous things that Othello taught me had guided my fall—all the way back to the earth I was still burdened to walk on.

I pulled my hand from its indecent place, and stood on the feet that would have to walk through another day of uncertainties. If only I could have been carried away by the ecstasy of those fleeting minutes; free of fear and forever existing on a feeling that's true instead of stuck in the life of a lie.

The knob beneath my hand turned, allowing me back to the reality I walked into through the open door. Adam and Othello stood in the hall, each with their back against a wall, halting whatever conversation they'd been having—silent or otherwise. I looked at Adam, the cigarette in his mouth providing me with the scent that my body now registered as arousing. Then to Othello, where my stare lingered on the face that knew what I needed and chose when to give it to me. That knew the answers I sought and the lessons that could be taught only by a life he guided.

I looked at the man that I knew to know everything that I didn't.

"Is it wrong for that to be the only feeling that doesn't make life seem worthless? It doesn't make sense to be able to feel that good when everything else in the world is terrible." My question made them exchange looks, and Adam took a drag as Othello lowered his brows and focused back on me.

"Fuck, Genevieve," Adam said, expelling the smoke held in his mouth with his words. "You're especially messed up if coming leaves you with thoughts as bleak as that."

My face turned shades, hating that he was confirming what I'd assumed of myself. I felt messed up, like I was doing the things wrong that they knew how to do so well. Want, acquire, be careless, be selfish. I thought I had been wrong to want what I wanted during the heat of the moment—but I was wrong to think what I thought after it was done. I couldn't hang on to selfish pleasures the way they could.

"Why does it scare you when you feel so alive?" Othello asked. I watched him wait for my answer, sifting through the information I thought out before I gave it. He was in my mind just the same as I was.

"Because I'm afraid that this is the best it gets. Temporary comfort from all the horrible things that I'm meant to spend my entire life trying to avoid and ignore." It wasn't just the pleasure I found with them, but the sick solace that was provided to me in the darkest ways. I'd found unexpected safety when I strayed.

"It's only temporary because you keep choosing to return to the life you want to run from," Adam said. I could see him inspecting my cheek while I looked at him, but whatever he wanted to say he didn't. "You'd stay alive if you abandoned the dying life you're holding on to."

My dying life. The structured one that was crumbling and turning to dust in the wake of its secret and the parts that I could admit that I didn't miss. I was separated, I felt disconnected from all of it and the people that I thought I knew. But there was one detail that kept me attached, kept me holding on to the only good that remained and fed light to my soul.

Gray.

"If I left it all, I'd be leaving everything. And some things don't deserve to be abandoned." My words were lined with insinuations, but Othello read between them. He saw the struggle in my eyes that thought of the one thing that kept me distanced from giving over to everything I wanted. I would wade through the life I feared so long as it meant I was with the one thing worth enduring it for.

Othello's head turned as Nora walked in the side doors. I took in his perfect profile, overcome with the reliance I had for a man that had given me more reasons to remain terrified of him than to trust him. His appearance attracted me the way that it should, but his resilience attracted me the way that it shouldn't. I fell for every word of wisdom he'd given me, and would continue to do so for as long as he'd spare me his knowledge. I followed who I feared the way that Gray followed the man that he didn't know to fear. I did so willingly; he did so blindly.

"Company's gone," Nora told Othello as she opened the kitchen door. "Luke and Genevieve are the only ones here."

He nodded his head, accepting an update on the house's activity as if it were normal for a home to be run this way. But it was more than just a home, it was a place of business, and Othello was the one whom all information was run through.

Othello looked to Adam before starting off down the hall, and I placed my back against the door to Adam's room as I watched him leave.

"He wants you to follow him," Adam said as he put out the half-smoked cigarette on the wood of his door frame, leaving a circular mark that looked like it belonged to the wood's grain.

"Then why didn't he say that?" I asked as I fell into step beside Adam as we both followed Othello down the hall.

"He did." He looked down at me as he placed the saved cigarette behind his ear. "Just not to you."

The secrets the two of them could share between their minds didn't concern me, though they were often about me. I knew the two of them spoke of me in their silent thoughts, the exchanges of looks and the agreements they made with mute conversations. I couldn't catch up to their abilities, and I was too sober to be brave enough to try. They could secretly speak of me as they pleased—it didn't affect me the way that the spoken secrets in my life did.

"I must not be meant to read thoughts the way you are," I said. Othello left the hallway through the side doors, our steps unrushed as we followed far behind.

"Or you're just too full of your own thoughts, already." He pulled back the hair from over my shoulder. His eyes focused on my neck, and I assumed he was looking at the mark his lips had left me. "All those same thoughts that kept you from touching yourself up until now."

My feet stopped. I looked at him, unsure if I'd heard him correctly until I played his words again over and over in my head. He stood with me, waiting for me to either continue or respond.

"How would you know that?" My eyes looked down, seeing my own body that felt so exposed although it was covered. There were no thoughts hidden from Othello, no facts hidden from Adam. I was opened to them both in ways that I wasn't opened to myself. If I wasn't meant to understand it, then at least they filled me in.

"Because you would have thought it was wrong to do something that made you feel that good in a house that makes you feel so bad." He took a step closer to me, setting two fingers over the bruise he left that I couldn't see. "Your feelings are just one more thing that you're afraid of. But I'm sure it didn't keep you from thinking about the way I showed you to touch yourself. Did it?"

His eyes lifted from my neck and peered into mine. He found the answer there that I wouldn't admit to the otherwise empty hallway. His fingers pressed into the sore area he caressed, and my breath exhaled with an audible whimper.

"And you like the pain because it makes you feel like you aren't going unpunished for the sinful things you're doing." He didn't bother to ask if he was right. The eyes that I didn't avert from him let him see everything that he wanted to know—everything he already did. "Only somebody that's giving themselves over to something they see as wicked screams like that." He traced his thumb over the lips that I'd surrendered to him, that shared the things Othello had taught me. "Did it feel so good to do something so impure? Did you find out for yourself just how good forbiddance tastes?"

He brought my hand up to his mouth and placed my fingers on his lips. Knowing where they'd been, the slow stroke of his tongue over the traces that were left of their fleshly exploration felt intimate. My fingers wanted to curve into his mouth, keep him from removing them from the warmth of his tongue. But he pulled them away, holding onto my hand as he smiled at the panting that escaped from my open lips.

"Because depravity is a flavor worth craving."

His head turned to look down the hall, and mine followed to see Nora standing outside the kitchen door. She faced us, and I didn't know what she saw or if she'd seen anything, but the thought of it made me flush with embarrassment.

"Is her watching me put your fingers in my mouth any different than Othello watching me get you off?" He was humored by the humiliation I couldn't remove from my face. I tried to walk away, but his hold on my hand just dragged him along with me. "You're already drawn to depravity, and Othello is the walking incarnation of it."

Othello was the vision of everything I wasn't meant to know, see, or want—but did.

"And if he's depravity, then what does that make you?" I asked as I opened the side doors. Adam was cunning, stealthy enough to be the gatherer of all the information someone as depraved as Othello would need. The same wicked tendencies led by depravity are what Adam had.

"The product of depravity's influence," he answered, pulling me to him when we entered the big room. There was no sound of the buzzing machine and fewer bodies than there were when I arrived. It felt more like the eerie place that I first thought it to be, and less like the home of chaos that I knew it was. "You broke a stitch."

"What?" I registered his hand on my cheek and brought mine up to it, as well. He pulled my fingers away, keeping me from touching or worsening the wound.

"It must have happened during all that aggression." He looked at it again, and I knew this was what he wasn't telling me earlier. He hadn't wanted to add any stress to my overwhelmed moment. "I can stitch it again. Or it's safe enough to leave how it is if you can refrain from anymore activity that could result in it splitting open. Up to you."

I looked at Luke and the sheer joy on his face as he and Rachelle showed each other the marks they'd permanently placed on their bodies, indistinguishable ink from this distance. His place now in my life was as unexpected as this night was, as was the fact that he was here with me and smiling in a place that most people avoided. We'd both somehow befriended the members of society avoided by most, brought to understandings by closeted encounters and violent occurrences. I didn't know what I could and couldn't refrain from, because I was already here and becoming something that I hadn't expected to be.

"I'm not making any promises."

"Not any that you can't keep," he clarified. He pushed his hair back, looking back at the side doors we'd just come from. "I'll go get my stuff. I hope to fuck this is the last time I have to fix you. I don't think I've ever met anyone so damn breakable."

Fragile, delicate, that's all that I knew how to be. My body, my emotions, my faith and mind and trust. Each would show me how quickly they could come and go, and how easily I could fall apart. I also hoped that I wouldn't have to be put back together again, and not just by the stitching of a skilled hand. I didn't want the last whole pieces left in my life to break and take me with them.

I watched Othello talk to Michael, their positions relaxed as the machine between them was unused. Othello caught me watching, and held up a finger to Michael before standing up to come to me. Michael began to change and clean utensils, setting his things up for more work to be done.

"How do you feel about permanence?" Othello asked, his stone face not giving any more details to his question. My eyes flitted between him and Michael setting up for another tattoo. My heart raced, knowing how easily coerced I was by the man who got what he wanted, and my desperation to be who gave it.

"I can't get a tattoo," I told him—far too weakly. My words came out with notice that they could be easily converted. He smiled, and the resulting panic snaked through me like venom. I would cave if he asked me again. He knew it.

"And you don't have to." He looked at the place of my cheek that was undone by physical exertion, and I looked at the lips that'd sent me into a frenzy so encompassing that I hadn't noticed the broken stitch. "Permanence of loyalty. A permanent place where you can be assured that you belong, and come to when you're running from the life that you can't let go of. Permanent protection." He placed his hands in his pockets, as calm as if he weren't listing off life's most significant offers. "What do you think of permanence?"

I wanted that something that I could depend on when the rest of the world was undependable. Something that didn't make me feel wrong after spending my whole life doing everything and more to always be right, live right, and do right by those that expected it of me. I wanted the safety that came with being shielded by the ruthless, the vicious, and the remorseless. The unforgiving was offering me loyalty, belonging, and protection—all the things that a lost soul longed for.

"I think it's what I'm missing," I admitted. My fingers reached for my lip, roughly grabbing the already abused flesh of it. The pain steered me away, forcing my fingers to drop to the thin chain on my neck. I immediately let go of it, aware of my anxious fumbling and that I couldn't rely on its comfort anymore. Othello followed my movements with watchful, dark eyes, observing my inability to control my telling habits just as I couldn't control anything else. I needed him. I needed the assurance of permanent things in my life after all the stability I had turned out to be temporary.

He grabbed my hand, and led me over to stand beside the empty seat and Michael's table of prepared machinery. I forced my feet to stand still and not relay the nerves I felt from whatever I was waiting for. Michael's smile as Othello pulled the knife from his pocket didn't calm me any. I looked between them both, and felt the imprint of the knife that was in my own, doing little to reassure me. I couldn't reach it even if I wanted to. Even if I needed to.

"Are you willing to trust me the way that you've learned that you can't trust anyone?" Othello asked, opening the blade and laying its edge against his palm. He wrapped his hand around it, and I waited for blood to appear through the seams.

No blood came.

His control, the way the world bent to his will and blades did no harm unless he bid them to—that's what I could trust. He openly displayed how he wasn't like any other person I'd lost my trust in, because he bared what everyone else hid. He didn't lie about who he was, what he wanted, or the unfavorable things he did. I trusted him for all the reasons that the rest of the world didn't, because I found in him everything that I didn't have. Everything that I didn't know to look for. Everything that I was warned not to.

He was asking if I could find it in me to give to him what I'd lost because of everything else.

"Yes." I could. I was willing to give to him whatever I was able after all he'd given me. Taught me. Shown me. Saved me from. I was willing to accept the inimitable favor of permanence—but I knew all favors came at a price.

"Give me your hand." His instructions came with an open palm, and I tentatively placed mine in it. The blade touched my offered flesh, and the magnitude of my offering became apparent. He was offering me all I wanted, but I was giving him something undefined in exchange. My fingers curled above the knife, my body fearing what my mind was set on doing.

"I'm not asking for your soul, Dove. Just your blood." I looked up to his mouth that spoke words so serious I swore that I could see them written on the air between us. *Not your soul.* There was respite in knowing what he wasn't wanting, but concern in my thoughts that said that it wouldn't have mattered. Would I not have given anything? "If you spare yours for me, I'll spill mine for you."

One strongly stated word of consent, and the blade carved its way across my palm. The lack of fight that accompanied this wound made every ounce of pain stand out, every burn and sting of skin willingly harmed. The blood draining from my head was rushing to my opened palm, which Othello held as he placed it over a small container of ink. One drop, two drops, three drops more fell from my hand and mixed into the dense color that Michael pulled away with a smile and began stirring.

I looked back to Othello as he tilted my hand back up and released me to remove the faded black shirt he wore. He placed the bundled cloth in my hand, pressing it down over the opened cut. My lungs gradually began to slowly intake the air I remembered they needed. My head was spinning, but I didn't lose focus on Othello as he pulled his hands away from mine, watching me as he licked my blood from the side of his thumb.

He sat down in the chair, his exposed chest and abdomen revealing all the tattooed marks always covered by his clothing. He watched me sway on my feet, and hands on my shoulders steadied me as they walked me back to sit down—on the altar steps that led to the unused stage. Adam tied the shirt around my hand, tightening the fabric's pressure meant to stop my sacrificed blood.

Othello's eyes remained on me, and I couldn't take mine from him. I couldn't focus on the previously placed ink that I wanted to see, or the final preparations Michael made before he wiped down the skin above Othello's collarbone. I could see, but all I could think of was how ceremonial every step of this felt.

"You're in it now," Michael said before returning the buzzing sound back to the room. "Welcome to the family."

He set the machine to Othello's prepared skin, the unseen needles penetrating the sensitive area of the base of his neck. My uncut hand reached to my own neck, tracing my fingers over the mirrored spot on my body. Where Michael was placing the ink that contained my blood, my own blood was pooled beneath the skin of my fingers. The bruise Adam's lips and Othello's teachings had left me with was my temporary mark that matched the permanent one Othello was receiving.

"I think maybe I just did something unforgiveable," I said aloud as Adam put his hands to my face to fix one of the many impaired parts of my body. I couldn't keep the pieces of myself together that I already possessed. My blood would be better cared for in the body of the invincible.

"You're in the perfect place to ask for forgiveness and find out," he replied as he pushed the needle quickly through my cheek. Eye-opening words like that forced mine shut, and I searched pointlessly for the ability to do such a thing. Of all the things I'd done wrong, asking for forgiveness over something that I didn't feel guilty about seemed the worst. Othello had promised himself and all he had to me in exchange for a small portion of my living body. The blood that ran through me was plentiful, as was the fear of the things he offered to keep me from. My small sacrifice wasn't the end of me.

Clarity was brought to my vision as I rested beneath the pain of Adam's needle and from Othello's blade. Hurting was becoming my natural state, and my body was becoming unnaturally accustomed to it. Was one person meant to feel this much, know this amount of injury and devastation, experience the mental toll of meeting the traumatizing faults of reality in only a couple of months? I wasn't new, but I was different. I wasn't whole, but I was still one person with one foot standing on each side of life's fine lines. I was still becoming—someone or something changed.

"Why would he do this for someone like me? Why would he make me a part of this?"

Adam continued unwrapping my hand, the finished stitch in my cheek only one of the injuries he now had to care for. He cleaned the excess blood with a white cloth, staining it with the crimson drained for a binding purpose.

"For the same reasons you're his dove," he answered as he poured the liquid of a brown bottle onto the cut. It reacted to the blood, white foam fizzling between the separated sides of my hand. "You're too pure to feel like you don't belong. Too good to deserve a life of fear. You symbolize everything that Othello isn't; you're the peace that was sent to the hands of mayhem. You brought the things that he doesn't have just like the good little messenger bird that you are. He'll give you everything in exchange for all he's taken."

"He's already given more than he's taken." I watched him close the simple cut with thin strips of tape. Somehow the wound that was easiest to fix was the most significant.

"You only think that because you don't know how to value the things you give." He sat beside me on the steps, pulling the half of the cigarette out from behind his ear. "You've given almost twenty-three years to a man who lies and taught you not to. A mother who thinks a child is a prop and not a person. You've given everything you had to perfection, an impossible charade to keep up with." He lit what remained of his choice of toxicity. His habit wasn't all that unlike mine, a vice that occupied the quiet and anxious moments. "You weren't acknowledged for the saint you are. Now the bad will save what remains of the good. He'll selfishly save what he knows doesn't belong to him."

"How can it be selfish if I want it?" Othello sat motionless beneath the needles, letting blood and ink flow beneath his skin without reluctance. He watched me observe, not understanding how he could sit so still beneath the carving of skin that I knew to be sensitive. My own tingled sympathetically.

"Because a snake isn't meant to keep a dove," Adam said, his smile growing around the smoldering stick in his mouth when I looked at him. He leaned forward, bracing his arms against his knees as he watched Othello stand from the chair. "But nobody rejects the unnatural, here."

Othello came over to Adam and me, and crouched down until he was at my eye level. The red skin of his neck surrounded the ink—the dove drawn with darkness and blood. Permanently placed, a promise made with my nature to give and his nature to own. Below his collarbone and beneath the dove was the image of a snake, and my eyes turned quickly back to Adam.

"So it is written," Adam said with a grin at the disbelief on my face. Othello's new dove, just above and out of reach of the open mouth of the snake. His body was marked with the traces of his life, and now I was one of them.

"No more fear of living," Othello said, capturing my attention as he put his hand on my shoulder, his thumb over the bruise on my neck. "No more holding down what wasn't intended to be grounded. Live, and I'll share with you all the life that I have."

He stood up, taking the shirt from beside me that was covered in blood and stained with the life I handed over in return for his. As it slipped over his head, falling around his neck and revealing that the dove remained high and exposed, I was able to make out the tattoo scrawled along the bottom of his stomach before it was hidden and covered.

Words that read like a motto, a demand that Othello's body silently gave.

Save yourself.

DUPLICITY

The house was quiet as I walked through the door, the late hours of the night not unsimilar to the usual order of a structured home during the day. I'd left my shift at Nancy's, no excuses of dates or other options to keep me from having to be here, silenced and unwanted. Each day that passed here was another where my secrets grew less heavy the longer I held onto my father's. I was becoming balanced by the weight of shared transgressions.

The dining room was brightly lit, the only room in the house that appeared to have light on. I peered around the corner, finding my mother sat at the table alone with a catalog in her hand. As expectable as the house's low volume.

"Where is everyone?" I asked her, making her head jerk up toward the doorway and her hand clutch her chest. Me being just as easily scared was a product of her raising.

"My goodness, Gene. I wasn't expecting you home already," she said as she flipped the page, the sound of it crinkling traveling through the room. I pulled a chair out across from her, opting to sit down instead of forcing myself into bed already.

"My shift ends at nine, and it's nine thirty," I told her, looking up at the clock that was on the wall behind her. It was set correctly, the second hand that moved proving that time didn't stand still in this house.

"Is it?" She asked her uninvested question and continued perusing her beloved pages. It was such a simple thing to be occupied with, and I wondered how long she'd been sat here looking through this one or one of the dozens she always had around. How was she so comfortably lost in the life I loathed?

"Where's Gray?" The ticking of the clock was more consistent than her attention was. Embroidering, browsing magazines, fulfilling the expected duties of a loyal wife were the things she devoted herself to. She was satisfied with her perfect life and didn't enjoy having it bothered.

"Son's with Amelia. He'll be home by midnight." Every whereabout able to be quoted, followed by the expectation of Gray to follow routine. Remain on schedule. Stay in line.

"And where's Father?" Why wasn't he here to wait on Gray the same way he always waited up for me? Were Gray and I to follow the same expectations, but with different enforcements? Or did my undisclosed failures reveal themselves to Father and keep him watching me closely, as closely as I'd been watching him? Everything here was the same, days repeated in and out with the refusal to change— and none of it felt right. Things shouldn't still be the same when I knew how different our lives were.

"He went up to the church for something," she answered vaguely. She wrote down something with the pen and paper beside her, and I watched the digits being drawn from my opposite angle. Backwards, upside down, just as we were. This life, our structure, the fact that she was okay with blindly trusting her husband when she shouldn't. Or maybe it wasn't trust—maybe it was the devotion of a wife who knew plenty and hid it just as well.

Here, I was still obedient and made the appearances of their perfect daughter. Here, I played the role that I was assigned and forced to memorize through a lifetime of repeated rules. But I was only still here because I had to be. I wouldn't leave Gray willingly behind when I didn't know what I would be leaving him to. But what was it that kept me from asking and saying what I wanted to? The chance of her seeing through the person I pretended to be? I shouldn't fear the odds when I wasn't the only one in this house pretending.

"When did you meet Father?" It was a simpler way of asking how well she knew the man that I didn't, how she found someone so perfect at pretending to be perfect, who condemned the wrong that he also committed.

She ceased the tapping of her teeth against the cap of the pen she had in her mouth. Her eyes remained on the paper, but mine stayed on her, waiting for all the answers that came from the things she wouldn't say. Why was such a normal question something she paused at?

"I've known him my entire life." She looked up at me and smiled, and I refused to hide the eyes that studied her lips. I wished that the lies she told were written across them, because her answer was perfectly believable. I didn't know how to smile through a lie, but that didn't mean she couldn't. "Almost like you and Luke. Why aren't you two together tonight like Son and Amelia?"

I couldn't sense a lie, but I knew when I was being avoided. I was used to avoidance. I avoided their disapproval, their wrath, their attention unless it was good. And they avoided me in return, only giving me notice when it was for their benefit. She was avoiding my question with one of her own.

"Luke is out of town," I told her, wondering if she would have heard a lie just the same. If I'd chosen that moment to tell her that Luke and I didn't care for each other the same way that Gray and Amelia did, would she notice? Her eyes and her attention were returned back to her routine, and I figured that she probably would, because she kept track of what she wanted—and the lie that Luke and I upheld was just that.

I opened my mouth to ask her more, to find out how two people so tirelessly set on remaining perfect in the eyes of all who looked upon them could have found each other. How does fate bring those people together, and then drop me in the center of surrounding souls so different? Before the words found their way out, before I could ask for the vague answers she'd give me regarding *how* just as she did *when*, the phone rang. An abrasive noise that stirred the tension in the room, loudly preventing any satisfaction I could have further found.

Mother stood and went to the phone, answering it with the sweetest of hellos. The start of her new conversation was the end of ours, and I left the room of insincere smiles to find direction of my own once again. She'd won the ability to avoid me and my inconvenience with the precise timing of the caller on the other end of the line.

I walked toward my room, set on remaining alone for the rest of the night. I'd give up the moment's desire to chase after what didn't want to be given to me, and settle for returning to my unbarred cage. A wooden door, four walls, and forced ignorance was as effective as a prison cell.

The hall walls were lined with few photos, our collection lacking in comparison to the dozens I could look through at the Hannigans' home. There were pictures of Gray and I when we were young, his little face holding all the innocence that he still retained. Our differences in appearance, hair color, and the gap in our age set us apart, as did the weakness of my soul and the resilience of his. But it didn't keep us from being close, remaining connected by the life we were both standing before and told to walk through together.

Only four more pictures through mine and Gray's changing ages, and one family picture of all four of us bearing smiles for the camera. As staged as it was, it reflected us well. My dark hair matched mother and father's, and Gray's fair hair made him the odd one out. I should have been the one that didn't look like I belonged. But then again, it was Gray's purpose to stand out and be the shining image of light.

No pictures of grandparents, no photos of more than just what my parents wanted any onlookers to see. The extensions of our life weren't meant to be looked into, and only the surface was provided as you walked this home and through these halls. The less they provided, the more shallow the understanding of this insincere life was to the eyes who saw it. There was a deeper end, and I was slowly immersing myself into it until I drowned in the vast truth that had to exist behind the lies.

My hand on the handle to my room waited to make its turn. The desperation to seek what was hidden was whispering to me. I could hear Mother's voice still cheerfully keeping up with conversation, more willing to speak to a faceless friend than her physically present daughter. She was occupied; so was my mind.

The door to Father's office was unlocked, his clean study coming into view as its wooden shield slowly fell open. The still-rising moon filtered through the slits of the window, shadowing the room in black and white lines. Lines I crossed as I ventured further inside.

A forbidden room, kept off limits by word alone and not by material restrictions. Father's insistence that none enter and the guilt he played on the last time I made this mistake was meant to be enough to keep out all but him. The lack of a lock fed into the belief that I was exactly where I should be looking.

I rounded his desk, spreading my hands on the bare surface. Everything too immaculate, too spotless for there not to be something that he was constantly cleaning up to cover. No evidence of the office's use made it appear insignificant, as benign and plain as my father himself tried to be seen as. I had to peer beneath the mask to find something, anything that pointed to proof of his shortcomings.

I began with the tome on top of his bookshelf. I opened the leather cover, half-hoping for a hollowed interior and a quick end to my search. Nothing to be found but the years of notes and highlighting that one man could do to just one copy of a book he had many versions of. I knelt down to the floor, quietly looking through the other two shelves as I kept an ear on Mother's voice.

My foot kicked back against the bottom drawer of Father's desk, and my hands froze in front of the books. I waited to hear pause in the phone conversation in the dining room, and when none came, I reached back to slip my shoe off and prevent further incident. Hand grazing the handle of the drawer, I turned around and looked at the stained wood. It shined with what little brightness the room had, reflecting the window's light.

I didn't know what to expect, nor what I was looking for. I just needed something. Something more. A single trace of the secret that I knew one powerful man held because of the knowledge of another powerful man. Here in the middle, I needed more reason to remind myself of why I was leaning more toward one side. I began my unguided search in the darkness—where I'd found more of my answers.

I opened the top drawer first, unveiling a collection of files that were kept in pristine order. My fingers walked through them and peered at the contents of each labeled section. The church's paperwork, receipts, exemption forms, the records of payroll for both he and the compensated members that kept the facility running. All business, just like the carefully organized process at the House of Sarris.

The drawer closed quietly beneath my fingers that gently pushed it, and I slowly opened the drawer under it. More files, all appearing to be unused because they were left unlabeled. But as my fingers raked over the manilla tabs, I could see all the contents living between them.

I pulled one out, the blank file holding the keepings of tracked payroll—officers with names I didn't know, but could guess to be the ones that kept him informed the way Kephum kept Adam up to date. Corruptly paid, I held the tangible truth of the things Othello had said about my father. There were officers being paid regularly, other receipts in the next file that were dated over two decades ago and written with vague shorthand of jobs done, tax forms that were in the next that had my father's name on them—and only my father's name.

I read through the first few forms, the taxes filed over the last three years, and everything was simply done with only Father's information. Filed as single, the name and information of the man that I knew, and no claims of a wife or children. With each page I turned, the same exclusions of three-fourths of the family, the less it made sense.

I frantically grabbed for the next file, my mother's laugh ringing through my ears and raking over my bones. My heart felt empty where it stopped, my eyes felt empty as they opened themselves to all that sat before me, and I was the shell of the empty life I'd been living as I buried my hands in the dirt that filled it in place of truth.

Birth certificates, with mine and Gray's names and the evidence that we really existed and the two of us weren't as made up as I was beginning to believe everything might be. The certificate behind Gray's had mother's name on it, and I held my breath as I turned to the next and prepared to see the real name of the man—my father—concealed and heavily guarded.

My breath remained in my lungs as I read the certificate. There was no room to exhale between me and the name of an unfamiliar woman. It was the most faded and discolored paper of them all, the worn signs of the authenticity of its age. The date read the same as my mother's, the only identical information on it. My mother wasn't born in Ohio, my mother's name wasn't Edith Moore, but this woman was brought to this earth on the same day and existed in the same file as my mother.

The voice in the dining room was quiet, and I closed the file and began to silently place it back in the drawer. When I heard my mother speak again, I reached for the file at the back of the drawer, unable to stop when I was finding so much. So much that I still didn't understand.

I opened the file in front of me, and a paper it contained within floated out. It drifted to the floor before me, the yellowed hue of a once black and white newspaper now standing out against the dark green of the carpet. I recognized the halved image I stared at, the unwanted section of a front-page article cut through and uncared for. But I knew what I saw, and I knew where I'd seen it.

The cherished memory of Nancy's daughter laid before me, the recognition of Ohio's beauty queen living immortally on the paper. Nancy's copy kept the entire image because that was her focus, but the focus of this copy wasn't meant to be the remnants of the awarded woman I was looking at. I turned it over, one section of the article centered and surrounded by other news that wasn't worth keeping.

I grabbed the next clipping, and the next—all of them the same story reported on different days. The progression and withering of a case that just ends with no trail other than the one I had spread out before me. The following of a single story that transcended time, states, and sense.

Decades ago: a woman is dead and two children are missing. In Ohio: a woman is dead and two children are missing. My father collected the details and possessed the records of a tragedy: a woman is dead and two children are missing.

My shock turned to confusion, my confusion grew to anger, my anger fumed to hatred, and my hatred made me sick. I stuffed everything back together, put away the file and shut the drawer hard enough to be heard by a distracted woman. A woman who existed in the same lie, same strange life that I did, whom I couldn't label as innocent because I couldn't label anything. Everything was wrong, everything was off, nobody was who they said they were, and we were all a part of something that we weren't meant to be—all names and numbers stored together in the collection of one man's private affairs.

I hurriedly put my shoe back on, my feet begging to carry me out of this room and away from this house. If I left, I wouldn't look back. No guilt could tether me to a father who was guiltier than I. I stood from the frantic cleaning of any evidence that I was here, and saw the single newspaper clipping that didn't make it back into its file. I reached to grab it, stuffed the aged paper into my pocket, and freed myself from the hold of that forbidden room. I hurried past the door to my own cage, past the fake family that lined the walls of the hall, past the mother who could ignore her daughter as well as the sins of her husband, and past the exit of a house that hid its horrors.

I ran to my car, not caring that I was leaving without explanation and with no intention of how or when I could return. This breaking soul had collided with its life's breaking point, and it had one place to go and one promise to rely on.

I pulled away from one life, the headlights of my car spotlighting the figure of a supposedly pristine door, and I sped toward a life that waited for me with blood-stained, opened arms—toward a house that didn't hide its horrors.

SEVERITY

I found my way through chaos, pushing my way through bodies I touched and didn't bother saying excuse me to. The house was filled with noise, filled with people, filled with music that drummed through my veins and kept the hatred running through me. I hadn't been looking for peace, and I wouldn't have found it here.

The air was riddled with smoke that my own lungs inhaled the deeper I pushed into the crowd of the big room. I didn't know how to find a familiar face, each one I looked upon had the ink and piercings of someone that I didn't know. The longer it took to reach my solace, the more the rage within me grew. It was looking for a target, one person with whom it could unleash itself, and it knew who it wanted. My body was a vessel that followed the path that would lead to destruction—destruction I would cause.

When I couldn't be sure of anything else, I could be sure of how I felt. This sensation, this loathing and the desire to release it upon a soul able to withstand its mass. I knew nothing but what I wanted, nothing but what I needed, and the anarchy that I was surrounded by wasn't enough to distract me before a notorious victim like me could find another.

"Where is he?" I asked Adam, my hands reaching to his chest. His instinctively captured my wrist, ready to rip apart the unwelcome contact of another body, but his grip loosened when he saw that it was only me. Seemingly harmless, unaware of the state of my mind.

He broke conversation with the man he was talking to, and I could feel the stranger's eyes watching the two of us interact with unexplained aggression. Posed like we could rip each other to shreds, Adam glared at me in silence as he recalled my question. He nodded his head in a vague direction, and then pulled me along behind him with his hold on my wrist, the man being left behind without a parting word.

Through the left side doors, the first time I dared go through them since the first incident they'd opened up to. I was dragged quickly through the people cluttered in the hallway, people removing themselves from Adam's way as he tightly held onto the body he was delivering.

He pulled us to a stop next to a door at the end of the hall, and opened it without a knock or polite signal. I stepped into the darkness of the room, the middle of it lit by the moon that was now sitting high out the window. The large space, the many components that made up the personal touches to his private chambers, all glossed over as my eyes went to Othello walking out of a separate doorway as he pulled a shirt over his head.

He looked to Adam and me, and the fumes of my distress waited impatiently for whoever was to follow to come out from the same doorway. I'd ask them to leave, tell him to ask them to leave, because I couldn't leave, myself. Nobody appeared, no disheveled or ravaged woman. Othello stood alone in the dim space.

The trail I blazed to reach him was ferocious. The most confusion ever felt, the most maddened mind I'd ever possessed is what I was warring with when I stood in his presence. His calm intensity coalesced with my outraged turmoil, and I hated the disagreement of our bodies, minds, and souls as much as I hated everything else in that moment.

"I know too much," I told him, our eyes intently set on watching for the other's next move; his violence or my return to standing down to every overwhelming emotion I felt. I was too manic to stand down. His violence would come before I could break. "And you know too much to be as still in the midst of this world as you are, this dark universe that exists on the other side of all I've ever known. I found you, and I found all the things that you know everything about. Deceit, destruction, *depravity*."

I reached out to him, my fingers pushing themselves onto his chest. The solid form of depravity, its walking entity, emphasized beneath my touch. He looked down at my uninvited hand laid on him, and back to the eyes that belonged to insanity. "You began all this by ending me. You *ended* me the day that you left the pieces of someone else in my hand, and I've lost pieces of myself every day since then. You brought me here, to a place where innocence dies, and now there's nothing left. Nothing but this same body that you saw in tears, and *smiled* at. If you loved the sight of my weakness so much, then why take it? Why lead me here, where I'm meant to be stronger because I'm so aware? I'm standing over the ruins of what you took from me, and now all I have left is what you gave. You've given me anger, and the light that darkness sheds on a false life, and I want to loathe you for it."

My hand shoved against his chest, a single push against the flesh where I knew a snake to be. His stance held, a step back of his foot keeping me from moving the immovable. He promised me a home of corruption, a family that was loyal to each other and the immoral deeds that kept us all tied, and I wanted him to fall heavily the way that I had into this place, this promise. I wanted him to feel the same ruthless force that I had. The darkness here that had lured me in was the darkness now in me that begged to crush him.

I put another hand to his chest, but everything I had wasn't enough. He was born to withstand all that someone shouldn't.

"Leave," Othello said, the single word packing the room with more restricted rage than all my words had. He captured my wrist, the demand not meant for me, and the sound of the door shutting followed the last of my control.

"I'm filled with hate." My voice came out like glass, cutting me open and letting the acceptance of my discoveries and inability to process it bleed from my mouth. This wasn't who deserved it, but it was who could take it. "I want to break something the way that everything is trying to break me. You're just indestructible enough to endure it. The only one capable of guiding me through the anger I need to lose myself in."

"You think that because you're pushed to the brink that there isn't more ground to hit once you fall over?" His hands around my wrists pushed my fists into my chest, his steps slowly forcing me backward. "When life gets this tough, as long as you're alive, there's always room for it to get tougher." He pushed my back against the door, our arms crushed between us. "And an angry woman is an alive woman. If I'm the life that brought you to this, then I'm the life with plenty of fight left. Break me, and I'll break you." His hands on my wrists tightened and pushed harder against my furiously thudding chest. "Over and over again."

My breathing rose to a yell, the only power I had left pushing me away from the door and against him. He fell beneath all my strength, and brought me down with him. He pushed me to the side, quickly climbing over me with little effort. He pinned my arms above me, his hair falling around his face as he looked down at the tears that were uncontrollably slipping from my eyes.

"You want to fight me, Dove?" His voice held no regard for my body's weakness and all it told. "Because I'll fight you until you surrender. I'll take every bit of control you have left. I'll win, and you'll lose yourself."

It wasn't him. It wasn't the right person to be here with, unleashing myself upon. But because he was the only constant I had, the one who showed me all I'd never done and never knew, it could only be him. The two of us, fighting and learning. Safely dangerous.

My feet connected with his legs as I kicked, and he let an arm go to stop my frantic movements. I turned my head and latched my mouth to his wrist, forcing my teeth down on his flesh. His hold on me vanished, and I turned over to crawl away. He grabbed my ankle, pulling me to him as my body dragged along the floor. My hands could latch onto nothing as my fingers raked along the carpet.

Pulled up by the hand in my hair, I knelt in front of Othello. My back was to him, his heavily breathing chest pressed against me. I reached into my pocket, refusing to lose this fight.

"If I bleed, so will you," he warned as I pulled out the knife. I reached back, grabbed his hand, and cut through the chunk of strands he held onto. My hair fell to my shoulder as me and the shed pieces fell to the floor.

The blade slipped beneath my hand, cutting open a new line of slowly rising blood. Othello rolled me over and knelt beside me as he pulled out his own knife and cut across his palm.

"And if you bleed, so will I." He tossed the knife away, two open blades on the floor that had drawn the blood of a snake and his dove. We weren't the same, we were hardly similar, yet he kept us equal. A leader that would reach down to the level of the lost to help them find their way.

Our palms met, our blood being shared as he pulled me up to my knees before him. A wreck facing the reckless. My cheeks were wet, my hair was uneven, and my body couldn't dispel all of my emotions as quickly as they came.

"Are you done?" he asked as his hand slid away, from mine, slick with red.

I shook my head. My system was overloaded, heated and incapable of shutting down. I put my opened palm to his face. "I haven't lost myself yet."

My mouth met his, continuing the fight I wouldn't surrender to. I bit his lip, inciting the pain I was still looking for. I told him what I wanted, that this was the same war, and he returned the force as he pushed me to the floor.

I tried to push him, to roll him over as our lips continued a rough back and forth. When I couldn't move him, I tangled my hands into his hair and formed fighting fists. His throat growled with my grip and he drove his body into mine. It was force that my body begged for, and I spread my legs for him to do it again.

Again, and again, the movements incited my madness. My back arched beneath him, pushing us closer together. His hand wrapped around my neck as his lips traveled slowly down, where he finally spoke next to my ear that heard the noise of the house through the floor.

"You should have surrendered."

He pulled me back up, his hands on my arms holding on tightly. My mouth set onto his neck as he reached behind him, and I began to suck and lick the same mark into existence that Adam had given to me. I could feel him pull the back of my shirt away from my body, I could hear the sound of fabric being shredded, but I never saw the knife that cut my shirt away. He pulled it from each shoulder, dropping it to the ground between us, and his hands met with the exposed skin of my back before the last covering of my chest fell away.

I wanted the lips, the mouth that didn't bear its scary smile, to stay on mine eternally. I wanted to taste the decadence of our souls' feud forever. But the lips left mine, and they set onto the peak of my bare chest where he took me between his teeth. I hissed, the pain just enough to thrill me and lock my hands around his neck. I held on, keeping his mouth tethered to me.

"Don't stop." The first command from the desires that I didn't cease. I was fighting him, the substitute for everything I hated, not my feelings. Not myself.

His tongue lapped, his teeth grazed, and my breathing turned to panting. Until he let go and I was left wanting and glaring at the face of a man who didn't relinquish his control. A face whose cheek wore the blood of my hand.

I pulled his shirt up over his head, equally baring him. He pulled me to him, his arm around me leading to fingers that dug into my side, and he held onto me as he stood us up and laid us on the bed. My fingers raked up his back as his tongue slid down the front of my body. He stopped at my pants, animal eyes peering up at me as I watched his fingers quickly unfasten them and pull them off of my body. He was opening me up to him, more attention being given to me than I'd ever paid to myself. I was a new person being presented for the first time to the man who'd created this version of me. The version that shook beneath the eyes that took in my vulnerability, but was insatiable. I wanted more of the things that I didn't know.

I wanted less to remain of me.

His hand moved up my body and settled around my throat. My eyes went wide, forgotten fear beginning to creep back in as his fingers slowly tightened. I grabbed at his arm, hanging onto something real before I slid into panic.

"This is not a fight I'll lose, Dove," he said as the fingers of his other hand traced over the thin covering that remained between my legs. "But I'll make you feel like you've won. I'll give you everything I shouldn't, and take all of you for myself." He grabbed the last semblance of my modesty and pulled it down, my legs working for him to free myself from what was left standing between the full collision of he and I.

He rubbed slow, wet circles between my legs. My grip on his arm tightened, pushing his hand harder over my throat. I already couldn't breathe, the pleasure beginning its attempt to consume everything else that I felt, but the lack of air began to turn my vision black at the edges.

He let go of my throat just before he forced a finger inside of me, and my exhale came out as a scream. It began slowly, the in and out of an unfamiliar touch, and I bit my lip to keep from crying out all that my body begged me to release. There was a slow and subtle stretch as he added another finger, and my hands clutched the bedsheets.

He came over me, his fingers buried in the depth of my pain and my pleasure having their own fight as the two of us fought on. His mouth met mine, greedily parting my lips and releasing the sounds of a woman willingly breaking, being set free.

My knees came up, my body trying to lift itself from the bed as he engraved his touch inside of me. I belonged to him, inside and out, and my body was beginning to submit itself to the heat that came from playing with fire. The most sensual burn grew within me with the speed of his sliding fingers, and I felt myself break beneath his guidance.

It flowed from me, a warmth that carried my voice through the room as he pulled his hand away from its work, stained in my blood. He took what no one else ever could, and the proof was on his skin.

He grabbed my waist, pulling me up with a slick hand just as strong as the other. I could feel what remained within me dripping onto his sheets under me. I looked down at the red marks left on white cloth, embedded there just as he was now embedded in me. I'd always remember when this fight broke me and took with it the last of my innocence. I could continue to fight freely, liberated from the hold of perfection.

My mouth crashed to his, pushing him back on the bed as I straddled over him. I slid against the skin of his stomach, leaving dark traces of purity's release along his body. His grip on my hips kept me against him, accepting the blood I shed.

I rubbed myself, openly displaying the selfish pleasures that he'd shown me. I sat up over him, my fingers sliding harshly to another carnal satisfaction. I grew louder with each second of the approaching ecstasy until I reached it, his name falling from my lips as my body trembled beneath my own hand. His face was all I could see, his poisonous darkness all I could taste, and my veins pulsed with longing that refused to be quenched.

"Beg me," he demanded as he put his lips to my ear. "Beg the man whose name you call when you come. Beg me to give myself over now that I own you. You're mine, and you're not meant to be." He pulled away, his eyes meeting mine as he grabbed my hand from his shoulder and brought it to his tongue. All I'd given, all I'd spared, caressed by the tongue that slowly tortured me. "Beg me to show you how good it feels to be this fucked up together."

"Show me," I pleaded as I reached to remove what clothes he still wore. "Make me forget who I was before you." My hands brought down all that shielded him from my view, and I looked back to his eyes as I took him into my hand, slowly stroking the only man who could make me dare to do such a thing. "I beg you."

He moved out of his clothing, entirely bare to me the way I was to him. Between my legs, he positioned himself against me and my teeth caught my lips as he slowly pressed in. My nails dug into his shoulders, trading slow pain for slow pain. He pulled away and my body tried to follow, not wanting the ache to leave. He slid back in and I stretched around him, no room within me spared. I was filled, complete, and painfully whole.

My legs wrapped around him, and his hands wrapped around me and lifted, sitting me up against our connected bodies. I began to slide down, the length of him pushing deeper into me and reaching past comfort. It was injury that my body could endure. I wanted him to have all of me, and my moans were strained as I warred with myself to persevere.

His hand gripped my jaw, forcing me to look down at him as he held us together. My hips moved back up, desperate for ease, before I began to fall back down against him. He kissed me as his fingers tightened on my face.

"Let it hurt," he told me as I shook with tension. I reached the point of agony, and I cried out. Wet with yearning and the blood I'd shed, my body slid against him until he was entirely inside. I bit his shoulder, muffling my labored breathing. He lifted my hips again, and I began the slow slide down once more, the pain beginning to dull. I released my mouth from his shoulder as the pain continued to transition.

"More," I said against his ear. He brought me up again, this time forcing me down quicker. He restored the pain to mix with the pleasure and I called out, gripping my hands around his shoulder as my head tilted back. "More."

One hand held behind my head, the other arm wrapped around me, he kept us joined as our bodies began to move together. He wordlessly showed me how to do what I wanted, my body working without thought toward its desires. I could hear his breathing, matching the force of mine, and I brought my head back up to look at the eyes that watched me learn—watched me lose myself.

He laid me back down, my body stilling as his continued to use mine. He became quicker, rougher, overwhelming me with all that I was meant to feel. The pain restoked my anger, the pleasure continued to build, and I gripped onto the stained sheets as I trembled against my approaching release.

I met it, and he continued to move into me as I got caught on sensation. I couldn't scream the way I felt, my voice caught in my throat as he pushed my ravaged body into the mattress with each thrust. Silent screams of satisfaction led to more begging as my body became alight with nerves too sensitive to his touch.

"I can't take it," I breathlessly said as I grabbed his arms, both wanting him to keep on and unable to bear how overwhelmed the inside of my body was.

"Then tell me to stop," he said as he slowed and set his mouth back on my chest. He sucked gently, making my hips jump and push him deeper into me. "Or tell me to fuck you until you bleed again."

I groaned at the words, seduced by everything wrong about him, about this, about us together. I wanted to spill all that was left, and remain here with the darkness. I wanted to be selfishly swallowed by the man who demanded the world. I wanted him to finish me the same way he'd made me, saved me, and bled me—with me losing my control.

"Say it, Dove," he said as I moved beneath him, forcing our bodies together again. "Say the words."

"I don't want you to stop," I told him as I brought his hand to my mouth. I licked the wound that was left by his blade, that prefaced this moment where we fought each other hungrily.

"Say what you *want*," he corrected. His hand slid away from my mouth, opening me to the words he wanted to hear. His fingers were splayed by my head, in the dark hair fanned against his sheets. I looked into his eyes as I allowed my tongue to relay such a vulgar thought.

"I want you to fuck me." One word, charged with forbidden definition and all the impropriety I'd always avoided. I wanted him to continue giving me everything that he was, all that I spent my life evading at the chance of being ruined. It was the enemy of what I had always practiced— pure words, pure thoughts, pure actions. My impurity was devoured here, and shed from me like the chain that it was. My desires now were heavy, but I was light. Weightless, and free.

His body listened, fueled by the words an inexperienced mouth like mine spoke. His moves weren't gentle, this wasn't the soft and caring exchange that I'd always intended to lose myself to, but it was what was meant for me. I was meant to feel all of this—blood, sweat, and tears—as I was safely consumed by reality. Heat, passion, and lust between two humans that bled the same color. I'd always imagined this moment to be one where my soul tenderly embraced another—but the darkness of our souls fought, each taking what they wanted from the other. He took the last traces of the me I was abandoning, and I took every indulgence that he taught me to savor.

Greedy. Selfish. Real.

I was overcome again, letting go of all that he'd built up within me around him as he relentlessly pressed on. I breathed his name into the humid air, the heat we caused lingering between us. He brought my leg up to his shoulder, moving deeper into me than before. I cried out at the punishing speed, the pain that racked through my spent body. More fervent thrusts ripped moans from my throat before he slowed, and I could feel warmth spill into me.

He held my leg to his shoulder as we came to a stop. He pulled out of me, damp traces of blood and all we'd shared marked all over his body. He looked at me, his face unreadable in the dark and its state of complete control.

I did feel like I'd won. This fight with myself, with him, with the things I'd been taught that I couldn't have. I felt like I won, but I knew that he didn't think he'd lost. As he stood at the foot of the bed and looked at me as he silently redressed, I refused to disturb the quiet atmosphere of victory.

I didn't want my clothes that belonged to the woman that came here. I didn't want to be near the temporarily forgotten article that was in my pocket and distanced from me. I wanted to stay on the sheets that proudly proclaimed the stains they'd earned. I wanted to remain in this dark room and away from all the people outside. I didn't want to leave this bed and have to retrace the steps that brought me to where I was.

Othello sat in a seat against the wall, leaning back to maintain the stare on me that I had on him. Beneath his clothes he hid everything that I still exposed. Covering it wouldn't keep me from forgetting. This was a lesson, a memory that would stay with me forever. But it was new, and I knew nothing past this feeling.

"What now?" I asked him as my cheek rested against a cold, unmarked place on the bed.

"Now, we wait for a new day where we will live without regret," he said with eyes that ingrained his words into my focus. Hypnotizing me with serenity, assurance, and control like nobody else had. His hold over me exceeded the explainable boundaries of my body and mind.

"Is this something I'm meant to regret tomorrow?" It didn't feel like something I would. Nor something I should. It was wrong in the ways that catered to my flesh, but didn't consume my peace. I felt satisfied, and seen. I'd lost myself and found something new.

"What do you think?" He placed his fingers around the end of the chair's arm, sat regally as I'd seen him numerous times before. The statue of a leader, the image of beautiful authority. He looked at his own hand, and even in the dim room I could see the discoloration dried upon it.

"I don't think I possibly could," I told him as I sat up, and his eyes followed my movements as I covered my body with a sheet. "This wasn't what I intended, but it wasn't regrettable. I got more than what I came for."

"Is confronting me really what you came for?" he asked.

I sat back on my knees, knelt on the massacred bed and robed in a garment as stained as I was. I'd come here because I was running. I ran from ruin and into the embrace of destructive bliss. He'd taken my fragility and broke it into resilience. I'd been trained to survive. I'd come for the promise of safety without condition.

"I came here to escape." Escape the distress and find my way through my furious confusion. I'd been blinded by it and he tended to the beast that broke free until it was tamed once again. I came here because I wanted to be far from everything I had, and all that I was, until I was unable to look back upon what I'd left. I came to distance myself, physically and mentally.

"And did you find that escape?"

I looked at the dark lines of the dove on his neck, free above the collar of his shirt. The snake hidden beneath it dwelled in the shadows.

"I found more than that," I admitted.

The commotion outside was slowly coming back into focus. I could make out the suggestive words of the loud music, hear clearly the excitement of too many people piled into one place where they could come and just exist without expectation—without rules. It led to havoc, and it led me to my haven.

"I found everything."

His smile appeared at the echo of a conversation since past, and I returned it instead of backing away like I had that night. It would be a smile that induced fear in others, but no longer in me. I'd familiarized myself with all his horrors, and was confident in his presence. He'd promised to never hurt me, to always give me my freedom and a home to turn to, and he followed through. He gave me the delightful aches of pleasure and this place that I didn't want to flee from. He was a man who gave me more than just his word when he knew only that wasn't enough for me.

My thighs became wet, and I looked beneath the sheet at the red and cloudy streams slowly running between them. I didn't know what to expect of my blood loss, but its continuation was alarming. I remembered wanting to die in the midst of sensation, to be taken while I was happy and felt alive and not deprived. Now I was removed from that feeling, and I wondered if I was slowly going to meet my end as the life drained from me.

"You're going to be fine," Othello said, and my hands gently placed the sheet back around my chest. "It's not as much blood as you think it is. It will stop."

"So now you can read my eyes when I'm not even looking at you?"

"I'm just familiar with the face of someone who's concerned about dying." His hands went behind his head as he leaned it back against the wall. "You weren't this concerned about dying when you got here with rage and a knife both readied."

"That was different," I told him as I sat down and crossed my legs in front of me. The sheets beneath me couldn't be saved. "I was angry then and didn't care." The feelings I'd come here with had been all-consuming.

"And you care now?" It was the most he asked, usually capable of reading into my thoughts and answers before they were questioned and given. Maybe all the questions and waited-for answers were a test of my comfort, because I knew that our connection wasn't broken. He was asking just to keep me talking.

"Now I can clearly remember that there are things still worth caring for and parts of life still worth living through." And I would talk for as long as he would listen.

He watched me contently as I waited for a reply, another question, but it didn't come. I pulled my gaze away from his and looked to the door, my eyes as adjusted to the dark as I was. I looked back at him from the noise of the lively gathering outside of this room.

"Am I keeping you from going back out there?" I asked, to which he shook his head slowly where it rested.

"You aren't keeping me from anything. I had my fill before you got here," he told me. I remembered him dressing as I came in, and my mind immediately returned to where it had been when I'd seen him. I'd expected there to be a woman, and now I wondered if there had been someone before me tonight; if he had his fill before I came as a surprise. I opened my mouth to ask, knowing he always answered, and he shook his head again. "There was plenty of blood spilled before you arrived and added to the night's list."

Changing bloodied clothes, just as easily predictable as him being with another woman. I hadn't been his first fight, but whoever had come before me hadn't fought the same. They lost their blood, maybe even their life, and I was still sitting here facing the man I'd warred with. They hadn't shed their blood to a man who'd already taken it from them and placed it under his own flesh—I had.

Each side of his neck had my marks, a bruise and a permanent brand. One would fade, just like these moments here in his room would. He could always remember that it had been there, as would I, but it wasn't going to exist forever. Sharing our bodies, giving over to intimacy, was only a temporary thing. That experience shared was past, but his promise was forever. The mark that would remain on him for as long as he lived reminded me that he'd give me all he could whenever I needed him. And as I looked to my clothes scattered on the floor, knowing what folded paper lived in the confines of the uniform life I'd shed, I knew that this was what I would need forever. I couldn't return to the place where rules were broken by the ones who enforced them.

"Tell me about what happened." he asked me, pulling my attention away from the unseen article put aside in my pocket. "Tell me what it was that has driven you to…this."

To the mess I was that sat on depravity's bed. To the open blades on the floor amongst my clothes; to sex, sin, and slashed skin. To voraciously commit the last of me to depravity himself.

"I know too much." The first words I'd spoken to him in this room would be the first ones in a confession that I only wanted to make once in my life. Admitting the faults of another person was harder than admitting my own. I felt sick as I relived the revelation I had in those last moments before I ran—before I was driven to this. "I know my father's a liar. I now know that everything you said was true, because I found the proof that had always been just out of my reach. And more. I found more, and I don't know what it means but I know that I'm scared to find out." I looked down at my clasped hands that sat still as I gave him all that only I knew. All that I was never meant to know. "I know too much, and I still don't even know his real name."

He accepted the vague details with a single nod. "He's unaware that you know?"

"He doesn't know anything. But he'll know something's wrong when I don't come back home." He kept a close watch on me. There were times these past months that his few words and stern expressions questioned me as much as I questioned him. He would come looking for me, but this would be the last place he would ever think to look.

"I'll take care of it," he said as he removed his hands from behind his head, and leaned forward to grab his knife from off the floor. "I'll make a few calls. Kephum will know that you're an adult who isn't missing, and your father will have to do the searching for himself when the authorities won't."

"And if my father comes searching?" I watched him wipe the blade with his shirt before he shut it, and held it loosely between his fingers on the arm of the chair the way Adam held his cigarettes. Knives and blood were a habit to Othello as smoking was to Adam. Neither could live without them. I looked down at the chain still hanging around my naked body, and quickly away. I'd forced myself to live without it, and moved on to finding comfort in pain.

He shrugged, the knife between his fingers moving as his thumb moved it up and down in his loose grasp. "That's nothing to be concerned about. If he comes to you, he'll come unprepared."

Because nobody knew what to expect from the lives in this church. I'd once been the one here, unprepared, and I'd found more than one twisted mind could imagine. A powerful man with rules wouldn't know how to face a powerful man with none.

The door opened, and we both looked to the heightened volume of the noise that filtered in around Adam. He immediately found Othello sitting in his chair, and they silently spoke before Othello stood from his seat.

He looked at me, the stained and naked woman beneath the sheet, as he placed his knife back into his pocket, conveniently concealed. "Stay here. I'll be back."

Adam blocked the doorway, watching me as my eyes followed Othello's approach to him. He looked between the two of us, the obvious marks on the sheets, and I knew the question that he asked Othello by the glare of his eyes.

"She's fine," Othello told him. Adam didn't challenge him further, the trust there between two deviants that had no reason to lie to each other. But he spared me a look before he closed the door as they left, and I nodded my head in agreement.

I was fine.

The door shut, and I laid back down on the bed, alone in the dark room.

I was safe, satisfied.

I closed my eyes and listened to the voices outside, the loud music that lulled a heavy heart, and the screams that came and rose above all the other noise of chaos.

I was able to give myself over to exhaustion, no fight left in me.

I drifted to the sounds of destruction, defying the taught definition of peace.

Gentle strokes stung my open palm. My sight returned, slowly adjusting to the dark as the pain pulled me to consciousness. I could still hear voices outside, but the music and the sounds of utter freedom were gone. The night was beginning to still, and Othello sat beside me with my hand in his lap as darkness was closing in on its final hours.

He cleaned my wound, unaware that I watched him. Softly, he ran a soaked cloth over my palm again. He was shirtless, his hair damp and pulled by the weight of the water it still held. Awake in the unknown hour of the night and healing the woman that was a stranger to his bed.

My breath pushed the sheet against my chest, and it clung to my skin. The room wasn't hot, nor was I, and yet I was damp. I pulled the sheet from me, looking at the body that had been cleaned of all the bloody traces. He continued his unrushed work as he spoke.

"As clean as you were before you met me," he said, smiling down at the cut on my hand.

"I was lost and searching when I met you," I replied as I pulled a pillow beneath my head and continued to watch. The light touch compensated for the sting it caused.

"You found more than most do in their lifetime," he said as he grabbed something from the table beside him. "Maybe more than a dove should."

The hard lines of his features were shadowed, his profile outlined by the dark. The lashes that extended from the eyes set on my hand, the straight bridge of his nose, the full lips that I knew to taste as fatal as they felt. No kiss should be that perfect, no face that flawless unless it was made to lure—and he was. His demeanor drew in victims, but his image left them hypnotized and able to forget the existence of harm. He led to violence, the sins of the flesh, and he was just immaculate enough to make me believe that he'd been doing it for eternity.

"How old are you?" I asked, and his hand didn't stop but his eyes strayed to mine.

"I'm thirty-three," he told me as he smeared a film of ointment over my cut. It was the first time that Adam wasn't the one tending to my injuries here, and the difference in their touch was noticeable. The scar of my cheek where my stitches had been would be minimal because of Adam's insistence to bear the temporary pain as he did his work. Othello's work was tender and the wound on my hand didn't meet the force that I knew he was capable of.

"Can I expect to know as much as you do when I'm thirty-three?" I couldn't help but smile. One more difference, our age contrasted by ten years. We were opposites brought together, a wise soul and a wandering one. The biggest thing we had in common was the bed we rested on, and the scars on our bodies left by blades.

"I hope you don't have to know as much as I do," he told me as he placed a bandage on my palm. "But I hope you know everything that you want to know."

There was plenty to learn in that amount of time. But as unpredictable as life had been, as relentless in its tolls it had taken on me, I knew not to even expect to see that age. I could close my eyes once more in this bed and never wake up again, because that's the way that fate worked. The way life was. If I wanted to know anything—and I wanted to know everything—then I had to ask while I still could. I had to know how someone like me wound up here, how I had changed this much.

"How did I end up where I am now?" I asked. He laid my hand back down, done with his careful attention. He leaned back on the headboard, and his fingers found their way to my hair. Gentle strokes caressed my head, and my eyes threatened to close as I looked at him and waited for an answer. Because it was one more thing that I couldn't figure out for myself.

"Because your soul is a light sleeper," he said as he stared into the dark room, "and it only takes a shift in the light to rouse one from their slumber." He cast his eyes down to me, continuing to slowly push my hair away from my face. I was enraptured by a man who could both say something so beautiful and commit acts so horrific. "The sun and the shadows of the world have stirred you, awakened you. You're just finding what living without an incapacitated soul is like."

I had slept through more than twenty years of life. My soul listened to what it was told, and remained benumbed. It was bound and leashed, and shadows that I'd avoided *were* what woke me. I questioned more, I became aware, I found the secrets that I was kept ignorant and insensible to in order to never discover them. Now I was alert, and knew enough, even if I didn't know as much as Othello did.

And I lived the back and forth between the sun and the shadows, and found the most consolation in the latter. I was fooled by the false light of the sun.

My finger traced over the words tattooed next to me, unconsciously attracted to the exposed, dark letters. There was no feeling to them other than the touch of my skin to his, the ink embedded beneath the surface. But I could feel the illusion of a current coming from it, the power behind something important enough for him to wear it for life.

I'm saved, I told myself as I scrawled my finger over the letters again and again. I'd awakened, walked through violent trials, and still had a beating heart within my chest and a soul that now searched for all the answers it demanded. I could sleep now, and wake up in the morning as this same version of myself who knew the world it faced. I could allow myself rest, because of where I was now and how far I'd come to feel this sure.

Tomorrow's light could shed more exposure, and with it more dangers of a soul that refused to stop searching. But for now, that soul that was awakened could allow its battered body to sleep.

Beneath the hand of severity's vessel that pet his dove with care, I was safe.

PURPOSE

My arm stretched across the cold sheets; no warm body next to mine any longer. I opened my eyes to the bright room, transformed by the sun that filtered through the window. It looked like a different space as I sat up and took it all in. It was even larger in the light, the sun opening up areas that were hidden before. Furniture I hadn't seen, the white color of the walls that I hadn't noticed; the spotted sheets and my clothes still on the floor assured me that I was exactly where I'd been left.

I couldn't hear any noise through the walls. The house slept through the day and lived through the night, and I wasn't on its schedule. My body wasn't conditioned to a routine this strange—yet. My internal clock was still wired to the routine I'd left, the charade of normalcy. It would take time to undo what had been formed over years.

I wrapped the dirty sheet around my cleaned body as I sat on the edge of the bed. I'd been washed by Othello as I slept, and that felt more intimate than anything. After all we'd done, he'd restored me, put me back together again just as he always did. My body was sore, but it was without the stains of impurity. He'd removed the traces of what I'd given him, and showed me that I can wake up and live this day just like the last.

But I didn't know how to live a day in this place. Of all the time spent here, I'd never seen a morning through these windows or began a day by stepping onto the ground in a room where I'd committed to changing. This bed didn't belong to me, but I belonged to it. I willingly let go of burdens and chose to fight here, and as I stood from the mattress where physical devotions were made, I filled the lungs of a new woman with the air of a new dawn.

I walked toward the empty seat where Othello had sat, wanting to see the bed, the room, the imagined picture of an unleashed woman from his point of view. The opened blade still on the floor stopped me as my eyes caught on the reflective metal. I stood above it, looking down at the knife that was left beside my ruined shirt, my own knife that had cut my hand. I looked at the wound, cleaned and restored as I'd rested. I thought of the intentional cut Othello had made across his palm, and all the pain he'd shared with me as well as saved me from.

I'd left behind my life's struggles and intangible pain, and I'd left behind the person who shared it. The one who lived that same life, and didn't know the corruption behind it. Gray was stuck in the place that I'd escaped because he was blissfully unaware, and so good at being compliant and never asking for the knowledge that didn't belong to him. But this knowledge that didn't belong to him did affect him. This knowledge that I had didn't just ruin me and my faith in a false family, it could ruin him to know that the man he admired wasn't a man worth admiring. Gray didn't deserve to be ruined, but he deserved to be saved. Saved from finding out our life's horrors the hard way, spared from falling down this same spiral that I had. The truth would come, and it should come from the lips of who he trusted and adored.

Gray deserved to be saved, and our father deserved to have to confess. Gray needed someone who knew the darkness to reveal it to him, as the darkness here had enlightened me.

After being the one who always needed to be saved, I needed to save him. I couldn't be truly free until I knew he was freed from deceit and not living blindly.

The one good thing that didn't deserve to be abandoned.

I dropped the sheet to the ground, baring myself to the light. I redressed, feeling the evidence still in my pocket and the wickedness of it that burned through to my skin. I put on my shoes, removing the comfort of walking freely in this lawless place. I put the knife back into my pocket and walked to the closet, putting on the first shirt my hands latched onto like the violent owner of these grounds would. I embodied all I'd been taught, conjured all I'd been given, and consumed the capabilities that flowed from all that I had of Othello's.

It was the first time I felt powerful, walking in the steps of the invincible.

I stopped at the foot of the bed, looking down at the carnage from a single night here captured by the white sheets. I would return, never the same as I was when I'd walked through this door. The chain around my neck unlatched beneath my fingers and I laid it down, replacing the crutch that a liar had given me for the courage bestowed upon me by the man whose shirt I wore. That was what I needed to get me through this, and to bring me back to freedom.

Courage is what I needed to face one man to save another.

I hurried from the comfort of the room with the power that came with it, and ran past the two sleeping bodies of strangers in the hall. Through the front doors I escaped my solace and burned beneath the sun's blaze. I rushed to my car, carried by feet that wanted to end the reign of the unworthy. I wanted to release the hold that he'd had on me by the one, truly pure soul in this forsaken family. I drove quickly, breaking the rules of the road as I sped down the path toward deliverance.

The outside of the house appeared harmless in the light, all its harm hidden within. I turned off the car, and inhaled once before I got out. I didn't look down for fear that the ground beneath me dissolved with each step, that I had no way to turn back. My heart crashed against my ribs, knowing that danger was imminent. I couldn't ignore it, but I swallowed the fear that I didn't want to show on my face as I opened the door.

Gray sat on the couch with his head rested against his hand as he stared blankly at the floor. He looked up, and the concern that was already creasing his brow magnified.

"Vieve?" He questioned everything with just my name. Where I'd been, why my face held the intent expression of a stranger. I heard it all in those five letters, and ignored it for the sake of pressing on. For his sake, too.

"Where's Father?" I asked as I pushed away from the door. He stood up and followed my every move as I looked into the hallway and saw nothing but dark rooms and a closed office.

"It's Saturday, he's preparing at the church like he always does." He put a hand to my shoulder, turning me to him before I could reach the dining room. "Genevieve?"

There was panic in his eyes, the tension of his face growing with every second I spent here, angry and determined. There was already something wrong, I could feel it in his worry. His cheerful demeanor had already been broken.

But he asked me before I could ask him.

"What's going on?"

I pulled him to me, my arms wrapped around the neck that carried a head whose thoughts were always generous, empathetic, innocent. One hug of the person I intended to spare from our life's shadowed troubles was all it took to spur me on.

"There's something I have to do," I told him as I turned back toward the front door.

"Genevieve Wren, where have you been?" my mother scolded from behind me. The disappointment in her voice did nothing to stop my actions anymore. There was no effect, no halted beating of my furious chest. I didn't bend beneath that burden any longer, and I walked out the door without paying her notice. Without answers.

"Genevieve!" Gray called as I got into my car. I watched him as I backed away, my eyes attracted to the blue that matched the sky of a day that would seem beautiful to anyone who wasn't me right then. But they were pained, and hurting, and I never wanted to see him look that way again. So I turned away, and toward the only action I knew to take to ensure he wouldn't be hurt the same way that I was.

I drove until I saw the steeple. The tires came to a harsh stop beside the only other car in the lot, and my mind tuned out the sound of the car I left running as I ran up to the doors. Past the place where I was conditioned to say goodbyes, and give thanks for prideful and wrong things. Unlocked, supposedly welcoming, I entered into the large, empty room where my father's voice spoke to the void seats. The sound of his own voice kept his face satisfied as I watched him from the end of the middle aisle.

The door shutting behind me crashed through his sentence; warnings spoken in anger, a practice he'd perfected. He looked up at me from words he didn't need to read, things he'd memorized and used against the masses to invoke guilt. His hand was frozen in the air, pointing a finger toward the nonexistent crowd. His eyes glazed over. The ferocity he was controlling could be seen and felt through the distance between us.

"You didn't come home last night." It wasn't an accusation, because it was known by us both. It was an acknowledgment of my wrongdoing that he declared. His chin was held high in his imagined state of superiority.

"That isn't my home." My veins threatened to burst. I'd never dared to speak against him, to do anything so defiant. I was laying everything down in the open and uncovering all that was buried, including the opposition in me that had always remained dormant. "I will no longer live beneath your roof."

Shock briefly showed on his lips before he regained control, pressing them together as he stepped away from behind his pulpit. His hand remained on its wood; he felt the same power from it as he did from his desk at home, another barricade he hid behind.

"Don't be fooled by impulsivity. You're too young to be on your own. You have my forgiveness for your disobedience, but I won't hear another word of this." He waved me off with his hand as he turned back to his work, assuming that his word would be the end of it—as it had always been before. "And you know better than to interrupt me again." He added as he looked back down to his notes, his lessons, his hypocritical words.

I took a step closer, forcing myself to step away from the urge to comply. It was ingrained so deep in me that it was my body's first response. But I took two, three steps nearer. My hands hung by my sides, near the contents I had in each pocket. Near my defenses.

"Too young?" My voice shook with the pulse of anger. With the life that had flowed through me for so many years now trying to burst free and escape. "You only want me to feel that way because you want me to stay reliant on you. You want me to continue to think I need you, and that your guidance is as perfect as you pretend to be." I knew my words were coming out loudly, because I could hear them over the drumming in my ears. I knew they reached him, because he looked up at me from his downcast face with mounting fury. "I don't want your forgiveness." I felt no remorse for the things he'd insisted made me guilty. "I want your confession."

The color came to his face, slowly drawing the marks of wrath beneath his skin. Red, as deep as the lies were that he concealed better than his body's reaction to accusation. He brought his face back up, and looked at me straight on. The threat was sent down the line, cast to the soul he looked down upon.

"You seem to have forgotten your place," he told me. His tone was severe, its volume held down as he hung onto the last threads of control he had. I could see them breaking, one by one, with each word he said growing louder. "I expect your respect. And I suggest you seriously consider the consequences behind whatever it is you intend to say next."

My hand went to my pocket and retrieved the folded paper. I opened it, looking at the title from an article of the past one last time. I wanted everything to make sense. I wanted to understand how this paper could appear in my life at a time like this, at the beginning of my wandering and the end of my search. I wanted to know what it meant to my father as he watched me closely, waiting to see how obedient my next move would be.

"Tell me why you have this." I held up the paper to him, and his eyes locked onto the evidence. "Tell me who you are and why you're hiding so much, and *then* tell me how you expect me to respect you."

He stepped slowly away from his wooden shield and down the stage's steps. I couldn't find any surprise on his face; it was smothered in outrage. I took a step back when he stopped at the front of the aisle, and forced myself not to retreat any further. This was my ground as much as his. He'd always told me I belonged here, and here I was, in the place where truth was meant to be set free. I wouldn't leave without it, and I wouldn't allow the remnants of fear he incited within me for so long to sabotage my strength. I would fight until I found what I came for.

"How dare you disobey my orders not to go into my—"

"How dare *you* hide all this behind those rules you put in place," I interrupted, my fist crumpling the top of the article with all the force rushing from me. "How dare *you* hide behind a name that isn't yours, and get away with everything you've always ordered us not to do." Gray's face appeared in the blur of my eyes, the hurt I'd last seen him with demanding me to discover answers. "Who are you? What is this? What is it you're lying to protect?"

He took another step forward, and I kept my feet planted. I looked for resemblances, how I could belong to someone so terrible when I tried for so long to be someone so good. I tried to be good for him, and now that I wasn't, all I could see between the likenesses of a father and daughter was the dark hair of their heads. He put out his hand, and a slow demand that I give up and hand all that I knew over to him.

"Give it to me, and we can let this go." I looked to his opened palm, uninclined to cooperate. The colors from the stained-glass window high on the wall behind him shed their hues on his hand. It was chaos coming to light. I could feel the anger running beneath his flesh that was disguised by those colors. This place had always been one of his best disguises. "You won't speak of this to anyone. You won't ruin all I've done to protect you. Give it to me, and you won't end up doing something that you'll regret."

"Protect me?" My hand grabbed the bottom of my shirt, clinging to the courage I'd come with and remaining close to the weapon in my pocket. "You can't protect me when I don't know who you are. What do I need to be protected from other than you? The world out there shows its dangers, and you hide yours. I've seen them all, and I'm not going to regret learning more. You tell me why *this* matters to you so much." I pulled the article in closely, keeping it to me and out of his reach. "Tell me who you are, tell me who *we* are. Tell me everything that you never intended for me to know, or you'll be the one with regrets."

I'd always feared milder expression from him than the one he had now. I had always cowered and bowed to the wishes of a father who kept me in line with just a single look. Always powerful, never defied. But now, I couldn't be intimidated the way I'd always been, because I held his weakness in my hand. I had the same control over him that he'd always had over me. And as he slowly walked forward and I discreetly reached to my pocket, I knew that this wouldn't end until one of us broke. I was done breaking.

I pulled the knife out just as he lurched forward, latching onto the wrist that held the aged and crumpled paper. The force of his shoulder that met my other arm knocked the knife from my hand, and it flew from reach into a place unseen in the empty church.

I tried to turn away, pulling all of my weight down over the contents in my hand that I refused to let go of. I could hear it tearing in the hold he had on it as he tried to pull it away. His arm around me pressed into my throat while I hung onto his weakness and my strength.

I could feel the warmth rising in my face the longer my lungs remained empty. I could hear the slow ripping of the paper in my hands as his power endured and mine was being exhausted. The loud demands for me to give it to him were being clouded as I weakened, becoming as dulled as my other senses were.

The realization that he would let me die for his lies to remain unknown was the last thing that I would remember about my father as the bright room filled with soft colors began to turn black.

It faded like my breath had, slowly and painfully, until the last moment before the void could take over entirely. Oxygen forced back into my pounding chest and my father's arm ripped away from my neck and took with it a handful of the torn paper. I clutched my throat with my own hand, feeling the pain from his pressure lingering beneath my touch as I rolled over and let the room come back into focus.

He couldn't lurch for me again despite the clear desire to on his face. The knife that was held to his throat as he sat in a pew kept him from acting on all his wishes to save himself. Othello waited for my eyes to lock onto his before he commenced the situation now held in the palm of his hand.

"Tell her what she wants to know," Othello said, his even voice the only one of ours entirely capable of control. "Then maybe I'll give you enough time to ask for forgiveness for it all before I let her watch the power you thought you had bleed out onto these seats."

I couldn't pull myself off the floor. I was stuck beneath the both of them looking down on me, waiting for me to use the authority I'd been given. My father's chest was moving as rapidly as mine. He wasn't used to being held under a blade like I was, and I wasn't used to being put in charge. I took a breath that burned through my strained lungs, and set my eyes on the man who had no choice but to answer this time.

"Tell me who you are." As slowly as the words came out, they were powerful. They were insistent. I watched his nostrils flare at the sound of his own daughter forcing his corrupt hand. I would let him remain here beneath Othello's knife until he told me.

"Nathanial Moore." The name scraped through clenched teeth. He hated to say it. It was a name he'd probably gone without hearing for decades, a name he hoped to never have to hear again. He looked at me like he would bury me for unearthing all the graves of information he'd dug.

I waited for explanations that I shouldn't have to ask for. He knew what I wanted, and I hated that I had to ask him as much as he hated to have to tell me. The man I looked at still had the face of my father, but the name of a stranger. He wasn't who I knew, or who I used to think I could trust. I severed the last of the affection I'd held for him, all that was left living in me from the hopes that things couldn't be as horrible as they seemed. But the secrets I was forcing from him had to be horrible for him to glare at me with such loathing. I wasn't the daughter he raised, and he was no longer the father I'd thought I had.

"Why does this matter to you so much?" I didn't bother raising the paper in my hand anymore. I knew the torn piece crumpled in one of his fisted hands beside him burned against his skin the way it did in mine. It led me here, and it fueled this violent confrontation. The story he held onto for years was a fire that wouldn't burn out until it was extinguished by confession.

Othello pressed the blade harder against Nathanial's throat. The invincible image of beauty that had once been a nameless stranger now lorded over the father who became a stranger to me by revelation of a name. Othello watched me, patient with my inability to take all this in as quickly as he could. But he wouldn't wait for the answers I deserved. The thin trickle of blood was enough to coerce words from refusing lips.

"I was watching. Keeping record of everything that anyone knew about what happened." The singular line of blood dripped to the neatly folded collar of his light shirt. He hissed at the blade still set between the fine cut of his neck.

Two kids, taken from a dead mother. It wasn't a record that should be kept by anyone but the officials, anyone involved. He was a man who proclaimed to be a simple family man, not anything less and not anything more. I couldn't connect the lines between every short detail he was giving me, and I pulled myself up off the floor to stand before him—to make him look up to me.

"Why?" The longer I remained unsure, the more furious I grew. I'd been kept in the dark long enough, and now the darkness I'd found for myself was what guided me out. Information taken by force was what this had come to, and I was grateful for how easily Othello could hold death against someone. I was grateful that he'd come before death had succeeded when it was held against me. "Why are you tracking someone's tragedy? Why is this something that you're also hiding? What does Nathanial Moore have to do with this?"

As the name left my own lips, I was able to piece together a sole part of my confusion. The name on the aged birth certificate, the one of a strange woman that didn't belong to the other documents of our family. Edith Moore. My mouth fell open as my brows drew together over the eyes that watched his every small move. I saw the sweat bead from his temple as he stared at the woman he'd raised who he now saw as his ruin. I saw the worry in his own eyes as he tried to guess how much I knew by the look I was giving him.

He couldn't read my face. He wasn't the one that knew me better than I knew myself. He wasn't the man who knew how to read my eyes for their questions and my body for their answers. The man holding the knife to his throat was. The one who kept me still in the presence of the end of a life half lived. With this closure would come the fall of all a father had built, and all the time I'd sacrificed to his rule.

"Who is Edith Moore?" I asked him as I took a step closer. The nearer I came to the frantic body imprisoned on those seats, the harder the determination thrummed through me. "Tell me everything. Everything that you don't want to tell me is exactly what I want to know." He closed his eyes briefly, refusing to accept defeat as I exposed that I already knew more than he hoped I did. I waited for him to open them before I spoke again, reaching the finality of my own patience. "I won't ask again."

It wasn't me giving in, dropping this whole thing like he wanted me to. It was me giving him one last chance, and my voice sounded strange to my own ears with the sincerity of the threat. Othello smiled, attracting my attention for a fleeting moment that propelled my will. There was pride in that smile, and it made up for all the disappointment that I'd always dreaded giving everyone else.

The sound of a car door slamming broke through the heavy breathing that came with being held at knifepoint. Worry showed on my face, but none reflected on Othello's as he drove his knife into Nathanial's arm before setting it back against his throat. The terrorized sound of pain rang out just as the door opened. Gray halted in front of the slowly closing door, the click of it shutting heavily behind him mixing with the grunts of a man unable to handle pain.

"Vieve?" Gray's small call to me matched the stunned expression of his voice. I knew he didn't recognize the person he looked at, because I wasn't the sister he knew in that moment. But I was the one that was able to do this for him. To expose everything he wasn't that was in the man who might be his father—because I'd decided that he was no longer mine. All the bad that Gray didn't possess was sitting in the room that he'd entered, that he'd come to just to find his sister.

"Edith is your mother's real name," Nathanial said as one hand clutched at his bleeding arm, every word coming out on ragged breaths. I looked away from Gray's disbelieving eyes and set mine back on the holder of the truth he needed—that we needed. "We changed our names after your grandparents turned us away."

I watched the blood seep from between his fingers and spread across the sleeve of his white shirt. The purity he'd always acted as if he had was stained, pried from his unwilling hands. That one answer echoed through my mind as I watched his blood spill, and a million more questions followed. I didn't know what to ask. I didn't know what was important to know before time ran out and Gray broke free from his shock—or Nathanial bled out before we knew enough. I looked to Othello, who read into me and did what I couldn't.

"Why is the changing of your name something that needs to be protected by the police you pay?" Othello asked, keeping his eyes locked on mine as he pulled the most pertinent question from them.

Nathanial's head turned, trying to pull away from the discomfort of the blade, but it only pulled a larger line along his neck. Othello didn't budge, he wouldn't release a man who had been given undeserved comfort for too long.

"Because our names hide more than just us," he answered indignantly. His chest was inflating and deflating with the breaths of a losing man. Anger, pain, everything I'd grown to embrace. He scowled, all of it directed my way as he put the fault of all that had happened on me. "They hide you and your brother."

No children were hidden by their parents. People hiding their own names were hiding me and Gray, and I looked to see if he understood, if he heard. There was confusion and shock written all over him in this violent interrogation. He looked for the sister he always knew in me, and for answers that had always been given by him. For once, I could be the older and wiser one. For once, I could be capable and save him. I could finish what I started and continue down this path that was led by blood and secrets.

"Why do Gray and I need to be hidden?" I asked as I came closer, and Othello's knife lifted the chin of a deserving victim. "How do you hide your own children?" Children that were heavily guarded, and unclaimed on the official documents I'd found along with the article in my hand. I looked back down at the nearly ruined paper, and read the bold title again.

Two kids.

Gray's blue eyes were full of worry. I couldn't claim to know everything he felt, but I knew he was just as lost as I'd been. He was finding everything I'd found all at once, the way I didn't want him to have to. But at least it was being found, all pieces of a broken family that had perfected pretending finally coming together to reveal the grave picture.

"Is this us?" My voice was low. It left its weight on my tongue, a question so heavy that I could already taste the answer to—a dreadful confirmation.

The deep red of Nathanial's face was draining away along with his blood. The weaker he became, the less he could fight his refusal to speak. The answer came out from the oldest person in the room, the one who should have been wise enough to know that a day would come when secrets had to be shed.

"Yes."

The answer tightened my fingers around the paper. My heart stopped as it looked to the sign I held, that had been hidden so near to me my whole life. The truth hurt just as much as it set one free.

I held the piece of a story in my hands that told of two missing kids, both standing in this very church surrounded by extraordinary color and the metallic scent of blood. Nathanial held the piece of a story that told of a dead woman, whose kids were never seen again.

"What happened to her?" I asked, my pointing finger extended from the hand that held onto the story dearly. It was my life engraved into those words, and I couldn't let go.

He didn't look down at the remnant in his hand. He knew what I asked as his eyes fluttered and his body slowly expelled all his strength. "You were born to an immoral woman who didn't deserve the gift of a child. I saved you—"

"You *stole* me!" I lost all restraint. No tears left my eyes, but the outrage I felt at being lied to and used and betrayed poured from my glower. "You're an immoral man who has no right to judge anyone the way you do! You took two innocent children and tore them away from a family they *should* have had! You've kept us running and hiding against our will, forcing us to be perfect and fill the empty spaces in your family that we don't belong to!"

I closed my eyes, focusing on the breaths I took in the space meant to cleanse. I took what I knew of this place, hoping that not everything I'd been taught was a lie. Slowly, I came back down into my own body. Slowly, I connected back to my purpose and the control I'd come here with. My chest still worked to keep my heavy heart alive and beating, but I knew this couldn't be the end.

My eyes opened and locked onto Othello's. He'd remained solid, practically silent, the support he'd always been to me. I drew strength from those dark eyes. I remembered how to press on and fight for life the way he'd shown me. He fulfilled his quiet role for me, and watched me live shamelessly as the woman I'd become because of him.

I opened my mouth to give more orders, demand more answers. But the voice that asked them wasn't mine.

"Why us?" Gray took a step forward. I saw him emerge from the chains of shock as he tentatively approached the sight of blood, the violence he despised. He wouldn't look anywhere other than the weak eyes that had all the answers. "Why are we the kids you took?"

I bit my tongue against Gray's gentle questioning. I wouldn't force him to bear my anger after our entire life had been forced upon us. He could be as kind as he chose to be—it was in his nature, not just his upbringing. I had left behind a lot on the road to discover this, but I didn't want to see him leave behind the only good I'd ever known because of our parents' betrayal.

"You're our cousin's children." My attention caught onto one of the words said by a dying man. Othello's eyes captured mine and told me he'd done the same. In the midst of violence and the expulsion of corruption, our minds were beginning to open to each other. "We'd seen Genevieve when she was just a baby. When she was still called Lydia, right before we left the family. We knew how much she looked like us." The slow breaths he took made the information inch its way out. The hand that gripped his arm wasn't holding on as tightly as before. "Edith kept losing our children. Each child born dead took a toll on her. I'd give anything to give her the family that she wanted, so I did."

His eyes settled back on me. "We came for you," he said to me, his tone accusing me of being ungrateful, "but we left with you both. We only intended to save you from the strung-out mother that you had, and by the time we got to you, she'd already had your brother." His head lolled to the side, and Othello's blade followed. He hadn't reached the point of offering mercy, because not everything I wanted had been given. "You two have different fathers, but you both made up for the two babies Edith had lost. We were meant to be a family; we all share blood." He looked away from me and to Gray—to the only eyes that had a chance of sympathizing. "We're the parents you deserved. We're what you needed."

Othello's raised brow told me that time was running short. That the time was closing in before we had to call for help—or he had to die. I took the message, saw the tear running down the side of Gray's face, and looked back to the man who I wasn't entirely sure I could spare or not.

"What did you mean by *our* cousin?" I asked, and his eyes closed as he let go of his bleeding arm and extended his hands to the seat on either side of him. "How was our mother related to both of you?"

He sighed, a tortured hiss that escaped through locked teeth. He opened his eyes at the very moment that my mind formed its own answer. *Moore.* Edith's birth certificate wouldn't have the same real name on it as his just because they were married. She couldn't be born with the same last name that he had unless they were—

"Edith is my *wife*," Nathanial spat defensively toward the shock on my face. "I've cared for her and loved her my entire life, and I won't let you look at me the same way that our parents did." Our. *Our.* "It's why we're here, it's why I've done everything for her. It's why you belong and were gifted to parents whose minds aren't muddled by the ideas of the world like ours were."

His breathing picked back up with the fight he had left in him. The fight he had for Edith; his wife, his sister. I was calmed as my stomach turned, replacing my outrage with sick understanding. One secret unleashed the flood of them.

He was once the outcast, he and his sister turned away by a family who refused to approve of a love so wrong, a devotion so twisted. He hid the two of them, and the children they stole to replace their own behind the guise of a perfect man—of a leader, a saint, a profession that's meant to be trusted and never questioned. We shared blood, and that was all. He was family, but he wasn't my father. Gray and I didn't belong to him, we were stolen. With all of the terrible things being revealed, there was one thing I still couldn't piece together to his story.

The story that stole my life until I found myself here, able to take it back.

"How is our mother dead?" I asked him. My hand instinctively reached for Gray's shoulder, and I could feel the labored rise and fall of his own system trying to take in so much information at once. "Our *real* mother. How is it that you knew to show up when you did, and take us from an already dead woman?"

Nathanial began to slide down in the seat, hardly able to hold himself up any longer. Othello put one hand beneath his chin and pulled him back up, forcing him to look at me and Gray again.

"You tell them," Othello said, watching as Gray placed his shaking hand over the steadied one I had on his shoulder. "Admit everything you've taken from them." The hand holding Nathanial's chin went to his shoulder, and he gripped tightly, making Nathanial groan and reach for the already injured arm. "I know a killer when I touch one."

Nathanial looked to Gray, but Gray looked to the floor of the aisle. He focused on the peaceful colors that didn't belong, and focused on false comfort. But I stole Nathanial's gaze. I made him look me in the eye, because I had to know. I needed to hear every last sin.

"The drugs would have killed her, anyway." The sneer of his lip as he spoke to me wasn't only there from his pain. It was the evil belief that he was still clinging onto that made him think that what he was telling me was justified. "And by the time it happened, you would have been ruined by her influence. So would your brother. You were both fatherless, and your mother was worthless."

His hand smeared across the front of his shirt, leaving red tracks from his fingers over his chest and on the tan seat he rested his hand back on. He was fading quickly, no longer the powerful man he thought he was—that Gray and I had always thought he was.

"I gave her that last dose, but she would have died for the drugs she loved more than you, anyway." It wasn't the same excuse to me as it was to him. It wasn't the same sort of mercy I knew a ruthless man could give. There were many differences between Othello and Nathanial, and one of them was that Nathanial was finally coming to an end that he deserved. "They couldn't even tell the difference in a murder and a strung-out woman who over-indulged. I did save you. I *did*." Nobody would be able to believe his words the way that he did, other than the only woman he loved. The only one that he was good to, and did the worst things for. We were all a charade that he had to keep up with for *her*. The woman we'd always seen as our mother was the only one that could feel like all of this was real. She wasn't just pretending, she was delusional. This life of simplicity and routine was everything to her.

"I came for you because I knew you didn't belong. You weren't what she needed; you were what *we* needed." Gray's hand began to squeeze mine as we both saw the pallor of his face turn bleak. "The proof is in the papers," he said, and I watched his hands turn to fists as his expression contorted in exhausted pain. "The world quickly lost interest because you both belonged to that drugged-up woman. I gave you a life with meaning. I gave you everything you needed."

The world lost interest, and he was able to hide behind society's flaws. The same, harsh truth had come from Nancy the first time I'd seen this paper—my story—and it was more bitter this time as it fell onto my ears. None of his reasons would save him. All the years of lies and work he'd done to silence his sins wouldn't change the fact that it all cost him his life.

And none of it felt good to know. These answers would cost more than just the life of a father we never had, it would cost everything for Gray and me.

Othello was my protector, waiting for my final call. I looked at the blade still readied against a dying man's throat, and gently shook my head as I clasped Gray's hand in both of mine. I knew what he was feeling, I remembered when I was the one frozen by fear and facing reality.

"He should suffer," I told Othello, and he pulled the knife away without hesitation. He allowed this to be my call, and he was only here to enforce it. I held the power as he held the weapon. Gray turned away from me, looking to the front of the room where the pulpit stood empty. The body that didn't belong there had been brought down. "We can call someone, and he can confess a second time." I looked at the light fading from the eyes that could barely stay open. "If they get here in time."

"Adam will be here soon," Othello said as he walked around the seat. He abandoned the limp body of a weak man to come to me, and he put his hand on my cheek. Warm, reassuring that some things in life could still provide comfort. I shut my eyes and took a breath, and opened them to share the weight of my soul with the brown eyes that cared to carry my burdens. "He'll make sure he lives long enough to recant his sins all over again."

I looked down at the paper on the ground I'd released to hold Gray's hand. It had been evidence, and now it was a reminder of all I knew. I couldn't process every disturbing detail that I'd learned, but I knew I'd done what I came for. I saved Gray. I set him free, exposing wickedness and leaving destruction in my wake.

I kissed Othello, relishing the touch of the one that continued to save me. My lips lingered as I pulled away, softly departing from the taste of true power. His body blocked the bleeding man from my sight, shielding me from having to face the remnants of that broken life anymore.

"Thank you." I looked up to him. To the face that saw me break down when I hadn't known my purpose, then had guided me to it with delectable darkness every step of the way.

The hand that still held his opened knife came up to push my hair from my face. I didn't flinch or shy away from his dangers anymore, I craved them.

"There's no false life to fly back to now, Dove." The uneven section of my hair fell back over my shoulder, and his fingers ran through the end of it as he looked through me and directly to my soul. "Embrace your freedom. Share it with me."

I smiled as I prepared to make a promise, this time not only making a deal. I would spend all of my freedom with the ones I owed it to, the ones who helped me find it. A new home, a new life, a new family.

As I turned around to look at Gray, to check on the one part of me that I wouldn't leave behind, I heard the call of madness. I heard the yell of violence that came just before Othello's hand tightened on my shoulder. Just before he turned around and slit the throat of the man who wasted his chance to be saved.

Blood sprayed the seats, the front of Othello, the part of my face that watched the scene unfold too slowly that I begged to not be real.

The body that fell to the floor had no chance. His last quiet moments were likely spent asking for forgiveness in the seat he sat in beneath the excellence of this church's covering. He now laid with his eyes to the sky, blood puddling on the sides of his neck as he wasted all he had left in his veins to ruin one more life.

Othello turned to me, his face still painfully stoic as he held the handle of the knife that was buried in his side. The knife I'd lost. Found by the wrong hands and pierced into the one who'd trusted me to use it for my own defense. I caught him beneath the arm as he began to fall, and the panic rushed through me as he grew heavier.

"Gray!" I yelled for the only person that wasn't bleeding, the only other person that I could depend on. My head turned to him as I held onto Othello while he continued to collapse, and all my body's desperation sent him rushing over to the sister he was always there for.

He helped me get him into the front pew and sit him down, both of us struggling even though Othello moved his own feet. Gray pulled away from him as he removed the arm from around his shoulder, and came away with blood covering the side of him and his light blue shirt. He didn't look horrified as he looked at the last remains of another's life covering him—him, the brother I knew to hate violence. Shock had its own effect on a body that still held compassion, and Gray was one to still be compassionate through his own mental suffering.

I dropped to my knees in front of Othello, my arm covered in blood and my cheeks covered in warm streams. I reached for the knife in his side, my instinct telling me it could be easy to free him from what was killing him. He grabbed my hand and put it against his chest, where I could feel it beating erratically.

"That will only speed the process," he told me, and my composure broke with every strong word. His voice was stable, though I knew everything in him wasn't. I put my hand beneath the blood that leaked around the blade and it slowly coated me in red.

I searched everywhere for answers, for any untold idea of how I could save him from being the second body to bleed out in this church. I couldn't give the wound pressure. I couldn't fix all it had ruined inside him. All I could do was look to the place where I found all the answers, with eyes that frantically filled with question.

"I don't need anything." It wasn't comforting. It wasn't an answer that I could take, and I put my hands to his face and begged him with my crying eyes to tell me something else. Through breaths that stole space in my hurting lungs,

I asked him to tell me how I could fix him the way he always fixed me. "It's all right, Dove."

My head went to his lap as I lost all the control and strength I'd come with. I could feel the hand he placed on my head as my sobs echoed through the room. I wept, feeling hatred for myself for having led him here. For having to have been saved again. If I lost the part of my soul that was withering beneath me, then I would be broken forever. I would be one of the people in my life that I could never forgive.

He slowly stroked my hair, the way he'd done the night before. He gave me all the peace he had that couldn't soothe me this time. My head turned beneath his hand and pressed his palm to my tearful cheeks. I saw the glint of gold that hung from his pocket as it shone beneath the colored lights, and I reached for it and pulled it out.

What had led him here. What let him know that I'd had more to do now that I had given in and broken free. What brought him to this place, where he knew I had to face the man who'd given it to me before I could live my life without question. Without guilt of leaving Gray behind in an undeserving home.

Othello reached for my necklace, taking the waning warmth of his palm away from my face. He held it between us, the simple cross I'd always clung to swinging gently back and forth. My eyes left the sickening motion of it and looked up to him, where his dark gaze waited with a terrifyingly calm smile. A smile that should have been as scared as I was. A smile that didn't relay its imminent end that was approaching.

"My reminder," he said as he put the chain loosely over his wrist and gripped the golden cross, "of what I took from a man who didn't deserve it." Of all his trophies, all his reminders, the piece of me would be the one that he possessed forever. I placed my hand over his, and held onto him as he clutched the comfort I'd always relied on. "You deserved to be saved."

He wouldn't close his eyes. He wouldn't look away from the tears that told him he was wrong. I didn't deserve to live when he couldn't. I didn't deserve to be the end of who I'd always known as invincible. And as Adam ran through the doors of the fatal, stained church, my lips began to move in defiance of the inevitable.

"You can't leave me," I told him as I put my fingers into his hair. "You promised that I could always come to you." I ran my finger through the blood that covered his neck, and exposed the dove beneath. "I gave you everything I had because you promised."

It all came out slowly, slurred by sobbing breaths. I saw him watch Adam halt behind me, the approach I'd heard and hoped would save him.

"The promise still stands." One heavy, soul-crushing look of determination was all he gave me before he looked back to Adam. I cried in the silence of the conversation that I couldn't hear, the last wordless exchange that the two of them shared before Adam pulled me away and I began to panic. "And if your god cares to even lay his eyes upon my soul, I'll thank him for sparing one of heaven's doves for me."

"No, no, no, please," was all I could manage as Adam pulled me up from my knees, and away from the body that gently seeped its blood onto the seat. I reached back for Othello, desperate for him to give me a final touch of fearlessness and all that I'd never have again. But he didn't touch me.

He smiled.

A wicked, intent grimace as he pulled the knife from his side and let the wound flow freely. Quickly embracing death, he put his arms across the back of the seat and hung his head as his body slouched. The cross swayed from his hand, and I screamed in all my soul's pain as I watched him sigh.

I watched him welcome his end as Adam pulled me down the aisle. I had no control of my body, my emotions.

My feet followed because I knew nothing and felt like I'd lost everything. I didn't register the rush of the motions, the hurry in the three still-living bodies that exited that church.

I was blinded by the blur of relentless tears as I was put into the seat of a car. I wanted to be numb as I heard the turn of the engine, and the car pull away with all of us inside.

But I felt it all.

I felt the hole forming inside of me that I was certain could never be filled again. I felt the pull of my soul's tie to Othello's as it refused to let go despite death. I felt the distance being put between me and the person who'd taught me how to survive, and fight, and *feel*.

I felt the final words that I'd never see again being spoken to my weary mind. I felt it register deep within as I tried to refuse to accept those words, accept his wishes. I felt what Othello had expected me to do so his dying body would take the fall for all that had transpired in that church.

Save myself.

1985

Families filtered out of the church without being forced to stop and say goodbye. They didn't have to praise a humble man. They didn't have to acknowledge the lessons taught by a gentle, good person when that person was Gray who didn't desire admiration for fulfilling his purpose.

Gray changed everything about the church that had molded our lives, and made it into the sanctuary I could return to. He thanked each person as they arrived, because he was grateful that they had come—not because they'd listened to him speak. And when he spoke to the people he was genuinely grateful for, he spoke of unconditional love and taught of all the things that a compassionate and selfless man would. It was nothing of the fear and hypocrisy of sins that we'd been conditioned by, but of forgiveness and understanding and guidance for life's realities.

Realities the both of us had lived through.

I'd been the first one that left through the doors. My place that was always open to me in the back row made it easy to exit quickly. The first sermon I'd come to hear Gray speak had been the hardest, and I put as much space between myself and that cursed front row as I could. And each time I'd returned, the space farthest from the brother I was entirely proud of was always available for me.

I stood at the bottom of the steps, and waited for Gray as I always did. The amount of time I could spend inside beneath the light and the colors was limited to the time it took Gray to speak to the congregation, and touch each soul with a reminder of the love that existed amidst the world's chaos. He had his own way of speaking to so many people at once and addressing them individually—because they wanted to listen and not because they gave their attention out of guilt.

"You look angelic beneath the sun like that, Gene," Mrs. Hannigan said as she descended the steps with a smile and outstretched arms. She was someone from the past that I could hold onto. She was also broken by the truth, and lost a friend when we lost the woman we'd always known as a mother when she was committed for a life of delusions. She'd been just as distraught at having never known the secrets of a woman that she thought she knew so well; a woman that was criminally sick, and needed a lifetime of help to recover from her shattered illusions. Sandy had held me this same way with her own tears falling from her eyes as we'd watched a mentally suffering woman be removed from her home, the façade put in place by a brother she loved disturbingly, and the two children that she swore belonged to her.

Gray and I could feel how deeply rooted her belief was that we were her children. But at that point, there was no added emotion that could make everything harder than it already was.

Sandy's face looked the same as it always had as I pulled away with my own smile. I looked between her and Mr. Hannigan and saw the two halves of Luke. The resemblance always brought back fond recollection, and I thanked everything fortunate that he'd made a life for himself outside of this town just as he wanted. He still had secrets that he shared with me upon his every return, but he'd found his own freedom with the distance from familiar eyes. There was never any disappointment expressed between the lie that Luke and I had upheld as it fizzled out in all of the chaos. Our lie was overshadowed by life's givings after so many things were taken.

Amelia walked out through the doors, carrying the spitting image of Gray on her hip as their daughter's head rested against her shoulder. The bulge of another growing life protruded from Amelia's belly as her father helped her down the steps, a family whole and loving.

Any time I looked at that little girl, saw the blue eyes that stole the heart of their father before he'd ever seen them, I remembered the moment that he'd shared his own truth with me as the two of us sat in the big room of a church without a steeple. Covered in blood and tears, the first words whispered after shock as we waited for Adam to return with directions of how life was to go on. We were hurting and clueless, but Gray knew what was prominent on his mind.

"Amelia's pregnant," he told me through the stillness of a dark room. I immediately reached out my hand to him, offering the only thing I had—the love for my brother.

He pulled me to him, and we held each other as we both cried. I cried for a life lost, and the pain I'd caused the both of us. He cried from all that overwhelmed him. Gray was still the most perfect human I knew, and what scared him was the outcome of what he'd been taught to see as a fault.

I assured him everything was going to be okay, and it was. I'd wished then that I would have been able to say the same thing the day that Amelia had come to me, looking helplessly at the face before her that had the scars of brutal lessons. I would have told her that it was going to be okay, too. I wouldn't have known then what I knew now, but I would have known that life didn't stop just because one was made.

Within twenty-four hours, Gray had both lost and acquired family. The night I'd left was the night he finally knew, and the day he found out all the same secrets as I did, he'd lost parents when he knew that he was going to be one.

He was given balance, and bettered himself and his life for the woman and children that I knew he would never lie to.

The halls we'd walked throughout our lives were now filled with pictures of a family that belonged. There was no pretending in those images, no coverings of secrets, just love in a home meant for a family that was real. I looked through those pictures each time I went there, taking notice of the difference. There were genuine smiles, a baby with the parents she was birthed to, and the extension of grandparents that children naturally had. Mr. and Mrs. Hannigan now had their precious photos of normalcy in two homes, and the house Gray and I had grown up in now had the traces of affection it deserved.

Amelia reached for me, the bracelet always on her wrist sparkling in the sunlight as she hugged me over her swollen stomach. Gray had bought it, intending to give it to a mother, and now it remained on the person it was meant for. Gifted to the mother of his children the night she told him about the baby as a promise that he would always provide. They married three months later; the bulge of her stomach had been apparent, but didn't prevent the sincerity of their vows as they married for love. She went without a ring for a year, promising Gray that the promise from that bracelet was all that she'd need. Given to a woman becoming a mother from a man whose word she could rely on.

Gray walked out of the church and pulled Amelia to him the moment he came down the stairs. He took their daughter and placed a kiss upon her small forehead, and smiled at his own reborn reflection. The way the two of them smiled at one another, loved each other, was what the world chased after. Innocent, eternal love.

To think that the ones who'd raised us would have seen her conception as a mistake made me grateful that they'd never had a chance to share their opinion, ruin the goodness of something so perfect. When Gray had told me that he would run the church that had once run us, I asked him how it was possible that his faith hadn't been shaken by all the trauma and abuse we'd lived through. How he could put himself willingly back into a place that had both hid and exposed all of our tragedy.

I remembered the determination in his eyes, and the sad smile that curved his lips as he looked at his transformed sister, and I looked at my same brother.

"Because I don't put my faith in man," he'd told me as he grabbed my hand from across the table. The one we'd spent so many hours at over the course of our lives together. "We're all imperfect creatures."

A hand on my shoulder brought me back to the present, both sets of blue eyes before me looking into mine as I grinned at both of them.

"Did we lose you there for a minute, Aunt Eve?" Gray teased, mocking the way the little one in his arms said my name. She reached out and traced the faded scar on my cheek and I reached out and pushed her strawberry-tinted hair behind her ears.

"Aunt Eve is never lost." I ran my fingers beneath her chin, grateful to have been found just in time for all of life's surprises. I was found by darkness, in my darkest hours, and now I could always see clearly ahead of me. I was given all the knowledge I would ever need to never have to wait to be found again.

I looked over her shoulder and saw the white car pull into the emptying lot. I would leave this church and go home to another, and spend my days content with the family I'd been promised. With the comfort and guidance of those who'd taken me in and assisted me through all my trials. With permanence established by a leader who'd left his mark on the world through me.

Gray and I had both decided not to turn back to the life we were stolen from in childhood. We each looked on, and pursued the families we knew we wanted. We made decisions for ourselves the way that we couldn't before, and chose what was best for us and paved the way for ourselves and the generations that would follow.

As I watched Adam get out of the car, I knew I'd never abandon the darkness that I'd soon return to. I belonged to the life I'd found through violence, and defiance, and the brutality that had found me. It's where I felt safest, it's where I was entirely accepted, and it was my home. My soul was tethered to the outcast that opened the car's door before he turned around and leaned back against the gleaming steel, smoke spilling from his lips as he looked to me and spoke without words.

Three years and counting. His mind had finally opened for me, and we spoke silent conversations as we lived together, worked together, and loved together. He told me with his eyes as he pulled another drag from his cigarette that there was no rush today. That there was no unspeakable business to hurry back to.

I took this time each Sunday to come to this church, where I knew blood had been shed and my new roots were planted by the life that had been slain there. I connected both to the light that Gray bestowed upon the masses and the unforgotten power that Othello still held over me as I sat in the back of the church each week.

My life was balanced. I could come here and be accepted as the family I was, and not questioned about the family I now belonged to. Gray looked to Adam and waved as he sat his miniature down, and she ran right to the boy with the lightest curls whose little legs were carrying him toward us with the speed of a free child. Adam lifted his hand to Gray, and returned the polite acknowledgment they often exchanged.

I watched the two kids on the grass, chasing each other with bouts of laughter as they played without care, without worry, without hesitation. I watched as my niece tumbled onto the grass, her small hands catching her fall. She turned over to the sight of a savior her size, who put his hands beneath her arms and clumsily helped her up. His bright hair caught the glow of the sun, just like a halo.

Gray and I looked to each other, seeing ourselves in each of them. He'd always been the one with the outstretched hand who saved me, until I found what it took to be the one to finally save him. We smiled, and I silently thanked divinity for always giving me what I didn't think I deserved. For gifting amounts of light to a soul who'd embraced darkness.

Light didn't belong to me, but I'd care for it for as long as it remained.

I would be its safety, and keep every promise I ever made as the permanent fixture in its life.

I would forever love what darkness had given me.

The laughter grew near, and I held out my arms to the joyful face of perfection. I pulled him up, and looked into the brownest eyes that beheld all the world's beauty. His legs kicked around me with energy and his smile greeted me with excitement. Our faces never grew tired of seeing each other, the images of each other's saving grace.

"Hi, mommy," he said in a voice so small, that would one day grow into all its inherited power.

I kissed his cheek, and pulled back to take in the image of the priceless gift that depravity had sent me. The product of a soul and a body who'd both made their sacrifices.

"Hello, my dove."

ACKNOWLEDGMENTS

To my extraordinary editor, Tasha, thank you so much for all you've done for this book. For the multiple read-throughs, for the attention you've paid to all the small and significant details, and for always eagerly being one of my first and most supportive readers. I'm so grateful for your hard work on this project, and for all the help you've supplied in order for me to give the world the best version of this story that I possibly could.

To my wonderful beta reader, Sabrina, thank you for being the honest person and perfect friend that you are. Thank you for being so excited about this book with me, and for giving me the amazing feedback that you did and helping me make the adjustments needed to bring this story to its full potential. I cherish our friendship and all the creativity you inspire within me.

To my outstanding cover artist, Mitch, thank you for all the art you've created and work you've done to make this flawless cover. For listening to my ideas, being a joy to work with, and having that uncanny ability to bring the thoughts in my mind to life the way that you do. Everyone knows that readers judge a book by its cover, and there's no denying that there's beautiful darkness to be found behind what you've created.

radpublishing.co

ABOUT THE AUTHOR

Gillian Dowell is a wife, mother, and self-published author with a passion for writing stories that leave lasting impressions.

Years after her debut novel, *Paracosm*, she wrote and released her second, *Found By Forbiddance*, and has found that the reward of writing doesn't only come from the completed stories themselves, but also from the readers who reach out to share their own thoughts, as well as their mutual love of memorable, fictional characters.

She's eternally grateful for all of her readers, old and new, and looks forward to a life filled with more stories to be shared with all who enjoy them.

@the.gillian.dowell

Made in the USA
Monee, IL
22 August 2021

76249959R00184